A REVIVED
MODERN
CLASSIC

AT HEAVEN'S GATE

Books by Robert Penn Warren

ROBERT PENN WARREN

AT HEAVEN'S GATE

A NEW DIRECTIONS BOOK

Manufactured in the United States of America
New Directions Books are printed on acid-free paper
This edition is published by arrangement with Random House
First published as New Directions Paperbook 588 in 1985
Published simultaneously in Canada by Penguin Books Canada Limited

Library of Congress Cataloging in Publication Data

Warren, Robert Penn, 1905–
   At heaven's gate
   (A New Directions Book)
   1. Title.
PS3545.A748A8   1985   813'.52   84-18980
ISBN 0-8112-0933-4 (pbk.)

FOURTH PRINTING

New Directions Books are published for James Laughlin
by New Directions Publishing Corporation
80 Eighth Avenue, New York, NY 10011

TO
FRANK LAWRENCE OWSLEY
AND
HARRIET OWSLEY

A REVIVED
MODERN
CLASSIC

AT HEAVEN'S GATE

One

IT was the brilliant, high, windless sky of early autumn. The blue was paler than the blue of summer, but not leached out, still positive, and drenched in sunlight as though treated with a wash which was transparent but full of minute gold flecks. When you stared at the sky, if you stared very long, it seemed to be pricked with those tiny flecks of gold, which winked and glittered.

Sue Murdock stared at the sky, northward, and narrowed her eyes against the light. She could see nothing in the sky.

She was leaning her folded arms on the white top bar of the paddock, with her chin braced on her forearms. On her left, her brother Hammond Murdock lounged against the paddock, and on her right, Slim Sarrett stood, not leaning, one of his long white hands laid on the bar, not for support but as in a position of control, as though it were a warrior's hand laid on a sword hilt, or a bearded mariner's hand laid, as in an old engraving, on a globe.

Slim Sarrett had just stated that he did not care for riding.

"Have you ever been on a horse?" Sue demanded, not taking her eyes off the bright sky.

"No," Slim Sarrett confessed quite candidly, and added that he did not think that riding a horse would be very interesting.

"Of course not, of course not," she murmured, "not at all *interesting*, oh, no," and did not look at him.

"For Christ sake," Ham Murdock said, amiably.

"The cult of horsemanship is a very peculiar thing," Slim Sarrett continued evenly. "It is probable that most people who devote themselves to it do so despite the fact that they do not enjoy it at all, in itself, or enjoy it very little. They simply enjoy the idea. They enjoy the picture of themselves on a horse. It is a symbol. It is a snob symbol derived from the Middle Ages. It—"

"You just read all that in a book," Sue said. "And you said it all to me on the way out here and now you're saying it for Ham's benefit."

He had said it all to her in her car on the way out here to see

Starlight, and there wasn't a word of truth in it, for she didn't enjoy the idea of being on a horse; she just liked riding and that was all there was to it, and he just said that to her because he said things like that. He was just that way.

He was saying that if you really did enjoy riding a horse it was because it flattered your ego. It was because you controlled a brute. You felt fully man because a brute, much stronger than man, was obeying you. "But," he said, "granting the perfectly normal desire to flatter one's ego, it is a cheap and easy way to achieve the end. The true contest should be to set oneself against another human being, not against a brute. It is too easy."

"If you think it's so damned easy," Ham said, "I'll just get one of the niggers to saddle Starlight out there—" he nodded toward the big, glistening bay stallion in the middle of the paddock, "and you can see how long you can stick on that baby."

"I wouldn't stick on a minute," Slim said, and laughed.

When she heard him laugh, she almost liked him again. One thing for certain, he never claimed to do anything he couldn't do. The trouble was he just knew exactly what he could do, and what he wanted to do, and that made him different from other people, and that was why people didn't like him.

"It wouldn't be half a minute," her brother said, almost snottily.

She turned her head on her arm and looked pensively at her brother, at the squarish shoulders under the old leather jacket and the squarish, strong face, which was smiling like he had the drop. He didn't have the drop on anybody. He didn't know what he could do and he didn't know what he wanted to do. All he could do was ride a horse, and she could do that as well as he could.

"It wouldn't be half a minute," Ham repeated, with relish. "Starlight would kill you."

"That doesn't prove a thing," she said distinctly, "just because Slim never had any riding lessons. I think what he said is perfectly true. People like to ride a horse just because they like to feel big. Especially," and she lingered on the word, looking at Ham, "when they can't do anything else."

"Yes," Slim Sarrett said, "that I do not have that particular technique does not prove anything about the principle. But," he added, "I imagine that one could become fairly proficient in the technique with a little practice."

When he said that she didn't like him any more. Why couldn't he keep his mouth shut sometimes? Sure, he could learn to ride a horse, any fool could learn to ride a horse, but why couldn't he keep his mouth shut?

4

"For Christ sake," Ham said again, but not amiably this time.

Why couldn't they both keep their mouths shut, she thought, and looked again at the sky to the north.

She wondered if you could see the plane from here.

She stared at the bright sky and thought of being very high up, by herself, absolutely by herself, and looking down and seeing everything so little that you couldn't tell what it was, and you didn't care what it was any more. Like that time when she got in trouble at Miss Millford's School, and Miss Millford had her in and dressed her down and said they hadn't decided on the punishment, though it was serious, and that they had notified her father, and so she just walked right out on them and packed one bag and went into Boston and got a plane home. She had fixed that old witch. She wasn't going to have anybody talking to her like that, and once she was up in the plane she felt all by herself and free and it was like nothing that ever happened mattered any more, and she didn't care what was going to happen, or how her father would be when she got home.

Now, looking at the sky, she thought of Jerry Calhoun, somewhere in a plane, high up in that clear sky to the north, and was struck by a stab of envy, a sense of being trapped and earth-bound and betrayed.

She stared at the sky, squinting.

"You can see the plane from here when the light is right," Ham said, as though he had read her thoughts, as though he had been eavesdropping or spying on her, and she felt a surge of anger at him.

"I'm not trying to see the plane," she retorted.

"I heard the old man say Jerry was coming in on the afternoon plane," Ham said.

"I told you I'm not trying to see the plane," she snapped.

"I heard the old man tell Anse something about meeting the plane. With the coupe," Ham said. "I reckon he's supposed to bring Jerry out here."

"Who's Jerry?" Slim asked.

"Jerry—Jerry Calhoun," Ham began to answer, "he's—"

Oh, she knew who Jerry Calhoun was, all right. She straightened up from the paddock rail suddenly, and turned away from the two boys, and moved toward the house.

Oh, she knew who Jerry Calhoun was. She knew all about him, all right. Oh, Jerry Calhoun was high up in the sky in a plane, and he was looking down on everything in the world like he owned it. But he didn't own her. Nobody owned her.

She strode across the firm, shaven turf, past the rose garden, toward the big red-brick mass of the house. She entered by the French doors into the back sitting room and traversed the length of the big hall to her father's library. The door was closed. She hesitated for an instant before it. It was a high white door, solid and dignified and deeply paneled. She knocked, heard the voice, and laid her hand on the cold brass of the knob.

Her father was sitting erectly in the wing chair by the window, a magazine on his knee. "Hello, Sue," he said, and smiled.

"Hello," she said.

"Have a seat," he invited, and motioned toward a chair.

She shook her head, not answering, and remained standing where she was, some ten feet from his chair.

"Sit down and have a chat," he urged, and dropped his magazine to the floor, with a gesture of flatteringly spontaneous dismissal.

He is so polite, she thought; *he is the politest man in the world.*

She continued to stand there, as by an act of will against the compulsion of his gaze.

Politeness, she thought, *it's just a way of making people do things.*

"Won't you have a highball?" he asked, and nodded toward the tray on which a bottle and glasses stood beside a siphon.

"Is Jerry coming out here?" she demanded, ignoring his invitation.

"Why, yes," he said casually, but for an instant she felt the probing appraisal of his eyes upon her, and then his gaze flicked away from her, as fingers flick over a page just read. "Yes, I sent Anse to meet the plane and bring him out immediately. He has some papers I want to see." He paused, glanced out the wide windows down the drive as though already expecting the arrival. "Yes, he has done a nice job for me in New York. Like a veteran." Then turning from the windows, he added: "That boy will go far, very far."

"I hope he does," she said, "and stays there."

She thought that that would make him jump a little. But it didn't. Nothing ever did. He simply regarded her indulgently, somewhat amusedly, then said, offhandedly: "I thought you and Jerry got along pretty well."

"Oh, Jerry—he gets along well with everybody," she replied as sweetly as she could. Then added, "simply *everybody,*" with just the slightest emphasis on *everybody,* and hugged herself inwardly over that one.

"So he does," Bogan Murdock agreed evenly. "It is an asset in business."

"Oh, of course," she breathed humbly, but her father did not seem to hear her. He was looking out of the windows again.

"He is coming now," he said.

She took a step forward so that she could look out. A half mile down the drive, the black coupe was coming serenely and powerfully up the rise between the cedars and handsome oaks.

"Will he be here for dinner?" she asked.

"I imagine so," her father said, still looking down the slope. "I had thought I would suggest it. The Governor and Private Porsum are coming out after."

She retreated toward the door.

"I'm going out back," she announced, and expected her father to say something, but he didn't say a thing, just looking at her like she was three years old.

She didn't bother to close the door as she left the library.

As she passed through the back sitting room, she heard the coupe pull up before the house.

She walked rapidly across the grass toward the two boys by the paddock. They were as she had left them, her brother lounging, Slim Sarrett with one hand laid on the top bar. They were arguing about something as she came up, but she didn't even bother to catch what it was. She broke in: "Slim, when I drive you in, will you take me to dinner?"

Slim regarded her detachedly for a moment, and she tried to read those chocolate-colored, agate-bright eyes. "Yes," he said, then, "if you will eat where I usually get my dinner. It is not a very good place, but I eat there because they give me credit when I need it."

"All right," she said.

Lulled by the triumphant and unremitting sonority of the motors of the plane, a sound which now, after so many hours, was unremarked by his mind, simply a background for all his awareness, a richly piled, dark velvet on which the bright center of his consciousness was cushioned, he lay back in the bucket seat; and feeling it give beneath the shift of his considerable weight, he relished that elegant resilience of the leather, the padding, the tempered steel of the frame.

He had thought to be able to sleep a little on the way down, for he had scarcely been to bed the night before in New York, but no matter how fully he relaxed, or how carefully he disposed his limbs, he was unable even to drowse. The present reality was too sweet, too flattering, to be renounced; and even as he tried to sleep, in some unsuspected nook of his mind his pleasure would flare up to a steady unwinking flame again; and then, if he kept his eyes closed, it was only to enjoy more unreservedly the truth of that interior illumination.

He could not surrender the present. Last night, after Mr. Burgess had let him off at the hotel, and had shaken hands with him, and said, "Give my best regards to Murdock," he had stood on the pavement to watch the big dark sedan whirl sibilantly away up the empty street, and had felt it impossible to enter the gleaming doorway behind him and cross the lobbies and cushioned corridors to lay himself down on the antiseptic sheets and, at last, shut his eyes on the powerful and tingling verity of the world.

But he had gone in, under the high ceiling, aware, as he traversed certain areas of uncarpeted marble, of the positive, rhythmic percussion of his heels, which seemed to strike down through the sheathing of marble, through the cement, steel, and superficial earth, to the fundamental center. Once in his room, he had lighted another cigarette, had taken a bottle of Scotch from his bag, and had telephoned down for ice and soda. He had stood looking at the bed: the sheet creased meticulously back, the folded pajamas, the decorously plumped pillow, gleaming, which waited for the impress of his head. The boy had come, had arranged the ice and bottle of soda, had opened the bottle of Scotch, had stood there, very erect, with his eyes, anonymous and unseeing and seeing, fixed at the level of the client's chest, and had said: "Will there be anything else, sir?"

Gerald Calhoun almost said, "Yes," without thinking, but he knew that everything was in its place, that every service had been rendered. So he said: "Are you often on night duty?" And waited, with a shameless avidity, for the reply.

"I am on duty this week, then I'll be off for three weeks, sir," the boy replied in that same anonymous tone, with the same inflection on the *sir;* but the eyes which, a moment before had seemed so anonymous, which by his inane question he had tried to stir to some warmth of personal life, now narrowed, ever so slightly, in their own self-assertion, which was cunning, appraising, vindictive.

Gerald Calhoun had felt resentful and tricked, as though he had reached out to fondle a dog, and the creature had turned on him in its true and snarling bestiality.

He had wanted to say to the boy, "My name is Gerald Calhoun—Gerald Calhoun—Jerry Calhoun—I have something to tell you—I—" He was full of things to tell people.

He heard the ice settle chinkingly in the full glass on the table beside him.

"Will there be anything else, sir?" the boy said, waiting, erect, insolent, uncompromising.

"No."

Then watching the boy turn away, he had, with calculated deliberation, separated a bill from the others in his wallet, and had held it out.

"Thank you, sir," the boy had said, and had taken the dollar, and had gone.

He himself had undressed and had got into bed. He had not touched the drink. Reaching up to turn off the bed light, he had seen the last few bubbles waver to the surface of the yellow liquid, each to explode there and release into the air of the room its infinitesimal charge of gas.

Suddenly now he felt the plane jolt slightly, encountering some irregular current of air, a cushioned, retarded jolt, as when the rubber-tired wheel of a surrey surmounts a stone in the road and drops over it. He straightened up in his seat, and looking out the window at the sunny emptiness of air, he smiled to think of the comparison which had come to his mind, thinking with momentary fondness which was patronizing, not entirely uncontemptuous, of the rutted lane, with the outcroppings of limestone, which had led to his father's house, and how he himself, a child on the back seat of the surrey, used to shut his eyes, as they drove up the lane after church, at noon or in the evening, and used to try to identify the stages of their progress by the special lurches and jerks. Well, the lane was pretty well graveled and fixed up now.

The plane, he observed from the instrument above the pilot's head, was losing altitude very gradually.

He looked down. The great valley was now below. It was richly tapestried and mottled brown for the bareness of the late fields, and red and dun and gold and adder-black for the wooded slopes and watercourses, and firmly, fecundly green, with scarcely an autumnal tone, for the pastures. Very far below, the valley spread out miles to the south, like an open fan, up the river, and the river lolled the length of the colored basin, and at last—near now, for he could see distinctly—coiled and contorted itself at the gap in the hills, as though to gather itself for the victorious free thrust, northward. It came gleamingly out of the haze of distance to the south, and the tributaries converged toward it across the land. He knew the names, Big Duck, Little Duck, Holly Mill Creek, Still

9

Deer, Pine-Away, and had heard, years back, or so it seemed, the ripple of their waters at dams, at fords, over stones, had felt it upon his wrists or about his ankles, and had called to friends across their easy widths. And now, looking down at their scarcely discernible courses, he thought how the earth, still soft from the lay-by plowing of summer, not yet packed by the fall rains, would crumble confidingly under the heel, and how some man or boy down there, going home across the fields, or lounging at the edge of the woods, would catch the silvery, fishlike glint of the plane in the upper light, and would keep his gaze fixed upon it as it dipped toward the city at the gap in the bluish hills.

That boy, or man, down there would see the plane, but he wouldn't know that Jerry Calhoun was up there. He wouldn't know that. But it was true.

That great valley, and these hills themselves, had lain—how many thousands of years ago—under the suffocating mass, and undifferentiating tread, of water. It had been a lightless slime, receiving as the meaningless seasons passed, the sediments and wastage of a life above. It had been pushed up. The epicontinental sea had been shouldered off and drained away. It had its history. He had seen the shell in the limestone which had once been slime; the print of the frond, its delicacy unimpaired. He had chipped these things out of stone, with his hammer. He had leaned above the dented, dusty boards of the laboratory table, and had sorted and classified them.

He was, or had been, a geologist.

Now he looked down upon the valley, and the late light, layered, striated, and rippling, was like the substance of a crystalline sea which had risen again, on the instant, to drown out that valley, but had done so with such subtlety that not a single item of its cunning and laborious perfections had been altered. He drifted effortlessly over those things, curious and detached, as once, when on a vacation in Florida, he had peered through the glass of a boat bottom at the glimmering intricacies of the world below.

But, presently, he would go down into this world. He took the telegram from his pocket and read it again: *Mr. Gerald Calhoun, Hotel Parkerman, New York City. Please bring papers immediately to house. Car will meet plane. Congratulations. Murdock.*

The plane was slanting off. He looked at his watch. It would be only a minute or two more. Then he would be down in that world, where he knew particular rooms, streets, names, and faces. There he would find, as though coming into focus beyond the fine sweep of the avenue of oaks and cedars, Bogan Murdock's face, strong, swarthy, shrewdly molded, blue-eyed, aquiline, smiling with closely set white teeth.

When Gerald Calhoun entered the library, Bogan Murdock, who had been seated by the window, rose with that balanced, lithe, and yet calculated motion, as of a force reined in its orbit, which was so characteristic of him, and put out his hand. "Well, well," Murdock said, smiling, and the level rays, which struck through the western windows, lighted up one side of his face, defining the high cheek bone and the long thrust of the jaw, and the upper lip, which was convolved in friendliness; and left the other side in shadow. "Well, well," he said again, shaking hands, "you did a fine job, Jerry."

"Thanks," Gerald Calhoun said, and all the stored satisfaction of the last two days, which had seemed so full in itself, ripened to the solidity of the moment, as when, at last, the check, which has been carried in the secrecy of the wallet, is laid, almost reluctantly, on the cool marble of the teller's window and is converted by the adeptness of the pale, flickering, ritualistic fingers into the newer, almost unanticipated pleasure of the neatly sheafed bills.

"Have a drink," Murdock said, and gestured toward the table where the bottle, siphon, and glasses waited on the silver tray.

Jerry shook his head. "No, thanks. I reckon I had a couple too many last night. Mr. Burgess took me around."

"You were in good hands," Murdock said, and laughed. "I don't imagine the speak-easy proprietors attempted to pass off any of their customary sorghum and benzine under those circumstances."

"We were at the Caraway Club most of the evening," Jerry said, conscious, even as he spoke, of the little touch of pride and rebuttal in his tone. And he was almost sure that Murdock was conscious of it, too, indulgently conscious, for he laughed and said, "Well, even the Caraway isn't above such things. In a promising situation. They're in business, you know."

"Yes," Jerry said.

"I don't suppose you got to bed very early, either, if you were with Burgess. He can stand a lot of punishment. Any kind. He can come out of his office as fresh as a two-pounder out of a mountain brook, and then put the Harvard boys to bed. I've shot deer with him in Louisiana, too, and that can be less than a picnic. And he's sixty, if he's a day."

"He said tell you he was coming down this fall for your quail."

"Fine," Murdock said, "he's a gun, now." Then, with only an im-

11

perceptible change in the casualness of his tone, he asked, "And you have the papers there?"

Jerry extended the brief case, which he held in his left hand. Murdock took it, and with the air of a man who chucks down an old hat, tossed it onto the broad ledge of the windows. Jerry had half expected him to open the case and take out the clean, crackling sheets which he himself, on the plane coming down, had examined and fingered so many times. He was almost disappointed, almost hurt, by that easy motion, and within him there was something like the echo of the little plop which the case made on the use-polished oak of the ledge.

Then he knew that he had been wrong to expect the man to sit and open the case and even glance at the contents. That action, which would have been so natural for another man, for himself, for instance, would not have been natural for Bogan Murdock. Bogan Murdock, after he had gone out, would sit again in that wing chair by the window, in this high, hushed room, where he so often sat alone—Jerry was surprised on the instant to discover how often he had thought of him in that way, alone in the late afternoon, in this room, unmoving in his rich potential. Now, he would sit down again, in profile to the windows, and while the last sunlight struck through the oaks and cedars and lay across the sweep of lawn, and while the few hickory chunks smoldered on the hearth, he would take a sip from his glass, and then, unhurriedly, reach for the convenient brief case. Jerry could see it with perfect clarity.

"Have a chair," Murdock was saying, and himself sat down.

"I won't disturb you," Jerry said.

"You certainly won't be, but if you want to stretch your legs after the plane, you'll find Sue and Hammond, and some boy Sue's picked up at the University, out at the stables. They've gone out to see Starlight."

"I reckon I'll walk out there, then." He turned away.

"See you got a new suit in New York," Murdock's voice said.

"Yes, I did," Jerry admitted, and glanced down at the satisfying sweep of the dark-gray fabric.

Murdock's gaze was accurate, friendly, paternal. "Very nice," he said.

"Thanks," Jerry said, and again started to go.

"The next time you go East," Murdock's voice said, "—and I'll probably be sending you toward Christmas about those Massey Mountain Lumber Company bonds—I'll give you a note to my tailor. Larkinson. Remind me."

12

"I'll do that," Jerry said, and with a slight sense of guilt, stole a look at the suit which Murdock was wearing. It was new, or almost new, he thought, for he had never seen it before. It was of a coarse tweed, dull blue-green; and the color of it seemed to come to twin focus in the man's eyes, which were smoky-blue around the hard, glittering black of the pupils. The suit might be new, Murdock might be wearing it for the first time, but you could not be sure. From the moment when he had put it on it would have been, and unmistakably, his. What another man might master by use, attrition, and long familiarity, and only in the slack decrepitude of the object, he mastered instantly and effortlessly. Jerry saw the heavy thorn stick, iron-ferruled, flung carelessly on the carpet by the chair, its handle polished by the intensity of that compact, not large palm; and the shoes on the man's feet, brown and heavy, but seemingly pliable. A 'ittle earth clung to the heel of one of the shoes. Murdock, on coming home from the office, must have walked out over the fields, probably to one of the tobacco barns. Now he sat there motionless, as Jerry had seen him sit in gatherings of people, motionless and silent, waiting, not quite with a smile, while the random voices, one after another, died away around him.

"By the way," Murdock said, "why don't you stay for dinner if you want. There's just the family."

Jerry said that he would like to stay, and said, "So long," and went out, and down the long hall. There, catching sight, in the great pier glass, of his own powerful, tall figure, draped in the new gray cloth, he hesitated for the fraction of a second. Jerking himself more erect, he buttoned his coat, inspected it, not too happily, in the mirror, and then passed on down the hall, toward the rear door.

After he had passed the rose garden, almost leafless now, he could see, over there across the stretch of lawn, the three figures leaning against the white fence near the stables. There was Sue in the center, standing on one long leg, the short skirt jerked up high, and tight over her narrow bottom, with the tension of resting the other foot on a bar of the fence. Her arms were crossed on the top bar, and her chin, as well as he could tell from that distance, was resting on her crossed arms. On her left there was Hammond Murdock, slouching against the fence, and on her right, the almost lanky figure of another youth. He was practically upon them before they heard him, for the turf on which he trod was deep and resilient.

Hammond, turning, said, "Hello, Jerry," and Sue, lifting her head a little but not changing her posture, said, "Well, I was expecting to read about the plane crash in the evening paper."

"No such luck," Jerry said; "we came floating in like a feather."

Sue indicated the lanky youth with a nod. "That," she affirmed, "is Slim Sarrett. And this—" she nodded toward Jerry, "is Gerald Calhoun. The sport writers used to call him Bull's-eye. But they've forgotten about him now."

"Glad to know you," Jerry said surlily, thinking that this was the way she was going to be, was it? On the way down he hadn't really wondered much how it would be. He had just put the question back somewhere in his mind, but it had been there, all right—he knew that now—and this was the answer.

Then, almost as an afterthought, he put out his hand toward the fellow named Slim. The boy took it, and Jerry, feeling at the first contact the narrowness of the hand, was suddenly surprised to find that the long thin fingers, which had extended, prehensilely, around to the back of his own heavy hand, were, with unsuspected strength, tightening like wires. And it seemed perfectly uncalculated. He met the candid, not too precise, gaze of the boy's brown eyes, and aware of an uneasy incongruity, released the hand.

"I'm glad to know you, Mr. Calhoun," the boy said quietly. "I'm sorry I wasn't at State during your playing days. I've heard a lot about you since I've been out there."

"It's nice to know that," Jerry said. "Even though—" and he nodded at Sue, "the papers, like she says, have forgotten about it now." He realized that he had not intended to say that last. It was a fool thing to say. But it had just slipped out. And he noticed that Sue, with her chin again propped sidewise on her crossed arms on the fence bar, was looking at him triumphantly, as from ambush.

"—and we could have used a little of your passing last Saturday. You missed the game, didn't you, being in New York?" The boy's easy, unemphatic, somewhat conciliatory voice was going on, as Jerry began to attend to it. "If we won, it was simply luck. You can't expect to recover fumbled punts every day, even if you have got a couple of good ends. What we need is some decent passing. Riley simply heaves the ball away, like the Russians used to throw the baby out of the sleigh to distract the wolves, and—"

"Oh, precisely, precisely," Sue said, "like the Russians," speaking as though to herself, with her gaze fixed on the big gleaming bay stallion, which was cropping grass in the paddock.

"—and if Morfee doesn't change his style of coaching in the backfield—"

"Don't listen to a word of it," Sue said. She rolled her head so that it lay on its side on her arms, as on a pillow, and regarded Jerry and the boy. "He doesn't know a damned thing about it. He

14

just writes poetry. That's why he wears his collar open like that. Like Shelley—"

"I have a tie," the boy said, in the same detached and yet insinuating tone, "but I must save it for Sundays."

The boy wore a freshly starched white shirt, with the collar open to expose the little V-shaped place where the tendons, which were thinly, almost painfully tight, joined the musculature of the chest. His old green pullover had gone drab in streaks, and was out at the elbows. His trousers, uncreased and loose about his long legs, were of some light washable fabric, probably the trousers of an old summer suit. Jerry observed these things for the first time.

"Oh, I beg your pardon, Slim," Sue continued. "I didn't mean Shelley. I always get people mixed up. I meant Byron. He wore his collar open, too, and I forgot that you like him so much better than Shelley. That—" and she addressed Jerry, "is because Byron could box, and Slim is a boxer, too."

"Not a boxer," Slim corrected, and laughed, "a college boxer."

"Well," Jerry said, sore at the girl and feeling, for the first time, a little kindliness for the boy, "you've sure got something on me. It just wasn't my dish. I didn't mind getting hurt, that is, I didn't mind more than the next man; I got hurt now and then playing football, but that seems sort of like an accident. But I just didn't like to stand up there and have somebody hack me down in cold blood. And when I used to try to connect with the fellow, he was always somewhere else."

"I don't like to be hurt," the boy affirmed, distantly. "Not at all. But the object of boxing is to hurt and not be hurt."

"I reckon I just never got the point, then," Jerry said, and laughed.

"Well, Slim," Hammond Murdock said, "if you don't like to get hurt, you better start weaving right now, before you meet that fellow Halleck from Tech. It looks like he's hurt a good many people." Then, again, he seemed to withdraw from the group, and again stared off across the paddock and the rolling pastures, to the fringe of hills toward the east.

"Oh, if Slim gets hurt too bad, he can always write some more poetry," Sue said, and then turned to Jerry. "Which is more than you can do. You can't even write letters. At least, you didn't."

"I was just away a few days," Jerry said, defensively. "And I did write you two cards."

"That isn't a letter. A picture of Grant's tomb, and something cute you wrote underneath. One look at that card, and anybody could tell you'd never been to New York before. It was so damned cute."

"It was very appropriate, then. For I hadn't ever been to New York before."

"You might have written a letter. Not that I wanted it. But considering all the meals you've eaten out here."

Speaking to him, she had swung to face him, but only from the hips, with her foot still propped on the lowest bar of the fence; and the torsion of the movement had pulled her skirt well up above the knee, so that a section of the flesh was visible above the neat roll of the stocking, which, ever so slightly, puckered the firmness of that flesh. His right palm tingled, and involuntarily his fingers curved to the precise conformation of that spot. And, precisely, he knew the degree of resistance which that segment of flesh had offered to his right hand, the sheath of softness, under the silk of her dress, and under that sheath of softness, the hardness of the semimembranous muscle of the experienced rider. It had been that unexpected hardness, plaited and expert under the superficial flesh, which had stirred him, on the instant of contact, more than any incidental softness or surrendering seductivity had ever done. It had, as it were, defined for him, violently, her basic reality. The night before leaving for New York, sitting on the divan in her father's library, he had leaned to kiss her, and that for the first time, and had laid his hand on that spot. She had kissed him, and then, as his hand had increased, ever so little, and unpremeditatedly, its pressure, she had jerked back.

"I won't be pawed," she had said. "Take your hand off me."

"All right," he had said.

"And get that expression off your face, too," she had said. "Nobody's abused you. I don't owe you a thing."

Now, he leaned against the paddock fence, and looked at that little patch of flesh, the quality of which the pressure of the roll of stocking defined, and knew that Slim was looking at the same spot; and knew that the girl knew that he himself was looking there and knew that he knew that Slim's eyes, in their arrogant and detached innocence, were fixed there, too. He felt the blood mounting, in anger and embarrassment, to his cheeks and forehead.

"At least," Sue said, "you've got the decency to blush about the way you've behaved. Look—" and she nodded at him, "he's blushing!"

Hammond Murdock had not turned.

"Well," she continued, in her discursive, unedged tone, "that shows he has some shame. He—"

16

"Oh, shut up," Hammond Murdock ordered. "You make me sick." He still leaned on the highest bar, and stared morosely across the landscape.

"I meant to say," Jerry said, "that I'm having another meal out here tonight. Your father asked me to dinner."

"Well, I won't be here. I'm driving Slim in, and he's going to take me slumming. We're going to eat at a dog-wagon."

"It isn't a dog-wagon, exactly," Slim said, in the tone of one who makes a correction merely out of a disinterested love of accuracy. "It's a sort of a restaurant. Down near the river. The food is not very good. It is greasy. But I eat there quite frequently because it is very cheap and is near my studio."

"Well, whatever it is, I'm going. And the Governor's coming out here tonight after dinner, with that fellow they call Private Porsum, I heard Father say, and you won't have to be bothered with me. You can sit around and smoke cigars with the big shots. You're going to be a big shot yourself some day, it just sticks out all over you—like boils—"

"You better not stay in town again," Hammond said. "You better be here for dinner. The Old Man will be sore as hell. I heard him tell you you had to study tonight. And you know what he said about you driving at night by yourself."

"You can tell him after I'm gone. If he doesn't guess when he sees my car going down the drive. That is—" and she swung toward her brother, "unless you want to make up a lie to protect me, Ham."

"I don't," Ham said.

"I'm going right now." She took her foot off the lowest bar of the fence, set it firmly on the ground, and laying the palms of her hands on the flatness of her hips, settled her skirt into position. "Right now," she said. "Come on, Slim."

"Sure," Slim said. "I'm glad to have met you, Mr. Calhoun."

"I'm glad to have met you," Jerry said.

The girl had started off across the grass. "Come on, Slim," she ordered, hesitating an instant. Then, as Slim followed her, she called back, "I'll see you all later."

Jerry watched the two figures move across the grass, pass the rose garden, and climb into the blue roadster, with its top down, which stood there at the back of the house. Then the car leaped forward, churning the gravel of the drive with a ripping sound, which, even at the distance, he could distinguish. As the car swept around the drive, and disappeared beyond the mass of the house, he watched the two heads which were just visible above the strapped-down top, the boy's dark and erect, hers thrust forward a little and with the blond hair lifting in the wind of the machine's passage.

He turned, and crossed his arms on the fence, beside Ham. Ham let his head droop forward over the bar, and meticulously pursing his rather heavy lips, let a globule of spit fall to the grass. It hung there on a grass stalk, white and frothy, gradually losing its color and identity as it spread slowly down the stalk. "The Old Man will sure give her hell," the boy said, still staring down at the spit.

Jerry did not answer.

The stallion had come closer, cropping the grass. The animal's rich bay coat had lost its sheen now, for the light was failing. The working of its teeth on the thick, crisp grass made a stitching sound.

"Slim," Ham said, as though he were making a complete affirmation, and again, slowly let a globule of spit form at his lips, and drop.

"Who is he?"

"You might say," the boy responded, "that he's a graduate student over at the University. He teaches some freshman class, or something. Then again, you might say he's a son-of-a-bitch. Born to the purple."

"Something sort of told me that."

"He's a good boxer," Ham said, "but that don't keep him from being a son-of-a-bitch. I saw him in one fight when he nursed some poor lumoxy twirp through five rounds when he could have kayoed him in the first. He didn't nurse him because he loved him. He just kept him on his feet so he could work on him careful. When the fellow looked like he was going down, damn if Slim didn't clinch to hold him up. He sure worked on him. They stopped the fight."

"He sounds like a fellow you'd like for a pal," Jerry said.

"He ain't exactly my pal," Ham said, "but I sort of like him. You can't dent him." He stopped, and seemed wrapped in his own reflections. Then he added: "Sue sure picked a post this time to sharpen her claws on. It's like the Woolworth Building." He sank again into himself, seeming to expect no answer. After a minute he stuck his right hand, fumblingly, into the pocket of his frayed leather jacket, and pulled out a squashed package of cigarettes and a pad of matches. Without speaking, he offered a cigarette to Jerry, who took it. He lighted Jerry's cigarette, and his own, and sank again into his former posture. They smoked in silence for a while. Then the boy said: "But I sort of like the son-of-a-bitch. Because he is the way he is, I reckon." Then staring morosely off

18

across the paddock and the darkening fields, he added: "I reckon a fellow needs a hide like an elephant's."

A figure had come out of the stables down across the paddock. Even in the bad light, its slow, hulking, uneasy mass was discernible in silhouette against the white wall of the stables. It moved along, lurchingly, weightedly, until it had come beyond the white wall, and then, without contrast, merging into the shadow of the land, it lost its definition.

"There's Grandpa," the boy said, "going up to the house. I reckon we better get on in."

"Sure," Jerry said.

During the meal, no one remarked the vacant chair, and the place at the table. Jerry had half expected some comment from Bogan Murdock, or if not some comment, at least some change of expression at the moment when, coming into the room a little after the others, he had first discovered the fact that his daughter was not present. That had to be the moment of discovery, Jerry decided, for only Ham had known, and he himself had been with Ham the whole time, out by the paddock and then up in Ham's room before coming down to dinner. No one even glanced at the vacant place, no one except Jerry himself, who, only half aware of the even flow of voices around him, now and then stole a look there. Bogan Murdock was talking about football, saying that the game Saturday had been ragged, that the win had been lucked, that Riley and Holmes were naturals but that they had not received adequate coaching; and Jerry, hearing the same things which he had been inclined to deny when that Slim had said them out by the paddock, now nodded in agreement, and thought: *Well, it was just because that bastard was saying them, I reckon.*

"As a matter of fact," Bogan Murdock said, "the whole system of football here needs—"

"I told him—I told him—" old Mr. Murdock said suddenly, very loud, and heaved his shapeless bulk a little forward, while he lifted his big head, as in command, shaking the sparse and dingy-gray, but yet leonine, locks, and stared from face to face with a widening flicker of his pale blue eyes.

"Yes, Father?" Bogan Murdock questioned, and inclined his head in that patient, schooled, and impeccable courtesy which he always showed the old man.

The old man focused his gaze, as with effort, upon his son, and laid his fork down, clatteringly, on the plate. He shook his head

19

again, with an irritable, baffled motion. "That hay—that hay down there," he said creakingly "—it ain't ricked up right. It ain't—"

Bogan Murdock waited for a moment, his head still inclined as though in invitation for the old man to continue, but those pale blue eyes were blinking now, seeming to withdraw into their blood-shot sockets. "I'll see to it tomorrow, Father," Bogan Murdock said. "Without fail." Then his voice resumed in its previous tone, as though the interruption had never occurred: "The whole system of football here needs an overhauling. I have recently talked to several of the more influential alumni, and have heard their opinions, which—"

The old man had sunk back in his chair, his head sagging pensively forward, its weight seeming to merge into the mass below. His mouth was somewhat open, and Jerry, sitting across from him, saw the gob of half-masticated food which lay toward the bearded lower lip, and which, with its wetness, gleamed a little in the light. Then he saw the gob withdrawn over the ruined teeth, and the big jawbone, under its sacked and folded flesh, begin to move.

"—which, on the whole, agree with mine. I do not maintain, I may say, that the sole, or even the primary object, of football in a college or university is to win games. But I have always thought that anything which was worth doing at all was worth doing well, or at least as well as one is capable of doing it. And I have never been able to see the necessity for constantly temporizing when one is confronted with a problem. If this institution should say that it did not mind losing games, and was going to play amateur football, I would be heartily behind such a program. But we—"

"I told him—I told him—" The old man started up, and his fork, clutched in his big, yellow, scaled fist, pointed upward.

"Yes, Father?" Bogan Murdock inquired, and waited.

But the old man made no reply.

"So," Bogan Murdock continued, "since we do not enjoy the satisfaction of virtue, we might at least enjoy the satisfaction of efficiency. And if there are to be victories, there must be a system. We can't expect players just to pop up these days—as you popped up, Jerry—just by the grace of God. Things have changed in the ten or twelve years since you were a freshman. You probably wouldn't come to State at all these days, would you?"

"I hadn't thought about it," Jerry said. "As it was, I just went where I could. And they had a good geology department."

"Well, in these days of recruiting, a lad with your high-school record would have a wide range of choices, with a nice little subsidy."

"Well, I didn't get any nice little subsidy," Jerry said, ruefully.

"Well—" Bogan Murdock said, as though clinching something.

But all the while, after the first few questions about his trip, Dorothy Murdock had said scarcely anything; but he was not sure that there was not, in her quietness, a restraint, a tautness, which only waited for the slightest contact of the appropriate circumstance to set it in vibration, or snap it. He could not be sure, for he had seen her, many times, that way, her small, clearly cut face, which always seemed pale in contrast to her dark, never too well controlled hair, lifted in polite attention, and her mouth set in its incipient smile, which was expectant, or appreciative, as the occasion might demand. But he had never phrased to himself that impression of tautness, and did not do so now; but he had, in the past, when left alone with her, or when the general conversation had sunk away, hesitated before addressing some commonplace remark to her, as though in fear of upsetting a precariously won balance. He had seen her knuckles whiten at the apparently casual contact with a banister, or whiten upon the bridle rein, when the horse stood perfectly still, or upon the steering wheel of a car, when the road was straight and open and the tires hummed comfortingly. Their color, then, would be a kind of mother-of-pearl, faintly tinted with blue.

He observed that whitening of the knuckles when, in the drawing room after dinner, she picked up a folder of music before adjusting it on its rack on the piano. "Let's have a little music," Murdock had said, sitting back in his chair with his coffee cup in his hand, "before the Governor comes. There's mighty little music in that pleasant old soul."

The white fingers, bluish-white against the ivory-white of the keys, had extended themselves, exhibiting, in that preparatory moment, their elaborate and almost fleshless articulation. Then they had proceeded, brittlely, accurately, to move upon the keys.

After a few minutes Dorothy Murdock went upstairs. She was not, she said, feeling very well.

For a minute after her departure neither Bogan Murdock nor Jerry said anything. Then Murdock moved to the bench before the instrument. Idly, luxuriously, he began to pick out notes from the keyboard, letting his dark, aquiline face droop forward a little. He plucked the notes with a slow relish, like a man who plucks grapes, one by one, from an arbor and lays them soberly and delectably upon his tongue. Stopping, turning to Jerry, he said, "Music—it's the only pure thing in the world."

He picked another note, and turned again. "If things had been different for me when I was a boy, I might—" Then he shook his head. "Well," he said, and spread his fingers upon the keyboard and began to improvise a slow, sweet, melancholy tune; and Jerry, attending to it, thought of his own boyhood, which, for the moment, seemed precious to him. That was strange, for ordinarily he shut his mind resolutely to any thought of that past.

"Well, well, Mr. Calhoun," the Governor had said, "I'm glad to know you, boy. I might have come nearer to recognizing you at first glance, though, if you'd had that old number six on your back and had your arm cocked back for a toss. Yes, sir, the old All American—that would have been easier, at first glance. Many's the time, boy." And the Governor had clapped him on the shoulder.

"Jerry's just back from New York," Murdock had said. "He's just done a nice little piece of business up there for me. The Atlas Iron properties."

"Still Bull's-eye, huh?" The Governor had laughed his easy, throaty laugh, letting his weight sink into an easy chair, and stretching out his legs. Then turning to the men who had come with him, he asked: "Didn't you ever see Mr. Calhoun on the field, Sam? Didn't you, Private?"

"Hell, Jeff, you know I never saw a football game in my life," Sam Dawson said, "but I've seen Jerry quieten a horse."

"Didn't you ever see him, Private?" the Governor asked, turning to the other man.

The tall, raw-boned man, now running to flesh, turned his sober, almost too narrow hazel eyes upon the Governor, and his clay-colored face broke into a sober, not quite apologetic smile. "I reckon I'm like Sam there," he said. "I never saw a football game in my life till I came down here. There wasn't any football up in the mountains. The boys just wrassled, and went to break-downs and got drunk and had fights, bare knucks or stomp and gouge, or went hunting, or had turkey shoots up there."

"Which was just as well," Governor Milam proclaimed. "I reckon it wasn't football you needed, Private, that morning you potted all those Germans."

"Governor," Private Porsum said, laughing, but with a laughter which was not quite true and comfortable, "it was luck I needed that morning."

"Luck," Bogan Murdock echoed, then said: "Luck never comes to the man who isn't ready for it, Private. Luck—you have to train for luck. Fortune—who was it said it?—is like a woman, and she surrenders easiest to the man who will take her by the hair."

The Negro brought the whisky then, and they settled back in their chairs, lifting the glasses, which in the firelight glinted ruddily. Sam Dawson took a deep gulp and set his glass on the floor beside him. Then, with the back of his hand, he wiped his red mustache. "Be damned," he said, "if I didn't take my first drink not more'n two weeks after I lost my virginity to a high-yaller out behind the haystack, and be damned if it don't taste better every time I pick up a glass. I was toddling home across the pasture in my little blue pinafore. I'd been down fishing in that little branch runs across our place, and had a couple of little sun perch on a string, and that high-yaller—"

"Sure, Sam, sure," Bogan Murdock said, soothingly, and laughed.

Sam Dawson grinned, showing his crooked yellow teeth, a slow grin, mischievous and sly under its heaviness, the kind of grin which, Jerry thought, he had seen in his boyhood on faces which leaned about the stove in the crossroads store. Sam Dawson had sat in crossroads stores and grinned that grin, Jerry knew, had sat by the pot-bellied glowing stove, in the nondescript, shabby clothes which he wore now, and had swapped talk with the loafers and had grinned and spat. But Sam Dawson's father had sat on the Supreme Court of the state, his grandfather had sat in the fateful room with Jefferson Davis that day in Montgomery, his great-great-grandfather had crossed the mountains from Virginia with the Continental Grant in his pocket and had built the house they called Northumberland, where behind the severe white pillars Sam Dawson led his slack and disorderly bachelor life, with riding crops and fishing tackle flung down on rosewood, with dust an inch thick in the corners, and had in his yellow wenches—so they said—and laid the schemes which bore fruit in the Legislature, on the stump, and in the upper rooms of hotels. When his father died, Sam Dawson, a boy then, had announced that a man with eight thousand acres of river land and Northumberland and a hand for handling horses and niggers didn't need to know more than to write his name. So he had steadfastly declined any more schooling. That was what they said, Jerry knew, but knew that Sam Dawson knew a lot more than horses and niggers and how to write his name. He knew what made men act.

"That's a likely-looking colored boy you got," the Governor said to Murdock, "that Anse."

"Yes," Bogan Murdock replied. "He's smart. He goes out here to this Negro college, every other term. He works a while for me, till he saves up some, then he goes back. I've promised to stake him to a hitch at Columbia University if he does well out here at Bollin."

"Bollin College," the Governor meditated, nodding. "I'm glad to hear somebody's getting some good out of it. We put up a hundred thousand this last legislature for it."

"Huh," Sam Dawson said, and picked up his glass.

"Only you mustn't call him Anse any more," Murdock said, and smiled. "He says his name is really Anselm. He read about this Anselm in a book."

"I know his pappy," Sam Dawson said, "and his pappy's name is shore-God Anse."

"His father lives on this place now, but his name is really Anselm, too. At least, that is what the boy tells me. So we call him Anselm."

"I'd be God damned," Sam Dawson uttered. "I'd wash my own dishes first. I'd die of thirst in the parlor with my tongue black like a dog's three days dead and the sun bearing down, before I'd do it. Look here, Jeff—" and he swung toward the Governor, "I elect half the senators in your damned legislature and that's the way you let 'em pass their time. Voting a hundred thousand so Dock's boy gets called Anselm. That's the—" He gave up. He sank his broad, flat, florid face until his lips were in contact with the glass, and then leaned his head back and drank.

"He's likely-looking," the Governor said. "He's light on his feet."

"Too God-damned light," Sam Dawson said. "I like to hear 'em coming."

Bogan Murdock laughed. "All right, Sam," he said, "I'll bell him the next time you're over."

"I'd like to hear him coming right now," Sam Dawson said, and drained his glass. "With that bottle rattling on his tray."

"It won't be necessary," and Bogan Murdock rose, took the bottle from the table, and poured the drink into the proffered glass. Then he brought the water. "And you, Governor?" he asked.

"No, thanks," the Governor said, "I'm lingering. Lingering, and with relish."

"Jerry?"

"No, thanks, not yet," Jerry said.

He sat back, fingering his half full glass, aware of the slow, gently unfolding bloom of the alcohol in him. He was a little drowsy, after the excitements and dissipations of the past several days, but he was glad he had stayed out tonight, for now, with the shaded lamps, the secure warmth of the hickory simmering on the hearth, and the easy flow of the voices, he found the satisfaction which the

24

earlier excitements had promised; more now than when he had turned the brief case over to Bogan Murdock. He himself said nothing. He only listened.

"—and Governor," Bogan Murdock was saying, "you know there's a little matter I've been meaning to speak to you about. But it has slipped my mind when I've been with you. You know, I've got a little tract of land over in the mountains, on Fiddler's Fortune Creek. Where I have a sort of lodge I use for fishing."

"Yes," the Governor said.

"Well," Bogan Murdock continued, "I haven't been able to use it much lately. The Massey Mountain Lumber Company, back before we took over their new bonds, made me an offer for the tract— it's not very big, just about six or seven hundred acres—but it's got some pretty nice timber—but I, well—" he hesitated almost as though in embarrassment, "I sort of had an affection for the place, so I didn't sell. It's a beautiful spot, and a few of our beauties should be retained unspoiled. I thought that, perhaps, the state might be interested in making that the nucleus of a park, a mountain preserve, you know, something of the sort. You see—"

The Governor coughed, and lifted his glass, not to drink but as though he had suddenly become concerned to inspect it. "Very interesting," he said, judicially. "Very interesting. I'll take it up with the Commissioner right away. Very probably he will see eye to eye with me, and something can be done at the next legislature to—"

Bogan Murdock lifted one hand. "Governor, you misunderstand me." And he smiled, again with that hint of embarrassment. "I was thinking about turning the tract over to the state—"

"Santy Claus," Sam Dawson uttered softly, toward the high, shadowy ceiling.

"I don't want to parade myself as a public benefactor, and—"

"You'd be a public benefactor," Sam Dawson said, "if you'd give me leave to pour myself another slug." And without waiting for a reply, he rose.

But Bogan Murdock had anticipated him, and was moving swiftly to the table. He pushed his friend back into the chair, and poured the drink, and brought the water. Then he resumed, as though there had been no interruption: "—and there's only one small stipulation. That the preserve be named for my father. The Major Lemuel Murdock Preserve. Or something of the sort. A sort of memorial to him, you know. He's old, and it might please him. And these days, the Lord knows—" he turned his glance to the fire, "he finds little enough pleasure."

"Very handsome, Bogan, very handsome," the Governor said.

"Our State has a great patrimony of natural beauty, and it is up to us to pass it on to—"

"To the future," Sam Dawson finished. "To our heirs, assigns, and a grateful posterity, but by God, Dock, I wish you'd take me fishing up there one more time before the Boy Scouts start giving eagle calls."

"Sure," Bogan Murdock said.

A car came up the long drive. From where he sat Jerry could watch it approaching, its strong beams striking between the trees. Then, a moment later, the lights swung past the library windows, following the drive to the rear of the house.

It would be Sue, Jerry thought. He knew it was Sue.

Well, let it be, he thought.

She had left Slim Sarrett standing on the curb a block from the river-front restaurant where they had eaten. He had stood there, tallish, in his thin trousers, unsuitable for the season, which wrinkled about his shanks, and his worn sweater, and his white face, above the open collar, smiling distantly and speculatively at her.

He had sat in the booth at the grimy, greasy restaurant as though a headwaiter, ushering him there, had whisked away the reserved marker. He had eaten his food with a fastidious precision, all the while watching her eat, watching her like a farmwife who prides herself on her cooking and wants to see how the guest takes every bite, or like a subtle and courteous potentate who luxuriously entertains a friend and watches for the first effect of the poison which is in the sumptuous dish. Afterward, he had laid a dime by his plate and had paid for their meals, overriding her protest, saying that he had just received a check from a magazine for an article. Then he had escorted her to her car.

After she was seated at the wheel, with the motor already throbbing under the touch of her foot, he had leaned to lay his hand on the door, as to restrain her for a moment, and had said, rather softly: "Sure, you're the sort of person who will get what you want. Because you will pay the price for it. Only—" and he had taken his hand off the door, releasing her to go, "you may not find out what you want until it's off the market."

"You think you know everything," she had retorted, and had slammed the accelerator to the floorboard, and the car had leaped away from the curb, and she had looked back to see him standing there amid the dark, enormous hulks of the warehouses, under the single street lamp, while children screamed in the next block.

He had sat in the restaurant and had made her talk about her-

26

self. Sure, she'd known he was doing it. She wasn't that big a fool. She'd seen him do that before. To other people. And to her. He would make you talk about yourself, and then he would tell you what it meant, what you had meant to say. "You're the sort of person," he would say, "you're the sort of person—" At least, sometimes he would, but sometimes he wouldn't do anything but sit and watch you and ask questions, questions which didn't seem to mean much but which were supposed to make you go on. Oh, she knew his tricks, and she had told him so. She had told him so tonight.

"You think you're making me talk," she had said, "but I know your tricks. I've seen you make people tell you all about themselves."

"I don't make them," he had said. "I simply give them the opportunity. Which is what they want. But they don't talk about themselves out of vanity. Oh, no. It is because they are mysterious to themselves, and they talk just to find out something about the mystery."

"Well, why don't you talk about yourself? Are you worried about what you might find out?" she had demanded triumphantly, preening herself on that one.

"No," he had answered candidly and thoughtfully, "it's not that. It's just that I'm not mysterious to myself. There're things I don't know, of course, but I know the basic line."

"Congratulations," she had murmured.

"And besides," he had continued, unruffled, "I don't have to talk about myself. Poetry is a much better technique for achieving self-knowledge."

"Oh, I must write me a lovely little poem some time," she had said.

But she had talked to him. She hadn't intended to, but she had. But she'd fooled him. If he thought she'd tell him everything, he was crazy. Everything—you couldn't tell everything, even if you tried. Because you didn't know what it was. Nobody knew, and talk was just jabber. It was just jabber. You did something and then you jabbered and told all the reasons, but the reasons were all jabber, and what you did was what it was no matter how much you jabbered, and if it was done it was done.

And caught at a red light, she raced her motor with the clutch down, and on the first flash of amber, she jerked away from the other cars with a roar, leaning forward as though she were putting a hunter to a hurdle, and tried to make the next light, and made it, and tried to make the next one, and made it by the barest with some fool nosing out from the side street and blatting his horn after her like a fool.

She was doing sixty through the suburbs, where the traffic was thinning out and where back across the lawns, under the black trees, you could see people through unshaded windows sitting around under lights reading newspapers or jabbering at each other. Jabbering, and God knew about what. Then she had passed the last houses and left the last lights, so she just gave the car what it would take. And it would take plenty. She sat up straight and let the wind snatch her hair back and half closed her eyes so she didn't see anything but the cement and let the long sweeping gray flow of the road swerve hissingly at her. Well, you didn't have to jabber all the time.

The turn was upon her almost before she knew it, but she took it, the tires screaming on the pavement, then grinding into the gravel of the drive between the big stone gate posts. Up the hill, she could see a few lights in the house, one room upstairs, the old man's room, and the light which marked the windows of the library, where her father would be with those men. As the car swung past the house she caught a glimpse of her father and of another form. She couldn't tell who it was. But it wasn't Jerry. But Jerry was in there, there wasn't any doubt about it, and that was where Jerry Calhoun belonged.

She ran the car into her section of the garage, switched off the light, and not bothering to close the door to her section, started for the house.

Very softly, she let herself in by the French doors of the back sitting room, then crossed the hall to the foot of the staircase. The door to the library was open, and she could hear somebody laughing. Standing there with one hand on the banister, she listened and tried to make out the voices. She moved up the hall cautiously until she could see inside the library. She saw, first, a man's shoulders and head above the back of a chair. That was that fellow Private Porsum. Then, moving a little more toward the front, she could see Jerry Calhoun, who was almost facing her. His legs were thrust out before him, and he held a cigar in his hand, and he was laughing.

That was what did it. Seeing him sitting there laughing fit to kill at something one of those men had said. Oh, she bet it was funny, all right. And sticking his legs out like he owned the world, and smoking one of her father's cigars.

So she began to look at him, hard. It took about three minutes, but it worked. Just the instant before he looked, she knew he was going to look, and she had her forefinger at her lips and was shaking her head warningly. Then when she was sure he saw her, she took her finger from her lips and beckoned peremptorily at him. He had seen her all right, and so she slipped over to stand by the drawing-room door, out of range of vision from the library.

He didn't come right away. She began to think he wasn't going to come, that he was going to say he hadn't seen her, but she knew he had—she had looked straight into his eyes—and if he tried to pull that, she'd fix him. Then he came out of the library, drawing the door almost shut behind him. He was coming toward her, not fast, not slow, but steady, steady and strong, steady, the way he went at everything like something heavy sliding down hill and nothing to stop it—not fast, though they said he used to be fast when he played football, but that was before she was big enough to like to go and she had never seen him, but she suddenly visioned him helmeted, shoulders great with the awkward pads, the ball tucked under one arm, the other arm outthrust, plunging toward her, knees pumping and cleated feet slashing into the turf, or the floor, and his face under the helmet intense and pure in its effort.

But as he came toward her steadily across the floor, there was a question on his face. He stopped at a discreet distance from her, and looked at her with that question. But he just didn't have the nerve to ask it. "Why don't you go on and say it?" she demanded.

"Say what?" he asked.

"Why don't you go on and ask me what I want?"

"Well," he said, and grinned warily—his square white teeth were set wide apart and he looked like a boy when he grinned, and that always surprised you—"what did you want?"

"Oh, I just wanted to ask you about your trip," she replied decorously. "You know, I just didn't have a chance before."

"It was fine," he replied, looking at her suspiciously.

"Did him sell all my daddy's big beautiful bonds in New York?"

"Sure," he said, grinning again.

"And did him have a whole lot of beautiful girls in New York?"

"No," he said, not grinning, "no, as a matter of fact, I didn't have any."

"Ah, me," she cooed outrageously, "is him losing him's little grip? For they say him just has all the beautiful little girls him wants in this town. They say him just has to bat little Southern belles out of him's little bed with a bootjack. Or—" and she inserted a forefinger in the slit between two buttons of his vest, and wiggled it and tugged gently, "was him just being faithful in the big city to little me?"

29

Then, while he seemed to be getting ready to say something and while she tugged her finger in the vest, she did want something, and she hadn't wanted to want it, but she did want, she did, and he was leaning over like he was getting ready to kiss her and was putting his big hand on her upper arm. She took a slight step backward, leaning against the jamb of the open door to the drawing room, with her finger still hooked in his vest. His hand was still on her upper arm and he was still leaning, but she sensed, or thought she sensed, some resistance, an unwieldy mass, the uncertain delay of weight. Perhaps she had only thought it, perhaps it wasn't real, for his arm was about her shoulders now and she felt the solidity of his chest against her, crushing her hand between them, as he kissed her. But the thought was enough. She jerked back, into the open doorway of the dark drawing room, saying: "Oh, you needn't worry, I'm not going to make you go in the dark. Oh, I know little him's afraid of the dark."

Then, as she surveyed him, she added: "You didn't have to kiss me. You don't owe me a thing, you know."

"Now, look here, Sue—" he began belligerently.

"Go on," she cut in, "go on back in there with them, where you belong," and snatched past him, as he stood almost blocking the doorway, and ran across the hall and up the wide stairs. She did not even look back.

Upstairs, in her room, she stood in the middle of the floor and thought: *I don't ever want to see him again.*

She stood there in the middle of the beautiful room, a young girl's room where the lamp gleamed under the rosy shade and the big mirrors of the dressing table reflected the pale-blue walls and the furniture was the color of rich ivory and the sheet on the bed was turned whitely, crisply, back, and she did not ever want to see Jerry Calhoun again, or her father, or mother, or Ham Murdock, or any of the faces she knew, or this beautiful room where, night after night, she had lain down.

Thinking that, she felt light, free, and clean.

Jerry Calhoun, re-entering the library, met the faces which were turned with mild recognition upon him, and experienced a sense of panic, of guilt detected, of fear and isolation. He expected Bogan Murdock's lips to open, Private Porsum's lips, Sam Dawson's lips, or the Governor's lips to open and utter some horrible and invincible accusation before which he would be sick and wordless. But he made his way to his seat, and they fell again to talking among themselves.

He sat in his chair, fingering the dead cigar, and scrutinized their secret and inimical faces. As he sat there, it almost seemed to him that the very walls of the room, the high walls which reached up into the floating shadows of the ceiling, were bending toward him, converging saggingly upon him with a soft and betraying mass, like wax. He gripped, with his free hand, the side of his chair, as though to assure himself that that object, at least, was not participating in the vast conspiracy which was the world.

God damn her, he thought. He hadn't wanted to kiss her, anyway. He was sure of that. One thing he was sure of: he was not in love with Sue Murdock. He didn't have to depend on her for what he got, and he thanked God for that when she was the way she was. He wasn't in love with her. And he never had been. He was sure of that.

"I won't be pawed," she had said, sitting right over there on that divan, a week ago, a week ago tonight; and he stole a look at the divan where Sam Dawson now sprawled.

"All right," he himself had said, and now he could almost hear the sound of his own voice on the words.

"And get that expression off your face, too," she had said. "Nobody's abused you. I don't owe you a thing."

They had sat there, side by side, saying nothing then until he had seen, as tonight, the lights of an approaching car on the drive, and had remarked that it was probably her father.

"Or mother coming home," Sue had said. "She's in town and Ham's bringing her home."

But it had been her father. He had come into the library for a moment, and had said that he hoped Jerry would have a pleasant trip, and had kissed his daughter good night on the cheek, and had gone upstairs.

The girl had risen and had gone to stand beyond the fireplace, looking down at the embers, which they had permitted to die almost away, for the night had been unseasonably warm. He had scarcely noticed her then, thinking of the next morning, of his trip. She had moved away from the fireplace, casually, as if she had been alone, toward the wall which divided the library from the hall. Her back had been toward him so that he had been unable to see what she was doing. On the instant of the little sound of the switches there on the wall, the bracket lamps and the desk lamp had gone out, leaving only one small, hooded light burning, across the room on the little table by the windows.

"All right," he had said, not quite humorously, getting up, "I reckon I can take a hint. I'm leaving."

31

Not turning, she had said: "Come here."

"What?"

"Come here," she had ordered, her voice hard, almost exasperated, and had turned to face him.

Even when he had felt her sharp fingers upon his hand, and her hand, ice-cold, on his, he had not fully realized her intention.

"Go ahead," she had uttered in that same hard, exasperated tone, more suppressed now.

"You—"

"Go ahead," she had said, and shook him as one angrily shakes a child.

Before his mind had actually seized on the fact, he had felt his heart bounce blunderingly, enormously, in the constricted cavity of his chest, like a basketball dropped into a dark locker, and then, as suddenly, go dead as he heard the passage of heels across some patch of uncarpeted floor in the upper hall. "Not here," he had said, his tongue thick.

"Here—"

"Let's go out—outside—" and he had tried to pull her "—there's my car—"

"No. Here."

"They're awake," he had said, "they're moving around up there, there's—"

"Go ahead. Now. Here," and her fingers had driven into his shoulder. "That is, if you want to."

Then, in that room, straining for the sound of feet above or in the dimly, mellowly lit hall, with his eyes fixed on the windows to catch any glint of light from an approaching car, clasped in that unnatural, awkward, frustrating posture, almost impotent at first from anxiety, he had violated her, coldly, desperately, without pleasure.

Before leaving—and he had been anxious to leave before he would have to face someone, Mrs. Murdock coming in, or Ham—he had been standing near the fireplace, with his arm about her, while he kissed her. He had felt nothing, beyond that gnawing impatience, except a sense of obligation, which made him bend his head and hold his lips pressed against hers, which, like her hands, had been cold. She had submitted to him for a short time, and then had jerked back from him.

He had been almost sure, as she lifted her head, that there were tears in her eyes, and had experienced for the moment a little start of tenderness. Then, as he put out his arm again to her, she had said, sharply: "You're such a fool!"

"A fool?" he had said.

"Oh, Jerry, Jerry—" and she had seized his arm, shaking him, "if only you weren't such a God-damned mess. But—" She had stopped, looking at him almost judicially while he stood there trying to think of something to say. Then, shaking her head, she had added: "but don't worry. It's a secret. I won't tell anybody."

"All right," he had said, "if that's the way—" He had felt a kind of twisted satisfaction at her words, which he did not try to fathom, for, in a way, they canceled the very act just performed. With difficulty, he had suppressed an impulse to speak the vindictive words which would have meant an open quarrel, which would have, at a clap, left him completely clean and free; but this impulse had risen, not in resentment and anger, but as an instantaneous calculation, mathematical in its dispassionateness. But he had, after that instant, only said, "Good night," and had gone out, leaving her standing there in the dim library, with one foot on the brass fender of the hearth, where the last wood was graying out to ash. "Good night," she had said, evenly.

He had written her the cards from New York. He had sat down a couple of times to write a letter, but had been able to think of nothing to say.

He started up, hearing his name. The men were looking at him, smiling.

"The boy had a pretty strenuous time, last night," Bogan Murdock said. "Old Burgess had him around."

"I'm sorry," Jerry said, embarrassed.

"I was just saying," the Governor remarked, rising, "that maybe we'd better be getting on in. And you probably won't object—you seem to be nodding off."

"All right, sir," Jerry said, and stood.

The men went out into the hall, where Bogan Murdock found their coats for them. They put them on, and went out to the porch, accompanied by their host, and stood there between the high columns, which were bone-white in the moonlight. "Well, Dock, I'll take up the park matter with the Commissioner," the Governor was saying, buttoning up his coat. "I know he'll—"

Jerry did not hear more. He was staring out over the broad lawn, where the oaks and cedars cast shadows which were inky-black and precise in outline against the moon-bleached grass, and out over the rolling fields beyond, toward the western rim of the valley. And the thought came to him how in rooms where the shades were drawn, in the city under the roofs which were frosted by that light, in houses and isolated shacks in fields and by crossroads, people were lying with their eyes closed and the life reduced to that wit-less susurrus of breath through the lax lips. Loneliness seized upon him, sudden and unspeakable.

In a moment they would leave. They would get into that black bulk of the automobile there, and go away down the white road, the Governor, Sam Dawson, who lived in Northumberland, Private Porsum, who, across the ocean, a long time ago, had killed all these men and was a hero, and he himself, who was Gerald Calhoun, who was Bull's-eye Calhoun, who was the man who had hurled the ball in the late sunshine while the stands cheered, who was the boy who had brought back the bacon from New York, who was Jerry Calhoun, who was Jerry Calhoun, who was Jerry—

His own name echoed in his head, over and over, like a set of nonsense syllables.

He would go up in the elevator to his apartment, to his room, where the objects and articles which belonged to Jerry Calhoun would be waiting faithfully in the dark. And while the other men stood there talking, he felt the impulse to walk away from them, across the lawn, beyond the trees to the open fields, simply and casually; across the valley, over which the moon so steadily pre-sided. *God-a-mighty, God-a-mighty,* he thought, and was not sure that he had not spoken the words out loud.

Then, he was only tired. He thought then that that was it, that he was just tired.

Two

Statement of Ashby Wyndham. Sheriff's Office, The Jail, Mulcaster County

THE PORE human man, he ain't nuthin but a handful of dust, but the light of Gods face on him and he shines like a diamint, and blinds the eye of the un-uprightous congregation. Dust, it lays on the floor, under the goin forth and the comin in, and ain't nuthin, and gits stirred up under the trompin, but a sunbeam come in the dark room and in that light it will dance and shine for heart joy. I laid on the floor, and it was dark. I wasn't nuthin. I was under the trompin, which was cruel hard. But a man don't know, for he is ignorant. There ain't nuthin in him but meanness and a hog hollerness and emptiness for the world's slop. A man don't think of nuthin but sloppin, and dodgen, when the kick comes. I laid on the floor, and didn't know, and the trompin. But the light come in the dark room, like a finger apointin at me through the hole, and it was the hard trompin had stirred me. I shined in the light.

It was so, and truth sober. Then, that time, and for a long time, me goin or stayin, on dry land or the river. Oh Lord, make me to be shinin agin, and do not turn away yore face. For I have spelled how it is writ, and water come sweet from the smote stone, and light in the dark place.

But a man don't know, nor was made to. Salvation has laid hid behind a dark bush, like a enemy man up to meanness and waitin for him was comin, when the moon had got down under the ridge. It holds out its hand, and there ain't no sayin what is in it. A stickin knife or a five dollar bill. But the Lord, He made the world and what walks on it, and it out of pure love. The copperhead, and him layin for sun in the path where the women folks and the children goes down to the spring for water. And the wicked man in his power of meanness, he puts out his hand, and he don't know, but the Lords love is in it, in a far country, and it only retches out to lay holt and come home. He figgers he's grabbin for the toys and garnishments and the vain things which is his hearts desire, but it ain't so. The Lords love in him is retchen out for the light of the Lords face, and is pore and peaked like a potato sprout in a dark cellar, where the sun don't come. But the Lords love in him, it knows what it hones for. It's him what is ignorant, and deceit laid on his eyes like a blindfolt at a play party, and him retchen out to lay holt.

Take Pearl. She et and lay down in the house of the abominations, and it was the roof of that house kept the rain offen her. But the time come, and it never kept out the light of His face. They ain't no ridgepole hewed nor shingle split, red oak nor white, will do it, when the time comes. Her hand retched out to lay holt. It was my blessedness to be standin there. The Lord led me, and He laid the words on my tongue. I named them, and it was ample. She come down the river with me and mine, frost or the hot sun, freshit or drout and the mud stinken when we tied up. We all broke bread and taken our sop in rejoicin.

I done what was moved in me. What I knowed to do. And what I wouldn't know, it may be, to do different and it to do agin. I figgered on tellin her of salvation, and us movin and rejoicin, which we done. And now she lays there, and the dungeon key turned in the lock, and her heart is full of hate. She won't unsquinch her eyes, they say, nor take sup nor morsel. How does a man know, not made to? She retched out her hand to lay holt on salvation, and done it, back in Hulltown. Her hand retched out that night, and it has retched nigh three years, and laid holt on that old squirril rifle.

If I han't never come, and named the words on my tongue, she would been there yet, and it the house of abominations, but her face smilin. Salvation, what good has it done her? She taken off one sin, lak a man his shirt sweat dirty, and flung it down, but she has done swapped one Bible sin for anuther, and hate in her heart, and the cold stone wall round and about where she lays down. And my wife and them what follered and trusted me, movin on the river, they is come amongst strangers, and the bitterness. Gods will, it runs lak a fox with the dogs on him, and doubles, and knows places secret and hard for a man's foot. But a man wants to know, but it is his weakness. He lays in the night, when the Lord has done turned away His face, and he worries his head and shakes his mind lak a tree, but what fruit falls, it is tart-lak and wries up the tongue. He looks back on what is done. He tries to see it lak it was, and recollect. But it don't do no good. Rememberin is lak the smoke what still hangs over the rifle barril, but the squirril fallin, bumpin the limbs. Oh Lord, I have laid down in the night.

They treat me good. I ain't got nuthin agin them here. They is doin accordin to their lights. If they turn the key in the lock, it ain't in man meanness. It is laid on them so. They told me to tell them all what happened, and it would be more easy. They said tell them and they'd put it down, and it would help Pearl when the time come. And help me. But me, what help I need, it ain't in feeble man to give. But I said, I would give testifyin for the Lord. I would write it down myself, I said, for a man can't say it all at once, how it was. Sometimes it comes when a man ain't thinkin. It comes before you lak you was there, and it daylight but gone in a blink. So they give me paper and ink and a pen staff. I will put it down, spare not, fear nor favor, and I will write it as fair as I can. . . .

Three

WHEN Sue Murdock first laid eyes on Jerry Calhoun, she was seventeen years old. It was late winter, one month after she had got into trouble at Miss Millford's School and had walked right out on that old witch and had packed one bag and taken a plane and flown a thousand miles home to confront her father, who, with his face high, composed, and sad, and his eyes brightly fixed upon her while he did not speak, had been sitting in the library, where he always sat in the late afternoon. When, a month later, she saw Jerry Calhoun, she was standing in the hall just outside the library door, listening to Dan Morton, who had a job with her father's company, who had inherited some money from his grandmother, who was runner-up in the city golf open and could ride a horse like nobody's business, who carried a lean, pale, imperious face above very good shoulders, and who had, just the night before, in the intimate darkness of his coupe, kissed her several times and had managed to slip his hand down under her evening dress and lay it on her right breast, where she had let it remain for a minute, considering her sensations and making up her mind. Standing there in the hall with Dan Morton, listening to him but scarcely attending to his words, toying idly with the recollection of the night before, she glanced into the library and saw Jerry Calhoun sitting alone on the divan.

She had seen a good many young men seated on that divan, young men from Meyers and Murdock whom her father brought out to ride or shoot with him, or young men who came to see her, but she had never seen a young man there who resembled this one. Slumped forward with his elbows on his knees, with a lighted cigarette unused in his right hand, he looked big and shapeless, and, obviously, as alone as a man waiting for a train. A gray flannel coat hitched up across his collar in the back, and the sleeves, somewhat too short, seemed to bind his arms at the armpits. He was wearing khaki breeches, new, thin, and formless like a Boy Scout's, and new boots. They looked absolutely new, the boots. They were set carefully, woodenly, on the carpet. They were absolutely vertical, like posts. They did not seem to belong to anybody, and they shone with the spurious luster which they had worn in the show window of the Army and Navy Goods Store.

Sue Murdock could not make out the face very well, for it was hanging forward, as though to inspect the boots. But the young man did not seem to be happy about the boots.

"Who is that?" she demanded, breaking in on Dan Morton's conversation.

Dan Morton turned his head and regarded the young man in the library very slowly, as though he had never laid eyes on him before. Then he said: "Named Calhoun. He works at the firm. Dock brought him out to ride with him and me this afternoon."

"Ride?" she questioned, still looking at the young man on the divan and at the boots.

"That," Dan Morton said, "was the rough idea. And," he continued, lifting his lips back in a smile and nodding toward the library, "you see he's got the idea. He's all fixed up. He's all set to go. Tom Mix."

Sue Murdock looked up into that pale, complete, confident face, let her glance flick down like a pullman porter's deft, ritualistic brush over the weather-mellowed tweed jacket, and the flared, shabby, whipcord breeches and boots, which made the legs look lanky, hard, and expert. Then, again, she met his smile, which seemed to define her absolutely, predict all her responses, absorb her into its own brittle certainty.

"Tom Mix," he was saying, "just give him his trusty six-gun and—"

But she had walked away from him, through the doorway, into the library, toward the shapeless young man on the divan.

She stood before him, put out her hand, and said, "I'm Sue Murdock," and the young man heaved himself up to assume his proper shape, heaving himself up uncertainly as though he were balancing on a fence or as though the legs inside the boots had gone to sleep, and tried to crush out his cigarette in a tray before he offered his hand, and succeeded in knocking the tray to the floor.

"I'm sorry," the young man said, as he crouched heavily before her, one knee on the carpet, the new, scarcely scarred sole of that boot twisting painfully to one side with its stiffness, the big hands picking up the tray, picking up the cigarette butts, trying to sweep up the ashes.

"Oh, let it go," she ordered, looking down at the broad back

39

and crisp dark hair; but for an instant he continued as though he had not heard her.

"Let it go," she repeated impatiently, feeling impatient and irritated, as though she herself had been trapped into clumsiness.

At that tone of her voice, he lifted his head, still crouching, however, and she observed, for the first time, the ruddy, or flushed, strongly fleshed face, with positive, black brows and good nose, a somewhat sullen face which, on the moment, was not sullen, for it smiled to show very white teeth which were set far apart, like a boy's.

"All right," Jerry Calhoun said, not moving, but his face lifted.

Then, looking down at him, as though he were some strange object washed ashore at her feet, some survivor from a distant storm whose most peripheral air had not even brushed her cheek, some kindly, awkward, humble monster which had wallowed up on the beach before her, she wondered where, where in the world, he had come from.

Crouched on the floor before Sue Murdock, feeling his cheeks flush at his own clumsiness, watching his hands fumble to collect the scattered butts, Jerry Calhoun suddenly saw, in his mind's eye, his own father; a big man, his blue shirt soaked with sweat, stooped to some small occupation—to buckle a harness or set a staple over a strand of wire—while his breath came in quick gasps, or while he held his breath and his face grew purple, while the thick, scarred fingers crooked ineptly and the sweat rolled down his cheeks into the neatly trimmed black beard. At that moment, Jerry Calhoun, tangled in his own clusminess, aware of the sweat starting at his own temples, had that vision of his father, or rather, felt himself somehow as merged into, and identified with, that image.

His father was a strong man, and his shoulders seemed to be stooped from the knotted pads of muscle. He was a man who would sweat easily, and his shirt would stick to the flesh, showing the twin humps of muscle knitted into the crevice where the backbone was. Jerry had seen him crouch and grapple his hands under the hub of a wagon wheel stuck in the mud, and heave it out while the mules strained forward. "You always put your feet together, son, this-a way, and lift straight, just rise up, son," he would say. "You don't want to be spilling your bowels in the road." But when he had some small thing to do, he was no good. The stiff fingers could not hold the buckle, the wrench, the staple right, the face would work with the agony of its intenseness, and the sweat would start. He did not break into fury on these occasions, as big, clumsy men

40

often do, but, when the effort became too much for him, he would lay down his tool, or the object with which he had been struggling, laying it down very gently, solicitously, and would stare at it and shake his head almost imperceptibly, while the sweat streaked his face and his breathing subsided to a normal rate.

That was the image of his father which had dominated his childhood, not the image of his father performing his casual and unprideful feats of strength, or holding him on his lap to read to him, to make him spell out the words, on Sunday afternoons, on the front porch of the big old brick house, or, in winter, before the fire in the draughty living room; and that was the image which now struck him more painfully, involved him more deeply, than ever before.

Jerry, when he was a little boy and was often with his father on the farm, could scarcely bear those moments. He would sometimes pick up the object which his father had laid down, and would hold it as though in readiness, as though in encouragement, but there would be a small, sickening congestion in his stomach, and he would avert his face from the scene; and, especially as he grew older, this sickness, this confusion, this unformulable distress, might suddenly coagulate into a cold core of hatred, and he would suppress the impulse to hurl the object to the ground and strike out at his father or run away.

At those times he felt as he did the time his setter puppy fell into the old well by a deserted tenant house on the place. For hours he crouched on the crumbling brickwork and the rotting boards, trying to snare the animal with a loop of rope, trying to make it cling to bits of planking tied to the old rope, trying to make it get into the old bucket which he let down, while the sickness rose in him and his whole consciousness was possessed by those thin, mechanical, gargling, accurately timed yelps which, strangely resonant despite their thinness, came up from the deep shaft. Then, involuntarily, he dropped the rope and watched it spin down to the water, and sink. He grubbed an old brick from the sod, and with the icy assurance of hatred, or something like hatred, hard in him now, leaned far over to observe the small target, which was the animal's head, in the middle of the glimmer-fractured blackness of the water. The one brick did it. It struck without a splash, with only a flat, surrendering sound. He leaped up and ran home, across the fields of young corn, while the sunlight rocked giddily over the unfamiliar landscape.

That night he told his father about it. "You did right, son," his

41

father said. "You'd done all a body could do. You couldn't leave the poor little thing down there to be suffering."

He had wanted his father to say that, and his father had said it. But the words, he knew, were a lie.

It was that way, sometimes, when he watched his father. But he felt better when his Uncle Lew, his mother's brother, was standing by and said something, as he never failed to do, about his father's ineptitude. "By God, Jim, by God," he would say, and his small black eyes would sharpen, and his sharp nose and all his bitter, twisted, pale face would seem to concentrate to the malevolency of the eyes, "why don't you put yore arms in a buzz saw and then try to pick yore teeth with what's left?" His father, slowly, would look up, with a sort of smile, and would say: "I reckon I ought to, Lew." Or something like that. Then, with a sense of relief and cleansing, the hatred in the boy would find its focus on Lew. That was all right. Hating Lew was all right. Lew never did anything nice for him, or anybody. Lew was not his father. It was all right to hate Lew.

His mother was dead. She had died at his birth. She had left little tangible record of herself. There was the wedding picture of her and her husband. She was seated, in the picture, wearing a white dress which came up high to the throat, with her hair combed smoothly back from her small intense face. Her husband stood behind her, and a little to one side, big and black-coated, one hand laid cautiously on her shoulder, black-bearded and with the black hair plastered down and parted with an artificial precision. There were a few other pictures of her, too, with that same small face and intense eyes. "She was a quiet sort of girl," his father had once said, "but she moved light on her feet, and nimble, and was clever with her hands. And she had a good voice for singing in the church, didn't she, Lew?"

"I reckon so," Lew had said, grudgingly, "but I never was no hand to take on much over singing."

She had left the pictures and a few objects, which year by year had grown fewer. There had been the set of blue dishes, once referred to as hers and rarely used, but as the years passed, the surviving items, a cream pitcher, a butter dish without its cover, and a few saucers, merged into the nondescript general collection. Once some time after he had left home and gone to work at Meyers and Murdock, Jerry, on one of his visits home, missed the butter dish. His father, noticing his glance, had said, "The cook broke it." And Jerry had suddenly experienced a startled and inordinate sense of release. His father, years before, had broken the red glass vase,

42

which had stood on the table in the parlor before some of the up-stairs rooms had been abandoned and the parlor had been converted into a bedroom for Aunt Ursula. He had come out of the shuttered, never-used parlor one Sunday afternoon, and had closed the door behind him with that awkward carefulness of his, and had announced: "I broke Holly's red vase."

Uncle Lew, hunched before the fire in the living room, had looked up with his air of shrewd and wry triumph and his lips had pulled back as though to speak; but he had said nothing. The pieces of the red vase had been left on the table for a long time. Jerry had seen the smears of the glue with which his father had tried to fit the thing back together, but finally the fragments themselves disappeared; exactly when, or by whose hand, Jerry never knew.

She had left these objects, and had left her brother, Jerry's uncle Lew, and her aunt, Jerry's great-aunt Ursula. At the time of her niece's death, Aunt Ursula had been some sixty-five years old, spry, competent, amiable, and fanatically clean. She had raised her niece, Holly, and nephew, Lew, through years of privation and tight-lipped scrimping, and then she had raised Holly's baby, Jerry. She had never married. She had raised Lew and Holly, the children of her dead brother and of a woman whom she had never seen. She had sweated in summer and had been cold in winter for them. She had lain awake at night, hearing the window sash rattle in whatever draughty house they were lucky enough to have over their heads or hearing the young frogs chirruping from the cattle pond, and had thought of the money which she would need the next month, or the next week, or the next day. She had never known these two children, neither the bitter and quarrelsome club-footed boy nor the silent girl. But the first few years with the baby of her niece had been different, a strong child, affectionate and never sickly. It had been hers more completely than the others. And she had not been forced to worry about the roof over her head or the food on the table. And she had not been aware of, or had shut her mind to, Jim Calhoun's worries; for he never talked of such things. The old Calhoun house which she kept so orderly, the big kitchen where she quarreled at the Negro cook and spied for the slightest spot of old grease or soot, the grassless backyard where the chickens fluffed in the dust or huddled from the rain, the voices about her—it had all been like a late and difficultly won harbor; and the problems and disorders of the life there had rocked her, in that new security, no more than wavelets.

She had loved the child, but as its strength increased, her own

43

diminished, and as the circle of its existence widened her own contracted, until it was nothing, until the whole world lay outside its periphery. By the time the child was ten years old she was nearly blind, and was confined to her chair. She had fallen against the kitchen stove one day, and had lain on the floor, unconscious, with the flesh of her left arm burned almost to the bone, until the boy had come in and had found her there. When, months later, she had been able to leave her bed and sit in a chair, he had not been able to fit her back into a place in his world. She had never again seemed real to him. "Go and talk to your Aunt Ursula," his father would say to him sometimes. "You ought to talk to her. She was always mighty good to you, son." But he would stand before her and the words would stick in his throat, like dry crumbs. Then, afterwards, when he was alone at night, or when he would be doing something during the day, he would see, suddenly clear before him, the way the flesh sagged off her cheek bones and her eyes lay back in their sockets, or the way the scarred flesh of her left hand seemed to crust off the bones, and he would be overwhelmed by a conviction of guilt and unworthiness.

One fall, after he was in high school and could make a little money of his own, he had saved everything he could for three months so that he could buy her a present. He had paid eleven dollars for a shawl and had given it to her for Christmas. He had put the package on her lap and had stood there to watch while her fingers plucked at the cord and the paper rattled. His father, finally, had opened the package. "Put it on her shoulders, son," he had ordered, and Jerry had obeyed. "It's a present," his father had said, "it's a present Jerry bought for you. He saved his money and bought it for you, Aunt Ursula. It's a shawl, a blue shawl. Feel it. Feel the fringe on it." And his father had picked an edge of the shawl and had dangled it before her as though she could see. Then his father had reached out to take up one of her hands—*Oh, God-a-mighty, God-a-mighty,* Jerry had thought, but his father had picked up her right hand, her good hand. His father's hand had lifted her hand and had guided it, making it stroke the soft woolen texture. "It's a pretty shawl. Jerry got it for you."

Then the boy had seen the tears fill up the hollowish sockets of her eyes and break over, and run unevenly down her cheeks.

"Jerry got it for you, Aunt Ursula. He got it for you because he loves you."

The boy had gone abruptly out of the room, leaving them there, out to the backyard, where the crisp icy crust over the bare ground gave down to the mud under his tread. He had leaned over the

44

fence to the stable lot, and had said, out loud, deliberately, over and over again, the vile words he knew, which reduce everything to the blind, unqualified retch and spasm of the flesh, the twist, the sudden push, the twitch, the pinch of ejection and refusal.

But his feeling toward his Uncle Lew had never changed from the time when he first became aware of the individual qualities of the people around him. Nor had Lew's face changed during these years. The skin on his face pulled back tight from the thin, uncertain mouth and the bridge of the nose, over the sharp angles of the bony structure, which under the skin seemed paper-thin; and the skin itself was pale and delicate, like the skin of a child. The texture and color of that skin never changed, even when the black, too glossy hair had begun to turn gray. His hands were narrow and spidery, deft at small tasks, when he sat by himself. He would hunch down in a chair, or on a bench in the yard when the weather was good, his high shoulder blades cocked up, his elbows sharply cut, the knee of his good leg crooked, and his bad leg thrust out before him, and in the midst of these angles and ineptitudes of bone, the fingers would move flickeringly, a small center of competence and certainty. When there was nothing else for him to do, he often occupied himself with his carving. He carved peach stones, walnuts, and small pieces of oak, hickory, and cedar, into complicated geometrical designs or into grotesque faces, not animal and not quite human. He never seemed to have any desire to show these things to anyone, but kept them in a big box by his bed, and the box had a padlock on it. On rainy days he would sometimes lay the objects out on his bed or on a table and handle them and study them, one by one. His big clasp knife was always sharp as a razor, both the big blade and the little blade, and when he was tired of his carving, he would draw his bad leg up to him, and lean over and hone the steel, with a slow, meditative, caressing motion, against the leather of the shoe sole.

He knew a few coin tricks, too. "Come here, Jerry," he would say, "here's a quarter I'm gonna give you. Look at it good. Here it is. I'm gonna give it to you." Then he would do the tricks. "It's gone. It's done flew away. Ain't that too bad. I'm sure sorry. Naw, here it is again! Here, take it, quick! Aw, durn, it's done gone again."

Finally, Aunt Ursula would say: "Quit pestering the child, Lew. It ain't right."

Then Lew, grinning, would stop. But his father, if he happened to be present, would only watch, saying nothing. But once, after it was over, while the child stood in the middle of the floor, hurt and baffled almost to tears, his father had said: "Come here." Then

45

he had reached into his pocket and had taken out a silver dollar. "Take it," he had said, and had held it out on the humps of his big palm. Slowly, the child had reached for the coin. "It's yours," his father had said. "Don't lose it. And when we go to town Saturday you can buy anything you want." The child had taken the coin.

"I'll be durned," Lew had said, "Mister Astor," and had spat suddenly into the fire.

He had never played the tricks again on Jerry, but Jerry, a long time afterwards, when he was in high school, had seen his uncle call some little nigger child to him: "Hey, little nigger boy, I'm gonna give you a quarter. Come here!"

Jerry never learned much about his mother's people. He had never heard his uncle mention the past but one time, and then only to say: "That nigger Jeff told me today they've done pulled down that little old house on the Moffat place, down toward Hamill's Crossing, putting a road through. I was born in that house." Then his lips had jerked back in a grin. "They oughter burned it down long back. It never was worth a gol-durn." And he had given three or four shrill, constricted cackles of laughter, before subsiding into one of his spells of silence. The old woman had said a little more. She had been born down in Alabama, Jerry knew, and he had heard her say once that down there she had seen Indians. "Indians, and I saw them, I recollect, Indians walking down the big road, just like folks, and me a little sprig of a girl standing in front of our house. Indians, but it was a long time back, and I don't know how come." There had been a big Bible she said, with names written in it for a long time back, back into the time when her people were in North Carolina before they went down to Georgia, and the last names in it were Holly's and Lew's; but she had lost it, moving around, when the children were little and troubles so thick her mind nigh turned and she was past praying, but she never asked, nor got, mite nor morsel not proper hers, and no hand to stay her.

Georgia, North Carolina, Alabama, Mississippi, Tennessee, Kentucky: these people whose names Jerry did not know had moved, for two hundred years, across the marshes, up the slow rivers where the water was black with rotting vegetation, over ridges where jutting limestone baked white in the glare of sunlight and the oak leaves steamed, through pine flats where the dead needles underfoot masked the sour yellow ground, across the valleys of Alabama and Mississippi and the green slopes and hollows of Tennessee and Kentucky. They had built log cabins, log houses with the logs hewed square and limestone chimneys, little clapboard houses which they had intended to paint, but they had always left them, and had moved on, and had left the dead in cemeteries at cross-roads or in untended plots near the houses where the sassafras and the love-vine took hold. They had always come too late. The best ground had always been taken, the best springs and the good place for the mill dam, or the place near the ford for a tavern. Jerry did not know their names. From them had come his mother, Aunt Ursula, and Uncle Lew. And once or twice, catching sight of Lew's face in repose, he had discovered that that face was the face of his mother in the old pictures, even in the wedding picture.

Jerry had that blood in him, but he looked like his father. Even when he was a child he had the face of his father. As a boy he was rangy and stringy, growing fast, but by the time he was fifteen, when he entered high school, his body was thickening out and by the time he was eighteen he already had his father's powerful shoulders. His hands were big, and like his father's were good with animals, when he was handling lambs and chicks and turkey poults, or doctoring a sick horse or breaking a colt. Jerry's hands had the same capacity. By the time he was fourteen he was making a few dollars, now and then, breaking horses in the neighborhood. But his hands, though big and clumsy-looking like his father's, were not clumsy. At the first, heart-stopping whirr of the quail from the sage or the brush harbor, the gun would be at his shoulder and the reports of the two barrels would almost merge; and he could lay a fly back under the willows along the creek bank or beside a sunken snag. All his boyhood, he had practiced these things, and his father, who had, however, no concern for sport, had never discouraged him. Sometimes, when he practiced casting out in the sideyard on Sunday afternoon, his father would come out and sit there, propped back against the wall of the house, smoking and saying nothing. After he entered high school, another boy would often come out on Sundays, and all afternoon they would pass a football back and forth, until it was too dark to see. His father would watch that, too.

During the first two years when he was in high school, money was very tight with his father and every penny which went for clothes and books was that much which might have gone to relieve the increasing pressure of debt. Aunt Ursula was completely blind by that time, and often ill; and there were bills for the doctor for her. Mr. Calhoun let the cook go for a while and tried to do for himself, but it was impossible. By the time he had managed to get the simplest breakfast together and had washed the face and hands of the old woman and had settled her in her chair, the morning would be half gone and none of his own work done. Jerry would get home just at the early winter nightfall to find the old woman propped in her chair in the cluttered room, which would be lighted by the fire, and Lew hunched down in his chair, staring into the fire, while the blade of his knife, glintingly, caressingly, moved over the leather sole of the shoe on the bad foot. The whole place would stink of burnt grease and stale food, even the living room. Jerry would go back into the kitchen, which was filthy as a sty, and light the lamp, and after a moment in which the nausea and fury mixed in him, and he gazed wildly about at the disorder, he would begin to clean up as well as he could, hoping to finish before his father got back to the house from the evening chores. After several months, Mr. Calhoun gave up and took the cook back. "I don't reckon it saved much, and me as unhandy as I am, and you having to go to school, and Lew not being able to get about good," he had said.

"I didn't have to go to school," Jerry had retorted, angrily, why he did not know.

"Sure, you did, boy," his father had said, "don't be talking like that. But I don't reckon a few dollars made all that much difference. I'd taken out the telephone and saved something there if it wasn't for Aunt Ursula, her being porely and maybe needing a doctor any time. And it was hard on Callie, letting her go, with her depending on her work up here to get something for her young ones. And the place here the way it was. It was a mistake, and I made it. It was no way for a man to be living. A man ought to live like a man, as long as he can, I reckon."

But at her best, Callie was not a good servant, and as the years passed, she grew more and more incompetent. Later, when Jerry was living in town and would drive out to the house for a visit, he might find his father with a broom and a dust pan trying to clean up the living room or the kitchen, or standing over a pan of dishes. "Callie didn't come this morning," his father would explain defensively.

"You ought to fire her and get somebody who would come."

"It ain't exactly her fault," his father would say. "She's old and ailing, and she's been on the place a long time."

"Ben's no good, either. And he never has been. You ought to have got rid of them both, long ago. They've got children, haven't they? They could go to their children."

"It ain't that easy, son," his father would say, lifting a dish with painful care and swaddling it in the drying cloth. "It just ain't that easy, I reckon."

48

"Well, you ought to get somebody to come in and help her, some young nigger."

"I can't afford it, son. Not and things the way they are."

"I'll pay it."

"No, no, anything you've got free that-a way I want to see put on the place. It'll be yours some day. But you—" the old man would be concentrating all his effort on the dish and the tangled, sodden cloth—"you do plenty as it is, and I'm grateful."

But there had been two or three good years, when Jerry was still in high school, the years of the War, good prices and good crops. His father had paid off the obligation on the place, obligations incurred years before; then, in the fall of 1918, he had bought a tract of fifty acres which lay between his place and the river, which had once belonged to him but which he had been forced to sell off before Jerry's birth.

During the years when that strip of bottom had been out of his possession, he would sometimes take a walk in the late summer evenings along the line. "The corn in the bottom is doing right well," he might announce on his return to the house. "That always was good ground for corn. Not better on the river." He was more excited about the purchase than Jerry had ever seen him about anything, not able to sit still that evening, pacing the room and picking up small objects from the mantel shelf or the table and setting them down, going out in the yard, though it was a cold night, to stand by the gate and look at the frosty, brilliantly starred sky or up the empty road. "Maybe I oughtn't done it," he had said. "Maybe I oughtn't. But it always looked like the place was sort of lopsided the way it was—"

"Lopsided," Lew had said, and had snapped the big blade of his knife shut, "like me."

Then, after Lew's cackle of laughter had stopped short, as though bitten off, Mr. Calhoun had resumed: "That bottom strip went with the place. The place lays natural to the river. It come to me from my folks that-a way, and I'd like to be a-leaving it that-a way. I hate to be running back into debt, just as I get shed of—"

"You paid too durned much for it," Lew had said, "Mr. Astor."

"Maybe so." Then, after a while: "But it looks like a good place is due some corn bottom. Now, don't it?"

Once, after she had known Jerry Calhoun some two years, but before she was in love with him, or thought she was in love with him, Sue Murdock went to the Public Library and hunted up the files of one of the local papers for the years when he had been in school and in the University. Her action was uncalculated. She had simply been walking down the street and had happened to glance up at the building and had, on the impulse, entered. She had found the stories in the sport sections, and the pictures. The pictures were all very much alike, from the first one—*Bull's-eye Calhoun Passes County High To Championship*—to the last one—*Bull's-eye Calhoun All American Choice.* Picture after picture, always the high, square, robotlike shoulders, the helmet above the face which was scarcely identifiable on the yellow newsprint, and thinner-looking than now, the pictures posed against the empty stands. There was Bull's-eye Calhoun, hands set to hips in a kind of stiff alertness, or one hand cocked back with the ball as though for a pass and the eyes scanning a field which wasn't there, which was off the picture.

She studied the pictures, but they did not tell her what she had come to find out. That was off the picture, too, or behind the picture. What had she come to find out? She didn't know herself, exactly, but when the last picture—*Bull's-eye Calhoun All American Choice,* a big picture with the lifted face under the helmet looking like an illustration in the old copy of Caesar's *Gallic Wars* which she had used in school—revealed nothing, she let the heavy folder of papers slam shut, and the dust popped out around the frayed edges, and she felt cheated.

She had not wanted to find out anything about Jerry Calhoun as a football player. She didn't care anything about football. A game was something you went to on a Saturday afternoon, and whoever took you got drunk and there was the yelling and the band, and you held a big bunch of flowers. And she didn't care anything about Bull's-eye Calhoun, about Jerry Calhoun, who, a long time ago, had stood with his arm cocked back and a ball in his hand, posed against the empty stands, waiting for the camera to click. But he wasn't like any of the others she knew, not like Dan Morton or any of them. Oh, she knew them, all right, she knew them all. But she didn't know Jerry Calhoun.

She had asked him questions. "What did you do when you were a little boy, Jerry?"

And he had said: "I worked on the farm as soon as I was big enough, and went to school, and the damned big old house we lived in was about to fall down, and we were dog-poor."

"What did you do when you were in college, Jerry?"

And he had said: "I studied and played football, and hoped to God I'd be able to finish the semester before my dough ran out."

That was the truth, and he didn't want to think about it. It was all he could tell Sue Murdock, or anybody. He couldn't tell about Bull's-eye Calhoun standing, at night, on the campus among the winter-stripped trees, by himself, looking over at the accurately spaced lights of the big dormitory, and catching, from very far away, from the Student Center, where the dance was going on, the sound of laughter, then of melancholy, beseeching music. Or standing in the dressing room, the last man there in the gymnasium, under the glare of the single hanging bulb, which showed up the wet cement floor and sodden benches, breathing the heavy air which smelled of sweat, tar, urine, soap, and disinfectant, and hating the whole God-damned business. Or sitting in his room, his head in his hands, his book propped before him, forcing himself to focus on the page, while around him, echoingly, the boisterous, companionable life of the old dormitory surged until late at night —the card games, the wrestling matches with the tables shoved back against the walls, the endless smut and bellowed laughter. Or lying in bed, overwhelmed by something like homesickness— even though he went out there every Saturday out of football season—wanting to lie on his own bed, on the sagging, lumpy, familiar mattress, in the dark in that bare room upstairs where he had slept ever since he could remember. That was a completely unreasonable feeling, and he knew it, for he knew that as soon as he got out home, with Lew and Aunt Ursula and, even, his father, he would begin to be impatient for Monday morning, when his father would hitch up and drive him over to catch the local into town.

It was not that he could not get along well enough with the boys. He knew the easy secret, and had known it for years: the friendly shove, the smiling insult, the shouted obscenity, the casual good-by —"So long, keep off your knees"—"So long, name it after me"—"I'll see you in church"—"So long." And he practiced the easy secret, and he liked the boys, and they, he thought, liked him well enough, as well, he told himself, as he wanted to be liked. But he had no special friends, no one who went out to his place with him, or with whom he loafed on the grass in front of the dormitory when the evenings lengthened out in spring.

Now and then he got drunk on corn whisky with some boy, sometimes with somebody he scarcely knew, one of the hangers-on who liked to run with the football players, and went down to one of the whorehouses along the river. They would come roaring into the dormitory long after midnight, slam the doors, and burst into some boy's room and jerk him awake and sit on the foot of the bed or astride of chairs, and try to reconstruct the blurred and aimless violence of the evening. "By God, I tell you we got stinking. I mean stinking. By God, I'm stinking right now, aren't you, Jerry?" And Jerry would say that he was stinking. "I tell you I sure learned something tonight Aunt Maggie forgot to tell me. We had a time. I tell you, we—" There, still drunk, slapping themselves on the knee, while the room swam and sleep encroached insidiously upon them, they tried to stir the envy of the boy there in the tangle of bedclothes and to extract from their own insistent and reiterated affirmations a triumph which had, somehow, been lacking in the experiences themselves. Then they would jerk the covers off the cursing boy in bed, and trailing them across the oily floor, run out the door and down the hall, guffawing and shouting.

Looking back, Jerry Calhoun did not like to think of anything in those years, not even his triumphs. They, too, were somehow tainted. It was hard for him to identify himself with the Jerry Calhoun, the Bull's-eye Calhoun, who had found it possible to live by, to be sustained by, certain things, books, laboratories, football, dissipation, which now seemed ugly, monotonous, fumbling, and dirty, like the play of some stupid, snotty child. Now and then he would wonder what had sustained him through all those years. He had forgotten the savage, joyless, implacable blind drive which, working itself out, was enough in itself, and which, in its very joylessness, was a kind of joy. He had forgotten how, in his room, solving a problem late at night, or how on the field, caught up into a pure, rhythmic, fluctuating but patterned flow of being, he had felt protected from the disorders and despairs of his life. He had not known what he wanted in those years; and had not asked himself what he wanted.

He could not even look back comfortably on the last two years of his life at the University, when he had been somebody, a big shot, when he had been on the team, when he had made good grades, when he had sat on a fraternity porch with his feet cocked up, or in the lounge, in the evenings after dinner. He had enjoyed that life, but memory of the enjoyment was not what he had carried away with him.

He had had a chance to join one fraternity earlier, and he was to thank God he hadn't joined that one. It had been toward the end of the football season of his sophomore year, a few days after the Saturday when he had been sent into a game in the last quarter—a game already in the bag. A boy he knew asked him, quite casually, down to his fraternity house for dinner. A week later he went back again. In the end, they asked him to join. He said he'd have to think it over. "It's a good bunch of fellows," they told him. "And they stick together. It's not like some—I don't mean to be running anybody down, but you know how it is—in some fraternities it's just a name. They don't really take it to heart. Now it really means something to the fellows down here. Our boys, they're picked for what's in 'em."

Jerry did not join. It was not one of the good fraternities, but that had nothing to do with his decision. If he had had the money he would have joined. When he told the boys no, they pressed him. Finally, he said: "I can't afford it."

He saw their quick, stealthy, embarrassed exchange of glances, the look people have when they tacitly agree to ignore a breach of decency or decorum. "Well, now," one of them said, giving a preliminary cough, "you see, you see—"

"God damn it!" Jerry burst out, astounded at his own violence, "I said I can't afford it."

For a second there was a dead silence, and the eyes focused upon him and ringed him round. Then one of the men said: "Well, if you feel that way about it—"

"It doesn't matter a God-damn how I feel," Jerry said, "it's a fact, and—"

"If you feel that way about it," the boy repeated, and shrugged.

But the next year he did join a fraternity, a good one, one of the best. When the boys began to come around, he knew what was up, despite the pretenses of casualness and idle goodfellowship. *I ought to stop it,* he told himself, *I ought to tell them how it is.* But that was impossible, he decided, for he couldn't tell them unless they said something to him.

When it happened, it happened with the naturalness of a foregone conclusion. One day, after class, one of the boys, strolling across the campus with him, as he had done on other occasions, said: "One of our alumni, a big shot round here, was out to the house and got to talking to me. He asked me why we hadn't pledged you a long time back. I just told him we just figured you didn't want to, that you could about have your choice of pins, but that you boned pretty hard, too, and all—but of course, Jerry, you know a lot of our boys hit it pretty hard, too. We like to see our boys doing some good and we don't go in for hell-raisers—and he said, 'My God, that's the kind of fellow we want.' Well, he gave me the devil, and he said some of the other alumni felt the same way about us not getting you in. I told him we all knocked round with you and were pals and hoped you liked us. Then he said he wanted to do something for the chapter—he's always doing something for the house, and the boys; he's got stacks of jack—well, you know how it is, and all—"

Jerry joined the fraternity. The anonymous alumnus paid the fees. No one knew this, Jerry was somehow given to understand, except the President and the Treasurer of the chapter. The boy who had strolled across the campus with him was the Treasurer of the chapter.

Despite the urging of some of the older men at the house, and despite the pull of the life there, he did not go there to live. He stayed at the dormitory. The reason for his decision he never quite framed to himself. Something made him keep that room, made him cling to that corner of the old life and the time when he had been nameless and alone. The demands of the new life did not steal much time from his work, but his week-end trips to his own home became more and more infrequent, and when he did go it was usually before quizzes or examinations. He would take his books out with him, and all Saturday evening, and all day Sunday, would hump over them, his brow warped and his pencil clutched in his fingers, ready to underscore the important passages. He found it almost impossible to study in the same room with Lew and Aunt Ursula, and when it was not too cold, he would spend almost all day Sunday in his own old room, upstairs. His father got the habit of coming up to sit with him while he worked. His father would rap softly on the door, and enter, and say: "I just thought I'd come up for a minute or two. I'll just sit down over here for a little spell. You go on working, and I'll just sit over here. I'll be leaving after a little spell."

Then his father would sit there, hour after hour, in a strained immobility, and Jerry would find himself listening for the small, throaty sound of the man's breathing, while his own fingers clutched the pencil hard or drove the point viciously along the page. Then, when he himself couldn't stand that silence any longer, he would begin talking to his father, at random, about the events of his life at the University. His father rarely asked questions, and usually only general ones. But the first time he wore his fraternity pin home, after his initiation, his father, seeing it, asked: "What's that, Jerry?"

"It's my fraternity pin," Jerry said.

"Can I see it?"

Jerry took off the pin and passed it to his father, who did not hold it in his fingers but let it lie on the humps of his open palm while he peered down at it in the lamplight. "It's a pretty pin," his father said. Then he took Aunt Ursula's hand and guided it to feel the pin. "It's a pin Jerry's got. It's gold and it's got some sparkles on it. It's his fraternity pin. A fraternity is a kind of club Jerry belongs to over at the University."

Lew looked up. "They wear brooches and spangles," he said, "over at that college. Like girls." He hawked up a glob and spat into the fire. "You wouldn't catch me wearing no brooch," he announced. All the while his eyes were fixed on the pin.

Mr. Calhoun moved toward Lew, and holding out the pin, said: "Don't you want to look at it, Lew?"

"You didn't see me busting no hame to, did you?" Lew said. But he took the pin.

"It must have cost something," he said, "Mister Astor."

"Not much," Jerry said. That was true. It was the cheapest pin he could buy. But he had borrowed the money to buy it. It was the first money he had borrowed since entering the University, except the money he had borrowed from his father the first year when things were still going well out at the place. After that he had worked in the summers, and during the winter and spring terms had had jobs through the Student Employment Agency.

He had entered the University with two intentions: to make the team and to learn something about geology. He had made the team as a regular in his junior year. In his senior year he was an All American. His grades were better than fair, with a low *B* average, and some *A*'s in Geology and Physics. In April, his senior year, the Professor of Geology told him that he could have a graduate fellowship the next year. The fellowship would pay fifty dollars a month, and he would have the job of laboratory assistant. He could live on that, he told himself, or just about. And he would have something over from his summer work to pay back to his father, not much but something to help tide over until the crops were in and sold.

In early May he received a letter. It read:

> Dear Mr. Calhoun:
>
> I have followed your career with great interest and admiration, and have often wished that we might become better acquainted. I should be very happy if you would drop by some time before long to see me at my office in the Meyers and Murdock Building. I have a proposal to make which might work out to our mu-

tual benefit. In any case, the meeting would give me great pleasure.

Sincerely yours,

Bogan Murdock.

P.S. You may, perhaps, recall that last fall we met at the fraternity house, and had a few words of conversation.

Jerry remembered perfectly well.

He entered the lobby, which was of marble and bronze and glass; high, dim, cool, and austere. To one side were great panels of glass, and beyond the glass he could see the rows of mahogany desks and the rows of heads bent above them. At the end of the lobby, the electric indicators of the elevators flashed on and off in the gloom, indicating the positions of the cars, floor by floor. A uniformed attendant stood in front of the elevators, a tall Negro, very black, and when he opened his mouth to answer Jerry's question the flesh of his inner lip showed innocently pink and the teeth white. Jerry entered the car, and felt the confident, noiseless surge of the mechanism.

"I'm delighted," Bogan Murdock said, "that you could come."

Jerry sat in a deep leather chair, while Bogan Murdock stood easily, cigarette in his fingers, before the large windows, which were open to the slight breeze which moved in, over the roofs of the city. Beyond the roofs Jerry could see the lift of the green fields toward the bluish fringe of hills. The individual noises of the street blurred out, here, to a steady pulsation, like the sea.

"I have hoped, Mr. Calhoun, that you could see your way clear to taking a position with us. I think that it would hold a real future for a man of your qualities. I know that—"

"I don't know anything about the business," Jerry said. "I've been studying geology."

"And you've been studying it very well. From what I have been able to gather. That is all to the good. What you know of geology will, no doubt, be useful to you. It is well never to forget—at least, I try never to forget—that finance is not abstract. That its only function is to answer the needs of the land itself and the life which is dictated by the nature of our land. That is what I preach to our men. But, of course—" and he smiled, "it will be unnecessary to preach that to you. And as for special training, there is only one teacher. Experience. You remember MacCallum, the track man.

56

Well, he was studying medicine, but he has been with us now for several years, and is one of our best men."

"Yes, I know about him," Jerry said.

"As for opportunity, I think that our section is on the verge of a great awakening, that it is about to take its rightful place in the life of the nation. I would be proud to think that I had had some part in that awakening—and for a young man—" His words trailed off. He turned away, and looked out the window, over the roofs, where the glare swayed dizzily. To Jerry, that form against the glare was almost blacked out to a silhouette.

The man turned from the window, and spoke in a different voice, more quietly now. "I didn't mean to make a harangue. You will know what you want to do, and I shan't urge you. But—" he gestured toward the window and the scene beyond, "it's a beautiful day. Come out to my place and have a bite of lunch with me. It's a shame to waste a day like this completely indoors. These days when you're not quite sure whether it's spring or summer, just at the turn, they're about the finest we have in this section, except, of course, the fall, when the bird season opens. They tell me you're quite a shot. You'll have to come out some time with me next fall on my place. I've got some right nice dogs—"

They went down, and got into the automobile, and left the city, and with the wind fanning their faces, drove west. They passed between the square-piled gate pillars of unhewn limestone, and up the long drive which swept between the oaks and cedars to the house, with the gleaming white portico, on the green hill.

When Jerry told him that he had the job, Mr. Calhoun was obviously pleased, though he only said: "If it's what you want to be doing, son, it suits me."

"Murdock, Murdock," Lew said, "that's old man Lem Murdock's boy, ain't it? He ought to rotted in the pen. I'd a-pulled the rope if they'd a-hung him, if they'd took him outer the jail and hung him I'd a-stood on his shoulders and tromped till the neck bone scrunched. That blackguard and murderer, and him high-stepping. And, Jerry, you gonna work for his boy?"

"It was a long time ago," Mr. Calhoun said, "and hard to know the rights of what happened. Men have done things like that, and not known themselves how it was."

"I'd lay in the ditch and lap water like a dog," Lew said, "before I'd work for his boy."

"I don't reckon it's all that bad," Jerry said, and laughed. He was not irritated by his uncle's words, and the laugh came easily.

57

After he had once decided to take the place, he felt at ease with himself and with the world, even with the things in his own world with which he had never before been able to come to terms. But during the few weeks between his interview with Bogan Murdock and the final examinations, he tried to put even his satisfaction from his mind and to finish up his work as well as he could. He did well on the examinations, better than ever before. Everything seemed easy, now. And Commencement was at hand.

His father went to the Commencement exercises, but Lew did not. Mr. Calhoun urged him to go, even begged him, in a way unnatural for him, for usually he never put any pressure on people, never insisted. Off and on, all the Sunday before Commencement, he kept returning to the subject, while Lew seemed to take more and more relish in his refusals, and even when Mr. Calhoun was silent, Lew sat, with his eyes gleaming and the knife blade sliding on the leather of his shoe, waiting. "You ought to go," Mr. Calhoun would say. "You want him to go, don't you, Jerry?"

"Yes," Jerry would say.

"I ain't a-going. Naw, sir. That college, they ain't nothing to me," Lew said, "and I ain't nothing to them."

Mr. Calhoun went, on the early local. Jerry met him at the station. Mr. Calhoun wore his blue serge Sunday suit, which during the last two or three years, with his increasing weight, had become a little tight. He wore a high stiff collar and a black tie, which Jerry had given him one Christmas. A heavy gold watch chain, with a dangling seal, hung across his vest. He and his son went into the station restaurant, where, sitting on high stools, they drank coffee, not talking. Then they got on the streetcar and went out to the University.

Shortly after eleven o'clock Jerry, sweating under his black gown, stood on the platform, waiting his turn to step up to the table and receive his diploma, and looked over the crowd which packed the big barnlike auditorium. He tried to locate his father's face, but could not.

After it was over, Jerry found the Professor of Geology and told him that he wanted him to meet his father. They joined Mr. Calhoun at the appointed spot. The men shook hands. The Professor of Geology said to Mr. Calhoun that he was sorry that his son would not be back with him, that he thought the profession was losing a real geologist, and that Jerry had made a name for himself at the University. Then he said good-by, and walked away. Then Jerry caught a glimpse of Bogan Murdock. "There's Mr. Murdock," he said, "I want you to meet him."

"It'd suit me," his father said, "if you want me to."

Jerry ran ahead to catch Mr. Murdock, but somehow he lost him in the crowd. He came back to his father. "I lost him," he said.

"A big man like that," his father said, "he must be pretty busy and not have time to be fooling around. He must have been in a big hurry."

"I reckon so," Jerry said.

They walked through the crowd, under the beating noon sun.

"You heard what that perfesser said about you, son?" Mr. Calhoun remarked, but did not wait for an answer. "He said you'd done right good," he went on. "And him a big man like that, too."

Those were the things Sue Murdock could never find out about. She knew that there were things there which she could not find out about, but she did not know what they were. They belonged to a world she had never known and would never know, even though she saw the marks of that world on the big young man in the too-tight coat and the shapeless breeches, like a Boy Scout's, and the new boots, who had knocked over the ash tray and had crouched on the floor of her father's library, at her feet, looking up at her and smiling embarrassedly to show the white teeth, which were set far apart, like a boy's. For a long time she tried to interpret those marks, to understand what life and meaning, what patience and strength and fortitude, lay behind them, but she did not have a key for the hieroglyphics. Gerald Calhoun could not tell her what they meant, even though she asked him, for he had forgotten their true meaning or had put it from his mind. Then, after a while, the marks themselves were worn away, smoothed out by the daily abrasions of the world she knew, the world of Dan Morton and her brother Ham and all the other young men like them, the world of her father.

Four

Statement of Ashby Wyndham

. . . I WAS born and had my raisin in the County of Custiss, which is a good country yit if a man can git him a patch of bottom or on the hill before the washin and rain scourin commences. But it ain't what it was before the change of time, lak in the days of my grandpappy, who was a old one but spry and his hand never shook and him nigh ninety, when I was a sprout. He told me how it was, ground idle for the takin and clearin, or slashin and burnin, and the timber there for a mans ax to square and lay for his four walls, when he left his pappys and taken him a wife. And the woods full of varmints yit, and squirrils fat in the trees, lak apples when the limb bends, and turkeys gabblin whar the sun broke through to a open place where they taken forage. And the skillit never groaned empty, he said, save once in a spell when the Lord laid down His hand on mans neglectful pride, and a woman never had to grabble in the lard barril nor a mans gut rumble dry and the young uns standin round about, big-eyed for the famish. Which I seen, and not me only.

But come the change of time and newfangleness, with the ground wore out and the washin, it ain't what it was, lak my grandpappy named it. My grandpappy was a godly man when I knowed him and had been a long time, he said, but there was a time he stood amongst the scoffers and scorners or lay down in the bushes to lewdness and carnal carryins-on. There was always sin and human meanness in Custiss, and he never said no contrary, but now they is churches in Custiss with the door done sagged off the hinges and the weather beats in where the roof leaks and sassafras and elder quick-growin where folks used to stand and talk before the bell rung, and in the walkin-out season, not even waitin for dark and it more decent, they is abominations under the ridgepole of the Lords house. I know it because I misbehaved and put my immortal soul in danger, but for the mercy, and I sweat in the night for it yit. And what churches they is in Custiss ain't full lak I seen when I was a young un, women and old folks now and the chillen too little for devilmint, and the men folks too few so you don't much hear a good bass burden to the song worship. Folks has got one eye cocked hot after lewdness and the other on the almighty dollar, and the Lord, He has seen and has laid down His hand, for He is the Lord God and is a jealous God, lak it is writ. Times hard in Custiss and misery, and folks lays the blame on one thing and another, how the ground's done washed and the rich folks done bought up or took the country for the timber or the coal down under the mountains, but they forgit the Lord God and how He don't have to be huntin for a stick to lay on the bare back of wickedness. What comes to His hand is His, and His hand clever past runnin or hidin.

They is good folks in Custiss yit, I ain't denyin, but for the blindness. My Mammy was good and feared God. My Pappy was a good man and stout for work and providin, and he never did my Mammy no meanness, but for likker and fightin. He couldn't take nuthin off no man it looked lak. He was not going to be no lackey boy to no man. He was good, but he was not God-fearin and never taken his sins to Jesus, not for all Mammy prayin and pleadin. He died sudden and it nigh dinner time, and the vittles what had been put in the pot for him scorchin on the stove. He went out in the mornin and put his ax to the tree, and the tree what looked true, it slipped and back-bucked of a sudden. The butt hit Pappy on the side of the head. The men brung him to the house and laid him on the bed, him breathin but his eyes closed. Mammy prayed by the bed, and the folks washed the blood off. He opened his eyes one time, and it looked lak they would pop out of his head, and they went wild around the room like birds what batters to git out when they done flew in the house. Then he was dead, and gore blood on the piller. Him buried, Mammy set in a cheer for three days, nor said nuthin. Then at night time and the third day she stood in the floor, and us young uns looked at her.

He died a unsaved man, she said. Jesus give me salvation, and I'll never see him agin. Oh, what to pray for, and me a woman ignerant and weak.

Then the tears come, and for the first time, quick as a freshit. And we put her in the bed. The next mornin she et a little somethin.

My Mammy was a Porsum, and they was good folks and clever. What they laid hand to, good or bad howsobeit, they taken it hard. They was wicked men amongst them, but they never had no name

61

for corner meanness, and folks give them a name for drivin a true furrow, once they set to it. My Mammy was a cousin to Private Porsum, what was in the big war over the other side of the ocean and made a name for himself and for Custiss that folks can read in the books. He was quiet talkin, they said, for I never seen him but one time, and he testified in the churches for salvation, but he was a man with a rifle you never seen the lak of, nor nobody in Custiss. He come back from the war, and there was big carryins-on over him in New York and in Washington, and in the city, and folks standin in the streets half a day, not workin nor nuthin, to see him come ridin past in a automobile, settin with ginrals and senators and sich. And him Private Porsum from Custiss. They wanted to make him a ginral or sumthin and put trimmins on his coat, but he said naw, he was Private Porsum, and he had not done nuthin but what come to his hand, and what air man would, with Gods help to uphold him. And they named him Private Porsum. He was book clever, and when he come back from the war he went to the Legislature. He done good there, and after a while he never come back to Custiss much except to be makin speeches. He has got him a little place up in Custiss yit, where he goes to be huntin and fishin, but he has got him a big house down nigh the city, here. My Mammy was his cousin and blood-kin, and me. But the Wynd-hams, my Pappys folks, was good folks, too.

The Porsums laid hand to the plow and held on, and my Mammy never was one to be turnin and laggin. She done what she could, and reared us in sweat and Gods name. I seen her barefoot in the field and the plow lines hung over her neck like a man, and her humped to it, afore us young uns was big enuf. And her not no big woman, and slight-made. I seen her, nights after she done put us to bed and me the biggest layin wakeful, I seen her settin weavin or patchin and the fire so low she squinched to see, or plaitin them hickory baskits, to sell in the settlemint. I shet my eyes for sleep, her settin there the last thing in them. We growed up and done what we could, and taken over the plowin. She did not work in the field no more, but to chop corn when we got in a tight and the grass taken a strangle holt after the wet. But she never was no sluggart, and taken no ease, with times hard till the day the women folks come in to wash her and I heard the hammer in the shed where they put the nails in and made her box staunch-tight.

Jacob my brother, he laid holt on Jesus afore Mammy shet her eyes on day, and it was a joy for her. But me, I never and I groan to deny it to her. It was not in me, for blindness. I worked and done, but Saturday toward sun, it was me down the big road, and many is the time I come back the dew done dried on a Sunday. Lak yore Pappy, Ashby, she said to me, a hand for gallivantin and revellin, and him dead in the dark past Jesus sight. He would not take nuthin offen no man, and the strong man is done brought low. Her heart grieved. And what she said last, and her lips blue lak a vilet, was to name my salvation. Ashby, she said, and tried to lift up her hand what was feeble on the cover, lay holt while it is yit day. I stood there. My heart in my bosom, it was lak flint rock for hardness and sharp edges cuttin, but I could not git out a word nor a tear to the eye socket. I tried to retch out and tetch the foot-board of the bed where she was layin, lak that was somethin to do. But my arms was lak frozen. It was the last she said, and then the black vomit.

I seen three die mortal on that bed, and me standin there. My Pappy, lost and his eyes poppin, and my Mammy, safe in Jesus, and that pore old man, the Frencher, wayfarin and far from home, comin off the big road and died amongst strangers. It was a time after my Mammy was done gone, and Jacob and me lived there and made out, him livin by Jesus word and me hittin off ever Saturday with my hat cocked on the side of my head and lookin for what mought be. It was gittin along in August, and the sun not down yit and the day was a scorcher. I come round the corner of the house from the woodpile, my arm full of stove wood, and I seen a wagin comin up, and Jacob awalkin afore it. I went on in and throwed down them stove lengths, and heard Jacob callin. I went out there, and Jacob was pickin up a old man out of the wagin. He handled him lak he was nuthin for lightness, him wropped up in a old quilt and his arms ploppin out to drag down. His eyes was open, but he never looked at nobody nor noticed, but he looked up at the sky and never blinked. Then him was drivin the wagin jumped down and come runnin round to the old man, and leaned over to grab holt of the old mans hand, and the big old straw hat fell off, and I seen it was a woman, not more than a gal, and long black hair come undone and tumblin down. Then Jacob yelled fretful at me standin there gapin, it's a pore old man sick to die, and you standin there. Git the bed ready! And I done it.

Jacob had done met them down the road, and the gal ast him where to git some drinkin water for the old man sick. So Jacob brung them in, lak air man would, and him Christian. We put him in the bed, where had laid the saved and the unsaved to taste the bitterness. We unwropped that old quilt offen him, and it dirty from the journeyin, and taken off his pants and shirt. There was not no meat to him, for the wastin and fever, and the skin hung

63

off him lak a tow sack hung on a barb wire fence. The gal washed off his face and hands, and give him water to sup, but he never said nuthin. He laid there. He had a white beard, and his head was bald like a punkin on top, and yeller, with white hair bristlin off the sides. His eyes was blue lak a babys, and he looked up to the ceiling, and it the house of the stranger, where he had done come all that wav and all that time, from Canady, whar they is the deep snow.

The gal never said a word. She set there and leaned towards him and had holt of his hand. She did not cry, but they was dust from the journeyin on her cheeks, and you could see how the tears had done come down from her eyes and made streakin down her face. Her comin down the road in the wagin, and the old man layin there, and the sun bearin down, and the tears come down from her eyes. She set there till he was dead, after Jacob had got the doctor from Cashville. He was a gone goslen, the doctor said, and taken his leave. It was nigh midnight when Jacob come with the doctor, and he did not stay no time to speak of after he looked at the old man. It was towards day the old man crossed over. That gal did not cry none. She looked at his face for a minute real hard. She still had holt of his hand, lak all that time. Then she put her head down on his chist and let it lay. She shet her eyes, and for all you could say, she mought been asleep, and her hair loose over his chist. I taken a look at her, and I went outside and stood there lookin off towards Massey Mountain. The first day was comin over the mountain, the sky there the color of blue-johnny spilt, and the mountain black under it.

They is good folks in Custiss and they taken holt. They buried that pore old man and was Christian kind to Marie, which was that gals name. Old Mrs. Marmaduke, who had the place next ouren, she taken her in for four days, till she got ready to leave. She was goin on, she said, to some place where she could git some work. She had been headin south, she said, to git the old man where it would be warm in the winter time, lak she had heard tell. They had been comin down a long time, she said, nigh four years, stoppin and workin to git a little somethin to eat, and movin on. She mought as well keep on goin that way, she said, not havin nobody of kin nor kind. She would make out, she said.

The mornin she was leavin, I got up and started out the door and towards the gate. Whar you goin, Jacob said. I didn't say nuthin, but kept on goin. I went down the road toward Marmadukes. I got to a place whar you can see the house, then I squatted down lak a man will to take his ease. I seen smoke comin out the chimney, and knowed they was stirrin, if haven a name for late risin. A time, and Old Man Marmaduke brung the wagin out, and I seen that gal Marie come out, and Mrs. Marmaduke. That gal was wearin a dress now, lak she done after her pappy died. Then I seen her put her valise up in the wagin, and git up, and the wagin start rollin, and the folks wavin after her. Then Old Mrs. Marmaduke went in and Old Man Marmaduke went off towards the shed. I moved down the road a piece, round the bend, and squatted down, where the cedars was.

She come down the road. She was settin there straight, and lookin down the road, not this way nor that, till I riz up by the cedars when she had done got nigh, and said good mornin. And she said good mornin, in that way she talked, not lak ouren. I kept on walkin alongside the wagin, not sayin nuthin for a spell, nor she. Then she not sayin nuthin, I said, I am goin a way down towards Cashville, I wonder can I ride with you. She said I could, and I laid hand to the side board, and lept up.

How far you aimin to get today, I ast her.

They say I kin git to what they call Tomtown, she said.

It is a way past Cashville.

Not too far, they say.

It is a heap too far, I said, for today.

Then I will rest where I can, she said. Lak we done, afore. I got a little somethin left yit, and I kin pay. She did not say nuthin for a minute, then she said right sharp, I tried to pay Mrs. Marmaduke, and not be beholdin for bread.

It is too far, I said, for tonight.

I'll git there tomorrow.

It is too far, I said, for tomorrow.

I'll git there when I git there, she said sober, lookin down the road.

No, mam, I said, you won't.

How far is it.

It is too far, I said, for mortal time.

And she looked at me right sudden, and her eyes was big and blue like her pappys.

And mortal time, it is, we live in, I said.

Then I told her how I had done gone to Cashville yestiddy, and she could git work to do there, and not leave so far from where folks knowed her name and had put forth their hand to her in sorrow, and where her pappy was laid in the ground. One of them boardin houses up nigh the Massey Mountain Company sawmills could use a woman could cook and was willin.

65

She did not say nuthin for a time. She looked down at her hands laying togither in her lap. Them wagin wheels screaked lak they do, and the dust puffed up where the mule put his hoofs down. The road, it was deep dust up over the rim, it a drout from way back. It did not look lak she was goin to say nuthin, settin there, her head bowed down. Then she said, I will do what I can, Meester Ween-ham. Which was what she called me, her comin from way up in Canady, where they do not talk so good.

Five

THERE were many other young men working at Meyers and Murdock. In fact, except for the people in the accounting department, almost all of the men were young, twenty-five, thirty, thirty-five years old. They accepted Jerry with a mixture of jaunty amiability and respect, with helpful suggestions, with an easy greeting in the morning when he happened to meet one of them in the elevator or in the corridors—"Good morning, how's tricks?"—"How's the old All-American?"—with a friendly and confident clap on the shoulder. He went to lunch with groups of them in the back room of a little restaurant, a dingy hole where the wallpaper was scaling off and where on the walls hung old Coca-Cola advertisements and calendars advertising undertaking parlors and insurance companies; but the tablecloth was cleanly crisp, the chops came sizzling and rich off the charcoal, the Swiss cheese was excellent, and the bootleg beer drinkable.

The faces about the table changed from week to week, for men would go away on trips to the firm's branches in New Orleans, Memphis, Atlanta, St. Louis, and Chicago; or the more favored and older ones, the ones who carried their easy comradeship and masculine freemasonry with more dignity and deftness, who seemed to nurse secretly some high, impersonal concern, would go away to New York or Boston or Washington, or to the capital cities of other states. Then, they would reappear at the table, and someone would ask, "How'd you make it?" and they would reply, "Fine, fine, good trip," and in their eyes, for an instant, would flicker up an abstract, inward light, quickly quenched. And sometimes men connected with the branch offices or with some of the affiliated banks would appear at the table, absorbed effortlessly into the circle, speaking the same language, wearing the same clothes, bringing news of politics and business and pleasures in other states and cities, telling new jokes, serene and at home, returning proconsuls.

After the office closed in the afternoon, Jerry would go down with some of the men, now and then, to a speak-easy, just beyond the business district, down toward the river where a few soot-crusted, two-story, turreted old brick houses, with stained-glass panels on each side of the heavy oak front door, still remained among the warehouses and garages and parking lots. The speakeasy was in such a house. Set in the stone pavement outside the iron gate, there was an iron hitching post capped by a horse's head in iron. Grass struggled sparsely in the trodden and carbolic soil which had once been lawn. To the right of the gate, in the middle of the open patch, there was an iron statue of Diana the huntress, tunic looped lightly from the breasts, bow in hand, the greyhound crouching before her. Men coming down the steps of the house at dusk sometimes cocked a hat on her head and stood back to laugh.

Toward five or five-thirty on the summer evenings the young men would come down the street in little groups, and turn in at the iron gate. They wore white linen suits or seersucker suits, crumpled now from the day at the office, and panama hats or flat straw hats. They mounted the stone steps, entered the dark hall, where the mirror of an old hat rack glimmered mottledly like stagnant water, and heard the burr of the electric fans and the chink of glasses and the voices from the rooms beyond. They leaned against the battered mahogany of the bar, thumped their hats back on their heads, and picked up their glasses. There would be the card-players in a corner or in the next room, a couple of seedy bookmakers, peddlers of gyp insurance, the aimless riffraff, the hangers-on, young with their nails carefully scraped and pared and with their coats buttoned, or middle-aged with their bellies pressing against their belts and the color of bulging flesh showing through the sweat-soaked fabric of their shirts. They would look up when Jerry and his companions entered and call out, "Hi, there," and the young men would respond, "Hi, Butch," "Hi there, Moon," for they liked to buddy with the toughs, to sit in for a hand now and then, to talk about the chicken fighting or about the races down in Louisiana or in Kentucky. And there would be young men from other banks and bond houses and insurance companies, ready with their greetings and with the clap on the shoulder. They were the same kind of people as the men from Meyers and Murdock, but between them and the men from Meyers and Murdock was a line of demarcation, thin and fluctuating, but real. They were "Murdock's boys."

Jerry fell in with the new life with scarcely an effort. After the first few weeks had passed, he began to feel that it was, after all, not quite so new as he had at first imagined. It was, in a way, the life of the fraternity lounge lived on more spacious terms, but, underneath the easy comradeship, with a deadly earnestness. Jerry worked hard at trying to learn something about the business. He read books on economics and banking and studied statistical reports of various companies. He would leave the speak-easy and go to his boarding house and after dinner would go up to his room and study, as in the old days at the University he had left the racket of the fraternity lounge to go to his room in the dormitory.

"Jerry," Duckfoot said to him one day, "they tell me you're living out at a boarding house on Pratt Street."

"Yes," Jerry said.

"Well, you better move," Duckfoot said. "The diet out there won't agree with you. Too much cabbage."

"Cabbage?"

"Sure," Duckfoot said, "cabbage. Cabbage don't agree with bond salesmen. Didn't you know that? The smell gets in the clothes and you can smell it. That good old boarding-house smell."

"It's a pretty good boarding house, I reckon. And it's cheap."

"You better move. You better see if they've got a room and bath, somewhere higher up than the fifth floor down at the Macaulay Arms. With a view. Or this new residential hotel—you know, what's its name?"

"Sure," Jerry said, "sure, if I could afford it. I don't save much now, and I wouldn't save anything, paying a big room rent and eating out."

"Oh, Gawd, oh, Gawd!" Duckfoot breathed, "who said you're supposed to save anything? You're supposed to make money, not save it. Suppose you do save ten dollars a week? Suppose you save fifteen dollars a week? Do you think you'll ever get rich that way? Hell, no. The idea is to lay for a killing and not be putting the dime in the sock. Say, where do you keep all your money, anyway? Under the mattress? It'll make you a humpback sleeping on it."

"Not what I've got saved, it wouldn't," Jerry said, and laughed.

"You better leave that boarding house," Duckfoot said, and wagged the pale, phthisic forefinger of his right hand at Jerry, "and fumigate the cabbage out of your pants and vest. Now, me, it don't matter where I live. Since our shack burned down out in the country, and my folks moved to town, I been living with 'em on a street that would make Pratt Street look like the Gold Coast. But I don't sell bonds. I'm an accountant. I'm a statistician. I've been everything from night man at a lunch counter down to a college instructor of freshman sociology, which is a point in the slime from which you look up at the pale bellies of the eyeless creatures of the ocean floor. But I never sold a bond in my life. I can eat my cabbage. I can live on Pratt Street. But you—" And his long, folded-over bony form shuddered in the chair, and he laced his fingers across his chest.

Duckfoot Blake had feet that splayed out from his bony, beanpole shanks, feet broad and flat as a hoecake, feet that seemed to plop loosely on the pavement when he walked, with a sound like a wet washrag dropped on the bathroom floor. He wore high shoes, laced only loosely and always too big for him at the ankles, so that the thin leg bone stuck down into that tubular container seemed as irrelevant as a cane dropped into the brass holder by the hat rack in a boarding-house hall. The shoes were always black, always unpolished, of soft leather which bulged to accommodate the bunions, big as shooting taws. When he talked he propped his feet up before him on the desk, and looked at them; meanwhile the slow, reflective motion of his toes worked the soft leather, first one foot and then the other, rhythmically. He talked about his feet. In the morning when the men met him in the corridors, they said: "Hey, how's your feet this morning?" "Gawd," Duckfoot would say, and would hold out one foot, "now this one, you consider this one, this morning now—" He talked to strangers on streetcars and in railway stations, about his feet: "Have you got good feet? You have? Well, let me assert to you that if you've got good feet you ought never cease giving thanks to the All-father. You ought to thank God on your knees, and that nightly. Oh, you've had kidney stones, have you? Yes, indeed, I am sure that it must have been trying, even painful, but again I say that you are peculiarly fortunate in the nature of your infirmity, in a world in which, I am told, all values are rapidly collapsing into an untidy welter of relativity. Kidney stones? I congratulate you—" and he would pump the stranger's hand, and with his own left hand wave his long carved ivory cigarette holder. "Let me assert to you that Milton in his blindness, Beethoven in his deafness, Job with his boils, Judas with his conscience, a debutante with the clap, nor a matinee idol with approaching baldness—the sufferings consequent upon their infirmities are not to be compared to the agony experienced by a man with bad feet—" The stranger, a farmer waiting in the station for a train, with a brown-paper parcel in his hand, a drummer who held his cigar between manicured fingers, a college boy, would begin to move puzzledly and uneasily, would try to withdraw, would say good-by, but a hand would be laid on the shoulder, the pale narrow face, not quite smiling, would hunch down closer from its superior height, the long ivory cigarette holder would stab the air and weave incantatory circles like a wand, and the high-pitched nasal voice would rise into the full sweep of its rhetoric.

One day after the office closed, Jerry walked down the street with him. At the corner, a one-legged man leaned against the granite of a building and held out his box of chewing gum and shoestrings. Duckfoot bought a package of chewing gum, stuck two sticks into his mouth, and masticating it, meditatively regarded the man. Through the gum, shaking his head sadly, he said: "His troubles are half over. He hasn't got but one foot left."

Duckfoot wore blue serge suits, winter and summer, the seat and elbows shiny, the side pockets of the coat stuffed with papers, the trousers and sleeves always too short, a heavy watch chain with a Phi Beta Kappa key across the vest, which sagged off his shoulders. He wore a black tie, and a white shirt, always very clean, the soft attached collar too big and hanging forward under his Adam's apple. His hat was of soft black felt. His blond hair lay thinly across his high, narrow skull. His eyes were pale blue, and his nose pointed. He smoked cigarettes constantly, using a long, elaborately carved Chinese cigarette holder which he stuck in the corner of his mouth. The men in the office called the holder *the false note.* Duckfoot knew that. He called it *the false note,* too. "Besides, consider the beauty of it. And what man does not yearn for a little beauty in his life? Even you—" and he would stab the cigarette holder at the bosom of one of the young men, "even you, stirred by a blind amoebal itch, looked upward from the economic slime of your daily grubbing, and groping, albeit feebly, for beauty, laid hand on that gaudy rag you wear for a necktie. Gawd."

He was nearly forty years old. He had worked at everything. He had farmed. He had taught a country school; he had taught sociology in the State University, where he had gone to college, and economics for two years at the University of Chicago, where he had taken a Ph.D. He had worked in a bank. He had been an accountant. And before that, there had been the numberless transitory jobs of the hungry years when he had been in school or had been wandering around the country or had been in college, dishwasher, night watchman, lunch-counter man, janitor, auctioneer at a gyp-jewelry joint. Now he worked at Meyers and Murdock. In an oblique, puzzled way, the men there liked him. They guyed him and patronized him; and they were a little afraid of him. On the days when he was sunk in work or in one of his fits of gloomy silence, they left him alone, and in earshot of him, their voices dropped.

71

Jerry liked him, and grew to like him more and more. He was, in the end, more helpful than anyone else in the firm, more helpful, even, than Morton, whose job was to break him in. Bogan Murdock had originally sent Jerry to Duckfoot. "Get to know Blake," he had said; "he can give you a lot of pointers. He probably knows more about the business than anybody. He's a highly valuable man."

So he had gone to Duckfoot Blake.

"Mr. Murdock said you'd give me some pointers," Jerry said to him. "I'm trying to learn something about the business."

"Business," Duckfoot uttered. Then: "Gawd."

"Yes, sir," Jerry said, "something about the business."

"Business," Duckfoot said. "Gawd, this ain't a business. Who told you this was a business? This is the Hindu rope trick."

"Well," Jerry smiled, "I'd like to know something about the rope trick."

"Know? Know something? What are they starting you off with?"

"Selling," Jerry said, "after a little."

"I oughta guessed that, you being an All-American and so on." Duckfoot paused a moment, then waved his holder at Jerry. "Do you think these boys round here know anything?"

"They know more than I do," Jerry said. "All I know is a little geology."

"Then you better forget it. You don't want to let anything tarnish that profound and fruitful ignorance which is the *sine qua non* of your chosen profession. At least in this place. You think these boys know anything? They don't know a God-damned thing. Somebody gives 'em something and they memorize it and run out quick to say it to somebody before they forget it. But do they know what it is? Hell, no. You might as well make 'em memorize the Rosetta Stone. You might as well give 'em the lost sacred books of the Etruscans. You might as well give 'em Longfellow's 'Psalm of Life' translated into the Indian Sign Language of the Plains. They don't have to know anything. I can tell you in five minutes everything you need to know—"

"That's why I'm here," Jerry said.

"Do you belong to a church?"

"I reckon I do," Jerry said. "When I was a kid there was a revival out near home and I joined up and got ducked. It was a Baptist church."

"Well, you better forget it. Baptists round here just don't buy as many bonds as Episcopalians and Methodists and Presbyterians. You just go round town some Sunday morning along toward the gospel hour and see which church has the most seven-passenger sedans and yellow sport-jobs sitting outside. Then you just wipe off your chin, and head in there. You get to be one of those fellows who stand at the door and shake hands with people and find seats for old ladies who wear black silk dresses. Do you play golf?"

"A little."

"Start playing golf. Play good enough so nobody can take much money away from you at it, but for God's sake don't get the habit of winning anything from those bastards out at the country club who might want to invest some money in waterworks bonds for Tierra del Fuego. Bridge, too. The same thing. Friends. You got any friends?"

"I reckon so," Jerry said.

"Rich or poor?"

"Poor," Jerry said.

"Don't be seen on the street with 'em. Get you some rich ones. It's easy. Rich folks love friends, especially new friends. They like to feel people really love 'em. For themselves. You can dance with poor girls, if they're so good-looking the rich boys are chasing 'em. But not chasing 'em just to tarnish and deflower. I mean with honorable intentions. But you, you do your going out with rich ones. And distribute your favors around. Don't start off wearing a brand while your little knees still wobble and your eyes have that velvety, confiding look for the wide world."

"It sounds easy," Jerry said, feeling a little uncomfortable, not knowing exactly what to say, wondering what was going on behind those watery-blue eyes and that pale, peaked, almost hairless face, which wagged from side to side while the nasal voice proceeded.

"It ain't," Duckfoot said. "It ain't a bit easy. It takes a hero, and him with but a single thought. Everybody knows the secret, but it takes a hero to hew to the line, and let the chips fly in anybody's eye who happens to be looking. All human frailty hinders and forbids. Vanity, sloth, cupidity of the flesh, false shame, and the tender promptings of our deluded nature. But you eschew the kit and caboodle. You dump 'em in and pull the chain. Go to the ant, thou sluggard. What does the ant do? He heads for the sugar bowl. But you—" He suddenly stopped speaking. His face assumed a rapt and distant expression, and the long cigarette holder, with nearly an inch of clinging ash on the cigarette, drooped from the side of his mouth. Putting his hands on the arms of the swivel chair, he meticulously lifted one thighbone off the seat. Then he emitted a gentle, flutelike fart. The ash from the cigarette detached itself, and fell to the floor. "I beg pardon," Duckfoot said. Then

73

he added: "But that's something you mustn't ever do. Brokers don't fart. But me, I'm an accountant. I'm a statistician. I'm an economist. University of Chicago, Ph.D. I have published twenty-three articles in the leading journals of economics. I can fart when I feel like it."

Duckfoot put another cigarette in the holder, and lighted it. "But you, as I was getting ready to say before my carnal envelope so richly asserted itself, you want to learn something about business. All right. I'll give you a book. You read a book, and it'll put you way out in front of these other fellows." He leaned over and fished out a chunky blue volume from the shelves along the wall behind him. He held it out to Jerry, who took it. "Read it," he said. "It's a good book—Balfour's *Logic of Statistics*. You read it, and then you come back, and we'll have something to talk about."

"I'll read it," Jerry said, "right away. Thanks a lot for talking to me."

He got up, and shook hands with Duckfoot Blake, who did not rise from his chair. "My feet," Duckfoot explained. "Pardon me not getting up, but it's my feet."

"Thanks a lot," Jerry said, and went to the door.

As Jerry reached for the knob, Duckfoot said: "Say, can you ride a horse?"

"Yes," Jerry said, hesitating, and turning.

"I mean really ride a horse. Can you take obstacles like a bird? Are you a centaur under pants? Do you hold your elbows in? I say, old fellow—" his thin, nasal voice rose in the nickering parody of the stage Englishman—"I say, do you ride?"

"I don't know about all that," Jerry said, almost embarrassedly. "But I used to break a few horses when I was a kid. I reckon I can stick on most."

"Boy," Duckfoot affirmed solemnly and oracularly, holding up his pale, bony right hand, "let Murdock find that out, and your fortune is made. Gawd."

Jerry made, that first year, enough money to pay the few debts he had accumulated in the last few months of his senior year, to pay his rent for a small and badly located room at the Macaulay Arms, to make five payments on a fairly good secondhand car, to buy his drinks at the speak-easy and his chops at the little restaurant, and to buy two suits, one dark-blue and the other medium-gray, and a few shirts and ties. The suits didn't look exactly like the suits worn by the young men who slapped him on the back when he met them at the elevator in the morning, but he couldn't tell exactly what the difference was, not even when, on those nights just after he had bought the suits, he stood before the mirror in his room and examined them, and himself, long and critically. He tried to remember, exactly, a dark-blue suit which Morton had worn at a party. He knew that his own wasn't like that, except at first glance. There was a difference. He said to himself: "I reckon I ought to have looked closer before I got them. I just didn't look close enough, I reckon. But I got to wear them now, all right. I'll just look closer next time." He was not vain. That person in the mirror there was just himself—that easy breadth of shoulder, the rangy, alertly hanging arms, the dark hair crisping off the square forehead, the even teeth, set a little far apart to give his not very frequent smiles a sudden engaging, innocent, urchinish quality, the heavy, almost aquiline nose and straight black brows which indicated a mature, confident, driving masculinity. That person was just himself. He lacked that detachment, that paradoxical disinterestedness, possessed by the person truly vain, whose self ends by being nothing, by being, as it were, selfless in its passive contemplation of that image which has its reality only in the mirror on the wall or the mirror of the beholder's eye. He was not vain. He would wear the suits as he wore his face, without thinking about them much. But next time, next time he would look closer, yes, sir. That was just common sense.

The second year he made more money, enough to finish paying for his car, to take a decent apartment in the Macaulay Arms, to invest a few hundred dollars in stock in Pretty River Quarries, which was handled and highly recommended by Meyers and Murdock, and to help his father a little toward meeting the interest on the mortgage. He was greatly excited when he made the investment, feeling that he had taken a momentous step, that he had crossed a ridge, like a pioneer, and had seen before him the green valley. To his younger, poorer, more timorous, or more ignorant clients, he said: "Sweet River, yes, I think that is certainly worth your attention. I have just put something into it myself. And I am a geologist. I don't want to insist, but that is my personal judgment, scientific and financial, and I'm standing on it." To the others, to those older men with minutely veined, red jowls and pouched, slow, unflickering, deep-set eyes, or with slack, sallow dewlaps and the quick, piercing glance, with white on their wide waistcoats or with the black cloth buttoned tight over the pectoral plate which you knew would be paper-thin, to the owls and the old sparrowhawks, he said: "By the way, I hope you don't mind, but I just wanted to remind you again about Pretty River.

75

I may be a sucker, but I guess I really believe in that—and I hope you do. You see, I just put my pants and shirt in it. You know, not much, but—" and his even, too widely spaced teeth would be exposed in that boyish, almost apologetic smile, "but enough to keep a young fellow like me awake at night. Now don't be telling me I let Meyers and Murdock take me."

"Well, now, Mr. Calhoun, well, now—" they would say, and smile back, unwittingly, difficultly—"I wouldn't say that." Or: "Well, Bull's-eye—" If they knew him pretty well.

It was all easier than he had imagined. They talked to him about football, about the team, about prospects for the next season, or they talked to him about fishing or hunting. He listened gravely, as he always did when anybody talked to him, nodding his head very slightly, his eyes fixed on an imaginary point on the floor some fifteen feet ahead of him. If they asked him questions or asked for his opinion, he would answer not too discursively, nodding slightly, his manner respectful but authoritative. He was not afraid to disagree with them. He knew football and fishing and hunting; and they knew that he knew those things. When the men talked to him about business or politics, he listened in the same way; and when they asked him a question he replied in the same way, rather briefly, respectfully, not afraid to disagree, not afraid to say that he did not know, nodding almost imperceptibly, with a slight corrugation of the strong, glowing flesh between his straight brows.

"I told you you didn't have to know anything," Duckfoot said. "Those old bastards who know something are so anxious to tell you about what they know—or think they know—you don't have to open your trap. And those who don't know anything, you can just tell 'em what pops into your head and it don't make any difference. Nobody has to know anything. I don't see why you keep on wasting your time reading books. Besides, I told you all you need to know a long time back. And it's working like a charm."

"Aw, Duckfoot," Jerry said, and smiled, "I'm not as big a heel as you tried to make me."

"You play golf," Duckfoot said.

"Sure, golf's a good game, and I've got to have some exercise. Sure, you make some contacts playing, but I've got to have some exercise. I don't want to be getting an alderman." He patted his stomach, then ran his fingers experimentally along the inside of his waistband.

"Pinch it," Duckfoot ordered. "It's slacking off." He leaned forward in his swivel chair, and thrust his cigarette holder at Jerry.

"Your organs will sag. Metabolism will alter. Hair will fall. It is the fate of man. Desire shall fail and the handling of bubbies in a convertible sport coupe in the moonlight shall be a burden. Put money in thy purse, then lay up thy treasure where nor rust nor moth decay. By which I mean don't be giving it back to Meyers and Murdock to invest. Put money in thy purse. But—" and he leaned back in his chair and morosely regarded his propped-up feet, "I must say you seem to be doing that pretty well. You must be learning the secret."

"I haven't joined the church yet, anyway," Jerry said.

"You will, Oscar," Duckfoot said.

Jerry continued to work at the books and reports which Duckfoot Blake gave him or recommended to him—Murray's *Theory of Banking*, Porter's *Principles of Financial Analysis*, Brubaker's *Banking Law*, Marston's *Statistics: Method and Meaning*, and all the rest. He looked forward to the evenings of work, under the soft light of his reading lamp in the good apartment in the Macaulay Arms, with the clear page before him and the clear flow of the reasoning in his head. It was so clean and sure, that flow of unheard voice off the page—a guarantee that the world was secure, was a pattern which you could grasp and live by. About once a week he and Duckfoot got together, at Jerry's apartment or at the jerry-built little bungalow where Duckfoot lived with old Mr. and Mrs. Blake. "Beat it, you two," Duckfoot would say to the old people a few minutes after he and Jerry had arrived. "You all go in the back room, while we work. I can't think when anybody's knitting or snoring, and that's all you all'll be doing. Beat it!" He would lean over and seize his mother by the shoulders, as though to trundle her short, broad bulk from the room, and she would go out, complaining and puffing: "Now, Jimmy, now, Jimmy, don't shove so. Stop shoving. Wait!—Wait, I want to get my stuff!—My glasses, Jimmy—Jimmy—" "I'll get your stuff for you, all right," Duckfoot would say, "but out you go, on your ample. Now!" He would shove her out the door to the little back hall, and while he turned back for the glasses or her stuff, she would stand at the door, her toes at the very sill, her small, bloated hand on the jamb, blinking, interested, like a child not quite daring to come in. Then he would thrust the stuff at her, say, "Beat it!" and shut the door on the old woman's very nose.

"That's the only way," he said to Jerry, seeing Jerry's face that first time they worked at the Blake place. "Kid 'em along. Make 'em think it's a game. You know how old folks are. They ain't got good sense in a way. You ask 'em nice can they let you have the room, and they'd say sure, and be so God-damned sweet and I'm-by-the-side-of-the-road-now about it you'd want to puke—you know how it is—and then they'd go in the back room and brood all evening about Lear on the heath. Which, by the way, they never heard of. Nor you either, probably."

"I read it," Jerry said.

"You got to kid 'em. You got to know how to handle 'em. Take my old man, now. He never did an honest day's work in his life. He tried to, but he just didn't have the gift. If it hadn't been for Mammy we'd all starved to death out there on that farm. But he thinks life just wore him out and worked him to death. He thinks he deserves to be able to tell you about his innards and his symptoms all day. Sure, he's a sick man, but it ain't all these specialists I pay for that keeps him alive. It's the pleasure of talking to me and Mammy about how he is dying by inches. That and dominoes. He wants to play dominoes all the time. Mammy won't play. Never has. Not even one game. Which is shore-God smart of her. She just says she can't learn it because she ain't got as good sense as he has. Which is smart of her, too. I play with him, but just one game a night, and if I miss one I make it up, and then he wants to charge interest on the game I borrow off him. If I miss ten games, I got to play an extra. He keeps books on me. And he wants to win all the time. I won't let him win all the time. If I did there wouldn't be any living in the house with him by the time he was a hundred. Besides I gotta raise him so he'll know how to face reality. To take the bitter with the sweet, the thorn with the rose, and the smell with the cheese. The old bugger!"

About eleven or eleven-thirty old Mrs. Blake would come back, carrying a platter of cake or a pie. Immediately behind her, would be her husband with cups and a pot of coffee on a tray, shuffling his carpet slippers dryly over the floor, rattling the cups, and quarreling aimlessly, almost to himself, in a thin voice: "Now, they ain't no place to put 'em, just look, they don't make no place to put 'em down. That's right, keep me standing here a-holden this truck, and my back about to break. It does look like—"

But nobody would pay him any attention, and he would put the tray on the table and subside, still muttering, into his rocker. His head, with its untidy, wispy white hair, just came up to the back of the rocker, for he was a small man. He held his tight, pointed knees together and set his two small feet, in their carpet slippers, side by side. His hands lay on his lap, the forefingers twitching a little, and his droopy, inadequate, white mustache twitched, too, with the mumbling.

"Put something in your mouth," Duckfoot would say, "then we can't hear you. We all got corns in our earns listening to your jabber. Put some angel-food cake in your mouth. For a stopper."

"You know I can't eat nothing," the old man would say. "Not nothing to speak of, and you talk that-a way. I don't eat enough to keep a bird alive."

"Come on, quit kidding," and Duckfoot would shove a slab of cake at the old man, "we know you. A bird alive! What you eat would keep a family of Rocky Mountain Bald Eagles in affluence and leave something over for the parish poor. Here, take this!"

The old man would take the plate, prop it perilously on his knees, and hunching forward, would pinch off small morsels and insert them carefully and reluctantly in his mouth, under the silky, sparse, droopy mustache.

"Atta-boy, old Rocky Mountain Bald Eagle, *haliaetus leucocephalus,* king of the crag, majestic monarch of the skies, atta-boy, glut! What you need to do is to stay out of the icebox and do more eating with folks. Eating is a social activity for civilized man. What you need to do is renounce the primordial privacy of the pantry and—"

Sometimes Jerry, sitting there and watching that comic, sickly, ineffectual, hunched-over old man pluck at his morsels, and hearing the voice of the son, who was a kind of elongated, violent, and distorted parody of the old man, and seeing the old woman, with her glasses down her nose, fix her sharp little eyes alternately on father and son, while her jaws worked ceaselessly with a decorous avidity—sometimes, sitting there, Jerry would feel himself absorbed into a powerful but nameless security, would feel within himself a certainty and a warmth. Feeling that, he would lie back in his chair, almost drowsily despite the coffee, the sweet taste of the food still in his mouth. Sometimes, but not always, for sometimes, that very same scene, the same high bantering voice, provoked in him a discomfort and revulsion, almost a hatred for these people, who had done nothing to him but who, for the moment, worked upon him like an insult.

Afterwards, when he would go out into the night, and get into his car and drive off between the small, jumbled-up houses, now darkened, of the deserted street, those feelings would be transmuted, that warmth and security into an elegiac melancholy, touched with envy, or that hatred into an aimless and diffused despair; but always, after that, when he tried to cleanse his mind by forcing his attention to some practical problem of his own,

79

there would be, instead of the melancholy or the despair, not the expected relief but confusion and an arid self-distrust.

His visits to the Blake house became more and more infrequent. He insisted, for one reason or another, that Duckfoot should come to the Macaulay Arms for their work, or he found excuses to postpone engagements. He was not doing so in terms of a definite and conscious program. When he made an engagement to go to the Blake house, he made it in perfect good faith. He really intended to go, and when he postponed an engagement, that, too, was done in perfect good faith; but the postponements were usually made without previous reflection, on the spur of the moment when he happened to meet Duckfoot in the corridor the day before. The postponement would be made on impulse, but afterward, even at the moment when, in great circumstantiality, he explained the situation to Duckfoot, the whole thing would seem so logical and necessary. "Sure," Duckfoot would say, "sure, I see how it is."

The crisis in the relationship came just at the end of Jerry's third year with the firm, when he was just beginning to take little trips to other cities on business. One Wednesday night he had an engagement to go to the Blake house to work. On Thursday afternoon he was to leave for New Orleans, for a two-week stay. On Wednesday morning, when, by accident, he met Bogan Murdock in the corridor, Bogan Murdock suggested that he come out that evening. "There's a little thing I'd like to talk over for a few minutes, then we might have a rubber or two of bridge." Jerry went directly down to Duckfoot's office and told him that he had to go out to the Murdock place, that Murdock wanted to have a talk with him. "I don't know what about," Jerry said, "but I reckon it's got to do with this Louisiana business. I'm leaving tomorrow, you know."

"Sure," Duckfoot said, "sure." Then, gesturing: "Sit down. Get your weight off your feet. It makes mine hurt to watch you."

"I got to shove," Jerry said, and edged toward the door.

"Sit down," Duckfoot said, "I want to say something."

Jerry sat down.

Duckfoot studied his propped-up feet for a moment, while his toes worked, slowly, under the soft leather. "Listen, Jerry," he said, quietly, not looking at Jerry, looking at the movement of the leather, "about this coming out to my place, now—"

"Damn it," Jerry said, loud, and almost with triumph and exaltation he felt the hate blaze up in him, "damn it! Ask Murdock. Ask him yourself!"

"Sure," Duckfoot said, softly, still not turning, "sure. I know

Murdock asked you to come out. I know the Great White Father thinks he's got something to talk over and all that. That's why you needn't look so damned much like you'd been sucking eggs. It's not this time. It's just in general—"

"All right. Last time. Take last time. I'm sorry, I was sorry as hell, but I just couldn't make it. You know that. Those people coming to town, and all."

"Sure," Duckfoot said. Then he turned: "Sure, any individual instance is on the level. But the whole is greater than the sum of its parts, and I'm talking about the whole. I don't go for Yogi or faith healing, but I shore-God do think it's miraculous how brute event can conform to the secret will of man. I wrapped some cheese-cloth round my head, stained my fair face with walnut juice, and gazed into my crystal ball, and I'm just telling you what I saw—"

"God damn it, now look here—"

"Pal," Duckfoot said, and he pointed the cigarette holder straight at Jerry, holding it so steady that the smoke rising from it never wavered, "you oughter get wise. If you don't want to work out at my place, if the old folks get in your hair, that's jake by me. We can work at your place. If you don't want to work at all any more, that's jake by me, too. We can just drink a little red-eye now and then and go to a chicken-fight. And if you got cirrhosis of the liver overnight, we can just say good morning when we meet in the elevator."

"You got it wrong, Duckfoot, listen here—"

"But you gotta get wise. It ain't me. It's the old lady. Some-body's coming out to the house and she gets all excited about making a cake or a pie, and she fools around for a couple of days. She ain't got any ideas to exchange with you. She'd just as soon I'd bring home the garbage man or a cigar-store Indian, if the Indian could eat. She just wants something that can reach for a piece of pie, so she can have this big excuse to putter round for a couple of days, trying to decide what she's gonna do and all. Then when the thing gets postponed it reacts bad on her. She gets along fine without anybody coming, just so long as she don't expect it. She don't say anything, but I can tell. Now if you don't want to come any more, if—"

"Duckfoot—" Jerry said, hoarsely, "Duckfoot, I—" The scene flashed before him with the stabbing vividness of reality, the dumpy, bloat-handed little old woman with those bright, mean-ingless eyes, standing in a room, in a kitchen, bending over some-thing, the perspiration beading somewhat on her temples and dampening the stringy gray hair; and he felt as though a kind of

81

clot in his bosom had suddenly dissolved. He had the impulse to weep, the forgotten sensation of a swelling and flowering, a release, within him, and coupled with that an almost desperate sense of loss and danger. "Duckfoot—" he said again, "I want to come out to your house. It's meant a lot to me, that's the truth. I want to—"

"Hey, take it easy," Duckfoot ordered. "Sure, you can come out to my house. Any time you want. But take it easy, sit down."

Jerry sank back into the chair. "Listen," he said earnestly, leaning forward, "I'll go up and tell Murdock I can't come; he can see me tomorrow morning. I'll go, right now—"

He started up from the chair, but Duckfoot gestured him back.

"Take it easy," Duckfoot said. "You needn't get so worked up. You go on out to Murdock tonight and listen to his sweet nothings. One time more or less for the old lady won't make any difference. Forget about what I said now, and go on and peddle your apples. Go on and sell 'em some Pretty River. Which, by the way, I just learned Murdock himself has bought a slug of."

"Is that a fact?"

"It's a fact, but don't you go and spill it. He had it bought for him, but a little bird told me. You know, a little bird with a cigar in his mouth and a derby on the side of his head. One of my low companions, the kind my old lady used to try to keep me away from when I was young."

"I got a little piece of it," Jerry said.

"Congratulations," Duckfoot said. "My guess is the new fashion in school houses, city halls, county courthouses, bastilles, spittals, bedlams, and public monuments in five states is gonna be Pretty River Limestone. For my little bird tells me Sam Dawson has a big slice, too. Sam Dawson, the feet of clay of our local democratic ideals. Gawd."

"I better shove," Jerry said, his tone preoccupied, and rose.

Duckfoot thrust out his long, thin hand at Jerry. "Shake," he ordered, "and don't let what I said prey on your mind."

Jerry took his hand, and shaking it, felt a surge of warmth and gratitude.

"Pardon me not putting my weight on my dogs," Duckfoot said, and winked.

Outside, in the corridor, Jerry paused for a moment. He stood there in the cool shadow, hearing voices somewhere beyond one of the doors, and felt detached, cleansed, and restored, like a man recovering, at last from a long illness. Then he thought: *I could have told Murdock I had an engagement, that I'd see him tomorrow. He won't talk to me five minutes. He just saw me and thought about a bridge game because I was handy.* And then he had the impulse to back in to Duckfoot and confess that he had, in a way, lied, that what Murdock really wanted was to play bridge.

During all of the following year, despite the increasing number of times when he took trips for the firm, and despite the increasing complications of his personal life as he met new people and grew more friendly with people whom he had already met, he continued his work with Duckfoot. The work provided a kind of uneasy refuge, a corner where he was still the Jerry Calhoun who had sat alone in the bare dormitory room, the Jerry Calhoun he did not want to remember but who could yet make some stubborn claim on him beyond his will. And besides, there was Duckfoot's infrequent praise: "Well, thank God, Jerry, your brains weren't entirely corroded by four years on the gridiron and in the halls of learning. Thank God, you studied some science, anyway. Something tidy. You've still got some respect for the fact that two and two makes four. Which is more than I can say for most of these birds around here." And then Jerry would feel embarrassed and happy as a boy. And scrupulously he alternated times between his apartment at the Macaulay Arms and Duckfoot's house. His experience at the Blake house did not change. Sometimes, as before, he suffered the same confusions of feeling, and afterwards, the same self-distrust. But he disciplined himself to accept that, and tried to steel himself against it. As for the work itself, he knew that it didn't amount to much. He didn't have enough time, in the midst of his obligations and distractions, to put himself wholeheartedly into it. And now, he could not see that it was having great practical value for him. But he had the stubborn, blind impulse to cling to it, even as it was shoved back, more and more, into an obscure corner of his life.

During the quail season and the duck season he went shooting as often as possible, with some of his clients, or with Murdock and some of the young men from the office. For Murdock liked to have the young men around him. He had an art which made them forget the relationship of the business, a kind of paternal comradeliness and a casual modesty; and at the same time the respect which they had for him at the office was replaced by another respect as they watched his brown wrists whip the golf club, or saw how his knees seemed to lift his mount over an obstacle or how easily and instantly the gun was laid on the whirring covey, almost as the barrel blazed and the bird dropped.

After almost five years Jerry was put up for membership in a gun club which had a duck-shooting and fishing lodge and preserve on a lake to the south. Who had sponsored his membership, he never knew. Murdock, he thought, for it was Murdock who had introduced him to the president of the club, old Mr. Pickering; though Sam Dawson had first invited him down to the lodge. The fees, at first thought, seemed too much for him; but he joined. It would, he decided, be worth it. Yes, it would be worth it. Not many young men belonged to the club. On his first trip to the lake he was sure that it would be worth it. After the day in the blinds, under the gray, sagging sky, beside the dead-looking, steel-colored water, the men sat in the big hall of the log lodge, before the enormous fire on the limestone hearth, glasses in their hands, their legs stretched out before them. They had removed their shooting coats and now wore jackets of soft wool or old tweed. They were, for the greater part, middle-aged or oldish men, bald, gray-haired, or streaked with gray, but in that firelight and with the flush of the liquor, the flash of those faces looked firm, ruddy, secure. Jerry had seen those faces before, most of them, but never like this. Saying nothing, holding his glass in his powerful, passive right hand, Jerry sat there and felt his skin tighten minutely and tingle with the heat of the blazing logs, and heard, almost unheedingly, the drawling voices, and felt that he had approached the secret focus of power and truth. Yes, it would be worth it, all right.

As the time for his work with Duckfoot grew more and more limited, so more and more limited grew the time he could take for his visits home. He tried to reserve Sunday mornings for at least a little drive out to his father's place, and sometimes for dinner there. He would get up on Sunday morning, forcing himself out of bed, with his mouth stale and dry from cigarettes and lack of sleep and with his stomach sometimes a little uneasy, and would go down to the restaurant on the first floor of the Macaulay Arms to have a glass of tomato juice and a cup of coffee. That was all he usually had the taste for, and all he ought to eat, anyway, to keep from putting on any more weight. Then he would get his car from the hotel garage. Sometimes, however, he would realize that there would not be time for him to make the trip out and back, and would have to content himself with a telephone call. But he went when he could.

Nothing was changing out at the place. Lew, Aunt Ursula, his father, they were the same, or at least, they changed so slowly that the change was imperceptible to him. And sitting on the porch in summer or before the fire in winter, they held the same postures and said the same things or said nothing, according to their habits, his father's voice slow, infrequent, and deep, Aunt Ursula silent, Lew cackling and bitter—"How you making out, Mr. Astor? How you making out working for Old Lem Murdock's boy? Old Lem Murdock, and him a murdering blackguard and swole with pride-pus? Him and his boy, blackguards. All blackguards—"

"How you making out, heh? Working for old Lem Murdock's boy? The old blackguard." And Lew had spat out toward the packed earth beyond the edge of the porch, thrusting his neck forward with his quick, viperish movement. But it fell short. The sun glinted on the glob there on the worn boards. Lew hitched his low chair toward it, grasped the sides of the chair to lift up his body, and thrust out his bad foot to smear the spot with vicious twitches and jabs of his heel. "Naw, naw," he kept saying, breathless from the strained position and the violence of his action, "naw, naw, they ain't no law a man has to set and look at what gob he hawks or filth comes outa him. Not me—no matter how pore. And that foot I got—that foot I got, let it look like something a mule's done tromped, but it's good for that, it's good enough to swipe out filth and hawkings. And good enough—it'd been good enough to tromp and scrouge on Lem Murdock's shoulders, by God, till the neck bone scrunched.—If they'd took him outa jail and put the rope on him.—Yeah, yeah—" And he subsided slowly, the thin, corded wrists letting the body down into the chair with the delaying ease of a gymnast on the bars. "Yeah, yeah, I don't have to set and look at what no man hawks, not mine ner no man's gob, no matter if he be rich and high-stepping. Naw, I ain't like some folks I know—" and he gave a sudden sidewise look at Jerry, a jabbing, twitching look like the motion of his heel on the gob—"naw, I ain't like some what loves it, to set and mirate on a rich man's gob, to paddle it, to git down and—"

"Lew!" old Mr. Calhoun's voice burst out, loud and sudden, louder than Jerry had ever heard it.

Lew stopped, and swung his head slowly to face Mr. Calhoun.

"It ain't no way to be talking," Mr. Calhoun said, slow and composed now, not looking at Lew but out over the sunlit meadow.

"Heh, heh, heh," Lew cackled, then stopped, watching Mr. Calhoun's face.

"It just ain't no way for a man to be talking," Mr. Calhoun said.

Jerry was not angry. Sitting there on the front porch, propped back against the wall, he thought how once he would have had the impulse to strike out murderously at that pale-skinned, sharp-featured, thin-boned face, under its too glossy ageless hair. But now he felt nothing. He lay back in the sunshine, relishing, like a bath, the lassitude, the sense of his body cleansing and renewing itself after the dissipations of the night before. He felt nothing, not even a momentary irritation, lying back and idly observing his big black roadster, its top down, pulled up under the maple by the gate. Yes, he could go out there and get in and be long gone. Yes, long gone, he thought. That made the difference, he thought, and added, to himself, the poor old bastard. Out loud, he said: "You know, I don't reckon I ever did hear the straight of the Lem Murdock killing."

"The straight of it," his father echoed, and added: "That would be hard to name."

"You know what I mean, you hear something all your life and you get so used to it you just don't realize you don't really know anything about it."

"It was before you was born, son," old Mr. Calhoun said, "and better forgot."

"Fergot!" Lew said, and hunched and spat.

"What did they fall out about?" Jerry asked.

"Politics, just politics, son."

"Politics, just politics!" Lew mimicked, "yeah, politics, and he shot him three times, in the guts, and him a man like you or me, and he lay there. Not in the head, mind you—naw, sir! not him, the blackguard—and not in the chest, like a man would. But in the guts, mind you, like you wouldn't shoot a dog and him egg-sucking!"

"Bad blood betwixt 'em," old Mr. Calhoun said. "Politics, they was both running for Governor, Lem Murdock and Moxby Good-pasture, and one thing led to another. I don't recollect exactly, but the way it is in politics—because it ain't personal, you might say, a man sometimes feels he's got the right to say worse'n if it was, because they's always somebody to be yelling and clapping. But I don't recollect—"

"I recollect," Lew said. "By God, I recollect, and ever word it was like outa God's own mouth and the breath of truth! Ever word he said about Lem Murdock."

"It don't do no man any good to recollect now," Mr. Calhoun said.

"Good!" Lew said, and cackled.

"No good, for a man can recollect too much, and the wrong thing. I've seen things I don't want to recollect, a power of misery on good and bad. No, it don't do no good."

"Good!" Lew leaned, and hunching, gathered himself. "I recollect, and I want to recollect. All the meanness I seen, and was done to me, what children called me in school, and I can name their names, ever one— Wiley Turpin, what he called me? I ain't never fergot. Yeah, I want to know how it was, all of it, and I ain't aiming to give over. I've laid in the night to recollect, for it's what a man's got to go on." He stopped, breathless, his eyes probing their two faces, his lips now thinly pink and glistening with the saliva of his vehemence.

"Well," Jerry said evenly, almost politely, before he could suppress the pure, joyful impulse which took him as he met the eyes in which shone avidity, challenge, and triumph, "what did that boy, Wiley Turpin, call you, Uncle Lew?"

"Son, son!" Mr. Calhoun uttered.

"Hell, I'll tell him! Yeah, I'll tell him and proud—"

"Son—"

"Yeah, he called me—" and Lew stopped, leaning forward, as though to relish the moment—"he called me box-hoofed, lard-headed trash!"

"Son—" and Jerry observed, dispassionately, the pain on his father's face.

"The very words, and if he's living he don't recollect, that Wiley Turpin, but I do. I recollect. And—" he sank back, more detached and satisfied, his eyes seeming to film a little—"I recollect what Moxby Goodpasture said about Lem Murdock."

"What did he say?" Jerry asked.

"He was out making speeches, and he made a speech at Essex, standing on the courthouse steps. My honorable opponent, he says —yeah, my honorable opponent—honorable, he called him, and if he's honorable—"

"It's a way of speaking," Mr. Calhoun said.

"A way of speaking, yeah. And he said, 'My honorable opponent, Lem Murdock, held the commission of Major in the Confederate Army, and he is the son of his father, Angus Murdock, who got rich after the war by land speculation in this State in partnership with Mr. Herman Tilford of Cleveland, Ohio.' Yeah, that's what he said—ever word like it was, for I seen it in the newspaper and I recollect—and he said, 'But I stand here before you, as I am, without a Confederate commission or a Yankee dollar.' And Lem Murdock shot him."

"He shot him," Mr. Calhoun said, "when he got off the train at Mulcaster and come into the station, two days after."

"He stood there in the station, waiting, while Moxby Goodpasture's hired band was playing, and when Moxby Goodpasture come up, with folks all round him, Lem Murdock bellered out 'Sir!' And he shot him."

"Some said, and on oath it was at the trial," Mr. Calhoun said, "how Judge Goodpasture looked like he was reaching for a pistol."

"Yeah, and some swore to God how he never!"

"They found a pistol in his pocket—"

"—and not loaded! And the cartridges in his pocket, in a box. Just like somebody give 'em to him on the train. It was swore to. And Lem Murdock shot him."

"Folks toted guns more, back there," Mr. Calhoun said. "They was too free and easy with pistols, it looked like."

"Yeah, free and easy, free and easy! Three times in the guts. And Lem Murdock stood there, so nigh he could a-put his foot out and touched Moxby Goodpasture laying there, and the folks standing all round, and he broke his pistol and threw out the cartridges left, and put the pistol in his pocket, and walked outa that station and got on his horse. And no man to lift a finger. And why? Because he was Major Lem Murdock and proud as pus! Lord God, if I'd a-been there, I'd stopped him, my foot like it 'tis. I'd laid hand to me a half brick. I'd a-took me a piece of iron. I'd a-stopped him. Major Lem Murdock, and him pus-proud—"

"He got on his horse," Mr. Calhoun said, "and went to the police and gave himself up. He never aimed to run away."

"Run away! Not him, swole up with pride—Naw, he didn't have to run away and lay in no brush with the dogs on him. Not him, knowing how it would be. How he'd walk outa the courthouse a free man—"

"He was convicted," Mr. Calhoun said. "It was the high court let him off, things being mixed up like it was."

"They oughta hung him, they oughta put the rope round his neck—" and Lew set his thumbs across his Adam's apple and his palms under his ears, and in pantomime horribly rolled his eyes, and stuck out his tongue, which was wet and pink, like a child's. His grip was tightening until the veins puffed blue under the pale soft skin of his temples. He suddenly released his hands, gasped, and sank back lopsidedly upon himself. A little saliva hung on his lips, wiped off there as he had drawn his tongue in. "Then—" he said, softly, "then there'd a-been two of 'em. Two blackguards dead—"

"Two?" Jerry inquired.

"Lem Murdock and Moxby Goodpasture. Both blackguards."

"I never heard much against Moxby Goodpasture," Mr. Calhoun said, "but that he had a sharp tongue and said what come in his head. I heard say he was a good man."

"Good! And him like Lem Murdock, high-stepping and swole.

Them kind, judges and governors and senators and sich, swole up with wind like a dead dog—My friends, my friends—" his voice rose to a falsetto of mimicry. "They ain't got no friends. They ain't friends to their mother!" Then, quietly: "Them kind, governors and sich."

"There's been good men—" Mr. Calhoun began.

"Yeah, and what good they ever done you—you set there and grabble and rot, and what good? You say it, and you got some swole in you yourself, Mr. Astor. Because your uncle was Governor of this here State—"

"He was my great-uncle," Mr. Calhoun said, "and he built this house."

"My great-great-uncle," Jerry said. "I hadn't remembered that since I was a kid. And he built this house?" He glanced to one side, inspecting the wall, and then up at the ceiling of the porch, as though to verify his father's statement, thinking, *It sure needs paint, it sure needs some work done on it. The first change I can spare,* he thought, *and I'll do it.* He turned, then, to his father: "What else did he do?"

"Yes, Ezra Calhoun," Mr. Calhoun said, "he built this house and he was Governor. What else he did, I never heard tell—"

"A land-grabber," Lew broke in, and spat, "like all them kind."

"—and I never saw him. He was dead before my time." Mr. Calhoun paused, meditatively. "No," he added, "I never heard ill spoken of him, as I recollect. He was a good man, for aught I know to the contrary."

"Him good, and one of them kind!"

"For aught I know," Mr. Calhoun said.

"Look at 'em, and you'll know! Lem Murdock and all his kind—"

"I know him," Jerry said. "I have seen him very often. He's just an old man now, and he's about gone in the head, sometimes. He stays down at the stables and talks to the niggers." And he wished, suddenly, that he had not said that, uncomfortable and, strangely, defenseless, as Lew leaned forward seizing on the words, triumphant.

"Yeah, you know him. You know him, all right! You know that Bogan, too, and you work for him. And you come when he hollers and you dance his jig when he calls it, and you fart when he farts. I know, I know, and I've heard tell, for folks got eyes, ain't they? But I never needed no telling. Not me, I can see—"

And all the sun-drenched autumn landscape seemed, to Jerry, on the moment inimical, its bright stillness watchful and treacherous.

"—not me, for I know 'em. All them kind. All of 'em. That boy gallivanting round the country, throwing money like it was millet seed and a high wind, betting on chicken-fights and carrying on. And that girl—"

Jerry's heart constricted, suddenly.

"—riding round the country in automobiles, and setting out with men, and it nighttime—"

He could almost see her there—out there in his car, in the broad daylight, now—her head back, and her pale hair loose and silvered in the moonlight, and the black trees around—but it was broad daylight now—and he thought of the evasive, provocative, vibrant arc of her waist under his hand, the twin firm-knitted small columns of musculature at her back under the soft thin sheathing.

"—yeah, and it nighttime—"

He thought how sudden, small, and sharp her teeth were above the fullness of the lower lip.

"—and her setting in automobiles and drinking outa bottles and throwing her head back and shutting her eyes and not knowing or caring what hand 'tis on bubby nor belly. Nor caring—"

Jerry stood up, abruptly. "God damn it!" he said, "God damn it, you—"

Mr. Calhoun rose and went quietly into the house.

"Heh, heh, heh," Lew cackled, looking after Mr. Calhoun. "Mr. Astor," he said, "Mr. Astor ain't had a piece in thirty year—heh, heh! but me—" he stopped, leaning forward, lifting his delicate, sharp, peeled face toward Jerry, who stood above him, "—me, I had me some."

He withdrew his eyes from Jerry, and looked across the yard to the fields. "Yeah," he said, "it's all the same."

Six

Statement of Ashby Wyndham

THEY hired her up at the boardin house on Massey Mountain to be cookin and helpin to give their vittles to the men what was workin. I taken her up thar, and I seen what it would be lak, them two big cook stoves, big as a sawmill boiler, and her havin to be firin up one of them stoves and cookin for it looked lak a army, them tables was so long whar the men set down. And dishes to wash and the floor to sweep and mop. And her not no big woman, no way. I seen how it would be, and I said, naw, you ain't a stayin here, not and you no bigger than a rabbit.

You brought me here, Meester Ween-ham, she said in that air way she talked.

Yeah, I said, and I kin take you away agin.

You brought me here, she said right quiet and looked at me with them big eyes, and I'm stayin, Meester Ween-ham.

Her mind was set, nor canthook ner crowbar could budge it. She taken her valise and put it in that air little room they give her, you could see daylight through the roof it was so shack-built, and she taken my hand. Good-by, Meester Ween-ham, she said.

So I got in the wagin and went home, for she told me to take it and keep it for her.

I stopped down at the foot of Massey whar a man could git him a bottle of moonshine whisky from Buck Barkus what made it and sold it and stirred up abomination and taken silver for it, for it looks lak ain't nuthin pore man won't do for money, and what he won't do for money he up and does for lust of his flesh and sinful pride, and it for pride the angels fell out of heaven and Gods sight. So Buck Barkus he taken my four bits and it was his sin, and me, I taken that air bottle, and it was my sin, for a man takes a pull on the bottle and it is lak he taken a fire in his bowels and lust its name and his fingers itch. I done drunk up that air bottle and bust it on a lime rock, and I come toward the house standin up in the wagin bed whuppin that pore old mule and the wagin jouncin and me standin up and whoopin and yellin in my lust and sinful pride.

My brother Jacob was standin thar and lookin at me when I come.

Ain't that that Canady-girls mule, he done ast me, and I said it was, and she said for me to keep it.

You nigh kilt it, he said.

Hell, I said, I ain't kilt nuthin but me a bottle of Barkus panther-piss.

You nigh kilt this here mule, he said, and I looked at him how his face was, and I spat over the wagin wheel on the ground.

Jesus Christ, I said, I ain't kilt no mule.

Git down, Ashby, he said, quiet, and I'll unhitch.

Jesus Christ, I said, for it was not nuthin them days for me to take the name of our sweet Jesus and it in vain. You ain't unhitchin nuthin. I'm unhitchin. It's my wagin and it's my mule and it's my woman, I said.

Ashby, he said, quiet again, you git lak this and you ain't fit to unhitch no mule. You ain't fit for nuthin.

I looked down and I seen him standin there nigh the mules head. I just looked down at him a half minute. Then I spat a spew over the wagin wheel, gittin ready slow to let fly lak a man will settin on his porch takin his ease nigh sun. Then all of a sudden I let out a whoop and I whupped that air old mule with that rope end fit to draw blood, and that old mule jumped lak it was a race horse, and Jacob jumped back just in time, and I whooped and whupped.

We come round the corner of the house, me whoopin and whuppin and headed for the lot gate, what was open. I never seen how it happened. But it looked lak a wheel got hung on the gate post, what was locust and deep-set, and I seen that air old mule go down and me flyin. It seemed lak I flew slow, lak when a man dreams he can fly. It seemed lak I whooped once and me in the air. It seemed lak I was in the air flyin nigh a half hour. That was all I knowed.

I must have hit my head on a rock or somethin. Or maybe the ground what was tromped hard, it being drout and the ground dry-hard. I didn't know nuthin till next mornin. I woke up, and I was layin in bed and a knot on my head the size of a simlin.

Then Jacob come in. How you feelin, Ashby, he ast, and I said I was feelin all right. I said there wasn't nuthin could faze me.

He didn't say nuthin. He just give me a cup of coffee. When I done drunk it, he taken the cup and set it on the table. Ashby, he said, that mule is dead.

I got out of the bed, not payin him no mind.

Ashby, he said, agin, that Canady girls mule is dead.

Well, I said, drag it off. Drag it off and give it to the buzzards. That old mule, it was not nuthin no way but buzzard bait.

It was the Canady girls mule, Jacob said.

Shore, I said, and I'll pay for it, buzzard bait or no.

We can't pay for no mule, he said. Not right off. We got to grabble to pay.

You can't pay, I told him, but me, I can pay.

You can pay, he ast me.

By God, I said, I can and will. I ain't stayin here to grabble. They ain't nuthin here. I'm sick of it here and primed to puke. I'm goin to Massey.

He shook his head, slow, and said, They ain't nuthin at Massey.

They's money at Massey, I said. I was puttin on my pants and bucklin my belt. They's payin hard money at Massey.

Yeah, he said, and chargin you for board and bed, if you ain't got a house over there you can stay in. And it's too far a piece to stay here and work at Massey. And ain't many's got a house over there now, the Company done throwed folks off the Mountain.

I'm goin, I said.

Leavin me, he ast. Leavin me and this here place.

I'm goin, I said.

It was your Pappys and Mammys place, he said.

And I ain't Pappy and Mammy, I said. I'm Ashby Wyndham, and I ain't stayin here to rot and grabble.

It was lak that, and I made me a bundle of my stuff, and I walked out the door.

Seven

"OH, LOVE me, Jerry, love me hard," she would say.

"I do love you."

"You've got to, Jerry, you've got to!"

"I do, I told you I do!" he would say, and find, as he seized her by the shoulders, or took her hand, that a defiance, an irritation, had crept into his voice, even as it uttered the protestation.

Perhaps she would slip from his grasp, with that effortless, easy sway of her body, a motion as perfectly timed and controlled as a boxer's, a kind of fluent sway from the waist and shift of the shoulders that always inflamed him and at the same instant set up in him a ground swell of undefinable unease. She would stand there before him, and his hand would still be outstretched. "You've got to," she would say, soberly.

Or she would, suddenly, be in his arms, with an almost preremptory violence, and he would feel in the midst of her kiss the sharp, small, even edge of her teeth upon his lip. And once or twice, on such occasions, she had burst into tears, clinging to him with a shameless, awkward abandon, like a child. At these moments, seeing the tears spill so innocently from her eyes, a great compassionate tenderness would surprise him, welling up like a flood from an unsuspected depth of sincerity, sustaining him and exhilarating him with its full sweep. "I do love you, I do!" he would exclaim. And he would know that it was true.

But once, even as he spoke, that betraying openness had gone from her face, and with the tears wet and trivially irrelevant upon her cheeks, her expression had sharpened to a probing intensity as, leaning back in his arms, she had gazed at him. Then, detachedly, appraisingly, she had said: "Do you?"

"I do, I do!"

"Oh, Jerry, Jerry," and she had clutched his upper arms, trying to shake him, "not that way. Different, different! Oh, Jerry, can't you understand?"

What was there to understand, he would ask himself. But he

could not frame the terms of the question for himself. Alone, at night in his apartment high up in the Macaulay Arms, the lights out in the room behind him, he would stare out over the lights of the city to the blackness of the country beyond, and turn the question over and over in his mind. Or he would lie in bed, his eyes on the dark ceiling, trying to define what he knew about her, and about himself. He would think back to the first time he had had her—months ago now—that night in her father's library, the night before his trip to New York, and wonder what had made her do it. It had been her doing, all right. He sure couldn't take the credit, he'd admit. Had she been stuck on him all the time? Well, if she had been, she sure had had a funny way of showing it. And before that night he'd never even laid a finger on her. Sure, he'd wanted to, all right, and who wouldn't, the way she stacked up? But he sure God hadn't been in love with her. He'd laid a finger on plenty of them he wasn't stuck on. Yeah, he'd managed right well in this man's town without having his littl⌒ heart go pitty-pat. He'd had some pretty good innings, all right. But what had she been up to? If she had been stuck on him, she sure God had had a funny way of showing it. Before and after that night. Why, after he had got back from New York she'd treated him like dirt for weeks. Hell, it had taken him weeks to get to first base again. Not that he had tried, as a matter of fact. And with that thought he would experience a little flicker of satisfaction, of pride. He hadn't had to take the sort of stuff she was handing out to him. Then, all at once, she had been sweet as pie. He had found her sitting in her car in front of his apartment hotel one evening when he came out on his way to dinner. "Take me to dinner, Jerry," she had said to him, just like nothing had happened.

And he had. Out to a steak and chicken place, twenty miles from town. They had sure taken a long time to cover that twenty miles back, too. That had started everything again. Oh, that had been her doing again, just like that night in the library. And almost every time when the recollection of that night in the library came back to him, he would think, *my God, suppose somebody had come, suppose Bogan Murdock had come!* She must have been crazy. And he must have been. He couldn't understand her, not a damned thing about her. And he couldn't understand himself. But he had to admit one thing. She sure had him hooked now. She sure did; and always, the question, and its importance, would disappear in some compelling image of her, the way the wind whipped her hair glintingly back and her lips parted with excitement as they galloped their horses side by side across the pasture, or the way her lips would part slightly and her face seem to smooth and unveil itself to receive a kiss. The image superseded and mastered, effortlessly, all speculation. The truth was there, and he could depend on that. That was what he needed to know.

But the speculation might return, fleetingly, to him in broad daylight, or even when he was with her, or more especially, when he took her to her rehearsals at the University and sat back in the empty, dark theater and watched her up there in the formal lighted rectangular area as she walked, gestured, and professed sentiments and passions which were not hers. Or, how much were they hers? That thought, coming to him as he sat far back among the empty seats—and the emptiness of the theater heightened the illusion of the action, and gave him the sense of being a spy, of having caught a naked, privileged glimpse of privacies not decently to be observed —that thought made him feel, on the moment, insufficient and betrayed. It was a rehearsal of the last act of Ibsen's *Lady from the Sea,* in which Ellida, discovering that the freedom of decision is her own, is suddenly redeemed from the mysterious power of the sea and of the stranger from the sea and can turn to her husband, crying out: "Oh—after this I will never leave you!" When, turning with that familiar fluent movement from the waist and shift of the shoulder, Sue uttered the words, her voice ringing with a free and pure fulfillment, he thought, that's it, that's it! That was what he wanted, and had not had, and now that fellow on the stage, tall, stooping, lumpy-faced, whom he had met but whose name he couldn't remember, who was playing a part, could make her turn that way and cry out in that voice. Then, in the midst of his sense of inadequacy and betrayal, the thought came: How much of that was really in her, her herself?

"Well," Sue said, as they stood among the actors and the hangers-on after the rehearsal, "I reckon I'm through with that silly bitch for tonight." She lighted a cigarette, and as she put her hands to the left side of her waist to jerk her skirt into adjustment over the hip, she let the cigarette droop from her lips and held her head back, with her eyes almost closed, and took a deep, slow drag of the smoke, and let it seep from her nostrils.

"Let's go eat," one of the actors said, "let's go down to the dog-wagon and get some hamburgers."

"Sure," Sue said, through the cigarette stuck between her lips and the cloud of smoke that puffed out unevenly with the words, "as soon as I get this skirt so it won't fall off and leave me like a jay-bird. Damn it, I need a pin, or something. Or maybe somebody's got a hank of barbed wire."

They all laughed, easily, standing about, waiting.

"I got a corn plaster," the tall, stooping, lumpy-faced boy affirmed; "you can plaster it on with a corn plaster." And he produced a box of corn plasters.

They laughed again, Sue, too.

"I don't have corns there," she said. "I don't have corns anywhere on this fair white flesh—" and she thrust her arms out theatrically.

There she goes, Jerry thought, there she goes, talking like that; she just talks that way around these people.

"—but I'm going to have corns, right between my shoulder blades, if you—" and she addressed the tall, lumpy-faced boy, "don't quit rubbing the palm of your hand there every time you take Ellida into your protecting, powerful, manly, masculine, tender arms."

So they all laughed again, their eyes seeking out the face of the tall boy, who flushed a little.

"Oh, don't discourage him, Sue," another boy said, "don't discourage him; Jake's just trying to branch out; he's just finding a new interest in life!"

The tall boy was flushing, but his mouth was open in a fixed grin, which showed his extraordinarily white teeth; and above the grin, in the lumpy, arid contours of the face, the eyes were large, pale blue, appealing, fresh, and innocent, like pools discovered surprisingly in a sun-bit waste country.

"Well," Sue affirmed, "he can find any new interest he wants in life. He can take up crocheting if he wants, but he doesn't have to give me a Swedish massage."

"Ibsen was a Swede," the tall boy said, and laughed very loud, in command of himself now; "I'm just entering into the spirit of the play. I am just sensing the mood—"

Then, as the laughter began, Jerry, not laughing, caught Sue's glance upon him, and he managed to grin, too, as though it all was amusing him and he was having a good time.

"No, Ibsen was not a Swede," an even, detached voice said, and Jerry turned to see Slim Sarrett leaning against the wall, there in the shadows. No one, apparently, had seen him come in. "Ibsen was a Norwegian. That is, he was born at Skien, in Norway, though his father was German, Scotch, and Danish by blood, and—"

"Aw, shut up," Sue commanded. "Let's go eat."

The group moved to the door, and Sue came up to Jerry. "Drive me down to Rosemary's place first," she said. "I promised her I'd pick her up and take her out to have some coffee when we got through rehearsing." Then she turned toward the group. "See you in a minute," she said, "at the dog-wagon."

Jerry followed her out, and they got into his car. Though it was not very dark there—there was a big light on a pole at the other end of the parking area—Sue leaned over and kissed him, slipping her hand under his coat and seizing the relaxed muscle just back of and below his left armpit. She hung there against him for a few seconds, her body twisted over on her left hip, her left leg crooked, and her right leg, pale in the shadow, thrust straight to a point just in front of the right door of the car, under the dashboard.

He heard some voices just beyond the evergreen hedge that bordered the parking area. He lifted up his head. "Somebody's coming," he said, and released his embrace.

"To hell with them," she said, not moving. Then, when he did not lean again, she jerked herself to a sitting position. "All right," she said, flatly, "let's go."

They drove across the campus, and then down a side street along the rows of dingy rooming houses. "Listen," he said, "let's shake 'em pretty soon—" He was thinking of the place beyond the big stone bridge on the way to her house, the lane that turned off there with the cedars growing close down. "—let's go early—"

"You," she said, "can leave any time you want to, but I'll leave when I'm ready. I can get somebody to take me home."

"You don't have to get sore. I just wanted to get you away, I wanted—"

"Sure," she said, "you just wanted— You heard somebody coming, so your little heart went pitapat, and now you think— Oh, you needn't try to make it up to me. You needn't try to apologize— You just wonder, is somebody looking, is somebody saying something. You're just like a rabbit, sometimes."

He made no reply, staring sullenly ahead down the street, which was littered with dead leaves along the gutters.

"And you just don't like my friends, that's one thing."

"Sure, I like them."

"No, you're just like my father. He doesn't like them, either."

"I like 'em all right," he said. "I just don't happen to have much to say to 'em."

"Well, they haven't got much to say to you, either."

"Look here, they may be wonderful folks, but I—"

"Sure, they are. Rosemary, now, she's wonderful. She really is. She's poor and she's crippled, but just because she's poor and crippled, you—"

"That's entirely unfair—" he began.

98

"Just because she's poor and crippled—"

"Look here," he said, "you know God-damned well I've been poor, plenty poor—"

"Oh, you'll be rich," she said, softly, "you'll die rich, Jerry. You've got what it takes, Jerry. You'll die rich, but—"

"Oh, hell," he said, and slammed on his brake, and skidded the car in to the curb, and got out.

She got out without waiting for him to come around. She stood there, waiting for him, her legs far apart, her hands jammed down into the pockets of her light coat, which was unbuttoned, the rays of the street light falling whitely across her loose hair and across her face. "But," she resumed, "you're a cripple, too. You're an emotional cripple."

She went quickly up the steps of the house, and entered its dimly lit doorway. Jerry watched her go, then inspected the house, dingy unpainted wooden gingerbread work on the porch and cornices, soot-streaked brick walls, a faint patch of colored light on each side of the front door, where the little panels of stained glass were. He looked down and saw the wooden sign stuck on a stob, askew in the sparse grass: *Rooms.* He knew what it would be like in there, and, involuntarily, he said out loud, "God, God."

The door opened; Sue came out, and behind her, framed against the dim light, one hand clutching the door jamb for support, was the figure of Rosemary Murphy. The girls came down the steps, Rosemary prodding at the steps with her cane. Jerry was sure he could hear the creaking of her braces. He did not know whether to go forward and give her his arm. So he occupied himself opening the door of the car and holding it back, unnecessarily wide. "Good evening," he said.

"Good evening," the girl said, and added, "It was nice of you to come get me."

"Oh, Jerry wanted to," Sue said brightly. "He insisted on it. It was really his idea."

The hell it was, Jerry retorted savagely to himself, and watched Rosemary while she transferred her cane to her left hand, teetering, clattering the cane softly against the metal of the running board, and while her right hand grasped the open door of the car. He could see, even in the light of the street lamp, how the veins stood out blue in her hand across the thin bones, and could sense a kind of desperate, wiry, clawing strength in the hand. And as he watched the hand, and even as he took her arm to assist her and she turned to him and quite naturally thanked him, he was torn by a kind of shame. But even in the midst of the shame, he reasserted to himself, *The hell it was my idea to come get you, sister, the hell it was,* and took some pleasure in the hardness he felt.

Hell, no, it was Sue's idea, like so many of her screwy ideas, and sitting beside Sue as he glumly steered the car down the street, hating her, he wondered why in God's name she had to have somebody like this hanging round. So she could boss them, that was it, he decided, so she could bully them, and try to cover it up in being so God-damned sweet and democratic. *Dear Rosemary, sweet Rosemary, oh, so brave, darling Rosemary,* he rehearsed to himself, and stole a look at Sue's calm face, triumphantly thinking that he had her number, that she couldn't fool him no matter who she fooled. Thinking that she wasn't going to bully him.

There the others were in the dog-wagon, talking and laughing, sitting on stools along the counter, leaning forward, rattling the knives and forks, shoving each other playfully, laughing. "We ordered for you all," one of the boys called out, "—hamburgers!"

"Good," Sue said, and somebody yelled that he had been saving a place for her, and she was absorbed into the group, laughing, saying, "Darling, darling, blessed one," to the boy who had saved her the stool.

Oh, she was the queen, all right, Jerry thought. Bullying them and saying "Darling, darling, blessed one," in that phony voice he hated, which wasn't her voice, which was a voice she never used except when she was with these phonies.

The hamburgers came, the plates clattering down on the counter, and the cups of coffee, the coffee sloshing out into the saucers. But the talking and laughing were unabated. The cook, unoccupied for the moment, leaned at the end of the counter near Jerry, his small eyes staring out of his broad, flat, animal face. A toothpick hung from the corner of his mouth, giving a jaunty cast to his broken nose. His hands lay on the counter, very big, extraordinarily white as though they had been bled, and thickly haired with silky black hair. The cook was staring at the group, dully, unembarrassedly, speculatively.

Slim Sarrett came down to the end where Jerry was, and took the last stool. "Mack," he said to the cook, "this is Bull's-eye Calhoun. You remember, don't you?"

The cook turned his flat gaze upon Jerry, and seemed about to shake his head.

"You remember," Slim continued, "he was All-American about six or seven years ago."

"Yeah," the cook grunted.

"And," Slim turned to Jerry, "this is Mack Mann. Mack was a fighter once."

Jerry set his cup down, and put out his hand. The cook took it. "Yeah," the cook said, "glad to meetcha."

"Mack was a pretty good fighter," Slim continued, evenly. "He had some good fights. He fought Leroy to a ten-round draw, he knocked Butch Haley out in the fourth, he stayed with Merry Morris all the way. He had some good fights."

"Yeah," the cook said, "but I wasn't no good."

"Mack knew a lot," Slim continued, "and he has taught me a lot. I've won a couple of fights on what Mack taught me. But Mack was slow. He fought as a middleweight, and he was slow for a middleweight. You can sort of tell from his build he'd be slow," and he eyed the cook, nodding. "He's put on weight now, of course, but you can see he never had the right build. He had power, but there are a lot of fast boys in the middleweight bracket. Choppers. Mack just had to take a lot of punishment, and he couldn't follow. It's a pity, because Mack knew a lot."

The cook took the toothpick out of his meaty lips, looked at it, then put it back in. "Yeah," he said, "I knew a little something. But I didn't know enough to stop."

"Hamburger," somebody yelled, and the cook turned away.

Slim nodded after him, saying, "He knew a lot," and when Jerry did not answer, he continued, in the same voice: "How did you like the play?"

"I liked it all right," Jerry said.

"The acting is rather good for this period of the rehearsals. Sue was quite good on that last beat. She has a real instinct for drama; I use the word *instinct* because she does not have an intellectual grasp of the medium. But she can rise to a moment, with a kind of self-abnegation, which means that she can get a pure effect. She doesn't insist on being Sue Murdock. Whether she'll ever turn into a really good actress depends, it seems to me, on achieving some sort of intellectual maturity—a capacity for understanding the structural line—" and his thin, long, sinewy forefinger traced an undulating line in the air, and his candid brown eyes then seemed to regard that line. "It is a matter of her intellectual grasp—don't you think?" And he leaned in polite expectation for Jerry's answer.

"I reckon so," Jerry said.

"You don't know a thing about it," Sue affirmed pleasantly, "not a thing. And you—" she looked at Slim, "don't either."

"It is a simple proposition—" Slim began.

"Yeah," the lumpy-faced, tall boy broke in, "you know so much about it, why don't you try it? Why don't you play Hamlet?"

"I don't want to play Hamlet," Slim said, not as a retort, but conversationally, patiently. "It does not interest me—acting, I mean —except in a purely secondary sense. It is a purely secondary and almost parasitic art, in any case. The special discipline is physical in a sense not true of the primary arts. Its discipline, as such, is not superior, I should say to that of a pretty good boxer—take Mack, here—" and he nodded in the direction of the cook. "And I happen to prefer to keep my special physical discipline disjunct from my esthetic discipline—from my poetry."

"Nuts," Sue said.

"And boxing," Slim smiled, his upper lip lifting back evenly and precisely, almost as though at the request of a dentist, "enjoys, as a physical discipline, one distinct advantage over acting: you can observe the direct effect on your opponent."

"I observed a direct effect on you after that Halleck fight," the tall boy said. "I observed your left eye was a mouse."

"Yes," Slim said, and paused reflectively. "I did not earn better than a draw with Halleck. I did not use my head. If I had pushed him in the fifth—"

"For Christ sake!" the tall boy said, and stood up.

"Let's go," Sue said.

"Let's go up to my studio," Slim suggested.

The group, rising, hesitated.

"All right," Sue said.

Damn it, Jerry thought, sullenly. They would go down to the river, to Slim Sarrett's place and be there half the night, sitting round in that big attic room he called his studio, four flights up to get there, and going up slow, step by step, so they wouldn't leave Rosemary Murphy, whose breath would be coming hard and whose braces would creak, and they'd sit around, on the floor mostly, and the floor so dirty you left your tail-print on it, with the copper pots and ash trays and greasy sofa pillows, and the parchment-shaded lamps, and the unwashed dishes, and the reproductions of paintings thumbtacked to the crumbling plaster of one wall and photographs of boxers in shorts with their gloves cocked, some of the photographs signed, and the cluster of old boxing gloves hanging above the fireplace, dry, shriveled up, crumpled-looking, dusty, like an enormous bunch of old raisins. Yes, damn it, they'd stay there half the night.

And they did, while Jerry sat propped back against the wall, hearing the excited talking, and occasionally answering some remark addressed to him, thinking how he had to get up early in the morning and how he wished to God at least he had a drink. It looked like they would yammer on forever, drink or no drink. And while they yammered, he looked at them, and they were sure a crummy lot to look at, and he thanked God he'd never got mixed up with any outfit like this when he was in college. And he wouldn't be mixed up with them now, he thought, if it weren't for Sue.

Then, late, he drove out of the city, Sue beside him, not talking, his eyes fixed on the empty, glimmeringly white, rushing, powerful sweep of the highway. Just as they crossed the stone bridge, she said: "All right."

He did not reply, and did not lighten his foot on the throttle.

"All right," she said again, her voice flat and hard now.

He'd be damned, he thought, not after the way she'd been going on, after what she'd said to him. And he felt a kind of surprising, victorious, clear-sighted ease in his detachment, in his freedom from desire. He had her number. He'd be damned if—

"Did you hear me?" she demanded.

"Yes," he said, "I heard you." Yes, he'd heard her, and he told her so, and she could make what she wanted to of it. She could boss those others around, but she wasn't going to boss him. She wasn't going to boss little Jerry. There'd been a time he hadn't depended on her for what he got, and by God, he didn't have to depend on her now. What did she think he was, anyway? What did she think a man wanted? Well, he'd—

Then, suddenly, sitting up straight, she said, quite coldly: "I've got to."

And her words rang in his head, as in a cave. She had to, and he had to, damn it, God damn it, he had to, and he knew he had to, and he knew he would, and damn her—but by God, he wouldn't. He'd see her in hell first.

He tightened his grip on the wheel, his foot steady on the throttle, his eyes fixed straight on the road.

"Oh, Jerry," she said, quietly, sitting up straight like a child, folding her hands on her lap and looking, too, down the spinning white highway, "I'm sorry I acted that way. I'm really sorry. I didn't mean what I said. And I didn't want to stay with those people—I didn't—I wanted to be with you, Jerry." And she leaned slowly toward him, sidewise, her hands still folded on her lap, and let her head lie on his shoulder. "Oh, Jerry," she said, moving her head slightly to and fro, as a sick person does on a pillow, "I don't know why I act like I do."

103

"Hell," he answered, a little gruffly, the bitterness and, for the moment, the desire supplanted by a cautious happiness, a hopefulness.

"Something just gets into me," she said.

"Hell," he said, "forget it."

"It's just the Old Scratch gets into me, I reckon," she said. "Just the Old Scratch," she whispered, and, after a moment, giggled softly. Then she blew gently into his ear.

The car drifted almost noiselessly to the lane, turned off the pavement, and the big tires bit the gravel with a dry rustling sound, as it moved slowly between the black rows of cedars.

"You've got that blanket in the back, haven't you?" she asked.

He said, yes, he had it in the back.

He blamed that gang she went with at the University. He reckoned there had been people like that around when he was there, there always would be, he reckoned, but he hadn't ever known any of them. He told Sue he liked them all right. But he didn't. He blamed them, at least in part. And he was pretty sure that Bogan Murdock blamed them, too, though he never heard him say a word to that effect. "He hates them," Sue had told him, more than once, and he had replied, conciliatorily: "That isn't exactly fair; he never says so, does he?"

"Say so!" and she had laughed sharply. "He doesn't say things. He doesn't have to. He just doesn't say a word, and people do what he wants. Look at my mother. The way she is. God, I'd rather be dead, I'd—"

"Now, look here—" he said, and he saw Mrs. Murdock's face, pale, chiseled, and flawless except for the tiny sharp V-shaped gathering between the eyebrows, the incipient, abstract smile which she would direct from face to face or, indifferently, to some far corner of a room, like the blurred ray of an almost burnt-out flashlight.

"I'd rather be dead," she affirmed; then, viciously, "but I won't be. And I won't be bullied. I don't care if he is my father. That's it—"

"Now, look here—"

"—because he made me, he thinks he owns me. He makes something, then he sits back and looks at it. He sits back—just like sending that nigger boy Anse to college last year. And he says he's going to send him up North, to Columbia or some place, next year. But does he do it now? No, he keeps him here this year, so he can look at him, so he can sit back and look at him. If I were Anse I'd walk

104

out of this house and get drunk and go down to nigger town and get me the blackest, stinkingest nigger girl I could find and lie in the gutter, or cut somebody up with a razor, or something— But I wouldn't stay here, and listen to him say, 'Now, Anse, I've been thinking—' Only he calls him Anselm, because Anse asked him to— Anselm, Anselm—" And she stopped, breathless.

Mr. Murdock had never said a word to him on the subject, but Jerry was pretty sure Murdock didn't like those people from the University. Not that he'd even seen but two of them, Sarrett and that Murphy girl, whom Sue had brought out to her house a couple of times. And not that Jerry had been able to lay his finger on a thing the time when he himself had been present: Mr. Murdock smiling gravely and impeccably, shaking hands with Sarrett, offering the Murphy girl a chair, directing Anse to bring Scotch and soda. And talking pleasantly while the Murphy girl hunched on the edge of a big chair, her ankles in their metal braces crossed stiffly before her, and while Sarrett's attention wandered from what was being said to the book-lined wall of the library, and while Sue, who had refused a chair, stood at the window, with her back to the room, and stared out. There was nothing he could put his finger on in Mr. Murdock's conduct.

That he had been right—yes, he knew he had been right all along, and was filled with a shrewd complacency—he discovered from Mr. Murdock's own lips, a few days after Sue had agreed to marry him. "Yes," Mr. Murdock said, "I am glad, Jerry. You are the man for her. You will be able to do—" He lifted his head and turned, his strong chin high, in profile, the line firm from chin tip down to the loose collar where the coarse dark-green tie was knotted, his gaze off through the window to some point on the reddening western horizon. He stopped, then began again, firmly, like a man who has faced a fact and made a resolution: "You will be able to do what I have failed to do. It is a sad thing for a father to say, Jerry, but it is true: I have somehow failed to be a good father to Sue. How, I don't know. I wish to God I knew. I am not a devout man—no, not even religious in the ordinary sense of the word—but my failure with Sue has brought me more than once to my knees. It has taught me—" and he swung his head, deliberately, to face Jerry, as though he had steeled himself for a confession, "humility."

The smoky-blue eyes, with the large black pupils, fixed upon Jerry, and Jerry looked into them, thinking how he had known this man a long time now, had known him to be kindly, tolerant, generous, had seen him, day after day, graceful and unaggressive in his quiet confidence of judgment or horsemanship—confidence worn like an old but good coat, without ostentation—had thought of him alone in this room by the window. And he thought how he had never suspected this other dimension, and was almost ashamed that he had not. He felt, suddenly, a warmth toward him such as he had never felt before.

"I have lain awake at night," Murdock was saying, gravely, the eyes with the large black pupils not wavering, "but—" And he lifted his hands from his knees and let them drop, and smiled. He turned his face again to the window, and was silent for a moment, looking off to the west.

"She was a strange little package when she was a child," Murdock resumed quietly. "Skinny and big-eyed and her hair loose—" And Jerry saw that face—he had seen it in the old photographs which Sue had showed one evening here in this room, sitting beside him on the couch, fumbling with the pile on her knees with a cigarette stuck in the corner of her mouth and the smoke curling up from it across her smooth, gold-colored, expressionless face, passing each photograph to him with a quick, contemptuous jerk of the wrist, saying, "God, I must've had the hookworm, look!" or, "God, I look like I was Saint Cecilia or somebody. I must've been constipated." Now, on Mr. Murdock's words, he saw that face as he had seen it in one of the larger photographs—when she was twelve or thirteen, she had said—the pale hair falling down evenly to the shoulders, with an almost carved, metallic look, to frame, narrowly, the face, which was lifted a little, as though in expectation, the eyes wide and candid, the lips parted slightly. Her lower lip, even then, he had noted, had had that slight, provocative fullness, that hint of disturbing, glistening laxness. He had noted, too, the way the white dress, in the picture, lay over the small, flat bosom, and he had felt a wild constriction of the heart, and a surge of tenderness, a sense of loss, and he had said, suddenly, "Sue—" and as she looked at him, he had waited for the words to take shape and come up out of the agitated depth within him. But they had not come.

But now, as Mr. Murdock spoke, he saw the face of the photograph, more real and compelling now, as though he shared the actual memory with the other man, and the constriction seized his heart.

"Yes, a strange little package. Sometimes, I remember, she'd hide out somewhere, in the barns or stables—once she crawled up under one of the tenant houses, and it built almost right on the ground, too, and lay there God knows how long in the damp and the filth—

and everybody would be hunting her and holding up dinner. That time she got under the tenant house, we didn't find her till late, way after dark, and we were frantic. We just happened to find her, because the nigger's dog happened to get started barking at her up under the shack, and when the barking kept on so long we went back there. Then, of course, she'd have to be punished, some way. Not really, you know, but something to impress it on her mind. She never did do that often, of course, and not at all after she was nine or ten.

"But she never got along with her brother—she'd devil him. It's comic now to look back on it, she was so cunning about it. And he was always sweet to her. He's devoted to her now, you know, though he's an undemonstrative boy.

"She was an affectionate child, too, though she'd go for weeks sometimes not showing it, playing by herself. But then I'd be sitting in here, and the first thing you'd know, she'd be right beside me—she'd just sneak in—and she'd grab hold of me and hug me, or maybe sit on the floor and put her head against my legs, and say, 'Dockie, Dockie—' She used to call me Dockie when she was little. She'd say, 'Dockie, Dockie, I love you so much.' And I remember a time or two when she woke up late at night and sneaked down, barefoot and in her nightgown, to find me and tell me she loved me. But—" He hesitated, lifted his hands again from his knees, and let them fall back. He looked out the window, then, again, slowly turned his head to Jerry, smiling wryly. "Somehow," he said, smiling, "somehow something went wrong." His gaze was sharply, probingly, on Jerry's face, trying, it seemed to Jerry, to extort some reply from him. But he could think of nothing to say.

"Maybe," Mr. Murdock said, his voice again even, "we should never have sent her away to school. Up East. But she was so set on going. And she wasn't doing any good in school here; she seemed to have lost interest in everything, though she had made a lot of brilliant marks, off and on. She just lost interest in everything, it seemed, except riding. And she was so reckless. She'd put a horse to anything."

"She's good," Jerry said. "She's wonderful."

"Yes, but it worried me to death. Sometimes, I'd be sitting in my office, and the telephone would ring, and I'd be afraid to pick it up, I'd be so sure—"

"Yes," Jerry said, and saw her, with her hair flat on the wind, her face raised, her hands precise and close before her, and almost felt the cry forming in his throat as when he had called out desperately, "Sue, Sue!" She had not looked back, and at the very lip

107

of the wash, she had risen in the saddle, as though releasing a great secret force of her own to be incorporated in the surge and lift of the animal's haunches. She had made it. She had made it, but by a hair. He had seen the turf and dirt shear off from the farther lip of the wash, and the mare's desperate, almost clawing lurch. He had ridden a little farther down the wash to the crossing, his stomach cold and his hands shaking with fury. He had crossed, and approached her. Her mare was standing quietly, the sides lifting and subsiding with beautiful pulsing, piston-like regularity, like a machine. She had not watched him approach. She had been looking back across the field, her hands lying idly before her, and her face smooth and peaceful with the sunlight striking across it. "God damn it," he had said, "God damn it, you—" "All right," she had said, flatly, distantly. "Don't you ever—" he had begun, and she had turned to him. "And don't you say a word about it," she had said. "You'll kill yourself, you'll cripple yourself up, you'll—" he had begun, but she had cut in, "What's it to you?" "You'll cripple yourself and that—" "And that's none of your business. Rosemary's a cripple—yes, and that's why you don't like her, oh, I know—but she gets along all right. Better than most people. Better than me. And—" her voice had subsided, "better than you, Jerry." God, you couldn't talk when she was like that. There wasn't any use talking. They had sat their mounts, side by side, quietly, there in the middle of the field.

"But she was set on going," Mr. Murdock was saying, "and I let her go. It seemed that she couldn't get away soon enough. Naturally, a young girl would be excited, but her attitude hurt her mother. The last night, she had some people out here, invited them without telling us anything about it. Just thoughtlessness. But it hurt her mother, who wasn't well then and couldn't take her East. And I was too busy then to get away. But that night, after everybody had gone, and everybody was in bed except me—I was sitting here in the library—I heard the door open, and there she was, just like when she was a little girl, barefoot and in her nightgown. 'Dockie,' she said, 'Dockie—' That was the first time she'd called me that since she was little. And she came and sat on the floor and put her head against my knee.

"She made very good marks at first, and I wrote and told her how we had expected it of her. And I sent her a check, a right nice little check, to get her a new fur coat. But she didn't get the coat, I found out later. She just frittered the money away. She stayed in Boston with some people named Thornton for Christmas. After Christmas her marks got so bad the school wrote. So I went

108

up there, and she said she was just homesick, and wanted Sissie—that was the mare she had then—and if I would send her Sissie, she would be all right. So I did it, against my better judgment. But her marks got worse and worse, and she got into trouble with the school authorities about her riding or something, disobeying the rules. So she just walked out on them before the year was up. Just like her—she's got spunk." He smiled, and then continued, "Then she finished school here, and started to college, and got sick of it, and quit. I wouldn't send her away again, unless she had put in a year at the University here. But she quit, and then she made her debut. She was awfully excited then for a little while, and happy. But it didn't last. Right in the middle of the season she said she was not going to any more parties. She said she was sick of it. She'd met some of these theater people over at the University, or at the Drama Club in town or somewhere. And so—" He spread his hands, and looked at his long, brown fingers with the strong nails, which were cut short. He flexed them slowly.

"I don't like them," he said. He stopped, and began again: "No, I cannot say that I don't like them. That would not be fair. I have only met two of them, that boy named Sarrett and the crippled girl. But I don't think they are good for Sue." He studied Jerry's face. "Do you think they are good for her?" he asked.

"No," Jerry said. "I don't." And speaking, he felt triumphant and secure.

"No," Mr. Murdock said, "I didn't think you did." He continued to study Jerry's face. "You haven't spoken to Sue about the matter?"

"No."

"Nor have I. But she accused me of not liking them. She called me—" and he smiled, "a snob. I'm scarcely that. Whatever may be my failings. Take Porsum, for example, one of my best friends. The Private was an ignorant mountain blacksmith, before he went to France, in the War. And now he's a power in the State. He made his own way, and with what dignity, always. I think that the Emperor Tiberius was right in his reply to the courtiers who remarked on the poor birth of the favorite Rufus: Rufus is his own ancestor. I have always thought that a noble remark. Don't you think so?"

"Yes," Jerry said.

"No, it's not that I'm a snob. Nor that you are, Jerry. It's just that I think they are bad for Sue. Just as you think so. But there was nothing I could do. Something had happened, a long time back, and I cannot define it, but—and I must confess it—I have little influence with Sue. But you, Jerry, you will succeed where I failed. You understand her, I'm sure. And you can help her to come to terms with herself. To overcome this restlessness, this unhappiness—this—" he rose from his chair, very erect, his chin lifted, "this recklessness."

"I don't know," Jerry began. I—"

Murdock had stepped to the side of Jerry's chair. He laid his hand on his shoulder. "My boy," he said. Jerry could feel the pressure of the fingers closing there, the pressure of each finger firm and distinct. "My boy," he said quietly, "I know." He released his grip, and stepped back. "I know that it will be all right," he said, "for you understand her. And she loves you." He moved away, toward the door, then stopped, and turned. "I cannot help but feel," he said, "that underneath it all she still loves me."

Before Jerry could say anything—he tried to find the words to say—Bogan Murdock had left the room.

Understand her? Maybe not yet, Jerry thought. Not yet, but there would be time. And he could wait. He could wait, and keep his eyes open. You waited, and you kept your eyes open, and you learned. He had done that before. He had waited, and watched, and he had learned things. And the time would come. He felt a little gush of pity for Bogan Murdock, who had said what he had had to say. But Bogan could take it on the chin, all right. You'd have to hand it to Bogan.

Sitting there in the library, which was shadowy now, alone, with his gaze off beyond the lawn and the distant lift of the fields, to the wintry red of the late sky, he felt relaxed, patient, and strong.

"I'll have to hand it to you," Duckfoot had said a long time back one day in his office; "they tell me you're making time with the Infanta."

"I don't know about that," Jerry said, laughing.

"They tell me that's why Red Sullivan, four-letter man, high-point man in the SIAA Meet in 1923—or was it '24—how time flies and what strong hand shall hold his swift foot back and the name is writ in water—what they tell me is that Sullivan, manager of our St. Louis branch, has taken to drink. Which, with the head start he had in that direction, means something. And all on account of your superior charm."

"Nuts," Jerry said.

"Well, keep at it, boy," Duckfoot said, waving his long ivory cigarette holder. "But if I were you, before ever the banns get read, I'd make Bogan make a cash settlement on the bride. A nice little *dot*. Cash, not paper. Not a scrap of Bogan's paper. Or some day you will be using it in the backhouse. And real property. I've got a great respect for real property, unencumbered, well situated, good drainage, good—"

"Nuts," Jerry said, "I just go riding with the girl. Besides, the old man is going to marry her to the Prince of Wales."

"So you think you're not swell enough, huh?"

Then, in the midst of a surge of painful confusion and resentment, as though he had been spied upon, Jerry managed, somewhat bitterly and grudgingly, to say, "All right, if you want to put it that way." And he lifted his head to stare belligerently into Duckfoot's pale, candid, slightly satirical eyes.

"Hell," Duckfoot said agreeably, "you raised the question yourself. I just put it in intelligible terms. Besides, you needn't think it's a secret between you and me. Half the town has got money one way or the other on it."

"The old bitches," Jerry said, and had a vision of women, of old women in black silk, the black silk tight or baggy over their swollen or thin bosoms, old women leaning over the cards held in beringed fingers and whispering, whispering, and their eyes were all fixed on him. And of young women, in bright dresses, with cocktails in their hands, leaning their slick heads together. *The bitches,* he thought, stung and savage.

"Oh, don't you fret," Duckfoot was saying, and grinning. "You've got an ace in the hole. Don't forget old Governor Calhoun. Pal, you come of a distinguished though impoverished family. Hell, don't you know that a Governor in the family a few generations back when every politician was a Roman statesman and the *res publica* was untainted is enough to make any outfit a distinguished old family. If you play the cards right. Blood will tell. The Governor is all the straw Bogan needs to make his bricks. Hell, he don't need any straw. He could cram a horse thief down the throats of the local rusty-butts, and make 'em like it. And he'd enjoy doing it. One thing I'll say for Bogan, he don't let the old biddies make up his mind for him."

Jerry felt the eyes of those clustered, leaning, female faces upon him, and hot and squirming, he knew that his face had flushed.

"But don't you fret," Duckfoot said soothingly, and waved his cigarette holder. "Just rely on the old Governor. Besides, such gross considerations will never be intruded into what, obviously, will be pure love."

"I—" Jerry interrupted, getting ready to say he did not know what, ready to assert some hidden strength which he knew was in himself, feeling that he was ready to tell that lanky, spindle-

111

shanked, grinning, pale-faced fool to go to hell and was ready to walk out the door, into the street and never come back into this building where the glass and bronzed gleamed and the elevators surged effortlessly upward and the heel rang on marble or sank richly into the carpet.

"It's a cinch," Duckfoot said, "it's like ham goes with eggs, your black-browed and somber masculinity is the natural concomitant of what the society page will term her delicate blond beauty. Delicate—"

He let the holder hang from the corner of his mouth and held up his hands, the thumb and forefinger of each together, as though he exhibited a fine cord. "Pal," he said, "did you ever try to clean your teeth with dental floss and find it was piano wire? But—" and he dropped his hands, "I don't blame you. She is a slice of Eve's flesh the like of which has rarely swum into my ken to throw a monkey wrench into my parasympathetic nervous system and make this learned old head toss on the midnight pillow. To comment upon one item—" He lifted his right arm and extended his pale, sepulchral forefinger to trace lovingly a light curve vertically in the air; and his eyes fixed intently, abstractedly, upon it. "One little item only," he continued, "she has that narrow-sided, flat though sweetly molded little arrangement of the rear which is the despair of the corset maker's art and which makes the palms of my hands feel like somebody had given me a dose of itch powder. It is an arrangement which one rarely encounters, and that, no doubt, is what keeps society on an even keel. I encountered such an arrangement once in my dead youth, and though the associated physiognomy well merited concealment in a pillow slip, the total effect was nigh disastrous for my intellectual career. The arrangement of which I speak is generally, I should surmise on the basis of my limited experience, accompanied by an almost acrobatic lissomeness and enterprise. You are perhaps aware of the special advantages of having the sole of a little foot placed transversely on the outside of each thigh some eight inches above the knee.—Ah, youth! —But, alas, the happy little contour to which I have previously alluded is not often discovered in the marts of trade. By which—" and he leaned back in the swivel chair, which creaked, and wagged his head at Jerry, "I do not mean the Stock Exchange, as you no doubt believed."

"The hell I did," Jerry said, and grinned. He could grin now.

"But now that love has come to Gerald Calhoun and brushed his heart with its regenerating wing, I reckon that toward three-thirty A.M. on Sunday mornings after we've wound up our poker

112

session, you'll go no more a-roving with me down toward the river where the player piano tinkles behind drawn shades."

"Damn it," Jerry said, "who said I was in love?"

"But you will be," Duckfoot said, reaching up to scratch, fastidiously, with the little finger of his right hand the pale hair plastered down across his skull, "The setup is too perfect. I do not mean to be cynical. And I envy you. But you are shore-God in for a little restless ecstasy, and love's sweet pain, for Sue Murdock is something to blow the fuses."

"Sue's all right," Jerry said. "She's a good girl."

"Sure, she's all right, and I envy you, but I ain't the man to take the punishment. I wish I was. But girls like that Sue skeer me. They disorder my categories. I like everything tidy. It's my mathematical mind, I guess. Tidy, and in its place. Now, take Ellie May. I know exactly where I stand. I take me five dollars and a bottle of argyrol and a handbag of home brew to give a festive touch and I go to see Ellie May. Once a week. Or in the season when a brighter crimson comes upon the burnished dove, maybe twice a week. Very tidy. No muss, no fuss. You see?"

"Sure, I see."

"I never maintained that Ellie May would make thrones totter. And she is past her first blush of youth. But I know how I stand. And she's so comfy. But you know Ellie May."

Yes, Jerry knew Ellie May, all right. Duckfoot had taken him there, a long time back, to the little shot-gun bungalow set in a narrow yard marked out by scraggly privet, out beyond a warehouse on the north side of town, on the river. It had been raining, and the starlight glistened oilily in a pool of water which stood in one corner of the yard, by the hedge. Decorously, Duckfoot had introduced him to the middle-sized, chunkish but not badly built woman, thirty-odd, perhaps, who wore a baby-blue negligee and white, somewhat stained mules with pompons, and had a mathematically round patch of rouge, like a housewife on Sunday, on each pale but apparently firm cheek, and who smiled honestly with good teeth and round, unspeculative brown eyes. She looked like the negligee and the pompons didn't belong to her. "This is my cousin Jerry, from the country," Duckfoot had said, and Ellie May had said, "Glad to meetcha, Jerry," and the other three girls who stood about in the tight, little sofa-cushioned parlor said, "Glad to meetcha." Then Duckfoot had sat down and opened his handbag and taken out some bottles. He had passed the brew around, and they had sat around for a while before Duckfoot rose, picked up the bag with the remaining bottles, and went out with Ellie May.

He had paused at the door, stooping his narrow head, and had said: "Now, girls, be nice to Cousin Jerry. But don't try to provoke the cupidity of the flesh. Just talk about the crops. He's from the country, and he's keeping himself pure for the vicar's daughter." The girls had snickered, and one had said that she knew a poem about a vicar, whatever the hell a vicar was. The girls had agreed that Duckfoot was a card. They had sat among the sofa pillows and fringed-and-tasseled floor lamps, and had finished the brew, and hadn't talked much. A man had come in and had taken one of the girls out. Another girl, not too bad-looking in a skinny sort of way except for a white scar on her cheek, had sat on Jerry's lap and had pulled back his coat and with her lipstick pencil had drawn a heart over the pocket of his white shirt, while the other girl, not really a girl at all, but older, had watched distantly and preoccupiedly, like a stranger in a railroad waiting room. Jerry had not been exactly embarrassed, but that other woman kept looking at him that way, and after a while he thought, *Oh, hell,* and got up and went out with the girl who had the white scar but wasn't too bad-looking. But he had wished that he had got that other girl the strange man took out.

"Ellie May makes me feel so homey," Duckfoot had said that night, afterward, walking across the yard, where the pools of water glistened oilily in the starlight; and now, months later, with his feet cocked among the clutter of papers on the desk in his office and his shoulders sunk in his chair and his fingers laid skeletally and mathematically on his breast, like the fingers of a medieval brass on a cathedral floor, and the cigarette holder hanging from his thin mouth, he was saying: "It's just that Ellie May makes me feel so homey. She don't skeer me like girls like Sue Murdock. And when you pass the *mezzo del cammin di nostra vita* and the candle flame begins to shiver on the wick, you begin to appreciate that homey feeling." Ellie May is the kind of woman I'd marry if I was the marrying kind."

"I reckon so," Jerry had said, laughing.

Jerry was to tell Sue, a long time after, what Duckfoot had said. "Duckfoot Blake said that he admires your flat little behind, but that you skeer him," he told her.

She got up from her chair and put her fingers lightly on her hips, and revolved herself, slowly, before him, swaying a little, like a mannequin. "Do you admire it?" she asked.

"I'll say," he said, ungrudgingly.

She circled his chair, coming around behind him, and he turned his head to follow her. She thrust her small, sharp fingers into his

114

hair, while he leaned back and tried to look up at her. "Do I skeer *you,* Jerry?" she asked.

"No," he said, and laughed.

She leaned above him, like a mother, caressing his hair, and spoke softly: "Don't I skeer you, Jerry? Not even a little?"

"No," he said.

"Not a little bit?" she whispered.

"No," he said.

"Jerry," she whispered, and twisted her fingers in his crisp, strong hair, "somebody ought to scare the hell out of you." And suddenly, she jerked his hair, hard.

He had lied. He had, even, lied to himself sometimes. But not always. Yes, she had scared him, sometimes. She had scared him by that wild jump over the wash in the field. She had scared him, differently, one rainy afternoon when he and she had been sitting in the library with her grandfather, who had a cold and couldn't go down to the stables, in the wet, to be with the Negroes. They were not talking, just watching the fire and listening to the gusty rain, and the old man was sitting lumpishly in his chair, his swollen, yellow-clayey old hands folded on his paunch, and his big eyes blinking. "Grandpa," Sue said, breaking the long silence, "tell me something. It's something I've always wanted to know."

"Hanh?" the old man demanded, swinging his head heavily, creakily, toward her, and blinking.

"Just this," she continued, "what made you kill that man? You know, the man you killed?"

"Hanh?"

"What made you kill him?" she asked patiently, tenderly. "You know, the man you shot in the stomach, and killed?"

"I shot him, I—" the old man muttered, and heaved his bulk in the chair, and the swollen hands slipped off their perch to fall on the thighs, and the maned head twitched heavily at her. "I—" and he blinked.

"Yes," she went on patiently, "yes. But why? What made you?"

"Goodpasture—Goodpasture—he said—" and the bulk heaved again.

"Yes, he said something about you in a speech. Yes, I know that. But what made you kill him? What was it really made you? Don't you remember?"

"Goodpasture—he said—he said—at Essex—" Lem Murdock croaked rustily. "It was a crowd and he said—"

Sue was watching him, and when the croaking stopped and his big yellowish eyes blinked at her, she kept on watching for a moment before she resumed. Then she asked, still patient: "How did it feel, Grandpa? How did it feel to shoot him in the stomach?"

"He said—"

"How did it feel to shoot him in the stomach, Grandpa," she asked, watching him, "and look at him lying there?"

Then, slowly, while the big, yellow-muddyish eyes blinked—and Jerry watched, fascinated and feeling himself horribly implicated beyond his will—the tears welled up, and one big drop spilled out of each eye and crept down the flesh on each side of the nose.

Jerry had risen abruptly and gone out of the house and stood under the high porch to look out across the fields where the rain fell.

And she had scared him, again differently—and the cold fright would come over him, tenfold in recollection—on those occasions when she had compelled him to take her there in the house, provoking him, wheedling him with a shameless innocence, accusing his love, cajoling him, calling him a hypocrite, impugning his manhood, daring him, until, anger and desire and humiliation mixed in him, feeling himself trapped in a complicated mechanism the meaning of which he could not solve, he would take her. There in the library, on the great couch in the shadowy drawing room, once in the upstairs sitting room, with people in the house, the sound of footsteps in the hallways, with Bogan Murdock in the house. And thinking back, he would feel the sweat break out on his forehead, and he could see how Bogan Murdock's face would be, white-lipped, stony, deadly, and the black pupils of the eyes fixed malevolently, glitteringly, upon him. God, God, he would breathe to himself, and in the confusion of his fear and his gratitude for deliverance he would feel like making wild vows for the future, God, God, I'll never, I'll never, never—

Or that occasion when he and Sue had gone to get Rosemary Murphy and had found her room empty. Somebody had been in the next room. You could hear them moving about in there, through the thin wall. There had been the calsomined, peeling walls, the pine table with the good typewriter on it, the neat piles of papers, the single greasy, overstuffed chair, the shredded window shade and the streaked cretonne curtains, the lumpy bed covered by a splotched pink spread. There had been no latch on the door. "You could hear her coming," Sue had whispered, "you could hear her coming up the stairs if she came." And he had thought of the creaking of the braces; he couldn't get the sound out of his mind, and with a revulsion and nausea, he had felt as though he clasped that other body, small, bony, twisted.

Yes, sometimes she had scared him, all right. He had to admit it to himself, sometimes. Hell, anybody would be scared, the way she acted, acting sometimes like the minute was all there was, like there wasn't any yesterday and there wasn't any tomorrow, or like what yesterday was or tomorrow would be didn't have any connection, not a damned bit, and damn it, a man had to think about those things.

Eight

Statement of Ashby Wyndham

MARIE said that old mule was not no matter. She said it was not
no use to her. She said it was Gods will and she taken it for a
sign. It was a sign for her not to be movin down the big road, and
her amongst strangers.

That was what she said when I kept sayin I was goin to pay.

I tried to pay. I tried and strove. They was money at Massey, but
it looked lak what they give you with one hand on Saturday night
they taken back with the other hand afore Monday morning. But
I kept on tryin, if air man did. I taken what I could ever week and
helt it out. It was not much, and me there two months. It was nineteen dollars, or nigh it. I could helt out a little more if I had not
bought Marie them pretties. I bought them pretties down at Cashtown where they got stores full of them things, and they is vanity
and no denyin. But a man, and a young man he is full of vanity
and flesh forwardness, and it ain't nuthin but his lust and flesh
hotness if you scan clost and name it. He sees a woman and he gits
her on his mind and he wants to put pretties on her so he can see
her with them things, but it ain't nuthin but Bible lust comin out
of his eyes.

I bought Marie them things. I bought her a necklace and it was
all gold or nigh, like the man said. It had a sparklet in it and it
had a shine lak a diamint, you let the sun git it clear. It looked to
me lak I had to git it for Marie. I seen it layin there, and I knowed
I had to git it. So I ast him how much and he named it and I taken
four dollars and give it to him. I didn't say yea nor nay. I did not
hem or haw. I just give him that money, for I knowed Marie had
to have it. Marie was one of them little women, and not too much
meat on them. She was spry lak them little women, and quick when
she aimed to. But she was a quiet one. She was quiet and still.
She would be settin or standin there, and you never knowed it.
You look at her and you did not think nobody could be that quiet,

118

and it natchel. You looked and you never knowed it was breath comin and goin in her bosom, it moved so gentle for a marvel. She was lak water layin in the sun, and it deep and nary a riffle. But a little wind what a man cannot feel blowin on his cheek, and a sparkle runs all over that water all of a sudden. She moved her hand just easy or it was her eyes got bright of a sudden, and it was lak that wind blowed on the water and it was all sparkle. I bought that necklace to wear on her bosom for that sparkle what was in her.

She would be done work and I would be waitin. Ax or layin to a crosscut all day, and I would see her comin out of that there kitchen and me waitin in the dark and the weariness was not nuthin. It was lak I was wakin up fresh and a sunbeam done smote you on the eyeball and roused you. We would go to them frolics at Massey on Saturday night. She would stand quiet and watch them folks dance and stomp and the caller called the figgers and them fiddles goin. She stood right quiet, but you could see the sparkle in her. If you looked clost. Then maybe we would dance a set or twain. But I did not git no more of Barkus moonshine, nor offen nobody else. At least not when I was with Marie. She did not lak for me to. And when I was with Marie I never felt no call.

I never taken likker lak I use to, and likker is a sin. But a man cannot be good out of plain humankindness. He cannot be good for it ain't in a pore man. He cannot be good unlest it is good in the light of Gods eye. Gods eye ain't on him and he just swaps one sin for another one, and it worse maybe. I laid off likker, but I swapped for another sin. I laid off likker for Marie but it was because of pore human love and not for Gods love. Then it was for pore human love I taken that there worse sin, and I shame to say it.

Week nights when there wasn't no frolic at Massey, we walked on the mountain. It was moonlight on them clearins, or stars, and on them roads where the wagins went in the day time, and dark under the bushes and them trees. You look off west at night offen Massey, and you know they is the big valley and the hills off there, but you ain't seein it. It is lak the world is way down there and black dark to yore sight, and the folks down there and the folks doins ain't nuthin. The sky is way up, and the stars. I was up on the mountain and it was Marie with me. It was right brisk to cold on the mountain with the fall comin on, but we never taken no mind. We set down on a log or on a lime chunk, and it was lak we done built a warm fire for a camp and put our hands to the brightness. We never taken thought on the cold. A man don't take no thought on what he was or is or what will come.

119

I taken no thought and it was my sin. I ain't never said it was Maries sin. When a man ever does a sin he ain't done it secret and him private. He has done taken his own sin on his shoulders, but another mans sin too to bear him down. You throw a rock in a pond and it don't make but one splash but they is ripples runs out from it. I sinned and I taken Maries sin on my shoulders for Judgmint. It was my fault she taken spot and had blemish laid on to her. It was for pore human mans love, but love ain't nuthin if it ain't in Gods eye.

It was after Christmas she told me she was heavy. She did not say nuthin or complain. She just named it and looked at me quiet. I just bust out laughin. Lord God, I said, it ain't nuthin, yore Mammy and mine come to it. Lord God, I said, it ain't a thing in the world. I bet he will be a buster, I said. I bet he will be a ringtail. We will just go down to Cashtown and git married. I got me half of Pappys place, and me and Jacob will sell it and me take my half.

She said would Jacob mind to. She said maybe Jacob wanted to stay on where his Pappy and Mammy was afore him.

Hell, I said, half is mine and I by God aimed to have it.

I said we would take my half and git us a place to stay in on Massey so I could git to my work. I said she would not be standin over them cook stoves to git vittles for other folks. I said she could stay home and git my vittles and the young uns for a change. I said I aimed to git my half.

I knowed Jacob would squeal lak a suckin pig caught under the bottom rail, but I never cared. I aimed to git my half. I come down the road on a Sunday evenin, and I seen Jacob settin under a cedar tree with his chair cocked back for it was onseasonable warm and January. I seen him settin there but I knowed he never taken his ease. I knowed it was the Bible layin on his lap.

I ast him how he was makin out. He said he did not have no complaint, and he made to git me a chair from the house. Naw, I said, I did not have no time for settin. I said how it was business I come for. I said I was gittin married.

That Canady girl, he ast me.

I said it was.

He said she was a good girl, and he knowed it the way she was to that pore old man the Frencher.

I said, yeah, she was a good girl but I never put my foot in the big road and come twelve miles to git him to tell me. I said I come on business, lak I done said.

He said, what was it.

The place, I said.

It is yores to come to, yores and that Canady girls, he said.

And mine to sell and git my half, I said. That was what I said, right out. Good or bad, winter or summer, cold or hot, I never was one to let no word git spit-soft on my tongue. I never beat around no bush.

He just stood there shakin his head and never said nuthin.

I come to git my half, I said.

Ashby, he said, and shaken his head, it ain't in me. Not to sell this here place and be leavin. Ashby, you ain't meanin it. Not and yore Pappy and Mammy dyin here, and the bed they was in.

They is dead, I said, and ain't no talk makin it diffrent. They is dead and ain't this place or no other nuthin to them now.

I ain't selling this place, he said, quiet.

This place, this place, I said. Lord God, you talk lak this here place was gold and diamints. This place is lak air other place. A place is dirt. And I spat on the bare ground where it was tromped hard in front with the comin and goin.

It is dirt, Jacob said. But man, he is dirt, he said. He ain't nuthin but dirt, he said, but the God All Mighty breathed His breath in him and he ain't common dirt no more.

I told him this place was common dirt to me, by God.

It is not common to me, Jacob said.

I told him I was not breakin no wind if it was common or not common dirt to him, but I was havin my half.

Ashby, Ashby, he said, ain't I yore brother.

I nigh wish to God you was not, I said.

Ashby, he commenst, and put out his hand lak to lay holt on me, but I never knowed what he aimed to say. I have laid awake in the dark and seen how it was, and ain't never knowed.

By God, I said, and I looked in his face, and I knowed he would not sell never for no mans price. But that was not it. It was some other thing come on me lookin at him.

By God, I said, and I give it to him. I give it to him on the side of the head.

I stunned him flat.

He laid on his back I ain't sayin how long, not lookin at me, just up at the sky and blinked lak a baby you put him in the light. Then he rolled on one side and got up, and stood there and looked at me.

You sellin, I yelled at him, but it did not matter what I yelled for I knowed he was not sellin and I never waited for him to say.

It was on me, and I was blood guilty in my heart. I give it to him agin.

I give it to him in the mouth, and he lay there and I seen the blood come out of his mouth.

By God, I yelled, by God. I looked where he laid. Then I turned my back and left him layin and started down the big road.

I walked down the road fast. I reckon I done gone a mile and I looked down and seen my hand was bloody. I done cut my knucks and they was bloody. I reckin I cut them on his teeth.

I wish I had kilt him, I said out loud, but they was not nobody there. By God, I said, I wish I had kilt the bastard.

I walked down the road and sucked the blood out of my knucks where they was cut, and spat the blood and spit out in the middle of the road where folks goes.

Nine

"WHAT are we stopping here for?" Sue asked, and Jerry, not answering, got out of the car and came around to her side and opened the door. Then as he held the door open, he said: "To see my folks."

"All right," she replied, and got out, looking at him without surprise.

They passed through the gate, which dropped back into place after them, with a chinking of the two plowshares which weighted it. The house looked pretty good, Jerry thought, with the roof and window frames painted, and the porch fixed and painted. It looked all right. Then, being up the walk, he thought how the living room would be, and Aunt Ursula sitting there, and wished he had done something about the inside—damn it, why hadn't he, but you had to put money where it'd do the most good—and he wished to God they hadn't come; then, hardening himself, he thought, *Hell, things are the way they are.* And he opened the door.

Aunt Ursula sat in her chair by the low fire. At the sound of the door she had, apparently, lifted her head, and the blind, sunken eyes were turned toward them.

"It's me," Jerry said, "Jerry. And somebody's with me." He could feel Sue just behind him and to one side, but he did not turn to look at her.

He walked slowly toward the figure in the chair, by the hearth. The room was shadowy, for the shades were almost down, the light showing through little rents in them, and the fire was nearly out. He saw her hands on her lap, the flesh on the bad one scarred and crusty. He approached with an even pace. He looked into the face and saw something clinging to the flesh below the left corner of the mouth: spittle—no—perhaps a gobbet of food—he could not make out. He stopped in front of her, and leaned, and put his lips to her forehead, which was dry to the touch.

He stepped back, and turning, saw Sue's gaze fixed upon him.

"This is Sue Murdock," he said, dropping his eyes from the girl's gaze. "She's come out here with me."

"Sue Murdock?" the old woman said. "Murdock?"

"Yes," Sue said, and moved forward.

"Hanh?" the old woman questioned.

"I'm Sue Murdock—a friend of Jerry's."

The old woman's face lifted, questioningly.

She laid a hand on the old woman's shoulder, and then, with the most natural motion in the world, kissed her on the mouth. She straightened up slowly, and again gazed directly into Jerry's face, which showed surprise and, less positively, confusion.

"Excuse me," he managed to say, having had in mind to go out and get his father, but on the saying of the words almost forgetting what he had intended to do, feeling that the apology applied to something else, to the fact that the old woman was blind, to the fact that there was that streak of something below the left corner of her mouth, to the fact that, inexplicably, Sue Murdock had kissed her. It seemed the natural thing to say, as when one stumbles into an embarrassing and shameful situation, and trapped and confused, accepts without knowing why, the accusation of the surrounding eyes. Then he remembered what he had meant to say. "Excuse me," he repeated, with a touch of asperity, "and I'll go hunt up my father."

When he came back a few minutes later, followed by Mr. Calhoun, who wore old wool trousers and a mackinaw. Sue was sitting in a chair by the hearth, beside Aunt Ursula. She rose as they entered.

"Sue," he said, "this is my father."

She put out her hand toward him and moved toward him, saying, "I'm so glad to know you, Mr. Calhoun."

"I'm mighty glad to know you, Miss Sue," the old man said, and his big hand, marked across the back with a smudge of oil, or axle grease, enclosed hers. "I'm mighty glad you dropped by." He released her hand, and made a vague gesture, gravely: "Won't you please take a chair, Miss Sue. And I'll be letting in a little more light. I musta forgot to raise the shades, with one thing and another."

"Thank you," Sue said, and resumed her chair.

"I'm mighty glad you all dropped by," Mr. Calhoun said again, fumbling at the window, "but things mighta been a little straighter, it looks like. If I'd reckoned—"

"No," Sue said, "we didn't know ourselves we were coming. Not till the last minute. You see, we came because we had something to tell you—something we just decided—" She turned her head to meet Jerry's puzzled gaze, and with her eyes on his face, continued: "You see, Mr. Calhoun, we wanted to tell you right away. We're going to get married."

That was how Jerry Calhoun found out that he was going to be married. That was how she announced it to him, sitting there in the disordered, dim room, calmly, with her eyes fixed on him with a clinical dispassionateness. At first the words came to him without any meaning whatsoever. He did not even feel surprised, for the words were just sounds, incredible, incomprehensible sounds, as though she had suddenly begun to speak Chinese. And then as his father spoke, saying how glad he was and telling the old woman how Jerry was going to get married, how Jerry was going to get married to Sue Murdock, the words which Sue had spoken began to take on some reality. "I'm mighty glad," Mr. Calhoun was saying over and over again, and as he came over and took Jerry's hand and said he reckoned Jerry was a good boy but maybe needed some attending to, she watched Jerry's face, and demanded: "We are going to get married, aren't we, Jerry?"

"Sure," Jerry said, not very distinctly, and kept on shaking his father's hand, forgetting what he was doing, and feeling that everything in the world was all right, everything was wonderful, everything was fine, and by God, he did love her. He really did.

Mr. Calhoun asked wouldn't she have a cup of tea; he wished he had something else handy, but he'd make some tea, and Jerry said he thought they'd better be going, but Sue broke in: "No, I'd like some very much, if it isn't too much trouble." So, after a long time, after Mr. Calhoun had gone out to the kitchen and Jerry had come over to stand by Sue's chair and lean and kiss her on top of the head, there beside the old woman, who wheezed softly, the tea was ready. Mr. Calhoun brought out four cups, already full, and a bowl of sugar, in which, Jerry noticed, drops of coffee had made little, hard, stained nodules; and Sue, sitting beside Aunt Ursula and helping her with her tea, talked to Mr. Calhoun. Then Mr. Calhoun brought out the picture of Jerry's mother—the picture of the woman with the small, intense face and the dark hair combed smoothly back, wearing a white, high-necked dress—saying that he thought she might want to see how Jerry's mother looked, but she was a slight-made woman, and nimble, not nigh tall as the average.

"She was awfully pretty," Sue said. And Mr. Calhoun said yes, she was.

As the car eased on down the gravel lane beyond the house, they looked back and saw the old man standing on the porch, waving.

"Well, Mr. Gerald Bull's-eye Calhoun," Sue said to Jerry, as soon as they had passed beyond range of vision from the house, "it looks like you're going to get married."

"It sure does," he said.

"Surprised?"

"I'll say! Here I been asking you every day for three months, and you up and spring it like this. It's funny—"

"It's not funny at all," she affirmed.

"Huh?"

"Well," she said, "you worked yourself up to bringing me home. You finally managed to do it. You see, Jerry darling," she continued, "I wasn't ever going to marry you unless you took me home."

"For Christ sake, why didn't you tell me you wanted to go out there?"

"Then it wouldn't have meant anything at all, don't you see?" she asked patiently, and then added, not waiting for him to answer: "Or do you see, Jerry?"

"No," he said, with the slightest trace of irritation.

"Well, you did it anyway. Though it would have been a lot more considerate of your father to let him know beforehand. But you were too proud for that."

"Proud?" he questioned.

"In a messy way," she said. "You were too proud to let me see things fixed up and ready. You had to show me the worst. But you did it anyway, and I'm going to marry you, Jerry Calhoun, now you've got the worst over, even if you did do it the worst way."

"The worst—" he said, not looking at her but down the lane, and laughed shortly. "Hell, you don't know the worst. You ought to see the upstairs."

"Shut up," she said, "and stop talking."

"You ought to see Uncle Lew if you've got so damned much morbid curiosity."

"To hell with Uncle Lew," she said. "I don't care about our dear Uncle Lew."

"He is clubfooted. He sits around carving nasty-looking faces out of wood and whetting his knife on his shoe and aggravating my father. He's a beauty. He's a gilt-edged, tax-free, double-indemnity bastard. And—" he hesitated, with a kind of wry relish, "he wouldn't come in to meet you this afternoon. You see, he doesn't approve of certain events in the career of your grandfather."

"To hell with my grandfather, too," she said, "and to hell with

126

you, Jerry Calhoun, if you don't keep your mouth shut, but I love you, and if I were you I'd kiss me quick."

He kissed her, and she leaned against him as he drove.

They drove on down the lane, between the leafless ironwood trees and the elder stalks and the tattered sumac, with the fields on each side. Jerry kept his eyes fixed on the road, as though, instead of idling easily along, the big car flung forward at a breathless speed. At last, not taking his eyes off the road, he demanded: "Aunt Ursula—what made you do it?"

"Do what?"

"Kiss her. What made you kiss her?"

"Why shouldn't I kiss her?"

"Oh, it just surprised me."

"And," she demanded, "what makes you want to know?"

"I was just wondering."

The car moved on down the lane, gritting the gravel.

Then she said: "If the old woman's going to be kissed, she's got a right to be kissed by somebody whose neck didn't look like yours when you did it. You looked like you were laying it on the block."

He made no reply.

She said, again softly: "You're such a God-damned mess, Jerry darling. Sometimes. But I'll marry you. I'll marry you, all right. I'll marry you because I've just got to have you. And I don't mind telling you. That's why."

Yes, he thought, he just had to have her, too.

Leaning against his shoulder, she whispered, "I'm happy, Jerry." And added: "Why can't we be happy, Jerry?"

He said that he reckoned they could.

Later, they came to a woods and parked the car beside the lane. They got out and walked in the woods, along a stream. The hickories were tall and straight, with spaces between. There was no undergrowth, and the ground was carpeted evenly with fallen leaves of the hickories. The shaggy boles of the hickories rose like columns, and the sunlight came through the high, leafless branches, to accent the gold that had not yet leached from the untrodden leaves. He told her how he had come to this woods when he was a boy. A crow was cawing, far off. He had come here to fish or hunt, he said. Or just wandering around. She held his hand, and they walked rustlingly over the leaves. Yes, he said, he had used to come here a lot, a long time back. But it did not seem possible. He thought of himself walking alone through this woods. But it did not seem possible.

✦

Light glinted on the lifted glasses, on the rings on the fingers of women, on the bare shoulders, on the white shirt fronts, on Sue Murdock's hair. There was music in a farther room. The fragrant smoke of cigars wafted slowly, dreamily, unreally, aqueously, across the scene, and faded toward the high ceiling, above the laughter.

He stood there and listened to the voices and the laughter, and clasped the hands offered to him. "Lucky, lucky!" the voices said. "Congratulations," they said, "and when will it be?" "All happiness," they said. And the young men slapped him on the shoulder, and called him lucky, and they smiled in good fellowship, but he could not read their faces.

Or he stood in the bar, the older men around him, and they clapped him on the shoulder and lifted their glasses in their heavy, soft hands, or bony ones, and talked of business and horses.

They talked of the new hunt club, twenty miles to the south.

"Jerry's place is out near there," Bogan Murdock said, standing there, smiling, a long, pale cigar between his fine brown fingers, "isn't it, Jerry?"

"Yes, sir," Jerry said, "in that neighborhood," and wondered why Bogan Murdock brought that up.

But Bogan Murdock was turning to one of the men, saying casually, "You, Morgan, you must know the old Calhoun place?"

"Sure, Bogan, sure," the man said, letting the cigar smoke puff from his old mouth, and his eyes blinked in the smoke, vacantly.

"They say old Governor Calhoun built the house," Bogan Murdock said to the man—"but you probably knew that."

The man nodded, agreeing dutifully by that motion that he knew that old Governor Calhoun built the house, everybody knew old Governor Calhoun built the house, naturally he knew old Governor Calhoun built the house, and Bogan Murdock, turning to Jerry, asked: "Your grandfather, wasn't he, Jerry?"

Jerry almost said no, his great-great uncle, but somehow, looking into Bogan Murdock's confident, smiling face, with the smoke-blue eyes steady upon him, he did not. And in a cold, remote corner of his mind, even as he said, "Yes, that's right," he decided he knew why Bogan Murdock had brought that up. And he knew that Bogan Murdock knew—or must know—that old Governor Calhoun wasn't his grandfather, for whatever Bogan Murdock knew had come from him, Jerry. For he, Jerry, had remarked, casually, very casually, one afternoon, there in the library, when Bogan Murdock had suggested a little golf, that he had to run out to his father's place. "The house is pretty run down—things haven't gone very well with my father of late years—but I'm attached to the place, and I don't want it to go to pieces. My father, he likes the place, being born there and his uncle having built it, old Governor Calhoun." He had started to say "his great uncle," but had not. And Bogan Murdock had said yes, of course, old Governor Calhoun.

And now, he said, "Yes, that's right," ringed around by those faces, the round, old, jowlish owl-faces and thin, soaped, razor-scraped, old hawk-faces, with their eyes on him through the delicious, unreal haze of the cigar smoke, and for one instant in that cold, remote corner of his mind he hated them, every one of them, every God-damned one. But he felt his face smiling, and saw Bogan Murdock's face, and felt Bogan Murdock's hand laid on his shoulder, and heard his voice saying: "Yes, and I reckon Jerry's a chip off the old block. Jerry'll be Governor some day. I'm putting my blue ones on Jerry." Then Bogan Murdock had gone away, leaving him there with the eyes on him.

But the eyes were just eyes, and the mouths opened and spoke to him. *What about your trip up to the mountains? What about the labor situation up there?*

I can only speak, firsthand, about the situation at Massey Mountain. A few agitators only—especially a man named Sweetwater— it seems, but plenty of men back at work now. And it seems the situation—both the mines and the timber—is improving. . . .

(There is music off yonder. Under the colored lights, the uncovered shoulders are swaying. The silken knees are moving under the sway and rustle of silk, to the music, precisely, under the silk.)

It won't last.

No, sir, it won't last. It's not natural.

(I love you truly, truly, dear, life with its sorrow, life with its cheer.)

Well, the whole thing's not natural. This slump, now. . . .

(A man is singing, far off. The music is soft and glistens furrily, like a plum.)

Temporary, temporary.

What do you think, Jerry?

(A man has his hand upon her back, lightly, and feels the swaying, delicate articulation of her spine, under the sheathing of flesh and silk. But he knows that it is not for him, it is not for him. It is for Gerald Calhoun.)

Well, speaking as a geologist—what little I know about geology makes me . . .

Boy, you're not a geologist. You're a banker now!

That's right, Jerry. I forgot to congratulate you on the Southern

129

Fidelity. Congratulating you on getting engaged, that just drove it out of my mind.

(I love you truly, truly, dear, life with its sorrow, life—)

What were you going to say, Jerry?

What little I know about geology makes me sure we just haven't scratched the surface in this section. The resources here aren't really touched. This little slump, now. In the face of the resources we've got in this section, and the need for expansion and development, it can't mean much. Just temporary. It just seems so to me—now you all know a lot more of course, and I'm just sort of guessing—

At this point he feels the deprecatory smile on his face.

—but it looks like what we need is simply a free flow of financing for the expansion this section can have—

"We must not be deterred," Bogan Murdock had said, "because of the apparent lack of stability in Eastern business at the moment. We must be bold enough and farsighted enough to grasp our own opportunity here. To make our opportunity, if necessary. And that is why some of us—myself, Sam Dawson, for instance—feel that the moment is right for the launching of the Southern Fidelity Bank. And we hope you feel that way, for, Jerry, we want you as vice-president, in charge of the securities department."

It had come as simply as that, as simply as an invitation to dinner, or for a round of golf, or a canter. Simply.

"Private Porsum has agreed to become president. He has served his country on the battlefield, and now he can render a new service. With his personal prestige, his sterling qualities, his instinct for finance, his ability to inspire confidence, he's the very man. And Blake—"

And later Duckfoot Blake, cocked back in his chair and weaving his toes under the soft leather of his shoes, had said to Jerry: "Sure, I'm gonna take the job. Who wouldn't? It's all screw-ball, the whole idea, but a man owes something to just experience. But I said to Private Porsum, 'Soldier,' I said, 'Soldier, this ain't like the army, if you don't obey an order nobody can shoot you; all they can do is fire you.' And he fixed those steel-gray, unflinching, Appalachian eyes on me, which used to strike terror to the heart of the Hun over there among the ruined vineyards and the quaint old-world architecture, and asked me what I meant. I told him I was just commenting on one difference between being a bank president and a first-class private in the A.E.F."

"Well," Jerry had said, "what *did* you mean?"

"Hell," Duckfoot had said, cocking his head analytically to one side, and letting the delicate lids droop somewhat over the pale

130

eyes which peered at Jerry. "I didn't mean a thing. Hell, didn't you know I'm the half-wit they keep in the attic? I am Jo-Jo, and I beat on the floor with a grisly shank bone and if the racket I make happens to be the International Morse Code it ain't my fault."

"Well, what did you mean?" And a shade of truculence came into Jerry's tone.

"I mean that the Private's got a nice wad of dough which Bogan Murdock and Sam Dawson made for him—outa Massey Mountain, to be exact—and they make their rich friends buy nags at the Private's horse farm. And Murdock and Dawson ain't philanthropists."

"Look here, now, Duckfoot—"

"Sure, Jerry, sure. Your father-in-law-to-be is an honest man. Dawson is an honest man. The Private is an honest man. I'm an honest man. You're an honest man. That's the beauty of it. I am merely indicating a subliminal logic in the affairs of men—"

"Now look here—"

"Hell, let's drop the subject. I'm taking the job. Let's just accept the hypothesis that the whole business is based on the fact that Bogan wants a vice-president of a bank as his son-in-law." And Duckfoot had grinned, and Jerry had grinned, and Jerry grinned now at a joke which one of the old men had just told and which he had not listened to, and the music was going on out there, and Jerry fingered the cool glass in which the ice rode glitteringly, and the cigar smoke wafted across his face, and the music absorbed, overrode, lulled, subdued all the voices, the voices around him now, and the voices he had heard, and the small voices in the mind, which had come from dry tongues rustling like leaves, it seemed.

All right, he thought, *all right!* The words came into his mind, hard, defiantly sharp and clear, with no context, brilliant and gemlike in the rich and velvety-dark center of his being, preciously swaddled there, not reflecting or refracting, giving off their own incandescence. *All right.*

He had not thought that she could be like she was during the weeks before Christmas, and in January. She would sit quietly with him, in the car as they rushed across the countryside, under the lemon-colored wintry sunlight or under the positive, frosty stars, or in the library at her father's house, listening to him, saying yes, yes, she'd like to go to Havana for the honeymoon—they were to be married in February—or yes, she'd like a small place, at first, but in the country so they could keep a couple of horses. But she didn't ride much now, at least, not as much as before. And she had not registered at the University after Christmas. It had just been something to do, she said, that was all, and they were to be married so soon, now. Or they would stand with people at parties, or at the club, with her hair glinting and her face smiling, and she would say yes, yes, turning her even smile here and there, from face to face, or aside, from any person's face, as though the reason she smiled was in herself. Even when she drank she was like that—and she still drank quite a bit; he'd have to hand it to her, all right, she could take it—she didn't have the old edge to her tongue, and the sudden bursts of laughter; instead, she kept that even, almost abstracted smile, meant, as it were, for no one, and springing apparently from her own inner secret, which seemed to be happiness. It must be happiness, he thought. It had all been easier than he had expected, he would think victoriously, with her standing quietly beside him; and he would catch the glitter of the big square diamond on her left hand, and be filled, too, with happiness, hard and bright.

"Yes, she seems so happy now," Bogan Murdock said to Jerry, and turned to Dorothy Murdock, questioningly: "Don't you think so, Dorothy?"

"Yes," Dorothy Murdock said. She sat in front of the fire, the reflection of which gave her face a factitious glow. Like somebody waiting for the telephone bell to ring and can't settle back, Jerry had once thought; but he did not think that now, for he had long since become accustomed to her characteristic posture and air. She might rise from her chair, and with her attention still decorously, smilingly, fixed upon a speaker, move to adjust the position of an ornament on a table or the mantel shelf. Of when her car spun easily down the open highway, and nothing in sight, her blue-veined hands, ungloved, might tighten on the wheel until the knuckles looked like alabaster—he had noticed that too. And now and then, idly, he had wondered what she was like in bed. Oh, she was good-looking enough, still was, no doubt about it, but she just didn't give him any ideas. She just didn't look like she'd sing at her work. Well, she was Bogan's greens, and he should worry. A man in Bogan's position didn't have to put up with something he didn't want.

And Bogan was saying: "Yes, just as I was saying to Dorothy the other night, Sue seems to have lost that restlessness. Wasn't I, Dorothy?"

"Yes," Dorothy Murdock said.

"She seems more at peace with herself than she's been in a long time. What I was saying before, Jerry—you understand her. You will succeed where we—no, Dorothy, I should say, where *I*—have failed. To see Sue happy—" he lifted his glass, and looked into it as though to find in the sparkle of its fire-lit depth the specific image of that happiness of which he spoke, "that gives me the greatest happiness. And my father, to see him happy—perhaps now he can have a little happiness—satisfaction, at least. It won't be officially announced for some days yet, but the State is accepting the little preserve which I offered in the mountains, and is naming it the Major Lemuel Murdock Park."

"That's fine," Jerry said, really not listening, but studying Dorothy Murdock and wondering, just offhand.

"My father fought four bitter years for the defense and honor of his native State, and when he was compelled to fight for his own defense and honor, ruin was visited upon him. Now, at last, he can feel that he has not been entirely unappreciated by his State. Honor—well, he knew the price he would have to pay to defend it. And he paid it. Honor," he said, letting the word hang there in the air, while he turned his head and stared into the fire.

Then Sue came in, ready to go, her fur coat gathered tight about her hips, her gold slippers catching the light, her face tranquil. "I'm ready," she said, and she would go out with him, and sit beside him in the soft, insidious gloom of the car, lit only by the little glow of the dashboard, and the headlights would slice the darkness and the motor settle into its powerful, even sibilance as it bore them toward a place where music, lights, and voices were, certainly awaiting them.

Everything seemed so sure during those weeks, as when one wakes up to find the first snow of the winter, and all the items of the landscape, the bare trees, fence posts, the contours of a hill, the distant houses, stand out in perfect definiteness in the astonishing sunlight; or as when one has struggled until late at night with a problem in mathematics and has given up, exhausted, and wakes in the morning to know, before the pencil touches paper, the key to the solution. That was the reason why he was so unprepared and undefended when it happened, and why he could find no reason.

It happened during the intermission of a dance at the country club, late in January, some two weeks before the date set for the wedding.

They were sitting with six or seven other people at a little table in an alcove during intermission, Coca-Cola and a bowl of ice on the table and a quart of bourbon on the floor, in plain sight but on the floor.

The men asked Jerry about the Southern Fidelity, and they talked about that, while the girls drank their drink through straws, and carried on a cross-conversation, about something. But Sue wasn't mixing in the conversation of the girls; she seemed to be listening to the men, not saying anything, just listening, and looking at their faces. Then Hugh Spiller, just to be polite, Jerry reckoned, said to Sue how he had seen the piece in the paper about naming the park in the mountains for her grandfather. He said he thought that was mighty nice.

"Yes," Sue said, "isn't it?" But she did not say it in a very nice way, nothing you could put your finger on but just not very nice. Jerry glanced at Hugh Spiller to see how he was taking it, but you couldn't tell a thing; you couldn't tell anything about that boy anyway. Then Sue smiled, as in apology, to take the sting out, but a perfectly artificial smile which made her look like a dummy in a store window but a damned expensive store.

"Oh, I'd think you would be thrilled to death," one of the girls said.

"Yes," said Sue, keeping that smile, "I am simply thrilled to death."

"Oh, I know I'd be—"

And another girl broke in: "And your grandfather, I'll bet he's thrilled."

"Oh, he's thrilled to death," Sue said.

"Yes," one of the men said, "it must mean something to a man—you know, when—when he's old—you know—" The man began to flush a little bit under Sue's impeccable, unwavering smile, and fiddled with his glass. He tried again: "When he's old, you know—you—"

"Yes," Sue said, "I know. When you've shot somebody and they name a park after you. It must be thrilling."

"Now, look here, Sue—" the man began, and one of the girls said, "Now, Sue, you know Tom didn't mean—"

"In my opinion," Jerry affirmed, looking around the group, straightening himself in his chair, and they all turned their faces toward him. "In my opinion," he repeated, "that is exactly what Tom ought to mean. In my opinion, that's what makes it important. He did shoot a man. Sure, he shot him and killed him. But he shot to protect his good name. He shot him because—" he really wasn't paying any attention to their faces now, and he felt big and free and clean inside, as a man feels when at last he sees what value to put upon his life, and laid one of his strong hands before him at arm's length, flat on the table, "because it was a question

134

of his honor. Major Murdock was trying to protect his honor. And the honor of his name. Nowadays, we just forget—"

Sue had risen very quietly and moved out of the alcove and across the room, beyond. The pairs of eyes swung away from Jerry, following her figure until it had disappeared beyond the groups of people, and then, flickeringly, they fixed on each other.

"We just forget nowadays," Jerry affirmed, and he heard his voice rising, taking on an exacerbated edge, "what it means. The idea of a man's honor, I mean. We—" then he noticed Hugh Spiller's face, that damned big round yellow-moon face, and you never could tell whether he was grinning or not, God damn him, you never could tell about him—"have lost something. And I think it is important that the State is naming a park for a man who defended his honor." He looked straight at Hugh Spiller, damn him: "Don't you think so?"

"Sure," Hugh Spiller said, "that's what I always say."

"Well, I mean what I say," Jerry declared hotly.

"Sure," Hugh Spiller said, "I just said that's what I always say."

One of the girls sniggered nervously, or coughed, and Jerry swung toward her, to stare at her pretty little enamel-smooth face, with its wonderfully thin arched black eyebrows under the mop of artfully tousled hair, which was black. "Oh," she said, "oh, I wonder what's become of Sue. I'll—" And she made as though to rise.

"She'll come," Jerry said, and thought, damn her, why didn't she come on back, and if she couldn't hold her likker why didn't she stop drinking. And found their eyes on him, ringing him around, and damned their souls, and those clean, close-shaven brown faces and those God-damned cute little slick enameled faces and those pipestem little white arms that would go tight around your neck while they pipped and squeaked and squealed, like a baby mouse you held up by the tail. Oh, he knew them, damn their souls—

He shoved his chair back from the table, sharply.

"Oh, I'll go," one of the girls volunteered.

"No," he said, and remembered to say excuse me, and walked away, aware of their eyes upon him.

He stood in the corridor near the entrance to the ladies' dressing room, and watched but she did not come out. Several girls came out, laughing shrilly together, and then stopped laughing very suddenly, when they found themselves in the corridor, as though the climate appropriate to their humor had changed. The music was beginning. A Negro woman, in maid's uniform, came out, and he approached her. "Do you know Miss Murdock—Miss Sue Murdock?" he asked.

The Negro woman said, "Yassuh."

"Is she in the dressing room?" he asked.

"Naw suh," the woman said.

"Are you sure?"

"Yassuh."

"Are you sure?" he demanded savagely.

"They's some ladies in thar, but they ain't Miss Murdock," she said, and he looked into her eyes, the furry, chocolatey irises against the floating, oleaginous, yellowish whites, and thought, *She's lying, the black bitch, she's lying to me.*

"Go back in there and look again," he ordered. "Look good." He fumbled in his pocket and pulled out a half dollar, which he thrust toward her. Her hand, as though independently of her body, received it with a soft, easy motion, like an oyster pulsing deep below the surface; while those eyes swam before him. Then she turned away.

She came back to say that Miss Murdock was not in the dressing room.

He started to go back to the table, to see if the group was still there and get one of the girls to go into the dressing room. Then he changed his mind, thinking how the girls would talk about it later. He could just hear that girl telling how she found Sue in there, and how Sue had about ten too many and shot her dinner— that delicious dinner they had at the party, that swell dinner, that damned expensive dinner. No, he would wait—and then he thought how maybe Sue wasn't in the dressing room, how maybe she'd gone outdoors. He went out and prowled among the shrubbery, and went out to his car. Then he thought what a fool he was; naturally she'd be back in at the dance now, probably dancing with somebody, and he rushed inside to stand at the edge of the floor, trying to conceal himself by a curtain, and looked for her among the dancers. He didn't want to ask anybody. No, by God, he wouldn't do that, he wasn't going to advertise it, they weren't going to make a joke out of him.

When the dance broke up, he stood just in the shadow outside the entrance, with his overcoat collar up, watching for her to come out. He'd covered the place, but maybe he'd missed her in some way. She did not come out.

The laughter, the cries of good night, the sound of motors died away. Lights began to go out in the building. He walked across the parking area to his car, his feet crunching on the gravel as on a country road at night; at least, he thought of that, walking down a gravel road, by himself, in the dark. He got into his car, and drove to the city, very fast.

He went to the speak-easy where the boys from Meyers and Murdock hung out. Nobody he knew was there; even the bartender was a stranger to him, and at first he was disappointed: he had wanted to talk to somebody, to get a few drinks down, and talk to somebody, just to get it off his mind for a minute. So he could think. He needed to get his mind clear of it for a few minutes, so he could come back to it and think fresh. He bought a pint bottle, ordered ice and water, and leaned against the bar. He put down two heavy ones, straight and quick, and then mixed a highball, and started on that. He looked down the bar. Four or five seedy and tough-looking customers were arguing at the other end of the bar. A card game was in progress in the far corner. A youngish man leaned against the bar near him, nursing a beer along, and staring at his own image in the bar mirror. He was seedier-looking than the others, and not tough-looking but sly, a small man with a drawn, white face, like he had fallen in the fire when he was a baby and they hadn't jerked him out too quick and his face had healed up that way. A snow-bird, Jerry thought.

He edged down to the fellow. He was just finishing his beer.

"Evening, buddy," Jerry said, and the man turned his tight, white face on him, a face that wasn't going to make any concessions until you put up something; you couldn't fool that face. Only it hadn't fallen into the fire; it was just that way.

"Hello," the man said, and closed his mouth like somebody shutting a cash register after giving change.

Jerry drank his highball down, and said: "How about a drink?" He indicated his bottle, in which there were left several stiff ones.

"Don't care if I do," the man said, as though he were calling a stack of blue chips and knew he had the tickets.

Jerry got another glass, some ice, and another bottle. The man put his drink away, not hurriedly but competently. Jerry poured out two more, and the man took a preliminary pull. "I want you to do me a little favor," Jerry said, "if you don't mind."

The man, who had his glass raised again, almost to his lips, set it down on the bar, warily. "What?" he demanded. He did not look at Jerry, but at the beauty of his own image in the mirror.

"Nothing much," Jerry said, and laid a folded five-dollar bill on the bar. "You won't have to move ten feet."

"What?" the man said.

"Make a few telephone calls for me. That's all. And tell me what they say."

"Right here?" the man asked, and jerked his head toward the end of the bar where a public telephone hung on the wall, beyond the group of drinkers.

"Yes," Jerry said, and took a little silver pencil out of his pocket and tore a strip off the margin of a newspaper lying on the bar.

The man's fingers had pre-empted the five-dollar bill and had stuck it into some pocket. He was finishing his drink now, his little shoe-button eyes on the bar mirror.

Jerry wrote three different numbers on the strip of paper. Then above the first he put a figure *1*, above the next a figure *2*, above the next a figure *3*. He felt very competent and strong and businesslike doing that, very much in command of the situation. Just as though he hadn't even had a drink. "Now, you call number one first," he directed, "and you ask if Sue has come in yet, and if they say anything you just say you thought Sue would be in after the dance. Then no matter what they say, whether she's there or not, I mean, you just hang up, see?"

"Yeah," the man said.

"And if she's not there, you just call number two—"

"Yeah."

"And so on. And you tell me what they say. You see, it's just I want to find out if she is there. That's all—" But the man's little shoe-button eyes unwavering upon him seemed to extort the words from him with a contemptuous authority, with a horrible ease, and he felt the words drawn from him and he couldn't stop saying them. "I just don't want to call, myself, see. I don't want to speak to her, I just want to know if she's there—I just—" He found his voice moving into weakness, apology.

"Yeah," the man said, and seemed to say everything.

Jerry took some change from his pocket and sorted out three nickels, which he laid on the bar. "For the telephone," he explained, as though in shame.

The man dried his lips on a filthy green-and-blue silk handkerchief, patted the handkerchief back into the breast pocket of his coat, hitched up his trousers, as if he were getting ready for a great effort, and picked up the coins. He moved the length of the bar, past the group of drinkers, like a man who knows where he is going. Jerry, dropping his bottle into his overcoat pocket, followed him at a respectful distance. The drinkers turned, propped their elbows back on the bar, and looked. Jerry swung out to avoid them, and their heads turned on their necks to follow him.

The man called the first number, asked if Sue was there, and, after a moment, hung up, and shook his head. Jerry felt like telling him he didn't have to talk so damned loud, he didn't have to advertise it. The men at the card game were watching now.

The man made the second call, with the same result.

"She stand you up, pal?" one of the men at the bar asked.

Jerry did not answer.

"She stand you up, pal?"

Flushing, Jerry pretended not to hear. He knew that he ought to say sure, and grin at them, but he couldn't do it.

"Yeah, she stood him up," one of them said, "monkey suit and all."

Jerry looked down at the exposed shirt front, glittering and puffy. He wished that he had kept his overcoat buttoned up.

The man at the telephone did not have the number yet.

"You, Bitsy," one of the men at the bar called to the man at the telephone, "you."

Bitsy turned his white, welted face.

"Yeah, Bitsy," the man at the bar said, "what you doing, pimping?"

Why doesn't he get that number, why doesn't he get that number, Jerry thought.

"Me," the man at the bar said, "I wouldn't do no pimping for no son-a-bitch."

He had the number now, yes, he had it.

"Yeah," a voice said from the card table, "and I never let no man call me no son-of-a-bitch."

Jerry jerked around.

Somebody at the table laughed.

"All right," Jerry heard his own voice saying hoarsely, "all right!"

The bartender had come down to the near end of the bar. The man at the bar who had first spoken met Jerry's eyes, spat cleanly into the spittoon at one side, and said, "All I said was I wouldn't do no pimping for no son-a-bitch."

From the table: "What you doing, Bitsy? Pimping?"

Jerry turned his head to the table, then somebody at the bar laughed, and said, "Yeah, what you doing, Bitsy?"

Bitsy said, softly, to Jerry: "She ain't there."

"You finished your pimping, Bitsy?" another voice said.

And Jerry started moving toward that man. It didn't matter which one, they were all alike, they were all alike, eyes and grin and dirty teeth, every God-damned one, here and everywhere, everywhere—

139

The bartender had tapped the bar top with a sawed-off baseball bat. "Look here," he ordered, "look here!" And he came through the little gate at the end, and stood there hefting the bat in his hand.

The bat had electrician's black tape on the grip, and on the sawed-off end where the lead load would be sunk in the auger hole.

"They ain't gonna be nuthen rough," the bartender declared dispassionately.

"Now, look here," Jerry said, "I came in here, just attending to—" He wanted to tell him how he had been attending to his own business, and how they started talking to him and grinning at him and how they had as good as called him a son-of-a-bitch and how a man couldn't take that and how he wasn't to blame, he wasn't to blame for a bit of it, hell no, he wasn't to blame, not for anything: it all flashed through his head. And then he looked at that face. It was wood. Just like the bat. You couldn't talk to that face. You couldn't talk to that bat. There was the face, and there was the bat, and he felt like bursting into tears.

He swung his glance around the circle of eyes and grins and dirty teeth, and looked at Bitsy. Bitsy was grinning, too. He had taken the five dollars and he was grinning, too, just like the others, and it was horrible, and horrible on his white, welted face.

"You better git outa here," the bartender said.

He sat in his car and took another couple of drinks out of his bottle. Then he drove to his apartment house and put the car in the garage. But he didn't want to go up. He stood in the street, looking up at the sky above the buildings. The sky was very high and it seemed to be moving. As he stared up at it, it seemed to be flowing oilily, curdling, sliding darkly, at that great distance.

He began to walk down the street between the buildings. Then the thought struck him that perhaps Sue Murdock had been kidnapped. She had been kidnapped and murdered and her body lay somewhere in a ditch, in the dark, with her head back, her clothing torn, her arms and legs sprawled out. The flesh of her arms and shoulders was glimmering white in the dark, against the black ground, and of her bare knees above the rolled stockings.

They would arrest him. He knew it. They would arrest him and say he had done it and nobody would believe him how he hadn't done a thing and they would hang him. "Oh," he breathed, "oh!" and felt like running down the street.

They would ring him around with their faces, and the light would be glaring on his face, and they would try to make him confess. But he wouldn't confess. They couldn't make him. They couldn't make an innocent man confess. He hadn't done it. He could have. But he hadn't. He hadn't known it before, but he knew it now: he could have brought himself to do it. There had been moments when he could have. He loved her, but there had been moments. Oh, he loved her, he loved her, but if he confessed and told the truth, he would have to say: "There were moments when I could have killed her, when it was in my heart to kill her, but I did not know the name of what was in my heart."

But they couldn't hang him for that. He wasn't different from other people, and they didn't hang people for that.

Ten

Statement of Ashby Wyndham

THE WOODS boss for the Company he give me the letter that lawyer writ me from Cashtown. He said he had some money to give me and for me to come to see him. I bust out laughin. I knowed no lawyer was not givin me nor nobody no money. I tore up that air letter. Then the next week the boss said for me to go to Cashtown to see that lawyer what had writ me the letter. So come Saturday I went to Cashtown. I seen that lawyer. He laid the money on the table. It was thirteen twenty dollar bills and them new and green lak sallet, and one ten dollar bill and three one dollar bills and a handful of chicken feed nickels and dimes and pennies and such, nigh a dollar. He counted it out, ever bit. It was two hundred and seventy three dollars and eighty five cents, that air chicken feed. It is yoren, he said to me, and you sign yore name here.

How come, I ast him.

To sell yore place, he said, and I ast him about Jacob, and he said Jacob done it.

Well, I am God durned, I said. And I said, Mister, gimme that pen staff.

I signed my name. I put my John Henry where he said and I taken care and pains for I never wanted no mistake. It was not plain writin. It was fair a pitcher of my name Ashby Porsum Wyndham for full. I always was a hand to write good give me time and a pen—not no old stub.

I ast him who bought the place and he said it was the Massey Mountain Company. They goin out yore way, he said, out Fiddlers Fortune Creek section. Yore timber was not nuthin to speak on but they kin use the house for a cook house and all. They give a fair price, he said.

I ast him how much.

Three thirty, he said.

Hell, I said, Jacob never taken much. He will be wantin to git more offen me.

He never taken any, the lawyer feller said, he told me to give it all to you.

Hell, I said, you ain't give it all to me, you ain't give me nigh sixty dollars.

It was for fees and titles and such, he said, lak them lawyers talk.

Who gits it, I ast him plain.

He said he did, him and the courthouse.

How come, I ast him.

He said the Company had to be shore me and Jacob owned it true and right.

Lord God, I said, my Pappy owned it. My grandpappy owned it, and nobody said him nay. And I heard say my great-grandpappy afore him.

Hearsay, he said, hearsay ain't the law.

I knowed it was not no use to argify for he done had the money.

Mister Wyndham, he said to me, you done thought how you investin yore money. I advise you to buy some stock lak they call it in the Company. You buy a piece of the Company. Then you will be workin for yoreself. You will git yore pay and you will git some more too. If you put yore money in the Company.

The Company ain't nuthin to me, I said.

The Company will make money for you, he said.

Lord God, I said, that fool Jacob give you my money and you taken sixty dollars, and I shore God ain't givin the Company none of my money.

You better put it in the bank, he said, and not tote it.

You taken sixty dollars, I said, and the bank, I bet they take a hundred if I give them the chanst.

He said they would keep it safe for me.

Keep it safe, I said, and looked at him square. Mister, I said, I am six foot and two inches and I weigh a hundred and ninety pounds and I can handle me a ax ten hours and never be blowed. Ain't no man I ever seen can take what is true mine offen me.

I taken that air money up. I put it in my pants.

And let air man try, I said. I said that and I went out the door. I left him standin there blowin his breath on his eye glasses and wipin them with his handkerchief.

I come back to Massey and I told Marie how it was. You can quit cookin and scourin, I told her. You can cook my vittles, I said. We was married aready, but she was still cookin for the Company.

Ashby, Ashby, she said soft, and it looked lak she was gittin ready to cry.

Hell, I said, ain't you glad.

She said yes. She said she was glad not to be doin that cookin and scourin. But it looked lak she was gittin ready to cry.

Hell, I said, what you look that way for.

Jacob, she said, it was for Jacob.

It made me mad for fair. I told her. I said, I do not want to hear you namin his name. Not no more. What is betwixt me and him is betwixt me and him, and not nobody else. Not nobody. That was what I said. It looks lak a man cannot bear and endure to look in the lookin glass when somebody has helt it up to him. He cannot endure to see his pore sinful face. She named Jacobs name and it was lak she helt up a lookin glass for me to see my sinful face.

Then somebody ast me where Jacob had done gone.

No where as I knowed, I said.

But they said, yeah, he had done gone.

It stuck in my mind. I never wanted it to, but it stuck. I was workin or I was eatin or I was layin in bed and Marie there sleepin alongside of me, and it would come in my head. How he had done gone. It was lak when you git a little bitsy fish bone stuck in yore throat, little nigh to nuthin, and you think it is done gone for you ain't feelin nuthin and all of a sudden you swaller or you turn yore neck, and it is not gone. It is there. It is lak you swallered a pin.

Saturday evenin I taken out for Fiddlers Fortune Creek. I come there nigh four o'clock. I seen the house. The door was open and I walked in. They was not nobody there. They was not nuthin there. Everthing was gone. The chairs and cook stove and the bed-stid. I seen a chunk layin in the fireplace not all burnt up on one end and the ashes layin there, white ashes lak when good hard wood is done burnt. I squatted down and tetched that chunk, lak a man will to see if may be the fire ain't long been out. But I knowed it had been a long time. But I squatted and tetched it lak I never knowed.

I stood up and looked round. I seen the place where everthing had been set. Where the chist had been set and the bedstid. It looked lak I could nigh see them settin there. I stood there it ain't no sayin how long. A man stands in a house and there ain't nobody there but him and he listens and hearkens and it is plum quiet but he listens lak he is tryin to hear somethin. It is lak somebody was tryin to tell him somethin. It was plum quiet.

I went up to Old Man Marmadukes place. I seen Mrs. Marmaduke and I ast her. She said Jacob was done gone. She said he come and taken his leave. He give her Mammys bedstid, she said. He told her he did not want strangers to lay in it and tetch head to piller. She showed me the bedstid.

I ast her where Jacob had done gone.

He never said, she said. He said he was goin to walk in the world. It was all he said, and she seen him walkin down the big road.

Eleven

WHEN Jerry said what he said there at the table in the alcove at the country club, Sue got up and walked across the room, where people were laughing and talking, and down the hall to the telephone booths. She telephoned for a taxi, and the voice said that one would be there within ten minutes. She said for it not to come to the club building, but that she would meet it at the gate. Then she telephoned Slim Sarrett's studio. She told him to meet her at Wooford's all-night drugstore in town, as soon as he could. At first he seemed hesitant, and seemed about to make some difficulty about coming, but she told him she wanted to talk to him and if he couldn't do her a favor once he could go to hell and she'd leave him alone in the future. Then she heard him laugh at the other end of the wire, and he said he would come.

She got her coat from the check room, and went out the side door. Nobody was in the corridor when she went out. She crossed the drive, where the gravel cut through her thin sandals, and walked on the grass. A little way down she saw the lights of a car coming up the drive; so she stepped back behind some shrubbery until it had passed. Before she got to the gate, the music had begun.

At the gate, she stopped and lighted a cigarette. There was no moon, but the ragged sky showed a few stars eastward over the black mass of the hills. She leaned against one of the big stone pillars, letting her cheek rest against the comforting coarseness of the stone, scarcely aware of the music, which came faintly here, stared across the valley to the dark horizon.

Her feet were placed side by side, her knees touching; she let her arms hang straight down, not bothering about the cigarette, and leaned her shoulder against the pillar. She was not conscious of her body, just of the enormous expansion of the darkness which seemed to revolve slowly around her, of the distant heave of the horizon, and of the contact of her cheek with the stone. It was as though without that contact she would have not been herself at all, but simply a part of the unbreathing, velvety motion of the dark. She felt very empty, very light, and happy.

The taxi was almost upon her before she noticed it. As it slowed down for the gate, she identified it by its lights, and stepped on to the roadway. It slid to a halt in the gravel, beside her; she stepped in before the driver could come to assist her, slammed the door, and said: "Wooford's Drugstore, on Manchester Street."

He was waiting in front of the drugstore. Almost a block before they got there, she could see him pacing back and forth with his almost prinking, elastic step, his shoulders in the slight slouch which he affected, a hat crushed on his head, and his old raincoat swinging free from the shoulders, with the loose belt trailing at both ends. He looked around when the cab pulled to a stop at the corner, and strolled over to her, and watched critically while she paid off the driver. As she turned to face him, he said: "You tipped him far too much."

"What's it to you?" she demanded, but not unamiably.

"Nothing. But I have noticed that quite consistently you tip too much. What makes you do it?"

"Not that it's any of your business," she said, as she started to walk down the street beside him, "but I'll tell you. I do it because I want to."

She had to take unnaturally long steps to keep in pace with him, and she had to hold up her full, pale-green skirts, her dyed ermine coat hanging open and her arms stiffly beside her to clutch the fabric of the dress.

"Naturally, you do it because you *want* to," he observed, "but the special complex of factors represented by the word *want* is interesting. The *want* is not just simple. You might graph it as you can the resolution of forces in physics. The want, even a simple one such as your wanting to overtip, would, of course, involve ultimately the complete structure of personality and personal history. But one might isolate out certain—"

"Oh, shut up," she said.

"—certain factors. In your overtipping there is, for instance, a vanity, an element of ostentation. Then it gives you a momentary sense of security, of being loved and admired. In addition, there is the not unusual easy, sentimental generosity, which it is probably not too cynical to believe has its roots in a preference for smiling faces around one. And there is the sense of guilt. You, with five hundred dollars' worth of clothes on your back—" He reached out with his long, white, hairless sinewy hand, and held a pinch of the fur appraisingly between his thumb and forefinger.

147

"To be more exact," she said, "it cost a little over nine hundred dollars. The coat, by itself."

"The figure was chosen at random. The point is that you with your expensive clothes feel guilty in the presence of your tastelessly dressed economic inferior. Then there is the sense of power—but that is enough to illustrate what I mean."

"Quite," she said.

"Even such a thing as sexual desire—"

"Oh, do tell me about sex," she said sweetly. "Did you enjoy your stay there? I have heard so many friends who have visited there say it is a lovely spot. And the climate? But, of course, we always go to the seashore."

"That is simply facetious," he remarked, "not at all witty."

"Yes, yes," she murmured, hanging her head as in shame and watching her gold sandals flicker in and out with her stride. "Oh, yes. Facetious."

"I mean sexual desire in the most fundamental sense—not as complicated by personal attachments and romantic interest, etc.— but in its most anonymous, pitiless, and naked—" He stopped for a second on the words, then repeated them lingeringly and with a hint of relish: "anonymous, pitiless, and naked form."

"Lovely words," she said. "You must save them for a little poem. You mustn't just waste them on me."

"Even in that form, if analyzed—if it were possible to analyze that *want*—the *want* would probably be found to be enormously complicated. For instance, I once knew a girl who confided to me—"

She looked up at him watching the narrow face with the curled yet positive mouth and deep-set eyes. The muscles seemed pulled down tight and distinct over the side of the face and neck, as in an anatomical drawing. He carried his head well lifted, and the rays of the street lamp striking across it made it look white as a stone. "Yes, yes," she said, "we girls all confide in you. Because you are so tender and understanding."

"No," he said deliberately, "people confide in me because I am *not* sympathetic. I do not blur out the issue with a gob of synthetic goo. Sympathy is not what people want— But that is beside the point. This girl confided in me that she was almost completely cold to the sexual act. It was not a question of frustrated desire, but simply of weakness of impulse. But she constantly practiced the act. Almost daily for years, she said. She did not enjoy it in itself. She never used it for any practical advantage, neither for prostitution or marriage. She had no personal attachments to the partners, for she was absolutely promiscuous and often had never seen her

148

partners before and never saw them again. None of the relationships ever lasted very long, for she would break them off, and she was never faithful, even temporarily, to any one partner. But she said she got an enormous satisfaction from observing her partners. She said she couldn't describe it, but she absolutely lived for it."

"I want some coffee," Sue said, "some hot coffee."

"We can go to Mike's; they'll be open," Slim said, and continued in his previous voice: "She observed the behavior of her partners with a kind of scientific detachment and accuracy—"

"Did she ever observe your behavior?"

"Yes," Slim said, "she did."

"Did she ever tell you what she observed?"

"Yes, of course, but that was afterwards when we had become friends. I cultivated her friendship."

"I don't imagine she observed anything very nice," Sue said.

"It was very disturbing, what she said," he confessed candidly. "At the time, that is. I was rather naïve at that time."

"Oh, never, never," Sue breathed.

"She was a very remarkable person, absolutely uneducated, but she had a remarkable gift for introspective analysis. She had, by the way, begun her career by playing with and agitating small children, when she was scarcely more than a child herself. She loved to take care of children for the families in her neighborhood. She'd offer to keep the children for people so they could go out. She described to me—"

"Slim," Sue said, looking up at him, studying him.

He ignored the interruption, apparently unaware of it, repeating: "She described to me how—"

"I don't want to hear about it," Sue said.

"But it's rather interesting," he said. "She told me—"

"You know," she interrupted him again, and paused to look at him, "you make me want to vomit."

"At times, perhaps, that is true," he admitted judicially. "I have noticed a very definite ambivalence in your attitude toward me. But in two senses, that ambivalence has nothing to do with me. First, in the subjective sense, it derives from your own confusion of mind. There is no reason why, since you can't clarify your mind about other things, you should be able to do so about me. Now, for example, take your attitude toward your father. From what you've told me—"

"It's none of your business," she said.

"All right," he agreed. "But to return to your confused attitude toward yours-truly. Second, in the objective sense, it has nothing to do with me as a person, because I simply present certain facts or ideas to you, and you respond to the facts or ideas, and then blame me as a person for their existence. But they are in the world. Which, I hasten to state, I did not create. I did not create the girl I mentioned or initiate her career of debauching infants—"

"You made up every damned word about it," Sue said. "About that girl."

"Not at all. An artist, a poet, never feels the need to 'make up' anything. He is the only person who never experiences that need. He finds in facts ample occupation, and he can afford to face them. He doesn't have to 'make up' himself or his own life, or 'make up' a sweetheart or wife or friends or children. He can accept people and things without reinterpreting them to flatter his needs. The artist is the enemy of blur."

She walked along beside him for a few paces without saying anything, with her arms down stiff to hold up her skirts, staring down the dingy, cobblestone street, where paper lay in the gutters and the glass windows, set in the soot-blackened cement and stone, murkily glinted under the inadequate rays of the street lamps. "You aren't any different from anybody else," she said then.

"Not absolutely," he said, "but enough. As artist, that is. In so far as I am artist. And you—" he reached out again, and again plucked at the fur of her coat, rolling a few hairs between his thumb and long forefinger, "you are different enough, too."

"I don't give a damn," she said.

"But you are. Otherwise—" he released the little twist of fur which he held between his fingers, "you wouldn't have left the dance to talk to me. And otherwise, I wouldn't have come to talk to you."

"You'd talk to anybody who'd listen," she said.

He did not answer, and when she stole a look up at his face, she found it smiling, looking off down the street.

They were within half a block of the patch of lighted window which marked Mike's Place when she remarked, as though idly, "I walked out on Jerry tonight." And she thought: *I said it, I said it and I didn't feel a thing.* She had scarcely been able to bring herself to say the words. She had held the words in the back of her mind, like an unanswered letter stuck in the back of a desk drawer, trying to forget them there; but she had known they were there, and had said to herself, *I've got to say them before we get there, before we get to that light, if I'm going to say them.* And almost with terror she had looked down to see her gold sandals advancing rhythmically, one two, one two, over the fouled cement. The words

150

would make it real. It wasn't real now. It hadn't been real when she stood there in the dark with her face pressed against the stone, empty and happy. But the words would make it real, and you could never tell how it would be, you never could know beforehand, you never knew how you would be. And a wave of desire swept over her, and seemed to suck at her in its wash and swirl. Then she had said: "I walked out on Jerry tonight."

Slim had said something.

"What did you say?" she asked.

"I said it was only a matter of time," he replied.

"What do you mean?"

"I mean it had to happen."

"I suppose so," she said.

"The only thing not predictable was the time."

"I want some coffee," she said.

They sat in a booth in Mike's Place, facing each other across the narrow table, which was painted red and was faintly filmed with grease and a little sticky to the touch. Two old men, very dirty and shabby, sat at the counter, with cups before them. The counter man leaned on the counter, on crossed arms, a toothpick in his mouth. An electric piano was playing in the back of the restaurant. When a piece had finished, one of the old men would shamble back and put in another nickel.

She told him what had happened, watching his pale, expressionless face. He sat very erect. His dark hair was meticulously parted on one side, and combed down, with a sheen on it. His long hands lay on the table before him in perfect repose, one on each side of the stained cup. Now and then, as she spoke, his eyes would blink deliberately, like the eyes of a nesting bird, and momentarily, as she spoke, even with his bright eyes upon her, she had the feeling that she wasn't talking to anybody, that he wasn't there, that the other scene which she reached back in her mind to grasp was more real than this one.

She tried to remember every word, exactly as it had been said, and she would repeat speeches, lingeringly, trying to remember how Jerry Calhoun's face had been, how his voice had sounded. She remembered how, leaning back in his chair, he had laid his big hand, at arm's length, on the table.

"It just came over me," she said.

How had she felt, what had she thought? She tried to remember.

"It just came over me all at once," she said. "It wasn't like deciding anything, thinking about it, you know. I just got up and walked away. It was like when you rehearse something over and over in a play, and in the beginning you knew how the character felt, and you felt something, you felt a lot maybe, but in the end you didn't feel a thing, you just did something, and if you did it right you felt beautiful and empty, like a dream. It was like that. I telephoned you—and you weren't very nice about coming—and then I went out and stood in the dark down by the road, and it all seemed like a million miles away and I didn't feel anything except just empty and light and I never wanted to see anybody again."

Why doesn't he say something, she thought, but he just watched her across the table.

"I guess it has been that way, always," she said, "and I ought to have known."

"Yes," he said.

"I thought everything was all right. I was going to marry him, and I thought it was all right."

"You had made him up," he affirmed. "He was just a fantasy of yours. To fit your own special needs."

"I thought everything was all right. We were going to get married. Right away. We were going to get married, and I thought everything was all right."

"You were making yourself up for yourself, too," he said. "It is a very complicated picture. You don't understand yourself, and therefore you have to make up a version you do understand. A simplified, conventionalized version with a little best-seller plot and a happy ending. It is a common situation." He took a last sip of his coffee, and set the cup down accurately in the saucer, so accurately that it did not make the slightest chink.

"Oh, I tried to tell him. I tried to tell him. Or show him. But I couldn't. He just wouldn't understand. I wanted him to go away somewhere, to quit his job and we'd go away—"

"That would not have struck at the root of the problem," Slim Sarrett observed, but she wasn't listening. She was leaning forward, speaking: "—just go away. He could get a job somewhere, and we'd be away from everything around here. But—" she sank back in her seat, "he couldn't understand."

"No," Slim Sarrett said, "he wouldn't be able to. He is a very stupid person. Essentially. However," he added judicially, "he was an excellent backfield man."

"He couldn't understand," she said.

"It had to happen," he said. "It might have taken a long time, but it had to happen. The time, I dare say, depended on the nature of his sexual relation to you. As long as you didn't have him,

152

you might have not made the break, for that issue would have been—"

"What are—" she interrupted, sitting up.

But he continued unperturbed: "—in the foreground, you might say, of the relationship. But as soon as you discovered that that indulgence—even the most frantic indulgence—left other matter—"

"Now, look here, Slim Sarrett, you can't sit there and—"

"It isn't necessary," he remarked, watching her, "to take the line of the injured debutante honor. Not with me. It is another universe of discourse."

"Slim Sarrett, you haven't got any right—"

"It isn't a question of my *right*. You—" and he nodded at her patiently, "are confusing issues. It is simply a question of my intelligence. If you are going to indulge in these absurd confusions of attitude, you'd better not raise such questions."

"All right," she said, quietly. "All right."

"It is a matter of logic," he resumed. "Since you had had no real sexual experience—"

"I had had," she said, not looking at him, but across the restaurant at the two dirty old men, her voice flat. They leaned on the counter over their cups, their withered old legs hanging down from their stools, and they listened to the music. "One summer," she said, "a long time ago."

"That surprises me," Slim Sarrett murmured. "I had thought—"

"I'm glad something surprises you," she broke in, but automatically, without change of voice. Then, still looking at the old men, she said: "It was in Maine, the summer after I finished school. It was a boy from Princeton. He was a nasty, slick little boy. I didn't like him. I really didn't. I just did it, I don't know why." She stopped, and looked at him as though expecting him to say something, to offer some explanation. But he said nothing. "It was my fault," she resumed. "I just decided I'd do it. Then, after that first time," she twitched her shoulders as with disgust, "he thought he was so smart."

"Did Jerry Calhoun think he was so smart?" he asked, softly.

"Oh, have you got to talk that way—" she began, and under his level gaze she sank back into the corner of the booth, and her eyes filled with tears. "We could have been so happy," she whispered. "If things had been different—"

"No," he affirmed.

"If they had only been different," she whispered, and let her head fall forward, and began to weep silently.

The old men had turned, and were watching.

153

"Sue," she heard him say, but she could not raise her head. She didn't think she could ever raise it. The old men were watching, but she didn't care. She didn't care about anything. She felt like sitting there forever, with her head bowed, while the piano played on and on and the tears flowed out of her eyes and down her cheeks, and she didn't care, and everything flowed away, and left her.

"Sue," he said.

But she didn't look up. Then she felt his hand touch hers on the table, and he said, again, "Sue."

She lifted her head, slowly. There—and she couldn't believe it, she couldn't, but it was true—there were tears in his eyes, too. He sat up very straight, as though the tears weren't there, or as though they had nothing to do with him, his hand extended to touch hers, and the tears made his eyes even brighter. But the rest of his face didn't show anything. He said: "I don't want you to cry, Sue."

She thought: *He has tears in his eyes. They are really there. Just because I was crying.* And she stared at the little bulbs of moisture brimming at the inner corners of his eyes as though they were the most remarkable and precious thing she had ever seen. And she continued to stare at him as, sitting very erect, with a complete innocence and lack of embarrassment, he reached into his pocket for a handkerchief and wiped his eyes.

She slipped out of the booth, and he followed.

"I'm afraid," he announced, "you'll have to pay for the coffee. I have just enough to pay for my car fare to the University in the morning. I am expecting some money in the morning. For a poem," he added, "which appeared last week in *The Contemporary Age*. It ought to be here tomorrow. They pay very promptly."

She took a dollar bill from her little purse, handed it to him, and watched while he went to the counter. Then she was aware that the two old men were watching her. They were looking fascinatedly at her face, where, she knew, the tears were still wet. *Let them look, let them look,* she thought, and defiantly and happily turned her face directly upon them. Then, looking straight at them, who were dirty, old, wearing broken shoes, she felt a pity mixed in her defiance and happiness, and thought: *They'll never cry over anything, any more.*

Slim brought her her change, and they went out.

They walked down the dirty streets, over the uneven pavement, on which a film of moisture clung and glittered greasily under the rare street lamps. There were no stars visible now. The sky sagged blackly, heavily down, just above the roofs of the black hulks of the warehouses, which seemed to exude a sparse moisture, like the pavement. When they walked down by the river front, a mist was drifting off the river. Through an occasional rift the black water could be seen, sliding sluggishly and monentously, like old oil. The mist drifted in clots and patches up from the river, blurring the street lamps, and seeming to crawl up the steep sides of the warehouses, insinuating itself into crevices.

They saw no one except a Negro man, who was sitting on the curb, with one leg stuck straight out before him and his head sunk on his other knee. An empty bottle lay on the pavement beside him. A gray cat, some ten feet away on the cobblestones, regarded the Negro. As Sue and Slim approached, it glanced at them, then disappeared into the mist at the river bank.

How long they walked under the black warehouses, through the patches of mist, she never knew.

Walking beside her, speaking in his low, sure, vibrant voice, he told her she had to learn to be alone, and she felt that that would be easy to learn, that you could pull the silence, the darkness, and the mist about you, like a blanket. He told her that she had to learn never to make up a picture of herself, never, never, to do that, but to be what she was, that it was hard to do but she had to do it. And she thought, wildly, *oh, what am I?* But his voice went on, and she said, yes, yes. He told her that it was hard, that it was much easier to make up a picture to suit other people, but that that was not to be alive. It was hard to be alive, he said. And hard to be alone, as you must be to be alive. He told her that, saying: "I know what it is like to be by yourself. I have been that way, always. No—" and he paused, "no—not quite always. For a minute, just a minute now and then, I—" His voice trailed off. They moved on some five paces, side by side. Then he stopped, suddenly, and turned to her, peering into her face, and his voice broke out huskily: "Oh, Sue, Sue—"

But he did not proceed. Peering at her, he reached and took her hand in his. Then he jerked his eyes from hers, as one snaps a thread, and looked off down the street. With his head lifted, somewhat averted from her, his face white and firm and carved-looking against the darkness, he walked slowly beside her. He still held her hand, and she made no effort to release it, but let it lie passively in the steely cage of his fingers.

"I am going to tell you about myself," he said." Something, anyway. Because I want you to know. If you don't mind listening—"

"Yes," she said.

"I haven't told anybody else. Not anybody. But I want you to know. I want you to know what I'm like. No—" and he looked

155

down at her, "I won't be able to tell you what I'm like, Sue. For I don't know, finally. If a man works hard all his life, he may find out. At the very end, when it is too late to tell. But I can tell you a little. What has happened to me, at least. And can hope that you will try to understand. You will try, won't you, Sue?"

"Yes," she said, "I'll try."

"I have a reason for wanting you to know, Sue. I shan't tell you the reason. Perhaps, sometime, but not now."

"Yes," she said.

"My father was a barge captain at New Orleans. I do not know anything about him, and I scarcely remember him—or I think I remember him—a man with a gray beard and wearing a rough coat of some kind. It was rough, for I can remember how it was when I put my face against it. I remember him screaming at my mother and her screaming at him. Or again, I may deceive myself, and think I remember, for my mother used to tell me about the quarrels between them, after he was dead and I was old enough to remember. He was killed when a boiler blew up on a tugboat. He was blown to pieces or his body was washed away by the river. In any case, it was never recovered. I remember my mother saying: 'I'd shore-God like to seen the look on the old son-of-a-bitch's face when the thing busted. I'll bet that fazed him.' And she said: 'The only thing he ever done for me was get blowed up, the old cheapskate. And he didn't mean to do that, not him. Oh, no, not him. He'd a-died in bed and had a big doctor's bill, given his say-so. It's the only thing he ever done for me, getting blowed up so I never had to pay no undertaking.'

"When I was a child I used to have a nightmare about him being blown to pieces. How his head—just his head, with something hanging out of the neck like a hank of dirty white clothesline—would come drifting through the air toward me, in the dark, dripping wet and muddy and with weeds in his beard and smelling of river mud and whisky. He had always been a heavy drinker. And his face would be straining and twitching, so that I knew it was trying to tell me something. It would come close to me and put the mouth to my ear, but I couldn't hear a thing, just a rustling, no matter how hard I tried—and I did try; that was part of the horror of the dream; I knew that mouth had something to tell me.

"And then, suddenly, its teeth would snap shut on my ear, like a dog snapping a meat scrap. I would wake up, crying and sweating. My mother would wake up and be angry, and would slap me if I didn't be quiet. When I was little I told her about the dream, and she said: 'Spit in his eye, and he'll leave you alone. The old son-

156

of-a-bitch knows better'n to come hanting me.' Then she laughed.

"I never knew what they quarreled about. He was much older than she was, in his fifties, I imagine, and she was about twenty-five when he died. She was from somewhere up in the country, near Vicksburg, I think, and he'd met her when he was up there doing something on the river. I suppose that she married him just to get down to New Orleans, and get away from home. I never knew anything about her people, but if my observation of little Mississippi towns means anything, she would have been justified in adopting any measures which seemed necessary for escape. In any case, she was from the country, and the city never—that is, until the time I left her—lost its fascination for her. She was constantly wandering back and forth on the streets, looking into the windows of stores by the hour, stopping in soda fountains to consume some brilliantly colored drink, standing on the corner to watch the people while she sucked on a piece of hard candy which she held in her mouth. I can remember her standing on some especially crowded corner, her large eyes—they were china-blue, that color so often found in the class called pore white trash—staring bemusedly while her head swung slowly to follow some unusually interesting passer-by. Her mouth, as I recall quite distinctly, would be pursed and her cheeks sucked slightly in, like a child's, from the effort she expended on the candy. I suppose I remember such scenes so vividly because of the candy. She occasionally would give me some of the candy.

"The fighting with my father may have been caused by her predilection for wandering about the city and neglecting the housework. The disparity in age, too, may have created a good deal of friction because of sexual dissatisfaction. Perhaps jealousy played its part, though I do not know for certain that she was unfaithful to him. She must have hated him with a peculiar intensity; during the years after his death, she might burst out at any time with a fragment of some old quarrel. She would seize me, as though to compel my attention. Her face—it was full-fleshed and roundish—would suddenly grow rapt and strained. The hatred, you might say, sloughed off the casual, deceiving softness of her face, and showed another structure. A structure much more precise and pure. Such a change of fundamental structure may sometimes be seen in a face at moments of great sexual excitement, for example. She never related the context or the issue of the quarrel which she recapitulated. She simply would burst out: 'He said to me—yeah, the old cheap-skate, he had the nerve to say to me—' Then she would repeat his words. 'But I fixed him, I fixed the old son-of-a-bitch's clock—I ain't let no old pig-eyed slob puke his meanness on me—and I told him and he nigh busted a hame. I said to him—' She would scream out what he said and what she said, the whole dialogue. Then, after a while, she would be exhausted and would let go her hold on me, and would sink back in a chair. Her face then would be full and overblown and lax, like the face of a satisfied sleeper. She had a wonderful complexion, rather milky. When she would sink back after such a tirade, and the fullness came back to her face, I used to have the impulse to touch her face, like you want to touch fruit or silk. When I was very young, those bursts of hers, when she held me by the arm till it hurt and made me listen, used to frighten me. But later on, I began to enjoy them. I would sometimes try to provoke her by repeating back to her something she had quoted from one of the quarrels. Frequently my stratagem would be successful. I have never been able, however, to analyze very fully the nature of the enjoyment which I experienced on those occasions. But it offers an interesting problem. Yes, very interesting.

"After the death of my father—or my presumptive father, but I'll come to that—my mother went to work in a restaurant as a waitress. It was the sort of work which, I imagine, she liked. She could see a great many different people, and since it was a cheap restaurant down in the old quarter of New Orleans, but not the sort of restaurant where tourists would go, she probably had the excitement of talking to the men who came to eat there. We had lived in a little shotgun house in another section of the city, but we moved when my mother got the job so that she could be nearer her work. We lived in an apartment, a couple of rooms, with a sink in a corner and the toilet down the hall shared with other people. It was an old roach-ridden stucco building, with a patio and galleries around the patio. There were scraggly wilted vines of some kind on the galleries, and clotheslines strung back and forth. It was the sort of place which, when given a little paint and stripped of the clotheslines, so enchants the starved sensibilities of aging, overfed female tourists. But I was getting ready to say that the larger room, where my mother slept and where the sink and gas plate were hidden behind a screen in the corner, was the outside room, opening on the patio and on the hall. The small room—simply a hole with one high window, to be exact—opened only into the larger room. I mention this arrangement because it has some bearing on the story, later on.

"Before I was big enough to go to school, my mother would leave me to play in the patio. Other families in the building would look out for me, more or less, and give me something to eat at noon and at night. My mother never got home from work until late. For a while, she was in the habit of bringing me cake or something of the sort from the restaurant, wrapped up in a paper napkin and stuck in her handbag, but by the time I was seven or so she quit.

"After I was old enough to go to school, my life was much my own. I did not mind going to school because I was very good at my studies, and some of the teachers made much over me, and I confess that I enjoyed exhibiting my superior talents. I very early got the habit of reading widely, and spent a great deal of time in the public library. The rest of the time I spent on the streets and on the waterfront. The children of the street gangs of the New Orleans slums and of the river front and the shanty-boats—unless they have changed considerably in recent years—are as precocious, violent, vicious, diseased, depraved, verminous, cunning, and enterprising a lot as probably exists in the world. I use each adjective advisedly. Constantinople, Naples, or Port Said—those cities might offer a competing product, but I doubt it. Certainly, in the two years when I was a seaman on a line out of Mobile, I never saw anything to surpass them in their special achievements. And I saw a good deal. Not that I was on the look-out for what is vulgarly called 'literary material.' I was not that naïve, even then. I have never had any intention of transcribing, by way of either protest or celebration, that life. I simply mean that it is enormously valuable for a poet to know something of the context in which poetry exists. Something, you might say, of the dung and offal which fecundates the plant. Which fertilizes it. Some day I shall write a *Prelude* quite different from Wordsworth's. I had the privilege of observing in a relatively pure form the impulses which are decently—or indecently—overlaid in ordinary life. Every poet should have a taste of the slum. A slum will sharpen the perceptions far more than the vernal wood, because a vernal wood never hits you between the eyes with a set of brass knucks if you happen to be somewhat dull-witted. A short experience of the slum will make the poet want to vomit whenever he hears any glib effluvium about art-and-life vented by some bald-headed, vandyked, low-arsed professor of English Literature. Or the effluvium of art-and-revolution. And, especially, it will teach him the discipline of loneliness. But this is beside the point.

"I got along very well with my friends. I was more intelligent and, in my own way, harder. The stupid person can never be really hard. He can only be insensitive or brutal, which is very different. And the more stupid a person is the more likely he is to be a prey to wavering purposes and incidental sentimental ties—things which are characteristic of the insensitive or brutal person. The gang code, for example, is a peculiar type of infantile sentimentality.

"As I say, I got along very well with my friends, and I was very successful in the slum and water-front life, as judged by their standards. We committed petty thefts and raids. I participated in these expeditions, and even planned and directed many of them, but I never took any part of the loot. It was not a moral question, for that question did not enter my head. It was not fear, for by participating in the actual thefts I laid myself open to all consequences. I suppose, upon looking back, that in the first place I didn't take any of the loot because I had some desire to keep my motives untainted: I participated in the crimes because the act somehow heightened my sense of life, whetted my awareness, defined me more sharply in my special relation to society. In the second place, my refusal to share the loot must also have been a way of defining myself more sharply in relation to my friends. They no doubt thought I was peculiar, but they trusted my judgment and were not often inclined to debate with me. Or try to settle an issue by force. I had trouble with the law only one time, when I was about ten or eleven. We were pillaging a box car which we had pried open, and I was caught. All because of the incompetence or cowardice of a boy who was acting as lookout. But a little later, I must say, I gave him considerable cause to regret his conduct. Anyway, I was caught, my mother was informed, I was brought to the magistrate who had charge of juvenile delinquency. But one of my teachers intervened on my behalf, and I was simply given a reprimand. My mother beat me when she got me home, something she rarely did. On other occasions she beat me simply out of personal irritation. Now she beat me out of some obscure notion that the world would expect it of her. She must have known previously the precise kind of life I was leading, and had never made the slightest effort to discipline me. But now that I was caught she responded with that pathetic automatism: she beat me, she exclaimed against my immoral companions, she said she didn't want her boy to be a thief. The recollection of the scene always makes me sad, and a little embarrassed. As when you look into the littered, stinking cage and see an old monkey or mandril or baboon nursing one of its young with the posture and expression—in a kind of crude and painful parody, as it were—which one finds in the madonnas of the Italian Primitives.

"After my mother beat me, she wept and put her arms around me. I wept, too. Not in pain from the beating and not in repentance. And not in sympathy either, for I must have sensed the fact that this was simply an isolated moment for my mother, that it had no continuity with her past or future, that it could not be judged by any ordinary standards of 'sincerity.' As a matter of fact, very few people, strictly speaking, can be sincere. It can be achieved only by people who are intelligent enough to have a considerable degree of self-knowledge. The stupid person can never be sincere, really—you know what I mean—any more than the incompetent technician can write a sincere poem. But I wept, too. My mother lay down across her bed, and drew me down beside her, and wept bitterly. I felt her sobs shake the somewhat rickety bedstead—she was putting on some weight by that time, the fate of that milky-skinned, large-eyed type of woman, when the diet is adequate. As it might very well not have been on a tenant farm in Mississippi. And I smelled the strong perfume with which her person and her bed were impregnated. I wept, I suppose, for something I had never had. I discovered what I had not had, it might be argued, only by confronting its false image. I did not phrase it that way at the time, but it must have been the moment when I discovered the fact of isolation. And when I discovered the tragic sense. My weeping, so interpreted, had a ritualistic significance. And certainly, lying there beside her, I knew that I would have to leave. The nature of my relationship to her had become by the fact of her weeping irrevocably confused. It had been simple enough before, but it could never be simple again. I did not decide on the time when I would leave, but the conviction suddenly germinated within me. It took almost two years for it to come to fulfillment.

"I forgot to say—though you have probably surmised it—that during the years after my father's death, my mother had had various men. She was not promiscuous. In fact, the first man was her lover for five years or so after my father's death. He was a Mexican or South American, with a clear golden complexion, large brown eyes, and a scrupulously trimmed black mustache. He wore violet, mauve, or pink shirts, with cuff links made of gold nuggets and always with a narrow black tie. His shoes were narrow, and yellow, and pointed. He smoked long thin yellowish cigars, which, I can remember, he held with inordinate delicacy between thumb and forefinger, with his little finger standing out from the hand. His hands were very small and soft—I know, for he used to dandle me and play with me—even though he was a large strong man and was beginning to have a paunch. He always smelled of perfume. His name was Almendro. My mother called him Al. He would take me on his knee, when I was little, and make me repeat his name after him. 'Ah, chiquito mio,' he would exclaim, laughing and hold-

161

ing me up, 'ah, amiguito mio! you know to say it better than the old woman. She call me Al!' Then he would almost always pull a box of chocolate creams out of his pocket and give it to me. He would want some too, and would make me put them between his lips for him to take. He would lean over to me and open his mouth. I remember how soft and pink his lips looked, and how white his teeth were. The chocolates, I thought, were the color of his eyes.

"Almendro, I decided later, was my father. I would stand in front of the mirror for a long time and inspect myself for resemblance. I had dark hair, and it grew on my head like his, or so it seemed to me. And my eyes were brown, too. Though not ordinarily as soft as his. But I would stand before the mirror and try to make my eyes look soft like his. I learned the trick. Much later I learned that that expression of the eyes, which I could muster at will as a result of my long practice, had a very definite effect on certain types of women. A type which ceased to interest me a long time back. But at one time it was an effect which I found to my convenience on certain occasions. If Almendro was my father, then my only patrimony was a trick of the eyes which got me a few little pieces of tail.

"But this thought that Almendro might be my father came to me only some time after he had left my mother. I would look for him in the street. I would make up long conversations to have with him. I would plan to confront him with the paternity. I was not concerned with his treatment of my mother, though as a matter of fact, he had beaten her soundly the night he left her, as the numerous bruises testified next morning. But I did not require the testimony of the bruises. I had heard the noise through the thin partition which separated our two rooms, a noise somewhat different from the accustomed one on his visits. She had not really cried out. First, there had been their voices at a higher pitch than usual. Then the sound of blows. Then her moans began and a low whimpering. The blows came regularly. I seemed detached from it all, but was filled with a very peculiar excitement as I lay there in my dark room. Then, after a while, I heard him go out, slamming the door. I thought of him walking away down the street, his face wet with his exertions, his thin cigar held between his thumb and forefinger, and his pointed yellow shoes, gleaming in the street lamp, set one after the other on the pavement in his precise tread.

"I never saw him, despite my sharp lookout. But, as I said, the idea did not come to me until some time after he left my mother.

162

Then, after a while, I ceased to speculate about him. If I had met him in the street, I would have passed him without a word.

"There were other men after Almendro. I saw them now and then. And I saw the presents which they gave my mother—new dresses, hangbags, loud jewelry. They took her out to the race track and to the bars and hot spots. I do not think that she ever took money from them—just amusements and clothes and trinkets. The first one came to see her for almost two years after Almendro left, and there were others for shorter periods. But they never had much to do with me, for I was getting to be a big boy then. I knew the names of only one or two, as a matter of fact. But, naturally, I saw them now and then, and more often, late at night, I would be aware of the movements and excitements on the other side of the partition.

"The last man—whose name, by the way, escapes me—crystallized my intention to run away. He liked to carry fairly large sums of money in his wallet—large, that is, for the circles in which he moved, say, thirty or forty dollars—and he liked to flaunt his roll. He was an innocent braggart, and once or twice, he showed off before me, while he was waiting to take my mother out somewhere. I noticed that he carried his wallet buttoned into his left hip pocket. I had been thinking steadily about leaving, but I had not made any plans. The money solved everything.

"For several nights in succession I went to bed with my clothes on, and waited until they came in. The fourth night I could tell from the stumbling about and giggling that they were drunk. I waited until all sounds had ceased. I knew that they would be sunk in a stupor. I tied the lace of one of my shoes to the lace of the other, swung them about my neck, and began to open my door. I had carefully oiled the hinges in preparation for the moment, but the door was old and warped, and despite my cautious movements made some creakings. It did not wake them, and the whole affair was simple. I found the trousers and took them with me, too, for I calculated that without them the man would not pursue me, even if he woke up just as I was leaving. I unlocked the front door, on to the patio. I stood there with my hand on the knob for some minutes. A little light came in through a transom. There was no reason to wait, for the thing was as good as done, but I had the mastering compulsion to absorb that scene. The man lay on one side of the bed, on his side, with the sheet pulled across the middle of his chest, and his top arm, which was large and hairy, was flung out toward the woman. The hand rested laxly on her body, just under the left breast, which because of that pressure was outlined

163

by the sheet. She lay on her back. Her arms were by her sides, under the sheet. Her hair was loose and matted on the pillow, and colorless in the faint light, from the transom. The face, too, was colorless, and doughy. I had the feeling that it was sinking in upon itself to become a featureless mass. The mouth had dropped open, and the respiration made a ruffling, sibilant sound. Each inhalation and exhalation seemed to represent a separate, painful, exhausting effort, having its own finality. I stood there and examined her, and thought that if I had seen that face in unfamiliar surroundings I would not have recognized it. But sleep is a strange thing. I believe that physiologists have, strictly speaking, no definition for it. I have always been fascinated by the sight of a person asleep.

"I crossed the patio, put on my shoes, and hung the trousers on the patio gate, where the man could get them next morning, if some prowler didn't beat him to them. I hoped my mother's friend would get the trousers, for I bore him no grudge. I went to an all-night coffee stand, where I ate a heavy meal of sandwiches, cake and pie, and bought some sandwiches to take with me. Then I started north out of the city. I hid all day the next day, eating my sandwiches, and drinking water from one of the swampy ditches you found just north of the city. Then I walked most of the night. By that time I felt relatively safe.

"The details of my life for the next several years are not very important. I made my way to Memphis, where I stayed until I was fifteen. I got odd jobs as errandboy, paperboy, grass cutter, gardener, etc. I even went over into Arkansas to pick cotton. I read in the library, but I didn't go to school. Nobody made me go, and I was afraid of the questions they might ask me about my personal history. By the time I was fifteen, I was almost full grown. I wanted to save some money, so I went to Birmingham, in Alabama, where I worked in a steel mill. In two years I saved a few hundred dollars. Then I went to a little college in Alabama, Moffat College. I had no high-school diploma, but they gave me an entrance examination. I had expected something difficult, I had some superstitious reverence, and was terrified. I saw the questions, I burst out laughing. I knew then that I was in a nest of fools.

On the basis of my examinations, they put me in second year in most of my classes. I was petted by my teachers, some of whom were desiccated old ladies, spinsters of Baptist preachers. I confess that I played up to them. I held my tongue and listened to their questions about my immortal soul in private conversation. I even amused myself by devising and acting out over a period of many months a grave spiritual crisis. At that time I had just finished

164

reading the *Confessions* of Saint Augustine and Saint John of the Cross and Petrarch's *Secret*. So I had some excellent materials. I became so engrossed in my little drama, of which I was author, angel, producer, director, stage manager, and cast, that I practically lived for it. On one such occasion, while talking to Miss Constantina Buchanan, I burst into tears, which, to my surprise and delight, were quite real. And Miss Constantina Buchanan held my hand and patted me on the head and drew me to my knees beside her chair and, finally, laid my head on her inadequate breast, while she wept, too. The musty, boiled-vegetable odor peculiar to old maids—an odor which soap and eau de cologne never quite conquer, I have noticed—did something to bring me to myself, I suppose. That and the tears of Miss Constantina Buchanan falling upon the back of my neck. But in the midst of the scene, I suddenly remembered, and relived, the time when my mother had beaten me and had wept and had made me weep too, lying on the bed beside her. I rose very abruptly, and left Miss Constantina Buchanan, who, by the way, was the daughter of a Confederate brigadier general, killed at the Battle of Atlanta under heroic circumstances, at least, that's what they were always saying at the College Assembly.

"That was in May of my second year at Moffat. It brought an end to my little drama. I avoided Miss Constantina Buchanan, took my examinations, and left. I had led a double life at Moffat, and I knew that I could live it no longer without doing a violation to my nature. It was not the double life which every artist is forced by his nature to lead. You see, actually in the tears shed on the bosom of Miss Constantina—poor old thing, a bosom like two little wads of stale biscuit dough with a dried raisin stuck in each, I imagine—I had been guilty of a confusion between art and life, I had blurred out a fundamental distinction. You may recall what Paul Valéry says about the emotion of the poet and the emotion of the reader—I told you about that once, you remember. Well, I had mixed myself up. But it wasn't the double life of the artist I was talking about. I was cutting myself off more and more from reality.

"For three years I didn't go back to college. I wandered around the country, working here and there, at all sorts of things. I discovered that I had the talent of being able to come into a town, dropping off a freight, for instance, without a penny in my pocket, and being able to make friends right away, influential friends, and get a job, and have a good time, and wear expensive clothes, and be invited out to dinner in nice houses. It's funny how easy it is to do that, once you get the trick. Then I'd blow my money, and leave. But I quit all that sort of thing. I saw that every time you

165

do that you actually surrender some part of yourself, you make some concession, some adaptation, of your own personality. The impulse to blow my money, and leave town, penniless again, I saw was an attempt at cleansing and expiation. But that wasn't enough. So I went to sea. Out of Mobile. I was a seaman for more than two years.

"On my last voyage, the ship docked at New Orleans. I got paid off, and walked down Canal Street. I had not been back in the city for ten years, or almost. Naturally, I began to think of my childhood there. I walked up Royal Street, and into the section where my mother and I had lived, and found the house. I asked at the corner grocery about Mrs. Sarrett, but they did not know her. I had no intention of presenting myself to my mother, for that life, I knew, was over. It would have been the same thing even if our relationship had been different, more pleasant. The past is valuable only in so far as one can recognize it as *past*. Living is, metaphorically, a temporal art, like poetry or music. It is dynamic and consecutive in its structure. Nostalgia is a vicious denial of this fact. So is the thirst for immortality. The chord must be resolved.

"But I had a certain curiosity about my mother. I continued my investigations, and finally found an old woman who remembered her. The old woman was evasive, and I sensed some mystery. All I found out was that my mother had after some years been evicted from the room in the patio. Had she been too poor to pay her rent, I asked. 'Pore!' the old woman said '—not her! She had ways to git money.' But the old woman did not know where my mother had moved, and so I had a new area for investigation. I did not find my mother, nor did I find the place where she was living at that time. But I did learn of a fourth address, where she had lived only a couple of years earlier. I went to the address. It was a crib on a filthy little side street in the French Quarter. It was just before noon when I arrived at the place. The prostitutes, wearing kimonos and wrappers, were sunning themselves on the little wooden stoops in front of the cribs. The shutters of the cribs were closed. The women were not talking much. They sat there in the sun, and I looked at them and thought of one of William Blake's epigrams. Concerning satisfied desire. But it had only an ironical reference to the scene before me. The colored stucco walls of the houses down the street had peeled and faded into a wonderful impressionistic patchwork of mauves and yellows and pinks, and the bright sunlight fell over it. There was also the effect of the steel-gray and dove-gray and blue slates of the irregular roofs from which the heat shimmered up against the remarkable blue sky.

"I realized that there was no need to hunt further for my mother. It was all predictable, and I felt a little ashamed that I had not guessed. Though, of course, there is always a margin of error possible. As for my feelings about the fact, I cannot honestly say that I reacted very strongly. At the first moment of realization, I was, I suppose, sorry for her. Then I thought that she would not have understood my sympathy, because she had simply fulfilled her nature. She might have felt sorry for herself because of individual misfortunes, but not because she was what she was. I suppose no one who has succeeded in fulfilling his nature, whatever that nature is, needs sympathy. The man who has not fulfilled his nature is the man who needs sympathy.

"And I cannot say that I felt, except at the first moment, any special shame. The world has provided you with a vast number of stereotyped responses, in which you are schooled from infancy. The son who discovers his mother to be a whore must be overcome by shame. The person who wants to live—actually *live*, actually *identify* himself—must struggle against the stereotyped. The traditional discipline for struggling against the stereotype is art. But at that time I was younger, and more uncertain. I admit that, at that first moment, I did experience shame. But even as I stood there and looked down the bright street, the shame left me. I felt completely at peace.

"Why had it left me? The answer did not come to me all at once. But as time passed, I began to see that the situation was right. My father was not the bearded man blown to pieces on the river. Not the muddy river-stinking head which drifted toward me in the nightmare, trying to tell me something. My father was not Almendro, who gave me the chocolate creams. He was, rather, those seamen who staggered up the street by the cribs after it got dark. Or the stevedores with their shirts still gummed with dried sweat to their backs. Or the sniveling little checker or timekeeper from the warehouse. My father was not one of them, but all of them. Those men I never knew. And perhaps, Almendro, too. And even the old barge captain. For the artist has no father. Only a multiplicity of fathers, who don't owe him a thing. Not a damned thing. Because they have paid three dollars, or two dollars, or fifty cents, or have paid in some other way, already. And therefore, the artist is free, because he doesn't owe them anything, either. But, as I said, this came to me slowly. A long time after I had left.

"Well, I finally came up here and finished college. Then I went off on the road, bumming over the country again, but I came back here. And here I am, Sue."

167

He still held her hand, walking beside her.

"Here I am, Sue," he said, "and here we are walking together while everybody else is asleep."

She did not answer.

"I'm sorry," he said, "I've talked so much. But I've never said these things before. Not even to myself, I guess. I'm sorry," he repeated, and leaned down solicitously to her so that he could see her face.

"Oh, that's all right," she said mechanically.

"I simply wanted you to know what I am, Sue," he said, softly. "In so far as I could tell you. Or rather, in so far as you can put these things together in your mind, and know the truth."

Truth or not, she didn't really care. But she left her hand in his, although it was almost numb with cold. They walked on beside the river, from which the mist was swelling and flaking off more thickly now, for it was near dawn.

She had scarcely been attending to the meticulous, rhythmical voice. She had been thinking about Jerry Calhoun, and wondering how she would ever, ever get along without him.

Twelve

Statement of Ashby Wyndham

I TAKEN Marie out of that kitchen where she was cookin and fixin for strangers and put her in my house. I give a man a hundred and fifty dollars for that air house and give him two dollars ever month till it was goin to come two hundred and twenty dollars. I could give it all cash money but I helt out for Marie. She was not gittin on so good and I helt that money for medicine and such if need come. She said she was goin to be all right when the young un come. She said she was not nuthin but a little puny.

The young un come. He was a buster. He was nigh as big as his Mammy. He come some afore his time and all of a sudden but he was a buster. He never said by yore leave. She was washin dishes. we et offen for supper and she yelled, Ashby, Ashby, all of a sudden. It was comin. There was not nobody there but me for we never knowed it was time. Ain't nobody ever knowin it is time for nuthin. Man figgers and calkilates but he ain't knowin. He looks at the sun and he knows what time of day it is but there ain't no sayin the time of what is comin. The Bible says there is a time for everthing, but pore man never knows the time. It ain't got no foot he can hear treadin. It comes lak an Injun. It lays lak a copperhead amongst the dead leaves. It lays on the bare ground, but a man never takes no notice for it has got the color the ground has got.

I done what I could. What I seen them women do for Old Man Marmadukes wife one time when she come to bed. Marie laid there, and it looked lak she was gittin ready to die. She yelled, and there was not nuthin I could do but name her name. Then I could not do that no more. It looked lak it was not Marie layin there. Maybe it was not me standin there, it looked lak. Lak that time my Mammy was dyin and named my salvation and I stood there and my heart was lak flint rock in my bosom. It was hard and it cut me, but I never even lifted up my hand. A hardness comes

169

on a man. He is done froze up, and there ain't thaw nor freshit. Pore human love, it is lak that unless it is in Gods eye. In Gods eye and in His blessed name.

I seen Marie layin there and moanin and yellin when the pain taken holt. I said, she is goin to die. I said that but it looked lak I taken no count of it. It was lak it was not nuthin to me. I seen her lay and twist. I heard her yell. And it come on me to just turn my back and walk out the door and leave her lay. I seen myself walk off down the mountain where it was dark and no stars to speak of, and it was quiet and no yellin. I never done it, but it come on me. It don't matter I never done it. It come on me, and I say it is my shame.

The young un come and she did not die. She laid there quiet. I taken it and washed it and done lak them women done at Old Man Marmadukes. I laid it down on the bed alongside of Marie, and I covered it and her up good. Then I chunked up the fire, what was gittin low to ash, and put on some more wood. Then I set down in a chair. I set there till day.

Thirteen

EVEN though one of the windows of the taxi was lowered slightly, she was hot. It was January, but the day was like spring, the early afternoon sun beating down on the glittering ditches along the highway slab and on the green winter pastures. Only the smoky leaflessness of the woods on the ridges to the west defined the season. A beautiful and promising day with a sense of slowly swelling, last-minute repose before the fecund stirring. But it was false. By night the snow might be moving up the broad valley, the flakes hissing at the surface of the river, swarming dryly among the leafless black branches on the ridges. Now, however, it was a bright, perfectly peaceful afternoon, and the taxi whirred evenly up the highway between the pastures. Not another car was in sight.

Sue threw back her coat, and in the act scrutinized again the dark-blue velvet of the dress she wore—blue velvet with a beaded embroidery around the skirt, and an embroidered collar. *My God,* she commented in her mind, fingering the beads. *My God, suppose we had an accident and they picked me up wearing this thing.* She looked down at her out-thrust feet, on which were the gold sandals which she had worn the previous evening, stained now from the damp and grease of the pavements down by the river. *My God,* she thought, *I look just like a whore.*

But Rosemary wasn't a whore, and it was Rosemary's dress. It was Rosemary's Sunday dress. A whore was sure one thing Rosemary would never be. God never meant Rosemary for a whore. Not the way Rosemary was. Rosemary could wear any dress and not look like a whore. She could wear this dress, and above all that beaded junk of the collar the eyes would look at you like there wasn't anything you could do or say to hurt her or help her, and her face would be pulled and white like it had been washed in alum, and her legs would stick out from under that beaded junk on the skirt, with the braces.

It was Rosemary's good dress, and Rosemary had made her take it. She began to pick at the beading on the skirt.

171

She had come, in a taxi, to Rosemary's rooming house, just before light. The front door had been unlatched, as she had surmised it would be, and she had tiptoed up the dark stairs to Rosemary's room. She had pushed open the door, gently, and holding it ajar, had peered in at the figure on the bed, which was illuminated by a little light from the street lamp outside.

Rosemary lay on her back, one hand laid across the covers on her breast, her mouth slightly open. She called her name several times, softly, until she opened her eyes and turned. Then she walked in, and closed the door, with her hand lifted to compel silence. She stood at the foot of the bed and looked down at the twisted covers, and said: "I want to stay here tonight. The rest of the night."

Rosemary, half rising, shoved herself a little to one side, and seemed about to speak, but Sue said: "No, no, I don't want to lie down. Not now, anyway." She sat on the side of the bed, aware of Rosemary's eyes fixed on her from the bedclothes, like the eyes of some small animal surprised in its hole or in the grass, and then looked at the streaks of light the street lamp made in the shredded window shade. She sat there a long time, knowing that Rosemary was watching her, and wondered how long it would take Rosemary to get up the nerve to ask her something. To ask her what was the matter. If anybody came in her room at four or five o'clock in the morning, she'd ask them something all right. But Rosemary didn't say anything.

"I walked out on Jerry," Sue said, thinking, *I've said it, I've said it again, and it's true.*

"Oh," Rosemary uttered sharply, as though struck by a sudden stitch of pain.

"I walked out on him," Sue affirmed, with a touch of defiance now.

"Oh," Rosemary breathed.

"He was sitting there, out at the club with a lot of people—God, how I hate those people, that slinky little slit-eyed Morgan girl, I hate her—and I just got up and I—" And she began to tell how it had been. At least, she tried to tell how it had been. The reason was slipping away, as if you tried to grab a handful of quicksilver. The reason—it was heavy and real and shining, but you couldn't hold it. But the fact was there, and the fact of the horrible way she felt, like they had cut her open and taken something out. She knew she could go back to Jerry and she wouldn't have to say a word about what had happened. She could just go to his apartment and sit and wait for him to come, and he would come in the

172

door. And he wouldn't say a word—not a word—and damn him, damn him, he wouldn't say a word—it would be like nothing had happened, and that was the horrible thing, for something had happened, and he ought to say something, get mad and do something or say something, but he wouldn't, oh, not Jerry! Oh, he would just act like nothing had happened. Oh, why, why couldn't it be like nothing had happened? Why couldn't she be what she had been, why couldn't you ever be the way you had been?

"Go to him, go to him," Rosemary was saying, staring at her, "go to him and apologize—"

"Apologize!" Sue echoed, and laughed almost soundlessly with a tight constriction in her throat, and laughing thought, *apologize, apologize.*

"Yes, yes, go to him and tell him you're sorry!"

"But I'm not!" Sue burst out, "I'm not sorry. Not that way."

"You mustn't say that, you mustn't," Rosemary said, rising on her arm so that the bedclothes fell off her bony shoulders. "Not after you've been the way you've been with him. And he loves you. I know he loves you, and you love him—"

"I don't love anybody," Sue said, quietly, and watched with astonishment while Rosemary began to cry.

Rosemary sat up in bed, hunching forward, her shoulders bare except for the straps of the stringy pink nightgown, and the tears ran down her tight cheeks, and she reached out one hand gropingly and imploringly toward Sue. The hand touched her on the arm, seizing the fur of the coat, clenching on to it with those thin, schooled, steely fingers, and drawing her. She allowed herself to be drawn sidewise, leaning, until her head lay in Rosemary's lap, the crumpled bedclothes against her face and Rosemary's hands holding her and smoothing her hair and Rosemary's tears dribbling down on her. She lay there like a stone, submitting herself to the grief which was not hers and which she did not understand, and wondered in self-revulsion why she always had to run to somebody, why she always had to spill her guts. After a while, lying there, she dozed off.

When Rosemary, still sitting up with bare shoulders in the cold room and holding her, shook her to wakefulness, it was daylight.

"I'm sorry," Rosemary said, "but I've got to get up. I'm sorry to have to wake you up, but I've got an eight-o'clock class."

Sue sat up. She scarcely remembered standing up to take off her coat and dress and kick off her shoes before she got into bed. The first shock of the sheet was cold, then she moved over into the patch of warmth which the other girl's body had left, and let her head sink into the already dented pillow, which smelled faintly of face powder. Before Rosemary was ready to leave, she was sleeping like a baby.

Around noon, Rosemary woke her, saying she didn't know but she thought maybe she wanted to get up. Yes, Sue said, she wanted to get up. Could she borrow a dress, she asked, anything, just something she could wear that wouldn't hang out from under her coat like her evening dress, so she could go get a cup of coffee and go home.

"Yes," Rosemary said. "Yes, if I've got anything you—you can wear—you—" She opened the wardrobe creakily, to exhibit the stuff hanging there. She fingered the several limp dresses, looking at them, then at Sue's face, then back at the dresses. "I don't know— I don't know what—" and she hesitated.

"Oh, anything," Sue said impatiently.

Rosemary took the Sunday dress out of the wardrobe, holding it carefully out from her body, toward Sue. "Will this be all right?" she asked, and with her free hand smoothed delicately the beaded embroidery of the collar.

"Not that," Sue said, "something old, you know, just something."

Rosemary, bracing herself against the foot of the bed, moved toward her, holding out the dress. "No," Rosemary said, a hint of anxious humility in her voice, almost belied by a sternness, almost as of command, which her face showed, "take this one. You better take this one. If—"

"It will be lovely," Sue said, and took the dress.

When she came back from the bathroom, Rosemary was picking up the evening dress, which had been flung to the floor, and was preparing to hang it in the wardrobe. "Hell," Sue said, "don't bother about that thing."

But Rosemary hung it carefully in the wardrobe.

"I've got to go," Sue said, "before my family gets out the police. If they haven't done it already. But families don't like to get out the police. It isn't good advertisement. They'll figure I stayed with one of the girls out at the dance, but they won't like it."

Then she added: "No, they won't like it at all." She turned to the door, and stopped. "Thanks for the dress," she said, and went out.

She went to the corner restaurant, telephoned her home and told Anse, who answered, to tell her mother that she would be home soon, and got a cup of coffee, and called a taxi.

That was how it had been, and now, while the taxi whirred down the white slab between the sunlit pastures, she sat up very

174

straight and thought, *Why do I have to always spill my guts?* Her fingers worked methodically, unconsciously, at the beading on the skirt. She got a bead off, and rolled it between forefinger and thumb.

"Turn in here, Miss?" the taxi driver asked, slowing down as they approached the stone pillars of her father's gate.

"Yes," she said.

The taxi moved up the winding drive, up the rise. There, flanked by the cedars and the leafless oaks, was the house, isolated, beautiful, the sun glinting on the white pillars, secure, shuttered, perfect. There was no sign of life there except a single wisp of smoke sprigged into the blue sky. She had lived there. She would go into the high hall and see herself in the big mirror.

She would go and change into riding clothes and get her mare and ride. She would ride, by herself, in the sunlight, across the open pastures and up the trail to the east ridge. At least, she could do that. Until night. By herself.

She paid the driver, and went to the door. It was not latched. She stepped into the hall, closing the heavy door softly behind her, and stood to listen. There was not a sound in the house. Then, almost with a sense of unfamiliarity, she moved across the hall to the stairs, and ascended. When she turned into the upstairs hall, she saw that the door of her mother's sitting room was open. She hesitated. She knew her mother would be in there—she knew as surely as though she saw her lying there on the chaise longue, her pretty ankles crossed before her, her hands whitely clutching an opened book on her lap, her head lying back on the cushion, her eyes closed, or wide and fixed irrelevantly on a corner of the room, and the brow constricted slightly and the flesh of her face tautened, ever so delicately. Then she walked down the hall, approaching the door.

"Sue?" her mother's voice called from the room.

"Yes," she said. She stopped at the door, and leaned against the frame.

"Sue," Dorothy Murdock began, and sat up on the chaise longue.

"Yes," Sue said.

"Where were you? Why didn't you—"

"I spent the night with a friend." She let her coat slip from her shoulders, and stood there, letting it hang across her arm, with an air of patience.

Dorothy Murdock seemed about to speak, then did not, her eyes upon her daughter.

"Go ahead," Sue said, "ask me who it was. If you don't trust

175

me. Go ahead and ask me. Father told you to talk to me. I know he did, didn't he? Just as soon as Anse told you I was coming, you called him up, and he said for you to talk to me. Didn't he?"

"Your father—" Dorothy Murdock began.

"Well, I'll tell you and you can tell him. When he comes home. Or go ahead and telephone him. I stayed with a friend."

Dorothy Murdock did not speak.

"Where do you think I got this dress?" Sue demanded. "Look at it!" She lifted her arms and half turned, like a mannequin. "Where do you think I got it if I didn't borrow it from a friend? Does it look like one I'd buy? I wouldn't be caught dead in it," she affirmed. Then, when her mother still did not speak, but only looked at her, she continued: "Look at it. It doesn't fit, does it? I'll tell you why it doesn't fit. It belongs to a cripple, and I'm not crippled—"

"Oh, Sue, Sue—" her mother said, and moved her hands on her lap.

"I'll tell you who it was. So you can tell Father. It was Rosemary."

"Rosemary?"

"Yes. Rosemary Murphy. You saw her. When she was out here that day. And this is her dress. It is her best dress."

"That crippled girl? That girl who—"

"Yes, that's the girl. Tell Father. I know he doesn't like her. But I like her. Even if she is poor and crippled. She's brave and strong, she's got nerve—"

"Oh, Sue, Sue—"

"Call her up and ask her if I didn't stay there last night. Make Father call her up and ask her. I'll tell you her number—4683W."

"Oh, it's not that, Sue. It's just you didn't think enough of us to let us know. You didn't come home and you didn't call, and I'm your mother—"

"I told Rosemary to call up this morning early," she lied. "When she went to her eight-o'clock class."

"And a strange man called up late last night and asked for you. And I was worried. And this morning your father was furious. He didn't say anything but he was furious. And I was so worried." Her hands moved on her lap, then subsided. "I would have thought—I would have thought Gerald would be considerate enough to telephone this morning. But he didn't. I would have thought—"

Sue laughed. "He didn't know where I was," she said, and watched the surprise on her mother's face. "And he won't know," she declared, "ever—he won't know anything about me any more—" and her voice lifted in a kind of echo of the triumph which she suddenly discovered in her bosom, "not ever! Because—" and she watched her mother's face, carved like alabaster into an expression of pained surprise, beautiful, white, static, commemorative, "I walked out on him. I didn't say a word. I just got up and walked out."

"Oh, Sue, you didn't!"

"I certainly did, and I'm through." She advanced into the room and stood directly before her mother.

"You didn't, you can't. Not now, now everything's—" she rose from the chaise longue and moved to and fro, her hands laid together before her at the level of her waist, "now everything's—"

"Nothing, nothing," Sue said remotely, "nothing at all."

"Now everything's—oh, we thought—your father thought—"

"I know what he thought. Oh, I know. You think I don't know, but I do. I know now. I know right this minute, and I'll tell you." Her mother stopped moving, and stood still and looked at her. "Yes, I know—he couldn't run me—like he runs you, like he runs everybody—and he thought Jerry could, and he runs Jerry—and it'd be the same thing. Oh, yes, they get off in corners and talk. They talk about me. Don't think I don't know. You think I'm a fool. Oh, he thinks he can make Jerry run me, like he tries to make you run me—like today—he tries to make you talk to me because he won't. And he won't run me. Not if he runs the whole world. Because—" her voice sank, and she paused, intoxicated and bemused by the sudden new thought which surprisingly was in her like a light. "Because—" and her voice sank to a whisper, as though she was not speaking to the woman before her, but to herself, "because I'm going to walk out of this house."

"Oh, Sue!"

"I'm going to, and I can. I've got the money Granny left me, and I can use it now I'm twenty and nobody can stop me. She was your mother but she left what little she had to me. Why—do you know why? Because she hated him—and she knew you'd never have the nerve to use that money for anything. But I have the nerve, and I—"

"Oh, Sue—"

"Oh, Sue, Sue—that's what you say—oh, Sue, Sue. But you don't care. Not really. Not any more. You used to, a long time ago, but not any more. You wanted me to marry and get out of this house. You wish everybody would go away. So you could just sit here— oh, I know, I know!"

"Stop!" Dorothy Murdock exclaimed, and lifted her hands imploringly, distractedly, toward her daughter, and moved her head from side to side with a lost motion like a head on a pillow. "Stop, Sue, stop!"

"You thought I didn't know, but I do. You get up here and drink. That's what you care about. Just that. Not anything else in the world. You don't do anything. Why don't you do something? I'd do anything, something, anything—" She grasped her mother by the arms and shook her, as though to awaken her or compel her. Then, looking into her face, she released her hold, and let her own arms sink with a motion of resignation. "But you won't," she said. "You won't even go. But I'm going!"

She rushed to the door, then turned. "Call up Father and tell him. He can't get here in time. And even if he did, he couldn't stop me."

She ran down the hall to her own room.

She took two suitcases from the closet, flung them open on the floor, and began to throw clothes into them, items seized almost at random from the racks in the closet, and then from the drawers of a chiffonier. She ran to her bathroom, laid a towel on the floor, and piled toilet articles and cosmetics promiscuously into it, and gathered it up by the corners, and returned. She sat on the floor by the suitcases trying to cram the stuff in. When something didn't fit easily she flung it aside. One big box of talcum came open and spilled into the suitcase. She cast it aside with unnecessary violence. It left a white trail across the deep-blue carpet, and poured the powder out in a heap near the bed.

She glanced up and saw her mother standing in the doorway, silently, as though she had stood there for a long time.

"Telephone him," Sue ordered. "Go and telephone him."

Dorothy Murdock did not answer.

"Go ahead. Tell him. If you don't he'll be furious. He won't say anything—oh, no, he won't say anything—and he won't beat you—oh, no—but you know how his jaws will be and you can see the white come around his mouth. Call him, call him up, or he'll be furious."

Dorothy Murdock's face was composed and still, her hands hung at her sides, and she watched her daughter. The girl seemed about to speak again, but, caught in that gaze, did not. Her right hand, which held a blouse ready to cram into one of the suitcases, stopped in mid air. She looked at her mother's face and knew that she had never seen it that way before, never before, unpained, unreproachful, complete in its ritual calm, victorious, the look of having

178

come through something and being on the other side of something. "Mother," she exclaimed, and thought, *Oh, if she were just like that, if I were like that, if things were only like that!* "Mother," she said, and dropped the blouse, and got up, and went across the floor toward her, and seized her by the upper arms, as she had done before.

"Oh, mother," she said quietly.

She heard a door open and close, distantly, somewhere in the back of the house.

"Mother," she said, "I lied. I didn't tell Rosemary to call up."

Then, as she looked into her mother's face, she saw it contort itself helplessly and distractedly, and saw the tears start.

"Oh," Sue burst out, and jerked her hands back from the contact of her mother, "oh, everybody cries! Somebody's always crying. You—you—" she stared into the contorted face, "you don't do anything, you just cry!"

She ran back to the suitcases, and slammed them shut, and began to strap them. "Call him up, and tell him," she ordered, not looking up. "Go on! Do it now."

She strapped the suitcases, not bothering to latch them, her hands moving with a frantic, jerky violence.

She stood up and seized the handles, and started toward the door.

Her mother stepped back from the door.

She passed through, took a couple of steps down the hall, and turned. "Call him," she said, and went down the stairs, lungingly, the suitcases straining her slender arms taut and banging against her knees.

She went out the back way, leaving the door open, and into the sunshine, which was blindingly bright after the shadowy house. She hurried across the cropped lawn by the bare rose garden, toward the garage, trying to run but unable to because the suitcases banged her knees and the heels of her sandals sank and turned in the soft turf.

"Miss Sue, Miss Sue!" she heard a voice behind her, but did not turn. Then there were running footsteps behind her, and she felt a hand seize one of the suitcases. "I'm sorry, Miss Sue—I was out back and didn't hear you ring—" Anse said, and took the other suitcase. "I just didn't hear you ring—"

"I didn't ring," Sue said. She ran ahead, braced herself to lift the garage door to her section, not waiting for Anse, who called after her, and got into her roadster. The motor started almost at the touch of the button. She raced the motor, and jerked the car out of the garage. Anse stood on the running board to open the rumble seat and then began to arrange the first suitcase.

"Oh, just throw them in!" Sue ordered.

The rear wheels ripped into the gravel, with a tearing sound, spraying it back, and the car plunged forward.

Anse jumped back as some of the gravel struck his leg, and then stood to watch the blue car skid and grind around the loop of the drive. The girl's yellow loose hair, as she leaned forward over the wheel, snatched back glintingly in the rush of air. The car disappeared beyond the house.

Anse Jackson was a well-made, clean, ordinary-looking Negro man, twenty-five years old, of average height, with definitely Negroid features but a skin considerably paler than chocolate and yellow flecks in the pupils of his large eyes. He had a mustache, the hairs in it sparse and individual, and he used a prepared oil on his hair, which, naturally, was kinky. He carried a small comb in his pocket, and in moments of idleness he was accustomed to run the comb carefully and meditatively through his hair, with one hand, while with the other he would pat the hair into place. At such moments, his eyelids tended to droop over the yellow-flecked eyes, and he seemed to surrender himself to the pleasure of that even, rhythmical, clean, tingling sensation across his scalp. Occasionally, a little stain of hair oil could be seen on the collar of his white houseboy's jacket. Otherwise, he was very neat.

He had been born in a dilapidated cabin not five miles from the spot where he now stood. The cabin still existed, more dilapidated and sagging, propped up on one side by fence rails. But it was still occupied. He had seen children hanging out of the door or squatting on the bare earth before it, staring at him when he passed. He did not know the names of those children.

His father, Old Anse, grizzled and wiry now, illiterate, given to silences, a good hand with horses, now lived on the Murdock place in a two-room, decent, whitewashed board house, with Old Viry, who was fat and sleepy and too feeble to do work out now. Four years back, Anse had moved out of their house to a room over the garage. Without reproach, without words of any kind, they had watched him get his belongings together, put them into an old straw suitcase, and walk away up the hill which was dominated by the mass of the big house against the sky. Many evenings, however, especially in winter, Anse would go to the whitewashed shack and sit with the old people, in the cluttered, lairlike, low interior, unlighted except for the fitfully burning chunks on the

180

hearth. On such occasions they did not talk much. He would sit there with them, listening to the old woman's difficult respiration, until her head fell on her breast. He would not even think, then, surrendering himself to the rhythm of her wheeze or snore, the deliberate rhythm of his own heart, and the hiss of the burning wood, until drowsiness deliciously overcame him, too, rising insinuatingly about him like an unlapping flood. Then he would force himself to get up, and leave them, and return to his room over the garage, which was lighted by a single, powerful electric bulb hanging from the ceiling and which contained a cot, the straw suitcase under the cot, a chest of drawers with a mirror, a table with a stack of books, and his two suits—once the property of Bogan Murdock, but still good—hanging against the beaverboard wall under the curtain.

Now Anse stood by the garage, looking at the blue car, which was again visible on the sweeping drive down the hill. It was going very fast, dangerously fast. He watched it puzzledly. But he had been puzzled by things teachers said in the classroom. He had been puzzled by things he read in the newspapers, and by things he read in books, which told what people had said and done a long time back and which told how the world used to be. He was puzzled by the way the world was now. He was puzzled by himself, and he did not know what he wanted in the world. But he knew the world was to live in. He knew that.

The car was out of sight now, going off somewhere. He stood there for a moment more, in his somewhat crumpled white jacket, and looked down the hill. Then he glanced down at the ground at his feet. He saw how one of the rear wheels of the car had scarred deeply down into the drive, showing the damp-stained gravel below. With his foot, he scraped the gravel back into smoothness, and tamped it with his heel.

Then he started to walk slowly back to the house, across the grass. As he walked, he took out his comb and ran it through his hair and patted his hair into place. At night he wore a cap to hold his hair in place, a cap made of the top of a woman's old silk stocking. Now the sunlight, striking on his oiled, patted-down hair, gave it the look of black metal, coarsely cooled and with its rippled puddling preserved in hardness.

As he approached the house, he put his comb back into his vest pocket, where his fountain pen was clipped, a good fountain pen, and unconsciously wiped the slight film of oil on the palms of his hands off on his trousers.

✦

181

Dorothy Murdock stood in the hall, and watched her daughter rush down the stairs, stumblingly with the heavy suitcases, and pass beyond her range of vision. Then, a moment later, she heard the motor of the car as it swung by the end of the house and down the hill. Then, the house was completely still. There was no one in the house, she knew. The servants would be back in the kitchen and laundry. The old man—the heavy, bearded, dandruff-maned, asthmatic old man who had flecks of food on his beard and who looked at her from his red-rimmed eyes and did not see her—would be down at the stables, sitting there in the ammoniac gloom, alone, or with Old Anse. She was alone, and she stood there, listening intently, one hand held before her at the level of her waist, the other, closed, laid against her breast, just under the soft V-shaped depression between the tendons of the throat. The house was so still she could hear distinctly the ticking of the great clock in the hall below.

She walked down the hall and stopped in front of the telephone by her sitting-room door. She reached out her hand to lift the instrument, and for a moment held it, not quite to her head, hearing the dry buzzing. Then she replaced it on the rack.

She passed by her sitting-room door and entered the door of the bedroom which she shared with Bogan Murdock, whom she had not telephoned. It was a large, beautiful room, with many windows to the south and east, giving over the rolling grass land and toward the smoky east ridge. Her step made no sound on the deep carpet, as she walked irresolutely to the center of the room. The door of Bogan Murdock's dressing room, to her left, was open and she could see, beyond it, the chest weights on the wall and one end of the rowing machine, and she thought how, on winter afternoons, late, when it was too bad to ride or play golf, Bogan Murdock, after using those machines and bathing, would come out of that door, a Japanese robe of russet silk draped loosely over his square shoulders, and would go to the couch and adjust the sun lamp and lie down, his torso bare and the silk folded across his narrow hips and private parts. He would close his eyes, eyes smoky-blue around the bold, black pupils—they saw everything, you knew they saw everything, they saw everything you did, but he never said a word—and would lay his arms by his sides, relaxed, palms upward, as in humility and resignation, or appeal, under the rays of the lamp. The body was brown, an athlete's body, not old yet, modeled steelily, almost sparely, over an Egyptian delicacy of bone, the long arms almost too thin, almost painful, with their plaited perfection of muscle laid meticulously on the bone, and the chest plates of muscle knitted tightly to the bone box at the hollows, where the few black hairs sprouted crisply, like curled black wires. She could almost see it as she stood there in broad daylight—like a carved figure on a tomb, or like a dead body laid out ceremonially under that lamp.

She could almost see it now—and sometimes in the past, as the winter evening came on, she had seen, under the glow of the lamp, the closed eyes and humble hands and that brown, glinting body, boyishly thin, modeled by the hard will locked inside it, and she had been struck by a selfless pain, like pure grief. But grief for what, she could not understand. What she herself had lost, she could scarcely remember now.

She went to the door of her own dressing room, to her right, and opened it, and entered. She took off her gray wool dress, and dropped it across a chair, and stepped out of her shoes and pulled off her stockings. She took off her slip, and selected a negligee and mules from the closet, and put them on. She sat down at the dressing table. Looking at her own face in the mirror, she let down her hair. Then she began to brush her hair, inclining her head to one side a little, and slightly forward, as though in submission. All the while, she watched the face in the mirror. Suddenly, she laid the brush down. "Oh," she said out loud, "I wasn't like this, I wasn't like this always!"

She let her head sink forward until her forehead was in contact with the cool glass of the table top. Her hair was loose among the brushes and cosmetic jars. The glass, cool, hard, smooth, against her forehead seemed to mean something to her. But after a little while the heat of her flesh had infected it. When she lifted her head, the flesh clung resistingly to the glass with a slight filmy stickiness.

She went into the bedroom, closed the hall door, and lay down on her bed, on her back, with a comforter pulled up almost to her breast. She thought: *It* is in the other room.

She lay still, with her eyes closed, and tried to control her breath, drawing it in ever so little, letting it go ever so little, so that her diaphragm scarcely moved at all—she had the trick all right; it had come to her a long time ago, and she had it down pat, all right—and so that everything around her, the mirrors and the chairs and the hills far away out the window, all those things she couldn't see with her eyes closed but knew were there in their full vindictive certainty, seemed to draw in, too, upon themselves, and be still, like she was. *It* is in the other room, she thought, and then she had the picture of the girl in her mind.

The girl is wearing a gray dress and it is not a very good dress, and her hair is in a braid which is coming loose. Behind her is a gray house, for the paint is peeling off. There are many trees, and the grass and weeds are uncut, though it is early in the season. It is early in the season, because the winged maple seeds are coming down from the old maple by which the girl is standing. There has just been a storm, for the leaves of the maple tree glitter yellow-green with wet in the now clear, but late, sunlight, and the trunks of the trees look black. Great hailstones lie on the grass-grown brick walk, and on the drive, and glitter whitely. The wet grass seems to have its own luminescence. The wings of the wet maple seeds glitter as they flutter down in the remarkable light.

She thought: *It* is in the other room.

The girl holds a kitten in her apron. The kitten has been caught out in the storm, in the tangled grass, with the hailstones falling. It is cold, its fur is plastered to it, and the girl holds it wrapped in the apron, against her own body, under her breast. But the girl has just lifted her head to look down the drive.

She thought: *It* is in the other room.

A man comes riding up the drive. He is riding a black horse; the horse's shoulders and left haunch gleam richly in the light, the delicate legs lift fastidiously, the man's body moves, ever so slightly in that same delicious rhythmical compulsion and restraint of power, and the man, who wears no hat, smiles. The teeth are white in the brown face.

She thought: *It* is in the other room.

The horse stands still now at the edge of the drive, beside the girl, and the man looks down at her, smiling. He says that he has just come by to see how things are after the storm. The girl thanks him.

She thought: *It* is in the other room.

The man, sitting straight in the saddle, looks down and sees the kitten. Only its nose and eyes and ears are visible from the little wad of cloth which the girl holds below her breast. The man looks down, and says: Poor little thing.

She thought: He said it, he said, Poor little thing. And it died from the cold, and I love it, but he said, Poor little thing.

She clutched the comforter into a wad, just under her breast, as the girl had held the kitten.

She thought: I don't love anything now.

She opened her eyes and sat up, still clutching the comforter. She thought: *It* is in the other room. And flung the comforter back, and rose from the bed, and without bothering to put on the mules,

184

went to the door and opened it and looked out into the hall. There was nobody in the hall. She went swiftly into her sitting room, her bare feet making no sound, and to her desk. From the desk she took a bottle, a quart bottle of whisky. She ran her thumb nail under the seal, cutting the paper, and then tried to pull the cap of the cork. It would not come. She grasped the bottle in both hands, lifted it as though to drink, and set her teeth at the crevice just under the cap. Then, with the lips drawn back, with her hands clutching the bottle until the knuckles were white, she began to pull, moving her head a little from side to side to loosen the cork. It came slowly; then, with a slight *pop,* was free. A little of the liquid spilled over her hands. She let the stopper fall from her teeth, to the floor, then drank from the bottle. She took a deep draught, stopped swallowing, and breathed without taking the bottle from her lips, and drank again. She lowered the bottle, still holding it in both hands, and breathed heavily, closing her eyes. She went to the bathroom, got a glass from a cabinet, poured whisky into it, and added a little water from the tap of the basin. Then she took another drink from the bottle, corked it and put it into the desk, and carrying the glass, returned to the bedroom.

She set the glass on the floor by the bed, and again lay down. She had locked the door.

With her eyes closed, she felt the whisky flower inside her, and then its tentacles reached out delicately into her body. She thought: The light had never been like that before, green-gold light and bright after the storm and you thought it came from the underside of the leaves, too, and from the grass, for it was everywhere, and I held the kitten in my arms and I loved it and I knew it was going to die, but he came and looked down from his horse and said, Poor little thing. She thought: But that was then, not now, and I was that then and I don't know what I am.

She controlled her breath, as she had before, reducing it to the barest minimum of movement. She thought that she might go to sleep. And if she didn't go to sleep, she could lie here. She could lie here with her eyes closed and her breath scarcely moving, and that was almost as good.

She thought: When I shut my eyes I am nothing but that burning where the whisky is in me and the rest of me just flowing away, and that is all there is, and if I don't think of anything I am not anything and nobody else is anything either and the feeling in me is all there is, but the feeling doesn't remember anything, and if every minute can be just that minute and not remember the minute before and not want the minute that's coming, then you can be happy like shifting downward in deep water and the water weak-green-silver-streaked-bright but your eyes closed and the water breathes into you like you were a fish and you love it and it is all around you and on you and under you like hands, and that would be all if one minute could not remember the last one and didn't want the next one, didn't want anything.

But she did. And she held her lower lip between her small, perfect teeth, and shifted her body under the blue comforter and let her head move weakly from side to side on the pillow.

She thought: I could go to sleep afterwards.

The immediately reality was her body, with its tensions and blind compulsions and aimless appetites, but she felt herself to be apart from it and from them. Yet she was horribly involved, and loathed herself for being thus involved. She was filled with that loathing, and at the same time with a pity, which was almost sweet. She thought: I could go to sleep afterwards.

But she gained a sort of strength, and sat up. "All right," she said, "all right."

She stood up, put on her mules, and went to the door, which, with a sense of shame, she unlocked. She went to the telephone by her sitting-room door and dialed a number. When the answer came, she asked for Mr. Porsum. When she heard his voice, she said: "This is Dorothy Murdock, Mr. Porsum. I understand you have a hunter, a three-year-old, for sale?"

Mr. Porsum said that that was true, that at the moment he had for sale several fair walking horses, one Arabian, two-and-a-half years old, and two hunters, both three-year-olds.

"May I drive out and see the hunters?" Dorothy Murdock asked.

Mr. Porsum replied that he would be at the farm all afternoon, and would have the hunters brought up to a paddock if she wanted to see them. They would be on hand by the time she arrived. His voice was deliberate and detached, and on the telephone somewhat more nasal than she had remembered.

She said that she would be there within an hour.

While she took a cold shower and dressed, and even as she drank off the glass of whisky and water, which she spied on the floor by the bed, she experienced a sense of competence, of moral certainty, even of victory, which was entirely new.

Dorothy Hopewell, who married Bogan Murdock, was the only descendant of a family distinguished in Georgia in the Revolutionary period and in later generations in the section across the mountains to which they moved. Her great-great-grandfather was a general in the Revolution, and fought in the Carolinas, at King's Mountain, and in Virginia. He could have made money by speculation in Continental paper and land grants, but because of a delicate conscience, did not; he grew rich more gradually. When his son went West, he carried with him the Revolutionary boots and sword, fifty-odd slaves, and two heavy money belts. Dorothy Hopewell's grandfather, a lawyer, owned at one time over three hundred slaves and was a Senator in the Confederate Congress. Her father, a kindly and incompetent man, with no head for business and a mystical streak, bowed to his strong-willed, vindictive wife and pampered his only child, Dorothy, and died a failure. When Dorothy Hopewell, at the age of eighteen, married Bogan Murdock, to whom Mrs. Hopewell condescended somewhat bitterly, the only dowry was a small, heavily encumbered property, the Hopewell name, and the Revolutionary sword, which was to hang, later, on the high wall of Bogan Murdock's library. The boots of her great-great-grandfather had long since rotted away in a family attic.

Dorothy Murdock, gentle, beautiful, and not very intelligent, inherited something of her father's temperament, remembered him with affection, was relatively untouched by the snobbery of her mother, who in poverty regarded herself as the vessel of a great tradition, bore Bogan Murdock two healthy children, rejoiced in the early successes of her husband, and enjoyed the luxuries which his increasing prosperity afforded. Looking back she could not put her finger on the moment of change. But she discovered before she was forty that she scarcely loved the children, that her husband was strange to her and self-sufficient, and that she was in the powerful grip of secret, insidious, and suicidal vices, which drained her life of all meaning and the world around her of all reality. She believed in love and wanted to be loved; she could not achieve even bitterness, richness of fantasy, or violence. And there was nobody in the world to whom she could talk.

When, on that bright January afternoon, she conquered herself, threw back the blue comforter, and unlocked the door to her bedroom, she felt that she was discovering something new in herself. She felt clean and strong, like one who gets on a train, with plenty of money in pocket, to take a long trip, to new places. She did not speculate about the source of her new strength. She did not reflect on the earlier events of the day. And she had no specific plans for the future. She was, simply, moving back into the world, and the world was real.

Fourteen

Statement of Ashby Wyndham

WE NAMED him Frank for the old Frencher her father who had a name like Frank in French talk. He had blue eyes lak the old Frencher had. He was a buster and he thrived good. But Marie was puny. It looks lak you can't tell about women. A man gits him one of them big stout-lookin women whats got good teeth and is full of laughin and bouncin, but she has her a young un and it ain't no time till she is draggin and ain't no good for nuthin. And I seen lots of them little spry women quick lak Marie when she had a mind what has a half a dozen kids and it ain't nuthin to them. My Mammy was little and spry and nuthin never fazed her. Marie, it got so she was not no account for nuthin. She taken yerbs and such what the women give her and boughten medicine. And it got so bad I got a doctor from Cashtown. But he could do nuthin but retch out his hand and say gimme when payin time come.

She done her work, but it was trial and strain. She done her best, but many a time I come in from work and she was settin there white in the face and it was me put the skillit on the stove. She always was a hand to set still and quiet, but now she was still and there was not no sparkle come. There was not no sparkle in her no more. Except may be and it rare when she taken up little Frank and helt him.

I spent money for her, but it did not do no good. She seen me when I taken money out of that tin can where I kept it, and she said for me not to. She said she didn't want Jacobs money spent on her. Hell, I said, it is my money. She said to keep it, that a time might be comin when we would need it worse. Hell, I said, we couldn't need it no worse.

But the time come. The Company boss said they wasn't goin to pay us like afore. They was goin to cut our pay ten cents for ever

188

hour. It come to a lot ever week. They said the Company wasn't makin nuthin and they couldn't pay it lak afore.

A man was there workin in the sawmill by the name of Sweetwater. Nobody knowed where he come from but he come there short after me. He was a chunky-built man and stout and he was a good hand at the mill everybody said. He never got in no trouble or nuthin. He was good-dispositioned and laughed. But he said the Company had plenty of money. He said he knowed it had plenty. He said he knowed who got the money and it was them rich fellers what taken the money from the Company. He said they was rich fellers what taken the money what by rights ought to come to them as had bought a piece of the Company and to us what worked for the Company. He said he knowed. He said if everybody quit workin for the Company all of a sudden and didn't nobody work for them, then they would have to pay us good. They would have to pay us more than afore. He said it was ourn, and that was the way folks done to git paid better. He got folks to listen to him, and them as listened to him talked to other folks. Three weeks and everybody quit. It was a strike, what they called it.

They was fellers from the city come to talk. They made speeches and talked and said how the Company couldn't pay no more and how folks ought to know it and git back to work. Unless they wanted to starve and not git nuthin. But they wasn't but a few and them not many what wanted to git back to work. Then they brung in strangers to the Mountain to work. They was all sorts of folks. They wasn't no tellin where they come from. They was goin to do our work, and them strangers, and us git nuthin. That was what Sweetwater said. He said was we goin to let them sons of bitches do it and us git nuthin. He said wan't no true man would do it. He said he wouldn't. He taken his stand and ast them as would be true men to git by his side. He talked good. They come to him. I wasn't the fust, but I never tarried. I was amongst them as stood by his side.

He said not let them fellers work. He said not let them git in the sawmill nor touch a ax or crosscut in them tool sheds nor lay hand to harness to hitch air mule nor put yoke on ox. He said to git somethin be it ax handle or canthook or lug hook or roll hook, and stand up there and keep them fellers off. But he said not to use no gun or cuttin knife. He said not to use no canthook nor nuthin but yore bare knucks if them fellers did not use nuthin else. He said just have them things layin there.

We kept them fellers off. They tried three times. Two times it was bare knucks and then they come with one thing and another they had laid holt to. Sweetwater picked him up a canthook and yelled, come on boys it is going to be a play party. It was not no play party for some of them fellers. It was busted heads and busted arms and legs. They was layin on the ground and they drugged them off. Them fellers didn't stay on the Mountain. Then the Company brung more fellers and constables and depities with guns. Them constables come up with guns, and told us to git off, and Sweetwater looked at them and said, hell, they ain't goin to shoot nobody, they shoot somebody and they ain't got enuf bullets to go round if the boys git mad. He told them to shoot him if they wanted to start. They never shot him. Them other fellers stayed there on the Mountain but they never bothered us for two days more. Then they said they was another big strike nigh Cashtown, and another one in the coal.

Then Private Porsum come on the Mountain. He made another speech at Tomtown, and told how the Company could not pay no more and how we was breakin the law. Folks from Cashtown and Tomtown come and told us. They said the folks hearkened good to the Private. Sweetwater said the Private was with the rich fellers and was lyin, and a feller said Private Porsum never lied, he was not no man to lie. That feller said he believed the Private because he come off the Mountain.

He has done come a long way off the Mountain, Sweetwater said.

He ain't forgot, the feller said.

May be he ain't forgot, Sweetwater said, but he ain't forgot neither how it feels to have money in the bank and he ain't forgot where he gits his money. He gits it from them rich fellers for talkin lak they tells him. And he gits it off yore back and gits it off yore table.

It is a lie, the feller said.

Then everybody looked for Sweetwater to do somethin, to hit him or somethin for callin him a liar. We seen how he told that constable to shoot him and give him the dare, and then Sweetwater didn't do nuthin but let that feller call him a liar.

I ain't sayin how Sweetwater didn't do right. Maybe he done Bible right. I swear and believe he done right. But then it made me plum disgusted. I was not no Bible man in them days. I was in the dark and the wicked world. I was sunk down in the worlds ways. I was plum disgusted for Sweetwater.

Then Sweetwater ast him, you got kids ain't you?

The feller said, yes.

They got shoes on the feet, Sweetwater ast him.

Naw, the feller said.

190

They got plenty cover on the bed, he ast him.

Shet up, the feller said.

They got meat and bread on the table, Sweetwater ast him.

The feller never said nuthin, he just looked at Sweetwater.

They don't stand round, Sweetwater ast him, and say, Pappy gimme somethin to eat.

The feller never said nuthin but I seen him squinch up round the eyes lak he was sightin down a gun barril, and aimin at Sweetwater.

They don't wake up in the night, Sweetwater ast him, and say, Pappy I'm hongry.

Then that feller just yelled, God damn yore soul. And he jumped at Sweetwater, swingin his arms.

But he never hit him. They grabbed him fust.

Folks was standin there and seen it. But they seen too how Sweetwater taken a lie offen him.

Then Private Porsum come on the Mountain. He stood on a wagin and made a speech. I knowed he was my cousin but I never seen him afore. I knowed how he was in the war and what he done to them Germins. I knowed how he never taken nuthin for killin no human man, and how he would not be nuthin but a private soljer. I heard him talk. He was a big fine-lookin man, standin up there on that wagin, and he talked good.

A feller standin alongside of me, he said, Ashby, ain't he yore cousin?

I said he was my cousin. He was my second blood cousin.

The Private said the Company was doin good as it could. He said they couldn't pay no more. He said if they paid more there wouldn't be no Company in no time, and everybody would be ruint. He said to git back to work lak the folks done nigh Cashtown and at Tomtown and down at the coal mine. He said he come to say it because he had not never forgot how the folks on the Mountain was his own folks. He said he come to ease his mind because he did not want to know of no trouble amongst his own folks.

Then somebody yelled, Private, how you git yore money?

I knowed it was Sweetwater. He was standin nigh me and I knowed his voice.

The Lord has prospered me, Private Porsum said, and said he give thanks.

The Lord and the Massey Mountain Lumber Company, Sweetwater yelled.

191

Folks stepped back from round Sweetwater. There was just me and him standin nigh.

The Lord and the Atlas Iron Company, Sweetwater yelled agin. Then somebody yelled for him to shet up.

But he never stopped. He yelled, Private, who sent you up here?

I come to ease my mind, the Private said, and do right.

Private Porsum, Sweetwater yelled, do you stand there and say before God and man nobody sent you up here?

I say it, the Private said.

And I, Sweetwater yelled, and he stopped and everybody looked at him, say it's a God-damn lie. And he laughed.

I was standin nigh, and I seen him when he called the Private a lie. He had done taken the lie hisself offen a feller and everybody standin by and no shame it looked lak. And now give the Private a lie. It made me disgusted and sick to puke when Sweetwater taken that lie hisself and just laughed, and now he give the Private a lie and a man as takes a lie and don't do nuthin but laugh, he ain't got no right, it looked lak to me, to be puttin the lie on nobody. I didn't say it so to myself all of a sudden, but it come to me later that-a way. I just seen him put a lie on the Private and him my cousin, and lak I got disgusted afore I got mad. I got mad all of a sudden. I give it to Sweetwater.

I give him a jolt on the side of the head. He come down on his knee, and I give it to him agin. But he was tough. Afore I knowed it he done butted me in the stomach and grabbed me. He wasn't no big man, but stout in the arms. He nigh throwed me and me beatin on him. But I snaked him with my leg and we come down. He got my arm twisted and nigh broke it and me beatin on him. He would broke it if I hadn't laid holt of a chunk of rock. I never knowed I grabbed it. I give it to him right in the face. He slipped his holt and I seen the blood on his face and him layin there. I seen the chunk in my hand lak I never knowed I had helt it. Then I seen him and it looked lak I didn't care if I had hit him with a chunk.

I done a lot of fightin in my time of sin and revelin. But I always fit fair. If it was bare knucks it was bare knucks, if it was stomp and gouge it was stomp and gouge. I always let the other feller call the tune and hist the burden. I never used no chunk on nobody. But it was a chunk I give Sweetwater, and it looked lak I didn't care. It was on me so. He started to git up and I kicked him. Right in the side.

Then some feller come at me. They was fightin all round of a sudden. Some fellers was aimin to help Sweetwater, but not no

192

plenty, and fellers was fightin them. Sweetwater tried to git up but some feller was beatin on him.

They was not many fellers with Sweetwater. Them others beat them good. Constables taken Sweetwater and some of the others with him and put them in jail down at Cashtown. I never seen him agin. They said he was bad beat up.

I am sorry and grieve I used a chunk on Sweetwater. I ought never kicked him. I ought never lifted up my hand agin him in no way. If I had helt my hand, may be nuthin would happened. May be they would not been no fightin. May be the Company would paid us good and decent. May be they would not come no bad times on the Mountain lak come, and not long. It has come to me Sweetwater was a good man.

But I ain't never said the Private was not no good man. A big man lak him what never taken nuthin for doin what he done to them Germins, he ain't goin to take money offen pore folks, and them his own folks and with young uns. I ain't never said he did not aim to do good lak he said when he come on the Mountain. It ain't for me to judge. Not him nor no man. Not and me what I been and what I am. Oh, Lord, I was dirt and you taken me up from the dark ground and blowed yore breath in me, but I am sinful and weak.

Fifteen

SLIM SARRETT, sitting at the long trestle table beside the windows of his attic room, removed his gaze from the swollen, muddy river below him, where the coal barges, and the plank skiffs half awash, and an old side-wheeler were tied up at the bank and where the grimy, black, stoical bridges humped to support the traffic, from which the sounds blurred out at that height. His tall, monkish skull, on which the dark hair lay neatly, leaned forward, and he began to write on a sheet of legal foolscap in a meticulous hand, which resembled printing. He wrote:

"The theme underlying Shakespearean tragedy—Elizabethan tragedy, in fact—is usually misstated. It is misstated because the terms in which it is cast are taken as content-absolutes. These terms are: (1) character, (2) situation and plot, (3) statement—by which I mean statement in a paraphrasably valid sense, and (4) language as poetic instrument. The terms in their special forms are the terms historically available at the moment of composition. But the business of criticism is, ultimately, to disengage itself from the historical accident—which, I grant, can only be achieved by mastery of the historical accident. When criticism immerses itself in the historical accident, it can only be, at its best, an inferior parody of the art-object, which has already manifested itself as superior to the historical accident; at its worst, it represents an attempt to disintegrate the rose into the dung which fertilized the root.

"To return: the terms are character, situation and plot, statement, and language as poetic instrument. Only the naïve critic takes the statement in a play as a content-absolute. A more intelligent critic complacently says: 'Because Lear says so-and-so, I am not to infer that Shakespeare meant so-and-so; we must remember that Lear is a character in a play.' And the critic falls back exhausted. But the same critic takes character or plot as a content-absolute. A bad man, King Richard III, commits various crimes to gain a throne. His faculties then begin to fail, he has bad dreams, becomes confused, commits tactical errors, and is enveloped in

194

ruin. The critic, who has just renounced statement as a content-absolute, accepts character and plot as content-absolutes, and says: We see from what happens to Richard III that Shakespeare believed in and depicted a universe operating according to a moral order.' Indeed? We do not *know* that Shakespeare *believed*, as he may have done, in a moral order—by which the critic means an awarding of benefits and punishments vaguely according to the Christian scheme of values. (And the critic forgets, or blandly neglects, the tissue of negative instances surrounding the central character—good men brought to ruin, etc.—ah, where are the pretty little princes in the Tower?) What we do *know* is, simply, that Shakespeare depicted a universe recognizably like our own—in which good men are brought to ruin. But, says the critic, Shakespeare never painted vice as prosperous. The answer is: He did something far more reprehensible; he painted virtue brought to misery. Which leaves us where we were: All we *know* is that Shakespeare depicted a universe recognizably like our own.

"On this shoal water of morality, criticism, even when flying the Jolly Roger of estheticism, has foundered whenever it has undertaken to investigate the tragic theme. It has foundered because it has taken character (good-bad) and plot (prosperity-ruin) as content-absolutes. The critic replies: 'But Shakespeare did write about these things and interpret them, in plot and character, in a certain way.' Certainly. He could use nothing else as an overt subject— for that was what his world offered him at his moment. And his 'interpretations'—by which I mean the logical correlation of character, plot, etc.—could scarcely have been different from what it was because it was what his world offered him—the frame of tragedy. But the critic has simply taken the several terms in which the tragedy is cast—the plot-character frame—and called them a content-absolute under the name of 'interpretation.' But this interpretation, so called, was, as I have already said, part also of the material offered by Shakespeare's world—the tortured residuum of the Christian tradition. That 'interpretation' is simply part of the stuff available—like Plutarch or Holinshed or Marlowe's mighty line or the condition of the language; it is no more an end-product of the Elizabethan creative process than are the other items just mentioned. The end-product is Elizabethan tragedy itself. The other items—character, plot, that is, the frame—are simply metaphors, items wrenched from the contexts of theology, ethics, Tudor and classical history, romance, etc., and employed as metaphor in a gigantic series of discourses—the tragedies.

"These discourses are upon one theme. That theme is not to be defined by an investigation, however necessary at one stage, of any one of the metaphors involved; this is the program of historical criticism. (Historical criticism can give us only the origins of the individual metaphors, and define them.) The theme is to be defined only by an investigation of the dynamic interpenetration of all the metaphors of the one discourse, and a comparison among the several discourses.

"I shall state the theme immediately and simply, and shall then turn to evidence: the necessity for self-knowledge. The tragic flaw in the Shakespearean hero is a defect in self-knowledge. Macbeth comes to ruin, not because he kills (Shakespeare could scarcely have been so naïve as to believe that men have not killed and then ruled in prosperity and dreamless sleep—he had, we know, read Holinshed), but because he does not realize upon what grounds it is possible for him, Macbeth, to kill. Bacon wrote: Knowledge is power. Bacon was thinking of knowledge of the mechanisms of the external world. Shakespeare wrote: Self-knowledge is power. Shakespeare was thinking of the mechanisms of the spirit, to which the mechanisms of the external world, including other persons, are instruments. In other words, Shakespeare was interested in success. By success, he meant: Self-fulfillment. But his tragedy is concerned with failure. Naturally. The successful man—saint, murderer, politician, pickpocket, scholar, sensualist, costermonger—offers only the smooth surface, like an egg. In so far as he is truly successful, he has no story. He is pure. But poetry is concerned only with failure, distortion, imbalance—with impurity. And poetry itself is impurity. The pure cry of pain is not poetry. The pure gasp and sigh of love is not poetry. Poetry is the impurity which an active being secretes to become pure. It is the glitter of pus, richer than Ind, the monument in dung, the oyster's pearl.

"To turn to evidence—"

That night, while waiting for the other guests to come to his studio, he read the passage to Sue Murdock.

"I have begun my essay for the Shakespeare seminar," he said, standing with his back to the fire in the grate, behind his head the cluster of old, dry boxing gloves, which hung on the wall above the mantel shelf. "That dry-balled, pismire-headed, old Timsey will not understand a word of it, and will therefore give it an $A+$. Grudgingly, but an $A+$. He will be afraid not to. Since the time he gave me a C on a paper, and when the paper was published in *The Bookkeeper* I sent him an inscribed issue of the magazine. But I have not taken advantage of his stupidity and timorousness. I have indulged myself by giving this subject careful thought, because it interests me deeply. Not only in its literary aspect. And I imagine that it will interest you."

She sipped her drink, a slightly murky mixture of corn whisky and grapefruit juice in which a jagged chunk of ice floated, and stared into the fire, and listened to his precise, somewhat brittle voice. A sentence ended with scarcely a falling inflection, existed cleanly, finally, and independently, like an object, there in the air, in her head, for the fractional moment of silence before he resumed.

"—the glitter of pus, richer than Ind—" and she saw it like a drop on a glass slide, quivering, swollen, its gold streaked emerald and amethyst and opalescent. Richer than Ind. She did not catch the words which came after. Then she was aware of his silence.

"I shan't read any more," he was saying. "Just that first part."

She did not answer, watching the fire.

"What do you think of it?" he asked.

"I don't know," she said hesitantly, "—exactly."

He laid the sheets of foolscap on the mantel behind him, pushed back a coal with the toe of his patched shoe—once black, now grayish, dry, and seamed from lack of polish—and turned to let himself sink lithely into an overstuffed chair by the hearth. "Yet," he said, "you acted Cordelia last year in the Drama School production of *Lear*." His voice was not brittle now, but modulated, rhythmical, hovering.

"I don't know—" she said.

"You were quite good," he said, "relatively. Quite good. You must have some idea of the applicability—or lack of applicability—of what I have read, to, at least, *Lear*. To the character of Cordelia—"

"I don't know—I couldn't put it into words," she said. She sat up straight in her chair, looking away from him, and held her glass in the folded fingers of both hands, on her knees, which were close together. Her feet were set side by side on the floor, almost demurely. "Oh, it wasn't exactly like anything you can say. At first, it wasn't anything, when I began to read it and study it and rehearse it. And the books I read on it, they didn't help, that stuff. Then it was different. I just knew it was different, all of a sudden, one night rehearsing, right there on the stage. I was saying:

What shall Cordelia do?
Love, and be silent.

Standing there, and then it was different, all at once. It was different from then on. When we weren't rehearsing, I just didn't want to see anybody. I was so afraid something might happen to

197

change it, to change me. But I was afraid of *it,* too. And happy, and I felt that everything was going to be different from then on, not just being in a play. I'd go to my room, in the afternoon, and lie on the bed. It was like when I was a little girl—like growing up—when I'd go by myself and lie on the bed, and be afraid, too, and happy in a funny way. It was like the first time—growing up—the first time—"

"Like first menstruation?" he asked.

She did not reply for an instant, then said, "Yes," a little flatly, took a sip from her glass, and leaned back in the chair.

"You know," he said, "that is a very interesting comparison. A very interesting metaphor. It is very subtle and precise. You say very subtle and precise things, sometimes. I have thought, recently, that you might become a very good writer. And the reading you've been doing lately—it seems to have stimulated you.— I can assure you there's very little waste motion in the books I've given to you. Or I wouldn't have given them to you.— Yes, it's quite possible that you could become a very good writer—"

"I don't want to be," she said.

"We shall see," he said, nodding his head. "You are one of the few people—take this gang coming here tonight—in whose perceptions I have any real confidence. Perhaps the only one. Yes, it's quite possible—"

"I don't want to be."

"It is not a question of what you want to be," he affirmed, the voice going brittle again. "It is a question of what you are. In the most fundamental sense, to be an artist means to *be* a certain way, not to do certain things, perform certain tricks. But if you happen to *be* an artist and repudiate the discipline of the artist you will be very unhappy. You can never define yourself then, you can never become pure, but will remain immersed in the blur of the world. You must be like a spaniel that comes out of the stream and shakes off the water. Those random drops shaken off glitter in the sun and are beautiful because entire, because no longer simply part of the blurred stream. The artist—"

"They are coming," she said, sitting up at the sound of steps and voices on the stair.

"Yes," he said, and rose from his chair, not shifting his feet and struggling for balance, but rising with his feet unmoved, and with an easy, poised, forward thrust of his torso, without effort. "Yes," he said, quietly, standing there with his feet together, his hands at his sides, inclining his almost too narrow head a little toward her, "and it is too bad they are coming, for I wanted to talk to you."

Then, as he moved toward the door, his face assumed the smile—somewhat boyish and innocent, somewhat ironical and detached—an opalescent smile, structurally constant, unpredictable and flowing in color—with which he was accustomed, on occasion, to greet the world.

His world, his immediate world, comprised the classrooms of the University; the University gymnasium and a dingy, rat-infested downtown gymnasium, in the back of a garage, run by a syphilitic ex-pugilist; the Campus Coffee Shop, and a couple of greasy riverfront restaurants; the library; and his studio.

In the classrooms, he sat erect, with his shirt collar open, his stained raincoat across his knees, and beside him a mountainous heap of books which had nothing to do with the course in question. There he was accustomed to maintain a reserved, almost respectful silence, unless directly addressed by the professor. He never took notes. Frequently he would examine his hands, which lay on the stained raincoat, flexing the long fingers slowly. His course marks were extraordinarily good.

In the gymnasium he critically inspected the style of other boxers, conversed in technicalities with other student athletes or with the bums and grimy preliminary boys who hung around the garage, and sparred with a smiling, flickering precision.

In the Campus Coffee Shop he sat for hours, at one side a cup of cold coffee from which he took occasional finicking sips, before him a book open upon the table.

In the library he never read a book, except the reserve or reference books which did not circulate. He checked books out, and left. But one afternoon a week he spent in the periodical room, reading the current magazines. He never sat down, but stood before the shelves, his raincoat draped about his shoulders, the magazine poised in his left hand, the thumb and forefinger of his right hand holding the margin of a page, ready to flick it over when he had finished. He read with tremendous rapidity, and without hesitation in selection, working around the alphabetical shelves. When he came across an item, especially a poem, which pleased him or irritated him, he walked over to the desk of a young woman who was in charge, read the piece to her in his ordinary tone, making no concession to the sign above the desk which said *Silence Please,* and gave her a short analysis of the case. He did not know the name of the girl at the desk. She was ugly and sick-looking, with a blotched skin. When he happened to meet her on the campus, they never exchanged greetings. At her desk, however, she always listened to him with a strained attention and never asked him to speak more softly. When one of his own poems appeared in a magazine, she would sneak the issue home with her when the library closed, and puzzle over it a long time.

In his studio, at the long trestle table of rough boards, he sat for hours alone, reading, writing, or looking down at the muddy, sliding, viscous coil and thrust of the river. Or he sat with friends who were accustomed to come there, silently watching them drink—he never drank and very rarely smoked—and listened to their conversation, until some chance phrase, or some idle topic, fired him to begin to speak. The studio was the center of his world. It was the spot to which he retired to relish his triumphs, and it was the garden of his secret anguish.

The studio—one big room, a boxed-off bedroom, and a kitchen of a sort with soot-streaked skylight set in the slates—was the attic of a once-fine three-story residence built in the eighties or nineties. Now it stood at the edge of the market and wholesale district, flanked by warehouses, backed by a river which had changed character, fronted by pawnshops and cleaning establishments and a cobbled street over which drays and trucks clanged and hammered all day, where children screamed in the evening, and where drunks, snow-birds, and panhandlers loitered at night.

The big rooms on the first and second floors had been cut up by board partitions to make more rooms, as the disposition of the windows permitted. Sinks and gas plates had been installed for the tenants, and the odor of old food and burnt grease was always heavy in the dark hall, where the green tapestry, faded and stained into designs of morbid fantasy, scaled from the walls. Day and night, people padded back and forth to the bathrooms, one on each floor. Many of the tenants stayed only a few days, a week, or a month, and then vanished, leaving no addresses, nameless, carrying with them the split suitcases and the parcels tied with string. But some of them were more permanent: the Jewish pawnbroker and his wife; the German delicatessen proprietor, a bachelor, who kept cages of canaries in his room and on Sunday afternoons lounged in an old Morris chair while the birds perched on his shoulders or clasped his big, hairy forefinger, like a bough; two old women; a stall keeper from the market, who was a wardheeler and fixer at the courthouse, and who drank noisily in his room late at night with his blue-jowled cronies; a foreman from the Freeman Foundries and his girl, a largish, sandy-haired woman of thirty-odd, with pale-blue, weak eyes, who, it was said, had once been a streetwalker. The only tenants who were friends of Slim Sarrett and who came to his studio were the stall keeper, and the foreman and his girl.

Into this world, Sue Murdock came, or came, at least, on those nights when she attended the parties in his studio. She began to recognize the faces in the halls, and the faces nodded at her, or spoke. And in the studio were other people, the people who, from their various motives, climbed the stairs to sit with Slim Sarrett.

There were two newspaper reporters, Jenkins and Malloy, Jenkins young, dapper, thin, speaking in a soft, confiding voice, like a salesman in an expensive shop, Malloy short, thirtyish, barrel-chested, dark, hairy, clenching a short-stemmed pipe between his teeth, and speaking in grunts. Jenkins wrote the book page of the Sunday supplement, and poems in which anatomical and ecclesiastical terms and the islands of the South Seas figured prominently. Occasionally, one of his poems in his simpler, lyric strain appeared in a box at the foot of the book page. Malloy had done police, but now covered sports. Both Jenkins and Malloy were given to obscenity, anecdotes of depravity and violence encountered in their daily occupation, and small ironies. Both were aware of the theatricality of their profession.

There was a girl in her late twenties, Alice Smythe, a native of Connecticut, educated at Vassar, who wore flat-heeled shoes, expensive and unpolished, and tweed skirts. She had grown to love the South, she said, its innocence and cruelty, its strange perverted hope, she said, and its delicious weariness. I'm an addict, she said, an addict. She often mentioned the pure, sculptural quality of the Negro head. She often watched an old Negro for hours, she said, for there was so much to learn. She had the habit of laying her truly beautiful, aristocratic hands together, palm against palm, the fingers just beneath her chin, as in prayer, while she said, gently, "My dear, my dear—I have been thinking, and, you know, it's queer what I have found—" while her eyes left her listener, and an expression of sweet, melancholy inwardness came across her strong face, which was not beautiful. And she would tell what, queerly enough, she had found to be true. Or she would say, spreading her hands before her: "I have been hurt by things. But—it's true—I don't mind. I want to be hurt by things. For I want to be alive. I think it's one's duty to be hurt by things. Don't you think so?"

What she said was true. She was hurt by things, and the strong face, with its flat cheek bones, was a mask through which the shy gaze came. The foreman's girl was her special friend when they met at the studio, though they never laid eyes on each other elsewhere. They sat side by side on the couch, and Alice Smythe held the girl's fattish hand between her own beautiful ones, and said: "My dear, you are so good for me. You have taught me so much." She made her living by managing the book section of a department store. She slept with Malloy, who was the only man she had ever had, who was unfaithful to her, and who hurt her in a thousand ways, even physically. She drank prodigiously, and with each drink became more gentle, while the stridencies and argument swirled around her.

There were a young assistant professor of French and his wife. Professor Hoxley had spent two years in Paris, was competent in his profession, had written a book on mystic symbolism in French poetry of the fourteenth century, referred to himself as a medieval-ist, spoke with a thin, creaky voice through excessive teeth, and after a few drinks began to move his small, neat feet in a kind of abortive caper while his small, curved, almost malformed body twitched under its clothes. "I'm Gothic, I'm Gothic!" he would exclaim, and twitch and wriggle above the uncertain feet, like a blissful puppy. "I'm Gothic—look at me. Aren't I Gothic, hein?" And he would thrust his uneven, prematurely bald head forward and upward for inspection, waving it on the little neck stem, like a flower, above the black tie. "I'm Gothic—I ought to be on a cathedral—I'm Gothic, hein?— Only gargoyles didn't wear spectacles. Oh, never, never. I shall remove my spectacles." And he would remove his spectacles. His wife was fat, wore cheap clothes of drab colors, often sighed with a soundless exhalation, and sitting alone, not regarding her husband's vivacity, seemed to be absorbed and condemned in the mysterious, sad, tumescent processes of her own flesh. Her skin was fair, and her face reminded one inevitably of a snout. "She looks like a prize Hampshire in the death row at Sing Sing," Sue Murdock once said of her. The remark was applauded and passed around. That was after Sue had become recognized as a wit.

There were the foreman from the foundry, his girl, and the stall keeper from the market. The two men were burly and nearing middle age. Sam Ball, the stall keeper, was loud, jovial, and dressy, and full of the courthouse lore, and a good friend of Malloy, flirtatious with Alice Smythe and Sue Murdock, whose arms he pinched and to whom he told long-winded, off-color stories, prefacing them by, "Gee, and I sure heard one today, now buckle up your bra, so you won't bounce, girlie, and I'll tell ya—" Jack Morris, the foreman, was silent and watchful, and sat with a half smile on his face while the talk went on around him. Now and then his eyes would wander to his girl. He was devoted to her, and had been faithfully with her for more than five years, but he wouldn't marry her. "It just ain't in me, I reckon," he would tell her; "I just ain't giving no dare. Not gitting married or no way. Just like I ain't taking no dare off nobody." At least, that was the way she quoted him, and said he never said anything else on the subject. She talked about the matter to anyone who would listen, loudly, good-humoredly, calling on their opinion—"Now you tell him, you go over there and tell him how he ought to be. Hey, Jack, listen here—" Whenever Sam Ball saw her he greeted her: "Say, Betsy, ain't you got him to marry you yet, huh?" And she would reply: "Hell, no, and you know what that lug says to me—" She made a habit of clipping wedding photographs from the society page of the Sunday paper and from movie magazines; sometimes she would bring one of the recent clippings with her to the studio and would show it to Alice Smythe, painfully spelling out the print below: "The nuptials of ——— were solemnized today at the River Drive Methodist Church. The bride—" She would examine the photograph critically: "She's right pretty, but that veil now, it don't seem—" And Alice Smythe would pore sympathetically over the clipping with her, while Professor Hoxley, who was inevitably drawn to Betsy Dodds and leaned toward her round, amiable, blunt face and chattered to her with learned allusions, tags of French, and giggles, stood before them, talking unceasingly and unnoticed and shifting from foot to foot.

There were two or three graduate students, one in economics, who professed to be a Marxist, Rosemary Murphy, who never said anything, and Duckfoot Blake, who came rarely, got along well with Malloy, the foreman, and the wardheeler, and argued with Slim Sarrett: "Now, Slim, you claim to be a bright boy. I reckon you are a bright boy. But why ain't you bright enough to leave literature alone?— Sure, it's wonderful, and sure I got a soul, and I've read Homer in Greek and *The Black Mask* magazine in whatever it's written in—the reading of neither of which, I surmise, you number among your achievements. Literature—hell, the human race has spent the last five thousand years painting its self-portrait, and by God, it's about time it chucked the old stub brushes out the window and washed its face and squeezed out the pimples and went to a skin doctor. What makes you think your soul is so damned interesting? Hell, literature is kept going simply by a conspiracy among introverts like you who like to pick their scabs, and intellectual tat-and-crochet boys like Prof. Hoxley over there—yeah, you heard me right, Prof.—and the women's clubs. Jesus!"

And there was Sweetwater, who worked in the foundry, was a labor organizer, spent much time with Jack Morris, and played poker occasionally with Duckfoot Blake. One of his front teeth was missing, toward the left, and a scar ran jaggedly upward from the lip at that point. When he drank much, the scar showed very white.

This world was held together by Slim Sarrett. He had created it. If Slim Sarrett had not existed, the special combinations of that world would not have existed. Most of the people who came to his studio had met each other there for the first time, and most of them never saw each other elsewhere. When a new person came, Slim prepared the situation carefully, defining the new person privately to each of his friends, not overtly, all at once, but by a meticulous whetting of curiosity, appeals for opinion which he had already planted and nurtured, confessions, tinged with humility but qualified by irony, of what he himself had learned from the as yet unknown guest, little criticisms, hints at a secret which he had fathomed—all done as scrupulously and as cunningly as a dramatist prepares the entrance of his hero. Then, one evening, the new footsteps were on the stairs, and the door opened, and Slim Sarrett, smiling, with something of the air of a prestidigitator, approached for the introductions.

He watched over the new relationships and combinations, spiritual and physical, like a mother. He knew—and he was the only person who knew—that Alice Smythe was the mistress of Malloy. He had introduced them; he had been piqued by the profound lack of interest they showed in each other; he had insinuated into the mind of Malloy, the braggart, the challenge of Alice Smythe's virginity, spiritual refinement, and superior social background, and into her mind the image of Malloy as a man tortured by a wavering, thwarted sensitivity and yearning for sympathy. He knew, before she ever told him, all about the relationship, and knew—though she had not told him—that she had been seduced upon the couch in the studio. He knew, for he had planned it like a director, taking the other guests out for hamburgers, leaving the key on the inside of the studio door; for he had observed, upon returning, Malloy's indolent, alcoholic preening, her stained cheeks, and certain details of evidence which their caution had not obliterated; for, after the departure of the guests that night, he had paced the studio like a cat and then had sat alone for a long time. He was accustomed to devote a great deal of attention to Mrs. Hoxley, sitting beside her and talking of motherhood, in whispers, persuading her to talk, to tell him of her childhood. But the relationship between Alice Smythe and Betsy Dodds was his masterpiece; he leaned over it like an orchid. "Yes," he said to Alice Smythe, "you are right, she *is* complete. She has—as you say—" though Alice Smythe had not said it, "earned her definition. She is complete and pure, because she knows what is so hard to learn: that we can only define ourselves in the terms which the world offers. I have written a poem on that theme—the one in the last *Bookkeeper*. That explains, of course, the reference to Martin Luther in the last line:

Or Luther's hope, who on the mirror spat.

It was, perhaps, the intuition toward which Luther was struggling, but for which—if he had achieved it—he would have found no frame of statement. I have argued the whole point with Hoxley. He doesn't agree with me. You know, I think it is possible to regard Luther as a kind of inverted Saint Bernard. What do you think?"

Slim Sarrett had created this world, but sometimes, even in the very midst of it, when the studio was cluttered by people, and the voices ran high, and people spilled their drinks on their clothes, he would seem to be completely withdrawn from it. He would lean against the mantel shelf, or sit in a straight chair by the trestle table, over at the end of the room, and his curious gaze would flicker incessantly over the company. He never drank—he didn't like the taste, he said—and rarely smoked. But he bought whisky for his parties, when he had the money—a vile, pale-yellowish whisky, which purported to be distilled from corn mash, back in the hills, by the loving hands of simple independent folk of pure Anglo-Saxon stock who had passed the skill down from father to son, but which had actually been distilled, in tin, by Negroes in a slum shanty from a mess of potato parings, brown sugar, corn meal, and anything else which would ferment. He paid three dollars a gallon for it, and had sometimes stinted himself in order to buy it. Though he did not drink, and, in fact, needed no whisky to sit up and talk and argue until the sky began to thin and pale in the distance beyond the river, he got a peculiar and profound stimulation from its effect on other people, from the mounting noise, the sudden, aimless laughter, the self-appreciated wit, the refractions and distortions of personality, the twisted glimpses and unveiling, the flashing eyes and moist lips.

Sue Murdock had first seen this world early in her acquaintance with Slim Sarrett, for he had invited her to several parties with people from the Drama School. But Jerry Calhoun had always been there with her, at her insistence, big, clean-looking, his dark hair crisply in place, with the sheen of tonic, standing solidly among the moving people, the colored prints of masterpieces, the copper pots, and sofa cushions, sober, drinking sparingly and with ill-concealed distaste, answering people with scrupulous civility while his eyes strayed to the door or to the watch on his wrist. It had always been different when he was there, even though, watching him, she had recklessly downed the yellow whisky, on which she gagged. But now these people at the studio were almost the only people she saw. Two or three evenings a week they came to the studio, and she went there to sit with them.

She lived now in a run-down, scarcely reputable apartment house on the river, at a point where the wholesale section merged into streets of small clothing stores with advertising streamers limp above the doorways, cut-rate drugstores, and cafeterias. The afternoon when she had left home, she had driven straight to a small hotel, had registered under the name of Mary Moran, and had gone immediately to bed. She had taken a bath and had gone to bed—it was then five o'clock in the afternoon—and had slept profoundly and sweetly until nine the next morning. That morning, immediately after a cup of coffee, she had gone to the office of a young lawyer whom she knew at parties, had said that her grandmother had left her some money—no, she didn't know how much it was, she didn't know how it was invested—and had said that she wanted him to get her a hundred and twenty-five dollars a month. No, she said, she didn't care whether it came from the principal; if the interest wouldn't do it, she'd just take that much from the principal. The lawyer said for her to come back the next day. She came. He told her that her grandmother had not left her much, but that careful investment by Meyers and Murdock and the accumulation of interest over eight years had trebled the bequest, and that it would afford her something like one hundred and fifteen dollars a month. He gave her a check for that amount, and with a professional air, adjusting his English foulard—which she knew was expensive and surmised had not been paid for—advised her against drawing on her principal. She made no reply. So she was going to live in town for a while, he half stated, half asked, smiling, like a friend. Going to try her wings out, he said, and said that he thought that was fine. He talked like an old man, she thought, and said yes. Could he come to see her some evening, take her out, or something? Where was she living? He smiled, and looked out the window. She didn't know, she replied, and rose to go.

"Well, tell me what hotel you're in," he said, "and I might pick you up for a drink late this afternoon, if you can be persuaded."

She said she had checked out.

"Well, let me know when you're settled. I'd love to come by, I—"

"You saw my father," she said to him, not in question but in statement.

He moved his gaze quickly from the window to her. "Why—why, naturally," he said, "—just for a moment—the money, you know—he referred me to—"

"Did he tell you to find out where I was staying?" she demanded.

"Why—no," he said, "of course not. I didn't realize—" He smiled deprecatingly.

She was at the door now.

"Let me know to what address I can send the next check," he said.

"I'll come for it," she said. "When I need it."

"Well," he managed, "if there's anything else I can do, you just call on—"

"How much do I owe you?" she asked.

"Why, Sue! Nothing, of course. I'm glad to do—"

"I'll send you ten dollars," she said, and shut the door, and passed through his outer office, where the typewriter clicked desultorily, thinking: *At least it'll pay for his God-damned tie.*

That day she took the apartment, a medium-sized room, with a table, a couch and overstuffed chair to match, greasy-green, a wall bed, a kitchenette with a breakfast nook, and a bathroom. She paid twenty-five dollars a month for the place. Slim Sarrett had found it for her. She had said she wanted something cheap. It had a view, he said, when he took her to the place, and pointed out over the river. Then he said so long, he had some work to do, but would she go out to eat with him that night. She said that she thought she'd just stay at home.

After he had gone—and she was anxious for him to go—and she had unwrapped her package of new sheets and towels and had unpacked her suitcases and hung her clothes in the rack or stored them in the bureau in the alcove behind the wall bed, she stood in the middle of the room, under the low, gray-plastered ceiling, and looked out over the river, and was happy. She was happy, she knew that. At least, she knew that.

Then she was hungry. She went down the unsure elevator and to a grocery, where she bought salt, pepper, bread, a head of lettuce, butter, a steak, and kitchen soap. She washed the dishes and pans which she found in the kitchen, dented, cracked, gummy, dusty, plunging her wrists into the hot, hissing, swollen, delicious suds which foamed up to overflow the sink. The water was so hot it was painful—or almost painful—but at the same time it sent through her body a tingling pleasure, which, with the rising steam, flushed her cheeks and made her lips moist. For several minutes she dawdled with the dishes in the sink, not really washing them, just moving her hands under the water enough to nurse and keep alive the pulsing stimulation, the awareness of her own blood, which it provided. Then the water began to cool. The suds subsided, and grease began to coagulate murkily around the edges of the sink.

She cooked her steak, dousing it with butter, then ate ravenously, though the steak was badly cooked, hunching over the platter at the edge of the kitchenette table, under the unshaded electric bulb. In the end she held the bone in her hands and gnawed the last shreds from it, her elbows planted on the table, while she stared out the window. The lights were on out there now, pinking the slight mist from the river, and beyond, where the eastern suburbs were, sparsely pricking the darkness.

She took a cigarette, lighted it, rose, threw the light switch in the kitchen, and went into the other room, which was dark. She stood there for a moment, waiting for her eyes to become accustomed to the darkness. Then she lowered the wall bed, which she had already made up, and kicked off her shoes, and lay down on top of the covers, on her back, with her arms relaxed outward. Now and then, she took a drag from her cigarette. The flow and hum of the city rose and penetrated to her with a sound like the pulsation of distant surf. More immediately, two or three times, the steam clanked in the radiator, with a subterranean hollowness.

As she lay there, remote events, and those which were recent, came into her mind, like smoke. But they had not been like that. They had been real. That was why she was here, now. But, she decided, nothing was real by itself; things were real because they were together. And that was why she was here, and did not want anything.

There was a knock at the door.

At first she did not recognize it for what it was. Then, upon its repetition, she said, "Come in," and rose on her elbow. The door opened. Silhouetted against the dim light from the hall, she saw a man's figure. "Who is it?" she demanded, scrambling to a sitting position on the bed.

"For Christ sake!" a voice uttered, and she knew it was her brother Ham.

"All right," she said.

"For Christ sake," he repeated, not entering, "what're you doing there in the dark?"

"There's a switch there by the door," she said.

The light came on, and she blinked. It was a strong bulb, set in a small gilded chandelier, and the objects of the room seemed to leap toward her, then drop, and huddle, as the light struck her eyes.

Ham shut the door, took a few steps forward, and surveyed the crumpled bed, and her sitting in the middle of it, one leg bent under her, the other thrust forward. She lifted her hands to straighten her hair; then did not do it.

"My God," he commented detachedly, then glanced about the room. "My God," he said, "in the lap of luxury."

"All right," she said.

He crossed the room, and slumped into the overstuffed chair, flinging one leg over the side. She noticed that he had on a new suit, and his shoes were polished. He lighted a cigarette, looked about him, then snapped the match butt toward one corner of the room.

"Don't do that," she exclaimed.

"Do what?"

"Throw that over there," she said. "I'll have to pick it up."

"Nuts!" he said, grinning, "you never picked up anything in your life. But a golf ball."

She rose, in a cold fury, and padded across the carpet, picked up the match, and flung it into a tin wastebasket by the table.

"Gee," he said, "you did it."

She didn't even look at him. She returned to the bed, and sat as before. He swung his free foot, with its polished shoe, and watched her. "What made you do it?" he asked.

"I told you I'd have to pick—"

"Nuts," he said, "I don't mean that, I mean—" and he waved his hand heavily from the wrist, "all this. Running out. Come to this dump. What made you do it?"

"I did it," she said, "because I wanted to."

"Sure," he agreed, easily, "just like you do everything else. Because you want to."

"It's a damned good reason," she said, "and I don't see why it's any of—"

"Of my business," he finished for her. He flicked ashes on the floor, and continued: "I don't claim it is. But you up and leaving sure played hell out at the house. It has sure been one round of gaiety. Dock—"

"I don't want to hear about it."

"Sure," he said, and sank into silence, looking at the ceiling, a lock of hair untidily down over his forehead.

She studied him for a moment, then asked: "How did you know I was here?"

"Easy," he said. "I just heard Dock tell Dorothy. Dock said—"

"Dock?"

"For Christ sake," he said, "look here. One thing about being rich is you know things. You got ways of knowing things. That's the way you make money. And Dock is rich. He is stinking rich, and you may not like your old man, but old Dock—"

"You always get along so beautifully with him," she said.

"—but Dock," he ignored her, "isn't anybody's fool. Don't kid yourself. I bet Dock knew where you were before dark the day you left. I bet he knew you were here before you got your suitcase unpacked. I bet—"

"Spying!" she declared bitterly, "spying! Sitting there spying on people, just sitting there and not saying anything and knowing something. If he's put somebody to spy on me, I'll—I'll—" She gave up and stared at him, white in the face.

"It looks to me like you've done pretty well already," he remarked.

"If he has, I don't know what—I don't know what I'd do," she said, and clenched her hands.

"Well," he said, "you've done right well in the last forty-eight hours. You're God's gift to the old hens. I bet not a telephone in the higher-income brackets has been quiet a half hour all day. Old Mrs. Tupper called Dorothy—"

"All right," she said, "all right, and damn them all. Every one of them. Spying and talking, and Dock spying—putting somebody to spy on me. And you—he didn't want to come himself—oh, no, he wouldn't come—he just sent you—"

"Now look here—" he interrupted, unruffled, heavyish, leaning back in the chair.

But she went on: "—and you can get right out!"

"I came under my own power," he said, not moving. "Nobody had to send me. I reckon I got some curiosity of my own. I just wanted to see how come it was."

She told him it was the way it was because she wanted it that way, and he could go if his curiosity was satisfied. But he did not go. He sat there for a long time, smoking, not talking much, lying back in the chair with his foot dangling. When he got ready to go, he stood at the door, and said: "Well, you're shore-God something, I reckon." And went on off down the hall.

Late the next afternoon the letter from her father came, by messenger, in a long envelope bearing the return address of Meyers and Murdock.

Standing in the middle of the room, her feet wide apart, the jaggedly torn envelope on the floor beside her, the crisp sheet held in both hands, she read it:

January 18, 1927.

My dear daughter:

At first I was saddened by the thought that you had left home so abruptly and without good-by or explanation. That was, of course, the natural reaction for a father. But upon reflection I realized that, for the moment, you might not have been able to do otherwise—that each of us must work out his personal destiny, and that you must work out yours. Nobody, I suppose, can really help anybody else, no matter how great the desire. I confess, though it is a melancholy thought, that I do not even know what impelled you to this step, and that I probably could be of no real use to you if I did know. Your mother, who seems to be suffering considerably from the shock of the event, does not seem to be able to bring herself to talk of the matter, and I have not pressed her upon the point. Jerry Calhoun, it appears, has not been himself for the past two days. I saw him for a few minutes on business, but he said nothing to me. I did not seek his confidence, for I only want to hear about the matter from your own lips, and that only when you are ready to tell me. Until that day, I shall possess myself in patience.

Meanwhile I am thinking of you—but you must know that already. And though, as I have said, I know I cannot be of any real help to you, and know you must work out your own destiny, I want to be of whatever small service I can. The income from your grandmother's little legacy is not much, and if you depend upon it, you will be forced to live in rather unpleasant circumstances, to which my little girl is not accustomed. I am having two hundred dollars deposited for you in the Southern Fidelity the first of each month. If you need anything for special expenses, which are almost certain to arise, please let me know.

I sit here in my office and think that all I can do for my girl is to give her a little money. At moments like this, one realizes how little money means.

Good-by, and all my love,

Your "Dockie"

She crumpled the sheet of crisp, strong bond savagely in her hands, and flung it down. "I won't!" she exclaimed to the empty room, to the smoky roofs of the city, and to the distance beyond them. "I won't—ever—not a penny. Not a God-damned penny!"

Later, she picked up the paper from the floor, and spread it out again. "Dockie," she said, and repeated, with an ejective twist of her mouth as though the word were actually repulsive upon the tongue, that childish name, which had not crossed her mind, and which she had not heard, for such a long time. "Dockie—Dockie—Dockie," she repeated again, her face changing, her voice changing as though she were trying a gamut of subtle variations of tone upon the single word. "Dockie—Dockie," she said, and began to cry, with the crumpled sheet in her hand.

He was—he was Dockie once—a long time ago, she thought. Then she looked at the sheet of paper in her hand, and the name there. "But he's not Dockie now," she uttered violently. Then, with a bitter satisfaction: "He would do it—he would sign it that way—Dockie!"

She had quit crying. She didn't feel like crying any more. She washed her face with cold water and felt all right. Then she went down and walked along the river, for a long time, under the warehouses, where the drays and the big trucks were, and the rough, dirty men looked after her curiously.

She did not answer the letter.

Sixteen

Statement of Ashby Wyndham

NEXT day they was work. Folks started cuttin and haulin and workin in the mill again. Nigh everybody went to work agin, but them what was in jail down to Cashtown or too bad beat up. But they was some said they be God damn if they would work for the Company no more, and left. If they had anywheres to go. But not many, for a man has to git bread and meat. The pay wasn't good as afore, but the Company did say they wouldn't cut it no ten cents ever hour. They cut it eight cents, what helped some. But it was tight, and I seen folks hongry.

I went to work agin. I worked five weeks lak afore. Then one Saturday the woods boss said to me, Wyndham, they ain't no use comin back Monday mornin, they ain't no work for you. And I ast him, why, ain't I done good. He said, good as the next un. I said, why, and he said, it looks lak they's cuttin down, and they said to git shed of these fellers. He helt a piece of paper in his hand and it had five names on it. They was five of us got told not to come back.

I tried to git somethin to do. I went down to Cashtown and tried to git it. But they wasn't nuthin. I tried the Atlas Iron Company and they wasn't nuthin. I went plum down to the coal mine, and they said they didn't have no use for me. It taken me a day to git down there and a day to git back and after night. I left Marie with Frank home and nobody there, but I had to git down and see. I went to Tomtown. It was the same. It was winter and I couldn't make no gardin patch nor nuthin. I couldn't help nobody farmin. I tried cuttin stove wood with a feller had a wagin and sellin it in Tomtown and we got a few dollars. But then we cut some more and couldn't git shed of it. I taken nigh all what money was left in the tin can where I kept it hid to git somethin to eat for Marie and Frank. They et somethin, and Marie made no complaint. I paid on the house one month, then I didn't pay. I wasn't

213

goin to take money for somethin to eat and pay on the house. I told the man I would make it up. I ast him to let me work it out, but he said he didn't have no work.

I was comin down the road and I met a feller named Bud Jeffers. I knowed him workin for the Company. He ast me how I was makin out. I said I wasn't makin out. He said he wasn't makin out neither. Ain't you workin, I ast him. Naw, he said, they told him to git out. He said they told some more to git out. Eleven it was. He ast me didn't I hear tell, and I said naw. Everybody, he said, what taken sides with Sweetwater at fust, ever one. Everybody what talked fer Sweetwater about not workin, ever one.

They told me they was just cuttin down, I said.

Cuttin down on them as was with Sweetwater at fust, he said, and taken his side. You taken his side. I taken his side. All them fellers taken his side.

It can't be so, I said, for it was me knocked Sweetwater down. For callin the Private a lie. It was me knocked him down.

You was a durn fool to do it, he said.

That was what he named me. A durn fool.

I seen a time I busted a man for callin me a durn fool. I come nigh bustin Bud Jeffers standin there in the road. It looked lak I was goin to. Then all of a sudden they wasn't no man-meanness in me. They wasn't nuthin in me, meanness or nuthin else. It was lak the bottom drops out of a bucket of a sudden and the water is spilt. I just stood there and they wasn't nuthin in me lak a old man done used up. I seen Bud Jeffers walk on down the road.

I looked up in the sky. It was gray, lak to snow. Not gray clouds seperit lak, but all gray and low hangin. I looked acrost the valley over them black trees what didn't have no leaves, and over them few houses I seen but they was little it was so far, and lak they wasn't nobody in them. Lak folks had done gone and left them. I looked acrost the valley where the sky come down to the hills, but it was mist-smoky it was so far, and a man couldn't say for sure where the hills left off and the sky begun. The sky was layin on the hills.

It was lak a man knowed how it was to be by hisself. To be by hisself and not nuthin. It was lak I was by myself in the world, and not nobody else. Not Marie. And not Frank. Lak there hadn't never been no Marie and no Frank and no Pappy and Mammy and no Jacob. Not nobody but me, and me nuthin.

It was lak the time Frank died. It was lak I was standin there in the road by myself and the time was comin and everywhere was so quiet I could nigh hear it steppin stealthy. Lak a man out at night hears somethin and stops of a sudden and hearkens. Then he says, naw, it ain't nuthin but the wind maybe. And he goes on.

A man listens quiet and he can hear the Lords foot mashin down the hills. Lak they wasn't nuthin but old ruts in the road with the mud done dried where the wagin wheel squeshed it up soft. He hears it but he don't know to name it.

Frank died in February. It was in his throat and it looked lak he couldn't git no breath. He died all of a sudden, lak he come of a sudden and his Mammy not ready. It was lak he come of a sudden and was in a hurry for he knowed he didn't have no time much to stay.

They put him in the ground, and we seen it.

We come home and we was in the house, but we never knowed one another. Marie laid on the bed and shet her eyes, and I wasn't nuthin to her. I kept tryin to git her to listen to me, but she wouldn't unshet her eyes for nuthin. It come dark, and I set there. Now and agin I put some wood on the fire. Marie laid there, but I wasn't nuthin to her. I looked at her, and I knowed she wasn't nuthin to me. She was lak a old coat somebody done flung down, and I didn't know who. I couldn't look at her of a sudden and know she wasn't nuthin to me. I knowed why she wouldn't unshet her eyes. She couldn't bear and endure to see my face. I knowed it. Ain't nobody nuthin to nobody of his own strength when the rub comes, and a man knows it of a sudden and it is lak he was crossin a river on the ice at night and the ice breaks. It is lak he goes down of a sudden. The cold water is on him, and the blackness, and ain't nobody to hear him yell.

I knowed Marie wasn't nuthin to me, and it was lak I went through the ice. I couldn't bear and endure to see her layin there and know it.

I stood up and I went out the door. That night when Frank come into this here world of sin and pain, I stood and seen his Mammy layin there and heard her yell, and it come on me to walk out of that air house, and it night time, and walk and keep on walkin where it was dark and there wasn't no yellin or nuthin. It come on me but I never done it. But this time when I seen her layin there with her eyes shet and I knowed of a sudden she wasn't nuthin to me and my heart was like a orange squoze dry and throwed down, I up and went out the door. I never made up my mind to git out. I didn't even know I had done left. One minute I was standin lookin at her lay and the next I was out in dark and I was runnin up the road with my feet hittin on the froze-hard ground and my head throwed back lookin up in the sky where

the stars was showin, lak they do in winter time. I never knowed
how I got there.

I run on the Mountain. I wasn't carin where. Just so I was runnin. I wasn't on no road. I was goin acrost rock and dead bresh.
I run into it and it snatched and tore me. I kept on runnin. I never
felt it. I fell down on them rocks, and I got up and run agin.

I fell down and I didn't git up. I laid and I didn't know nuthin.
Then I knowed the breathin was lak fire in my chist when I drawed
it, but it didn't matter none to me for it was lak it was somebody
else's chist. I laid and it was quiet and I seen how them stars was
in the sky and steady.

I was hearin my name. Maybe I was hearin it for a long spell
layin there and didn't know, lak when you ain't waked up and
somebody keeps callin yore name. You hears yore name named and
knows it, but you ain't hearin either. Then it was clear. It said,
Ashby, Ashby, Ashby Wyndham.

It was Frank callin me. He was callin his Pappy. He hadn't never
said mortal word in this world. He never got big enuf to say no
word true and proper. But I knowed it was him. I knowed it lak
he was a growed boy and I had knowed his voice.

Frank, I said, Frank.

And he said, yes sir, Pappy, lak he was a mannered boy.

Frank, I said, where are you.

I am right here, Pappy, he said.

Frank, I said, I can't see you for the dark.

It is dark to mortal eye, he said.

Oh, Frank, I said, and it looked lak my heart would bust, why
did you up and leave, why did you git up and go, didn't we treat
you good.

Oh, Pappy, he said, oh, Pappy, I grieve to tell.

Why did you have to up and go, I said.

Oh, Pappy, he said, I couldn't thrive none and it the vittles of
wickedness. I couldn't thrive and it vittles and sop taken in blood
wrath and wickedness. And from Jacob. It was from yore brother
Jacob you taken it. Them vittles come in my throat and my throat
swelled for wickedness and I had to up and go.

Oh, Frank, I commenst, but wouldn't no words come.

I come lak the Lord sent me, little and pure, he said, and the
Lord He taken me so.

Oh, Frank, I said, and the big tears bust like a freshet.

Pappy, Pappy, he said.

Oh, Frank, I said, what can I do.

Don't cry, Pappy, he said.

216

What can I do, I said.

You can git up and find Jacob, he said, and take him by the hand.

I can't never find him, I said.

You can walk in the world, he said, till you find him. He is walkin in the world amongst strangers, and you can walk in the world. You can ast folks. You can tell folks how it was with you, and how you lifted up yore hand agin him and them others, and how no man ought never to. You can ast have they seed him. And the Lord will lead you and put yore hand in Jacobs hand.

Frank, I commenst.

Give my Mammy a kiss for me, he said.

Frank, Frank, I said, but he was done gone. He had said his say, and he was done gone.

I got up offen the cold ground. I went down the Mountain. Light was just showin blue and weak over Massey when I come to my house and entered in it.

I seen Marie layin there. She was sleepin. I went to her and I lent over and I kissed her lak Frank said. She opened her eyes slow and looked at me. It was a kiss from little Frank, I said.

And I knelt down beside the bed and let my head lay and she put her hand on my head.

Seventeen

THE GUILT and terror which Jerry Calhoun had experienced that night in the speak-easy, when the bartender stood before him with the sawed-off bat and the men laughed, and had experienced more painfully when he stood between the high buildings and stared up at the curdling, darkly sliding sky and knew that Sue Murdock's disheveled body lay somewhere in a ditch and that they would hunt him down like a dog, struck him again the next morning as he opened his eyes in his own bed. But it came on him now without context. As he opened his eyes, and moved his tongue dryly between his lips, and stared up at the familiar ceiling, the feeling was already in him, but for the first moment, it was simply a feeling in him, causeless, without reference to any events which he could remember. He remembered nothing. Then, all at once, he remembered everything, and his heart lunged and jerked as though he had taken a too deep dive and had barely fought his way to the surface.

He lay in the bed, on his back, with the bright winter sunshine streaming in over the bed, and sweated coldly. He knew that his morning paper lay on the floor, in the hall, against his door, rolled neatly up. He knew that, in a minute, he would get up and go into the living room and open the door and pick up the paper and stand with it in his hands, waiting to open it, waiting just a minute before he got his nerve up to open it.

That was what happened. He got out of bed, cautiously as though some sudden motion might upset equilibrium or provoke an alarm, and stepped past his evening clothes, which were piled on the floor by the bed, and went to get the paper. After he had opened it, he was all right. There was nothing there.

He leaned back against the closed door, feeling like a fool, calling himself a damned fool, gradually becoming aware of the thirst and the queasiness in his stomach.

He went to the bathroom, gulped the cold water, took a shower, and began to dress. He dressed hurriedly, knowing that he would be late for the office. Then, at the thought of the bank, the sense of guilt, still tinged with terror, began to gnaw at him again. Bogan Murdock might be at the bank. He had not thought of Bogan Murdock. He might see Bogan Murdock. He could see Bogan Murdock now, Bogan Murdock's face, the eyes, smoky-blue around the hard, glittering black pupils, fixed upon him in vindictive accusation. He had never seen that face, not really. But the image came to him with the conviction of recollection, for he *had* seen it before, in his terrified fantasies in moments after Sue Murdock had made him take her there in Bogan Murdock's house, in Bogan Murdock's library, on the divan in the drawing room, in the dark, while footsteps moved across the patches of uncarpeted floor upstairs, in the moments when he had vowed prayerfully, thankfully, never, never, never again.

It was a face that would never tolerate failure. And he had failed. His other feelings were lost in the numb misery of failure. He did not define the nature of his failure, but he felt stripped and derided, standing there, before his mirror, with his comb in his hand and his wet hair tumbled on his head and the little drops of water, like sweat, beading down on his forehead from the hair.

Catching sight of his own face, mottled and somewhat sagging in the reflected sunlight from the mirror, defenseless in its misery, he suddenly set his jaw, and was filled with resentment and defiance, thinking, how, by God, it wasn't his fault, how he had worked and done without in those forgotten years of his boyhood, how he had been alone, how he had sat alone at night with the book before him, how he had stood alone on the dark campus hearing music far off, how he had slaved for Bogan Murdock and had never failed, and now, by God, just because of this there would be Bogan Murdock's face—but damn him, and damn Sue Murdock, damn her to hell.

He plunged the comb into the crisp tangle of black hair.

He had made himself, by God. You sweated and you took it on the chin and you were by yourself and nobody knew how you felt inside and it was every man for himself and by himself, and he knew that and he had made himself what he was, and by God, they weren't going to take it away from him now. Not Sue Murdock or Bogan Murdock or anybody. Not anybody.

But all that day, in his office at the bank, every time the telephone rang, he hesitated, steeling himself, expecting to hear the voice of Bogan Murdock. But Bogan Murdock did not call, and the evening paper was innocent of any mention of the name of Sue Murdock.

It was the next morning before Bogan Murdock called. "Hello," the voice said, "how about having lunch with me today?" Then, as Jerry fumbled to concoct the lie that would give him a reprieve for a few hours, that would let him slip off alone to some restaurant where nobody from Meyers and Murdock ever went, the voice continued: "Blake and the Private are coming, and perhaps Dawson."

That saved him from the lie. If the others were going, it couldn't be that Bogan was on his trail. "Sure," he said, "sure," into the transmitter, somewhat weakly, and scarcely listened while the voice replied, "Fine, make it the lobby of the Harpeth at half-past."

He walked to the hotel with Duckfoot. "What's cooking?" Duckfoot asked him.

"Nothing I know of," he said.

"There better be," Duckfoot said. "That trouble over at Massey Mountain isn't doing Bogan any good. That fellow named Sweetwater over there has sure raised hell. He sure hasn't done Bogan any good."

"I reckon not," Jerry assented, thinking rather glumly that it wasn't doing him any good either, not with what he had in the Mountain.

"I don't suppose it's cutting your bill for sleeping powders, either," Duckfoot said, and Jerry, startled at the clairvoyance, snatched a look at his face as he went on. Duckfoot added: "You've got a slice of that Massey stuff, haven't you?"

Jerry nodded, wishing fleetingly that he had that slice out of Massey and had put it in Mississippi Electric when Meyers and Murdock bought into that. Or had it added to what he had in Southern Fidelity. Well, Bogan had plenty of the Mountain, he thought, with an inward shrug, and that ought to be some comfort. You had to get up early to outguess Bogan.

"Atlas Iron, too?" Duckfoot asked.

Jerry nodded again, irritably, for it wasn't any of Duckfoot's business, was it?

"Well, don't take it too hard," Duckfoot said. "They haven't done any killing yet on the Mountain. That's just been in the coal. And you haven't got any coal. You're saving money on commemorative wreaths for deputies.

Damn it, he thought, where did Duckfoot think his own money came from?

"Naw, don't take it too hard," Duckfoot said; "the old boy's got something simmering on the back of the stove. If," he added, "he's paid the gas bill."

But it wasn't Bogan Murdock who brought up the subject of

business at lunch, as they sat there in the alcove off the main dining room of the Harpeth, which Bogan Murdock always reserved when he had guests for lunch, and ate their soup and chops and salad. No, Bogan Murdock was talking about China. He had been reading books on China, he said. Something was happening in China that had never happened before in human history. At least, never so completely and dramatically. "The modern world," he said, "the world of industry and finance and science—our world—" and he nodded at each in turn, at Duckfoot and Porsum and Jerry, implying *your world, your world, your world,* "is face to face with an old world. Not just a world—like South America, for instance— which is different because incompetent, but a world which is complete in its own terms, and wise. I would like—"

"Mother India," Duckfoot breathed gently and indistinctly through a mouthful of lettuce, "sex in the Solomons, philosophy among the Laplanders, whither China."

Bogan Murdock laughed. "Sure," he said, "sure, you're right, but I'm romantic enough to want to go and see it. I've been thinking about taking a year off and going to look at it. It might help a man take stock a little. He might see himself a little more clearly. What he—"

But at that moment Sam Dawson, red in the face and puffing, came into the alcove, and Bogan Murdock rose, and shook hands with him, and indicated the empty chair.

"Gimme a steak," Sam Dawson said to the waiter, jabbing his finger at the spot on the menu, "rare. And tell that cook I mean rare, see. And a couple of baked potatoes and two glasses of buttermilk." Then, as the waiter slipped away, he spread his napkin over his front, cocked his chair back, looked at Bogan Murdock, and uttered: "My God!"

"What's the matter, Sam?" Bogan Murdock asked.

"My God, that Milam," Sam Dawson said. "A hell of a Governor he is. He's in a sweat. He can't make up his mind for God's sake or goobers. He kept me there an hour and a half and me starving, to hold his hand and wipe his little nose. I said to him, 'Jeff, you're Governor of this State, you make up your own mind and don't ask me. I ain't nothing but a farmer.' And you oughta seen him sweat."

"That's what he's paid to do, isn't it?" Duckfoot demanded. "Do the sweating?"

"Well, he ain't paid to keep me from eating my lunch," Sam Dawson retorted, and shot a glance across the dining room toward the service doors.

"That editorial in the *Standard*," Bogan Murdock asked, "is that what's got him excited?"

"Yeah," Sam Dawson grunted.

"I hated to see that," Murdock reflected. "Of course, the *Standard* is antiadministration and could be expected to make political capital out of the situation by demanding that Milam put troops in the strike area if he can't control matters. But—" he said, and paused, and his brown, adept fingers toyed noiselessly with the silver, "I saw Allen of the *Register* at dinner last night, and he was talking about running an editorial to back up the *Standard*. And the *Register* is certainly not antiadministration."

"Is he gonna do it?" Sam Dawson asked.

"No," Murdock replied thoughtfully, studying the dessert fork which he fingered. "At least, not right away. I persuaded him to hold off to see if something couldn't be done."

"Damn it, I'm starving," Sam Dawson muttered. "I'm skin and bones."

"But I don't know what can be done," Bogan Murdock said, almost as though to himself. Then he glanced around the table, his eyes coming to rest on Duckfoot's face. "Have you any ideas, Blake?" he asked.

"Boss," Duckfoot said, "you know I don't ever have ideas. I just add and subtract."

Murdock smiled, but in his smile was a hint of duty. "It has occurred to me," he continued, after the smile had been switched off, "that Jerry might go up and study the situation for a few days and help us to some decision. That might—"

"There ain't time," Sam Dawson broke in, and then observed his steak approaching.

"No, no, I guess not. They may force Milam's hand. And if troops go, it will be tragic. Things aren't too easy for those people up there at best. And I wouldn't blame them for what they did if troops were sent. If they could only see where their interest lies. That co-operation is best. If they—"

"Listen, Dock, listen here—" Sam Dawson abjured the first great chunk of steak, which he held up on his fork, crusty from the charcoal, ruby-red at center, dripping its juices and melted butter, "listen here, why don't the Private—" and he pointed the chunk of steak at Porsum, "why don't he go up there and try to explain things to those folks? Hell, they'll listen to him. He's the only man in the State those folks in the mountains will listen to. And he knows how it is. He can tell 'em." And the chunk of steak disappeared into Sam Dawson's mouth, and his jaws began to work slowly and powerfully, the red flesh of his face shining, his blue eyes going blank with the inward pleasure.

And Private Porsum, his big face as wooden as a chunk of cedar above the dirty plates, his big hands propped on his knees, his eyes on Sam Dawson, who wasn't paying him any attention now, said, "I hadn't reckoned—I hadn't reckoned—"

And Bogan Murdock, breaking in, said: "Naturally, that is entirely up to you, Private. If you can, in good conscience. I don't want to urge you. But you know the facts."

That was how it was, and after they had risen from the table, and were waiting for Bogan Murdock to get his change, Duckfoot slapped Private Porsum on the shoulder, and intoned: "Blessed is the peacemaker."

And Private Porsum said nothing.

They walked out into the street. Sam Dawson said he had his car and would take them where they were going. Duckfoot said it would sure help his feet, and he and Porsum got into the machine. Bogan Murdock hesitated, then said that he thought he would walk. Turning to Jerry, he asked: "Why don't you walk with me as far as Third?"

This is it, this is it, Jerry thought, and said, "Yes," for that was all he could say, and knew that he was caught with his pants down, and watched the car pull off down the street, and felt, bitterly, that he had been tricked. That he had been tricked like a kid.

But Bogan Murdock said nothing as they walked along the afternoon street, past the moving groups of people and the glittering glass of the store windows, where objects were piled and where images of wax, male and female, draped in shining new fabrics, stared out at them with fixed, secure, unsympathetic smiles. Jerry kept waiting for him to speak, stealing glances at the man beside him, at the profile of the brown, aquiline, handsome, unrevealing face above the trim, almost too narrow shoulders, above the dark-gray double-breasted flannel coat and dark-blue tie, which was the color of the eyes. Or, looking down, waiting, he watched the shoes, the black, coarse-grained, stitched-leather shoes the man wore, move rhythmically, steadily, invincibly forward over the stained cement.

He couldn't stand waiting, not any longer.

"It's Sue," he uttered hoarsely, "it's Sue you wanted to see me about?"

He watched the black shoes move forward, not slackening.

Then the voice said, "My boy, I wish you every good thing in

223

the world. And as for Sue—well, Sue is my daughter. But what has passed between you—" the voice hesitated.

It's coming, Jerry thought, waiting, *it's coming.*

"—that has been between you. All I can do is wish you both the best. That's all I—"

"I tell you I don't know what happened," Jerry burst out violently, defensively. "I don't understand a damned thing about it, I tell you I don't know!"

"Patience," the voice counseled, "you've got to have patience, Jerry."

The black shoes kept on, in perfect regularity.

"All I wanted—" the voice resumed.

I knew it, Jerry thought, in arid triumph. Sure, he'd known Bogan Murdock wanted something.

The black shoes slackened their pace, and stopped.

"—was to give you this," Bogan Murdock said, and Jerry looked up to see him slip his hand under his coat, to a vest pocket, and take out a card. He held the card out to Jerry.

Jerry took the card. On it was written, in Bogan Murdock's firm, precise hand, *The Eudora Apartments, 342 Bollin Street, Apt. no. 42.*

"She's staying there," Murdock said, matter-of-factly, nodding at the card. "Ham went to see her there."

"Yes," Jerry said.

"I simply thought that you might want to know the address," Murdock said impersonally.

"Thanks," Jerry managed to say.

"I guess I turn off here," Murdock said, and with his stick indicated the corner a few feet away. Then, all at once, he thrust his right hand out at Jerry, and when Jerry had taken it, added, "Best luck," and suddenly smiled.

Without another word, before Jerry could answer, he had turned away and was moving rapidly across the street, with the flow of traffic, under the green light.

Jerry Calhoun stood on the corner, clutching the little white card with the black marks on it, and gazed after the erect, supple, gray-clad figure until it had been absorbed into the crowd; and was filled with an overpowering relief, with lightness, humility, and gratitude.

Then, jerking his shoulders, he straightened up, and strode down the street, past the dawdling, irrelevant people, striding past them, breathing the crisp air, carrying his hat in his hand the better to relish the sunlight on his face.

What a fool he'd been, he thought, patronizing the self he had been and all guilts and fears and confusions. Why, Jesus, what a fool! What had ever made him get in a funk like that?

You walk down the crummy street, where practically nobody is out now, for it is after dark and the pawnshops and groceries and clothing stores are closed, and the dummies wearing the new suits with the big red price markers carrying the slashed price have been carried in off the pavement, and only the drugstore and the delicatessen show lights in the block, and the wind off the river is so sharp that there aren't any kids running down the street tonight yelling and shoving each other. The wind drives a sheet of newspaper over the cement with a dry, rustling sound which reminds you of leaves rustling at night when you would be walking along a path in the woods, at night, by yourself.

You hesitate before the corner drugstore, standing on the pavement in the area of light cast from the drugstore window. You look up at the numbering above the door, squint at the metal numbers, which are blackened by soot and corrosion, and finally make them out. The number is 300. It will be this block, a little way down in this block. You hesitate a moment longer, then go into the drugstore.

There is a girl behind the soda fountain, a girl in a green smock, with too much lipstick and a few pimples on her face. She is serving a milk shake to an old man there, who leans on the marble with both elbows and holds the glass with both hands and bows over the milk shake, which is chocolate, and holds a straw in his mouth reaching down into the frothy, muddy-colored stuff, and suck it in, while the girl talks to him. You bet he slips off every night and comes down here and gets his chocolate milk shake.

You go past the old man and move toward the back of the store, and a man wearing an alpaca jacket comes toward you, on the other side of the counter, but you take two or three quick steps so you'll get a little farther away from the girl at the soda fountain before you ask him. You observe a look of surprise, of question, of alarm, on the man's doughy druggist's face, then you realize that he's afraid of a stick-up, that he's afraid of a stick-up every night when there aren't many people around and somebody comes in and walks straight back with his hands in his topcoat pockets. You keep your hands in your topcoat pockets just a moment longer, just to give the old bugger a thrill, and cast a side glance back toward the soda fountain where the girl is, but she is talking and is too far to hear, anyway. You take your hands out of your pockets,

225

and the doughy face shows a little relief. "What'll you have?" the face asks.

And you tell him.

He slips the little envelope into your hand, and you drop a dollar bill on the counter.

"Will there be anything else?" the face asks.

You shake your head and go out, but there will sure be something else. There will sure as hell be something else, or you will know the reason why. You walk along the street and take two or three deep breaths of the river air, which feels good, and you feel good and sure of everything.

You slow down and begin to look for numbers. A little light comes from a deep doorway, and when you get there you see that the light comes through some sort of frosted glass in the door. You look up and make out the name *Eudora Apartments* cut into the slab of limestone set in the brick above the entry. You don't bother to fool with the letter boxes and buttons hunting names. You try the door, and it is not locked, and so you go on in, into the hall, where the light is coming from a big brass chandelier with one good bulb and where your heels click on the grimy tiles until you reach the patch of reddish carpet running along the center of the hall. You do not fool with the elevator. You bet it is no good, anyway, and start up the stairs, which you see at the end of the hall. You stop one landing too soon, just to be sure, but the numbers there are in the thirties, and so you go on up. You go to the next floor, see it is the top floor, and walk down the hall. Apartment 42 is at the end of the hall, on the side toward the river. You see the number by the light of the hanging electric bulb.

You stop before the door, and take off your topcoat and hat, and wonder what you're going to say; you've forgotten what you had intended to say; you'd thought of a lot of different things to say and different ways to be; but now, suddenly, just like before an examination in school, you don't remember anything. *Well, what the hell,* you think, for you know it's going to be all right. it's bound to be all right. You know that. Then, all at once, you are cool and sure and everything is clear, just the way you used to be, and it used to be, when you lifted your head up and looked down the field and all the charging, plunging bodies seemed fixed in their patterns of motion, and you cocked your arm back for the pass. So you knock on the door. Almost before you hear the voice say, "Come in," you have turned the knob and have stepped inside.

She is standing across the room from you, and does not say a

226

word while you stand there, with your coat over your arm and your hat in that hand, and reach behind you with the other hand to shut the door. You do not say anything, either. You start walking toward her. Taking your time, but walking toward her, with the coat over your arm, for you've forgotten about it. Taking your time, for there isn't any hurry, but you are moving toward her. She is standing where she was when you came in, over there near the table, with her feet close together on the floor the way a child puts her feet together, and one hand touching the table top. She is watching you, and you notice how her hair falls down smooth on each side of her face and how pale her hair looks against the dark dress and how her lower lip, with the little provocative fullness which always got you all right, is glistening and slightly parted as though she is about to say something. But she doesn't say anything.

Then she draws the lower lip up a little, and sets her teeth against it in a way that must hurt, for you remember how sharp her teeth are which you see set on the small, strained, glistening rosy fullness of the lip. Then you think, but you aren't quite sure, you can't be sure, she begins to shake her head, weakly, almost imperceptibly, from side to side in a kind of incipient negation. But it doesn't mean a thing. Not a thing, and you know it—whether she's saying no to you or no to herself or no to what, it doesn't mean a thing—for you feel the measured powerful knocking of your heart inside your ribs. You have dropped your coat and hat on the floor, and your voice says "Sue," not very loud.

But that does it. It is as though the single word, the word you had not really known you were speaking, had resolved something, had with a kind of talismanic efficacy clarified everything, had unlocked and released something, for, on the instant, she is very still, her head doesn't have that motion any more and she looks straight at you, and then she rushes the three steps toward you, lifting her arms a little, lifting her face, which is suddenly illumined and transfigured as you have never seen it before, and uttering a small, breathless cry. It is a small sound, seemingly surprised from her, wrung from her, unintended.

She stands against you, her arms around your body, some six or eight inches below the level of your armpits, for you are so much taller than she, her head bowed and pressed against your chest so that your own face when you lean feels the smoothness of her hair, and she again utters, twice, that small sound, *oh, oh,* which is breathless, yet somehow full-throated, surrendering, without reservation.

227

She has never been like this before. You didn't know she could be like this. You didn't know that you could be like this, either, that things could ever be like this. You are filled with something which is not exactly happiness, or excitement, or desire, which is larger than, and includes, happiness, excitement, and desire, which includes and absorbs everything which has ever happened to you and makes all those things seem right and foreordained, a pattern leading to the present; and as you lean your face against the smooth hair and attend to that small sound she makes, you discover a tenderness and pity, a magnanimity mixed with your own sense of fulfillment and victory.

For you do have a sense of victory. You know that you have won, but against whom, or what, you do not define to yourself. And you had known beforehand that you would win. What surprises you is not the fact that you have won, but the nature of the winning. What surprises you, far down in the depth of your mind, is the fact that you have won more than you ever expected was possible. You seem to have won everything in the world which you wanted, or rather, what you wanted but did not know that you wanted. It seems to you now to be the only thing in the world which is worth winning. You stand there for a long time, your face down against her hair, and know that.

She disengages herself, somewhat abruptly, from you.

At the first instant, you stand there and do not know why. Then you see that her hand is reaching to the pull-cord of the lamp on the table behind her, to which she has retreated. But even as her hand goes back to the cord, she is looking at you. Her face is very still and smooth, and except for the brightness of her eyes, is like the face of the little girl in the white dress in the old picture which she once showed you, a long time back, when you sat beside her on the couch in the library. Then the light goes out, and in the first moment of darkness, which seems absolute because your eyes have not yet adjusted themselves, you feel that she isn't there at all, that it was all a dream, and that you are alone in the dark.

Then she whispers: "The door—did you lock the door?"

That is the only thing she has said since you came in. And that fact seems to you worthy of remarking.

You move toward the door, groping in the dark, find it, and turn the latch, and as you do so, you wonder where you put that little envelope the dough-faced man in the drugstore gave you, in your overcoat pocket or in the pocket of your coat. Then you discover that it is in the pocket of your coat.

You hear a small noise across the room; then realize that it is the noise made by one of her pumps as she slips it from her foot and lets it drop the few inches to the floor.

Later, you lie beside her on the bed. You lie on your back, looking up toward the shadowy ceiling. A little light comes into the room now from the street far below, and you are aware of the distant rustle and muted hum of the traffic. But it is not so positive a sound that you cannot hear her breathing. There has been no talking. You have lain there for a long time now, your hand clasping hers on top of the cover.

That is why, when she pronounces your name, you are startled as though you had heard the name, your name, coming out of the thin air, in the dark above your bed, in your room, alone, at night.

"Jerry," she says again, for you have not answered.

"Yes," you say.

"Do you love me, Jerry?"

"God, yes," you say, and say to yourself, *God, yes,* and hold her hand hard, for you do love her. You know that.

She does not speak again for some minutes. Then she says: "Let's go away, Jerry."

"Sure," you say, "sure, we're going away. We're going to Havana. Don't you remember? We're going to Havana on our honeymoon." And you laugh, and squeeze her hand.

She draws her hand away. "I don't want to go to Havana," she says.

"Well," you say, "name the place and we'll go there."

"I don't care where we go—I don't care," she says, "but I want to go—"

"All right," you say, and laugh.

She speaks very slowly and distinctly: "I want us to go away, Jerry. Somewhere where you can get a job."

"I've got a job," you say, and start to laugh, but do not, and feel the small germ of hardness inside you stir.

"Oh, Jerry, Jerry," she begins, and pushes herself up on one elbow, saying, "Oh, Jerry, don't you see, we've got to, we've—"

But you reach out and slip one arm about her shoulders and pull her down, and roll to your side, and as she says, "We've got to, we've—" you put your other hand over her mouth, and say, "Ssh, ssh," and draw her to you.

She seizes your wrist and jerks your hand from her mouth and says, "I mean it, we've got to go, we've—" But you put your hand over her mouth again and say, "Ssh, ssh," playfully, and repeat it, but when she seizes your wrist again, you press tight and don't let her jerk your hand loose. "Oh, no, you don't!" you say, and laugh, for you feel all right now, and sure again, saying, "Oh, no, you little devil—no, you little mess!"

But she's a strong little devil and hard to hold when she twists and squirms and tries to break loose as you pull her. She gets her hand in your hair and pulls, and she pulls like she meant business, but you know she doesn't mean business, not really. It doesn't really hurt much, at least you don't notice it too much, and you laugh with your face tangled in a mop of her hair.

Then she turns your hair loose, all at once. *All right,* you think, and it is. It is all right.

But is it? But you push the thought from your mind even when, later, lying beside her again, you try to take her hand again and she pulls it away. You do not try to take it again, not if she's going to act that way about it. But it will be all right.

You lie still drowsily listening to her breathing in the dark.

"I know something," she announces in a tone which tells you nothing.

"I know something, too," you say; "I know I'm just crazy about you." You try to take her hand again, but she moves it on the cover, away from you. You know you ought to grab it again, but somehow you don't, and experience a little flicker of resentful pride that you do not.

"I know something, Jerry Calhoun," she repeats, in a whisper this time, as though she were imparting a secret.

You do not answer.

"I know you saw my father," she whispers.

"Sure," you say, "sure, I saw him. I see him nearly every day."

"You know what I mean," she whispers.

"How the hell can I know what you mean?" you demand. "I know I saw him, like I do nearly every day, but if you don't mean that, then I—"

"You know," she whispers, softer than before, "you know what I mean."

She waits as though for you to answer, but you do not.

"I mean that my father sent you here," she whispers, more softly yet, so softly that you scarcely make out the words.

But you do make them out, and exclaim harshly, belligerently, "Aw, for God's sake! If you think anybody had to send me here—why, my God!" And you stop.

"He sent you here," she reiterates, whispering rushingly with a sibilant emphasis, "my father sent you here—he would send you here—oh, I just know he did, and don't tell me different. Oh, that's why you came. That's why!"

"The hell he did," you burst out, "the hell he did. He didn't *send* me. Nobody sent me. I got your address from Ham. Ham had your address. Now look here, you know Ham had your address!"

You scarcely believe that you have said that, that Ham Murdock gave you the address. You stop suddenly, surprised by the lie, appalled by it. You hadn't meant to tell the lie. You hadn't meant to tell any lie, and every word you'd said had been the truth, the God's truth, for nobody had made you come, nobody, not Bogan Murdock or anybody else, nobody had sent you here. And you feel your muscles twitching under the sheet, and are terrified by the lie, which seems to be a powerful hand clutching your heart.

You are so seized by it, so involved in yourself, that you are scarcely aware that she has pushed herself up on one arm and is staring at you in the shadows, saying measuredly, not whispering now: "It's a lie, Jerry Calhoun—it's a lie—a lie."

"It's not a lie," you burst out again, bitterly, for the lie wasn't your lie, you had to tell the lie to make her believe the truth, and if it's a lie you were tricked into it, if it's a lie it wasn't your fault because she made you lie. "I told you nobody sent me," you assert savagely. "I told you that. Didn't I tell you that? Nobody made me come! And that's no lie."

"Oh, it's all a lie," she is saying, soberly at first, staring at you in the shadows, "oh, it's all a lie, everything's a lie. Everything. And he made you come, he made you—" And her voice rises, and you watch her propped there, and see the dim shine of her eyes and the white of her bare shoulder where the sheet has slipped down; and as you watch her, the whole thing doesn't seem real to you, for you seem to be drawing farther and farther away so that her voice scarcely comes to you. "Oh, he made you come, and you came, oh, I know! And you brought those things. Oh, you brought them in your pocket. Because you're so sure—oh, you're so sure of everything, Jerry Calhoun, you were so sure of me, Jerry Calhoun. Oh, you stopped at some filthy drugstore, Jerry Calhoun, and bought them, because you—"

"It's a damned good thing I did," you say.

"Oh, I wouldn't have cared, I wouldn't have cared," she says, "I wouldn't have cared about anything. It wouldn't have mattered, if you'd just come by yourself, if he hadn't sent you."

She is sitting straight up now, with the sheet slipped down to her lap, but you do not move.

"Oh, I was a fool," she says, leaning toward you, "I was a fool, and I ought to have known, but I did it—I don't know why I did it, and it is horrible because—because—" her voice sinks to a

231

whisper again, "because it is just like he was sitting there—over there in that chair—" and she suddenly thrusts out her arm to point across the dark room to the chair by the window, "like he was sitting over there all the time, all the time we were here, and looking at us."

He walked down the abandoned street, and it was all inside his head. It was all happening again inside his head. It was like a movie inside his head. It was like there were two Jerry Calhouns, the Jerry Calhoun to whom it had happened and the Jerry Calhoun to whom nothing had happened. As the pictures of what had happened kept going past, and it all kept happening over again in its perpetual present, the Jerry Calhoun to whom it had happened kept trying scrupulously to explain it all to the Jerry Calhoun to whom nothing had happened at all.

Eighteen

Statement of Ashby Wyndham

WE GIVE what little truck and plunder we had to them as needed
it more than we did. We taken some clothes to keep clean and
decent in a bundle, and a skillit to cook in, and nigh four dollars
I had, and we walked down off the Mountain. We come to a settlemint, and then they was more settlemints and towns, and I ast
folks had they met with Jacob, and told them how I come to be
huntin him. I done forgot the names of half them places. We
stopped in them places and I done what I could git to do. We was
hongry and it no lie more than one night when the sun went down.
We laid down and the belly was drawed, and the sun come and it
was the same. But the Lord taken mind on the sparrow, and the
Lord taken mind on us. He give me work to do, and He put bread
and meat in our mouth. Folks taken us in and they give us bite
and sup and we give thanks. I never ast for nuthin. I done somethin
ever time to pay.

I stood in the street and I told folks how it was. How the Lord
had laid it on me to tell folks. I told them my wickedness and how
the wicked man will come down low. I met folks in the big road
and I told them. I told them how peace come in my heart and it
was lak sunshine when the clouds are done gone. And I met folks
as taken heed. You meet a man in the road as has got a coat on
his back and his belly full and folks give him a good name and
got a tight roof over his head and money in his pants. It looks lak
he ain't thinkin on nuthin but gittin and thrivin and takin his
ease, and you tells him how peace come in yore heart. But you
name peace in yore heart and you look in his face and it is drawed
of a sudden. It is lak they was a old stitch or a old pain in him
and he ain't thought nuthin on it and all of a sudden he knows
somethin is in him growin and he gits cold all over and knows he
is goin to die and wries up his face. May be he will make his
heart hard and he will tell you to git out of his way. But you

233

know they ain't no peace in his heart. And he knows it and wries up his face. But I met a man in the road nigh a settlemint by the name of Sumatry and I told him how it was. You got peace in yore heart, he ast me.

I told him I did, and give praise. He looked at me nigh half a minute. The Lord bless you, he said of a sudden. Then he said, and the Lord have mercy on my soul.

He was a big man with a black beard all curly, and he had on a black coat and a gold watch and chain and he was ridin in a buggy. He said that to me and then he went off down the road in the buggy.

I come to towns and I stood in the street where the folks was and I read to them folks out of the Bible. I give them the Lords word lak it come to me and I told them how it was with me.

It was eight months when we come to Mitchell Landin. It is a settlemint on the river, and they was buildin a bridge there. I got me work on the bridge, and Murry got him work. Murry was a big boy, and he could do work lak a man. He taken up with us from a town up the valley. He did not have no folks. He was a orfin in the world, and he come with us. He could not read none but he would set and listen and hearken when I read what the Bible said. I read it and he never moved.

They was a feller workin on the bridge by the name of Jasper Littlefoot. Me and him, we was workin alongside, swingin a pick and shevil where the road was goin to the bridge. I ast him did he live in Mitchell Landin, and he said, naw he did not. I ast him where he come from, lak a man will and him civil. He did not say nuthin and I reckined he did not ketch me good. So I ast him agin. He histed up his shevil lak he was gittin ready to bast me over the head, and he said, you son of a bitch. He said it again. I did not do nuthin. I looked at him and I said, you named me a son of a bitch, I am a pore sinful man in Gods sight but I ain't no son of a bitch. He did not say no more, and he put down his shevil.

They was a feller seen it and it was afterwards he said to me, that feller Littlefoot nigh killed you.

Why, I ast him.

He done kilt one man, he said.

Why was he fixin to kill me, I ast him.

Because you ast him where he come from, he said. And he laughed and he spat out on the ground and he said, he is right touchous if you ast him where he come from, he is touchous because he come from the pen.

He told me that feller was in the pen ten years for killin a man.

He had not been out no time, and he was touchous. He did not have nuthin to do with folks. He lived in a old shanty boat on the river by hisself.

The next day when we quit workin about sun, I seen Littlefoot start walkin off. I walked aside of him. I said to him, I was in a dark prisen and I laid in the dark.

He did not say nuthin. He just kept walkin and lookin down the road lak they was not nobody but hisself.

I laid in the dark, I said, and I was a lost man and somebody put a key in the lock and throwed the door wide open and the light come in so strong I blinked blind for the brightness.

Yeah, he said, yeah, they put a key in my lock and they throwed the door open but it taken them ten years.

He said it but he never looked at me when he done it.

I laid longer, I said.

How long, he said.

Not ten years, I said, it was more than a score.

He looked at me right clost, and he seen I was not no old man, and he said, they must have put you in for bitin yore Mammy on the tit.

Naw, I said, naw, but I laid in the dark nigh all my life, I laid in the prisen cell but it was the dark of sin and wickedness where I laid.

He looked at me agin. He stopped in the road and looked at me and scan me clost, and he did not say but one word. It was a word I ain't goin to put on no paper. It was a word of filthiness and abominations. But he give me a look and it was all he said. Then he started walkin down the road.

But when the job out at the bridge was done finished he taken up with us. I had done told him how it was with me. I had done read the Lords blessed word to him. We had done been down on our knee bones together afore God and Him Most High.

I done said he lived by hisself on a shanty boat. He taken us on the shanty boat with him. We was goin down the river and we was goin to tell the Gospel to them as had ears.

We come to towns and places on the river. We worked to git money to buy a little somethin to eat. We fished in the river. Jasper had him a old squirril rifle and we kilt squirrils and rabbits and et them. We was a long time on the river, comin down. We stayed at places a long time and worked and told folks about Gods blessed word and how peace come in our hearts. Then when it come on us to be goin we went down the river. A old man and his wife taken up with us at a town they named Cherryville. The house they had had done burnt plum down to the ground and the grandbaby they was raisin. That baby was all the folks they had. Our baby has done gone to the Lord, the old man said, and we done turned our eyes to the Lord. They had the name of Lumpkin. He was a old man, but he washed a lot and kept hisself clean. He had been a hand to chaw and smoke, he said, but when the Gospel taken holt he give it up. It was a filthiness, he said.

We seen days hongry and we seen days cold on the river. But we taken what the Lord sent and knowed it was good. We give praise and rejoicin.

I always ast if folks had seen Jacob. At one place they was a man as thought he had seen him. But he was not positive of a certain.

Nineteen

HER WHOLE life centered itself about the apartment, the studio, and the walks along the river. For weeks her car sat in a garage, untouched. She did not even go the few blocks which separated her apartment from the center of the city, except once or twice, at night, to a movie. She would walk along the river, which was swollen now by spring rains, in any kind of weather, watching the sunlight strike across the roofs to the water, or watching, far away, a squall of spring rain move up the valley toward her, blotting out the river; or when the rain reached her, she strode through it with the wetness on her face.

It was the same course she had walked that night with Slim Sarrett, but then it had been night and the mist had been coming off the river to modify even such precise contours as had been visible in the darkness, and the streets had been deserted. Now, in the late afternoons, there were people everywhere—the red faces leaning from the high cabs of trucks, the cigar butt in the corner of the mouth, the thin old faces with the yellow saliva dampening the unshaven chin, the round faces and the narrow clean-scraped fox-faces above overcoats buttoned too tight, eyes gleaming from the shadow of rooms that opened on the street, the cripple on the corner, with pencils and shoelaces, who swung on his crutch to stare after her, the old Negro woman, bent, shuffling, unseeing, whose gums worked. They were the difference between night and day, but for a while, even in the day, she did not look at them, was scarcely aware of them, and moving past them, carried wrapped about her something of the solitude of the first night. Later, the fact of their eyes upon her, the fact that she herself possessed some reality for them, made her observe them.

But sometimes, late at night, when she couldn't go to sleep, she took the walk. Even at that hour, however, she found that it was not quite as it had been the first time. It would be dark, as before, and the streets empty, but now, in the solitude, she sensed some residue of their presence—that is, of the presence of all those faces—

like the tainted vapor which hangs over drains. She mentioned to Slim Sarrett that she had walked by the river at night. He said: "It is extremely stupid. That is the toughest section in town. You must promise me not to do it again. If you want to walk at night, let me know, and I'll walk with you." He went with her a few times. On these occasions he did not talk. He walked along beside her in his easy stride, his shoulders free but not quite stooped, and his head held up, his face, looking straight ahead, white against the darkness of the buildings or the sky. He did not take her hand as he had done that first night.

In her apartment, she cooked and ate her meals, sat for long periods looking out of the window, or lay on the couch and read the books which Slim Sarrett gave her. Not infrequently he came and sat and talked to her about the books, and asked her ques· tions, leading questions, leading her on to argument, analysis, and opinion. He was enormously patient, enormously interested, it seemed, and his eyes rarely left her face. Or sometimes Ham came.

During the early part of this period of her life, when she went to Sarrett's studio, she felt a kind of timidity, a sense of being left out, for everyone there seemed so caught up in his own concerns or his own vociferations. Or somebody would make a remark, and people would laugh, but she would miss the joke, and sit there, looking from face to face. Once, at such a moment, she found that Sweetwater—Sweetie Sweetwater, they called him—who had been laughing too, was watching her, his coarse hair disheveled and the scar that ran back on his left cheek from the lip, white with the liquor in him. She blushed guiltily, and turned to avoid his eyes. But he said, "Hey, kid," and she knew he was addressing her. She turned again to him, and he was grinning at her. The grin was crooked, because the left dog-tooth had been knocked out. "Kid," he said, "don't you grieve. It probably ain't half as funny as they think it is."

She started to make some retort, furious at him, but she became aware that Duckfoot Blake, with that long, horrible, sissy ivory cigarette holder hanging out of his mouth, was looking at her, too, and grinning. But he was not grinning communicatively at her, as Sweetie Sweetwater had done. He was grinning as to himself.

But things changed, changing, however, so gradually that she forgot how she had been at first, and how strange Professor Hoxley, drunk, had seemed at first and how she had hated the way Sam Ball, the stall keeper, put his big face close and blew his breath in your face when he started to tell you a story. She had read some of the books, too, and had learned most of the words.

"By the way," Slim Sarrett would say, in the midst of the talk, "Sue was saying something about that the other day that I thought rather interesting. She was saying—" but he would stop, and turn to Sue, almost with an air of discovering her presence, "—oh, how did you put it, Sue, how was it exactly?" And he would turn again to the company, saying, "I want the exact phrase—that was important." Then everybody would be quiet, and would look at her, waiting. The first time, it had been horrible, everything suddenly quiet and the eyes all on her, and in the middle, Slim Sarrett's eyes, waiting, and he seemed to be nodding at her in encouragement, and for the flicker of an instant she hated his very guts for that, for by God, she wasn't a child. What had she said the other day, she couldn't remember anything she had said, she didn't even know what they were talking about, what had Slim said—or anybody else said? But she said something, something that popped into her head—maybe Slim had once said it, maybe somebody else—and she smiled with a brittle challenge at the company.

"Yes, yes," Slim was saying, "that was it. The exact phrase."

And she learned that she could make them laugh. You just sort of shut your eyes, and made your mind a blank, and said whatever crazy thing popped into your head. "Malloy, Malloy," you would say, just out of a clear sky, when things were quiet for a moment, "Malloy, you're just like a tuberose—you really are, darling. Only—" and you'd wait for the preliminary laughter to abate, "somewhere back Burbank got gay with the cow itch." Or: "Browning is just like rock candy. He looks so hard and shiny, and he makes your spit sweet." Or: "Tennyson is just like Castoria—awfully soothing and the children cry for it." That was it. Something is *like* some-thing else—oh, just like something—the "just" was important—and you shut your eyes and it popped into your head and you said it, and they would laugh. But you yourself did not laugh. You just sat there with your face straight, just as straight as you could make it. Unless nobody laughed at first. Then you looked off to one corner of the room, and smiled just a little bit to yourself, like you knew something, and then—it always worked that way—somebody laughed, like he knew something too. But once, when everybody was laughing at something she had said, Sweetwater leaned toward her, grinning, and whispered: "Get right in there and pitch, kid. They don't know a ball from a strike."

It was exciting to know that you could make them laugh. She did it more and more. A few drinks and your head got full of things, just crazy things—"like, like, just like—" And if nothing

239

else came, you could always make them laugh at Professor Hoxley. That was easy.

But sometimes she just listened, and that was fun, if you really listened, even to Professor Hoxley. "It is easy to underrate Hoxley," Slim told her. "He is worth listening to. He is very instructive in his way. Just as Duckfoot Blake is. Of course, both are sterile—and that is what makes them so instructive. I sometimes think of them as the two special forms of modern sterility. Hoxley calls himself a 'medievalist'—he sees history as just a grab bag and you grab something that glitters and he has grabbed the Middle Ages all for his own. And Blake is really an extraordinarily intelligent cynic—that rare creature, a cynic who is intelligent. He is that rare person who has the capacity for creativity and yet repudiates all creativity. He remarked once: 'You know, I can't find but one thing. that repays the effort you have to invest in it—and Divine Providence in beneficent wisdom has made it possible for you to do that in bed so you can go to sleep right afterwards.' He has a kind of wit, you know.—But I must say that, in a way, I prefer little Frey, with his half-baked Marxism and sociology, or Sweetwater, with his homemade variety—he at least tries to do something. But Marxism, of course, is a superficial diagnosis. What is—"

Or sometimes she sat on the couch, beside Alice Smythe, who would hold her hand and, looking into her face, would say: "My dear, I must tell you how much I admire you. For what you have done. You have been so brave. When you admire somebody, I think you ought to tell them. Don't you think so?" And the shy eyes looked out at her, imploringly, beseechingly, asking for something, for admiration, for kindness, for hope, for a word.

"All nuts," Ham said to her one night as he walked to her apartment with her after the studio.

"If you don't like them you don't have to go there," Sue retorted.

"Sure, I like 'em. I even like Slim Sarrett, who is a brass-bound son-of-a-bitch or I give up lip reading. Now, Slim—"

"Now, look here, Ham Murdock, if—"

"Easy," Ham said, "take it easy. You don't have to protect Slim Sarrett. He don't need anybody to protect him. He is brass-bound. But he's nuts. The only one not nuts is Duckfoot. Duckfoot really knows his stuff at the bank. He is a real banker. He—"

"Like you," Sue retorted. "A real banker. You're getting to be a real banker and you polish your shoes."

"Well, what do you expect me to do, if I don't go in the bank. Join the Marines?"

"I don't care in the slightest what you do," she told him.

But she liked them, all of them. Well enough anyway. Even Malloy, who tried to make love to her, and little Frey, who tried to kiss her one night when they were in the kitchen together, and whose breath was bad, and whom she pushed off as though he had been a nasty brat—it was easy, she just grabbed his arms and shoved him off, and his arms were like dry sticks—and who got tears in his eyes then, and insulted her and called her a damned middle-class snob. But none of the others ever tried to make love to her, for you couldn't call what Professor Hoxley did by the name of making love—what he said in French and then giggled while his wife sat there on the couch.

Certainly, Slim Sarrett never made love to her. He would sit with her and talk, never about them as people together, but about other people, about books, about people in books—never anything else. Or he could sit with her and be quiet. She had not guessed that about him, but it was true. He could be quiet, sitting there in her apartment and looking out over the river. And once, after sitting that way for a long time, he had risen, soundlessly, and had walked to the door. He had stood there an instant, looking at her—she couldn't figure out exactly what the look meant, but it made her feel the way she had felt that first night in the dirty café, when she had discovered his hand upon her own and had looked up, through her tears, and had seen the unashamed, unpredictable wetness of his eyes. Then, he had gone, closing the door softly behind him, as one closes the door of a sickroom or of a room where a child is sleeping.

One night at his studio, she had had too much to drink and had lain down on the couch, her head in Alice Smythe's lap, while the party went on around her. When she woke up, it was very quiet, the light was dim, the ceiling above her was strange, and in the midst of her first confusion, a great terror gripped her. Then she saw where she was, and started to sit up.

"Are you all right?" Slim Sarrett asked.

He was sitting in a straight chair, erect, his hands on his lap, some ten feet from the couch.

"Yes," she said, and looked about the room for the others.

"They've gone. They were all plastered," he said. "It's late," he said, "but I didn't want to disturb you."

She saw that a blanket had been laid over her, and a pillow adjusted beneath her head. He moved to the switch of the main light. "I turned it off," he said. "It was in your eyes."

The light came on.

"Thank you," she said, and stood up, weakly.

"I'll get you some ice water," he said.

He walked home with her, slowly, not talking.

At the door of her apartment house, after he had told her good night, he said: "You were very beautiful asleep. I watched you while you slept."

Then he turned, and walked off down the street.

It was a timeless world she lived in. It was what it was, without any past or future. The people in it would never change. They had been different once, a long time back, but that fact didn't mean anything now. What they remembered from the past was always something exactly like the present. At one time all their past which wasn't exactly like their present had disappeared, like a puff of smoke. And all their future would be more of the same present. Their bodies would change. Malloy would get bald and fat and slow, and whisky would begin to disagree with him. Little Jenkins would get thinner and would stoop and would quit writing about those islands in the South Seas. Alice Smythe would get to be a shapeless body swathed in tweed suits, or when Malloy left her she might drink poison, or she might join the Episcopal Church. But none of them would ever change; what was true inside them would never change now. They would always be sitting around in a kind of party forever, talking and talking and being just what they were. The sense of that unchangingness comforted Sue Murdock, like a warm blanket you snuggle under in the dark when you feel the cold air from the window on your face. You could just lie there and be warm, for if the present was just going to keep on being the present and never was going to be the past, then everything was just what it was. If you found the time when the present was all, then you didn't have to worry. You could just be.

She rarely thought of her own past, of how she came to be where she was. The way things were now was good enough; at least, for now. When she saw her brother Ham, or Duckfoot Blake, they seemed to come without bearing any mark of that other world which she had left. They came from that other world which was concerned with the past and the future, and they would go back into it, for they belonged to it, but now, when she saw them, they accepted, provisionally at least, the world of the present in which she was. Even Ham didn't ask her any more questions, and didn't tell her what was going on at home or among those people she used to run around with. She'd made him understand finally that she didn't give a damn and didn't want to hear anything about it. So both Ham and Duckfoot, when she saw them in Slim Sarrett's.

studio, sitting with their glasses in their hands in the middle of all the jabber, seemed purged of all taint of time. They seemed, for the moment at least, to belong to that world of the studio—to belong to it even more finally and fully than Slim Sarrett did himself. For, since Slim Sarrett had created that world, he was, somehow, detached from it, and was above it.

Ham had tried several times, before she made him understand, to talk to her about the world she had left, but Duckfoot had never tried. The time he talked about it, he did so because she asked him. At the studio one night she walked over to the corner where he was sitting, and asked him how Jerry was getting along.

He did not show any surprise when she asked him, and because he took it that way, just looking at her like she had asked about the weather, a sort of smile on his face, or almost there, she was furious at him. He ought to have shown some surprise that she could walk right up to him and ask about Jerry Calhoun without batting an eyelash. That would have been some recognition of her own achievement, for she felt it to be an achievement. But the fact that he didn't show anything seemed to say to her that the whole business, everything that had happened and everything she had done, didn't mean a thing in the world. All he said was, "Oh, Jerry's making out."

"Oh, he'll make out," she said, bitterly, but told herself that the bitterness was for Duckfoot Blake; "he'll always get along fine."

Then she was sure that there was a smile on his face. "Sure," he said.

"Who has he got for a girl now?" she asked. She hadn't meant to say that, but looking at that smile on his face, she felt like she had stepped into quicksand or something, and her floundering simply got her in deeper.

"I'm not exactly an ardent reader of the society page," he said, "but I seem to recall seeing that he took a Miss Marcella Thomas to a dance recently."

"That bag of bones," she said, and laughed, and thought, *My God, why can't I shut up?* But she didn't shut up. She asked, trying to smile sweetly, "Is he sleeping with her?"

"The paper didn't say," Duckfoot answered, judicially, "and I couldn't tell you. Why don't you ring Jerry up and ask him?" Then before she could think of an answer to that, he said again, in a different voice: "Why don't you ring Jerry up?"

"Why should I?" she said snappishly.

"Oh, I don't know," Duckfoot was studying her through the smoke from his cigarette, his head cocked back, "but you all might

243

find something to say to each other. Maybe Jerry's figured out a few things."

"I don't care what Jerry Calhoun has figured out."

"Maybe he's figured out how he would like to go West and grow up with the country. Maybe he's tired of his job."

"Oh, so he made you his little confidant, he poured out his little heart to you, did he?" she demanded.

"No," he said, "as a matter of fact, he didn't tell me a thing."

"Well, if you believe that's the reason I broke up with Jerry Calhoun, you—"

"I'm no prophet," Duckfoot Blake said, "but I still believe that two and two makes four, whether anybody confides in me or not. But, as I was saying, why don't you ring him up? Jerry's a good boy."

"If he called me up," she said slowly, "I'd hang the receiver up as soon as I heard his voice."

That was a pretty weak come-back, she admitted to herself. But she did turn on her heel and leave Duckfoot Blake sitting there in the corner. And she meant what she had said. She would hang up the phone or slam the door if it was Jerry Calhoun. All that, the past which was Jerry Calhoun, didn't mean a thing to her now. She was sure of that.

She did not ask herself what did mean anything to her now. But certainly nothing in that other world meant anything. She did not even read the newspapers. If now and then news filtered down from that other world, like fragments shifting down uncertainly into the dim, subaqueous world she lived in, she scarcely paid them any attention. The agitations of the surface—whatever they were, and she didn't care—created scarcely a waver of outline here.

Occasionally Sweetwater—she couldn't tell, really, whether Sweetwater belonged to this world of the studio or not, but he was there—and Malloy, or even Sam Ball and the foreman, talked about business or politics, but she never properly listened. She did know that Meyers and Murdock had done something about some insurance companies, and she knew that they had bought some more banks down in Alabama or Georgia, for Malloy had come in one night with the paper and had read the story about the banks, a front-page story, and Sweetwater had said: "More rope."

And Malloy had asked Duckfoot what he thought, and Duckfoot had said: "It ain't ethical for me to think." Duckfoot never took part in those conversations about politics or business.

"More rope," Sweetwater had said, and Malloy had retorted:

"Hell, that boy's got this State tied up so tight you can't grow a corn on your little toe."

"Tying up this State won't help when the time comes," Sweetwater had said. "You can't make water run uphill just by crooking a legislature."

"Hell, that fellow's smart," Malloy had said, "even if he is a—" Then he had stopped, and Sue had known that he was stealing a look at her.

"Is what?" she demanded, turning on him.

"Aw, hell," he said, good-naturedly, "gonna put me on the spot, gonna—"

But Alice Smythe cut in: "What we need is faith. We have to have faith in the goodness and courage of people. We know there are good people and courageous people. We know that." And she laid her hand on Sue's hand. "We know what Sue did. We know she had courage. We mustn't lose faith in that kind of courage—"

Sue felt like getting up and walking out of the room. She felt like she had swallowed a fly in the coffee. She jerked her hand back. "That's not—" she began.

But Sweetwater, ignoring her, just as though she weren't present, said: "Yeah, yeah, and how does she live?"

"Damn it!" Sue said, and she was mad now, good and mad, and glad to be mad, "I've got my own money, I've got—"

"And where does that come from?" Sweetwater asked, grinning with that broken tooth.

"It's none of your business!"

"It comes," he said, "from the same place where that kind of money always comes from. It don't make any difference how much it is—lots or little. It's the same thing. It's just the way—"

"It's none of your business," she cried, and felt her face red and hot, but he kept on grinning.

"Sure," he said, "sure, but I don't think anybody ought to kid himself."

"I don't kid myself."

"It is sure hard to kid yourself," he said, "if anybody round here would come up for air now and then. This park bill before the Legislature—my God, Meyers and Murdock trying to unload that Atlas Iron and Massey Mountain and Pretty River Quarries on the State, and it—"

"Meyers and Murdock?" Alice Smythe echoed.

"Who you think is behind it? Who the hell? With that Private Porsum making speeches—yeah, he killed a lot of Germans one time and he's a hero, sure, he's a moral half-wit—and going up before that Legislature and saying what somebody told him to say. Yeah, and I know what's up there on that mountain. They took the iron out and cut it over and blew the rock out and starved the folks to death and the ground's washed away—oh, I know what's up there, I been up there, I'll say I have, I got this up there—" and he laid his forefinger to the scar, which was very white now above the black hole where the dog-tooth had been knocked out.

"And," he said, "I am stinking drunk." But he did not show it. He never showed it except for the way the scar got.

The foreman was drunk, too. Quietly, sleepily drunk. He had a right to be drunk. He had been fired that day. "Got the wrong friends," Sweetwater said. "Me."

That was all Sue heard from that other world, until the second letter came from her father. It came, as the other one had come, in the late afternoon, by messenger. But this time, the messenger was Anse, who handed her the envelope, and seemed to be embarrassed as he stood there in his chauffeur's uniform, with his cap held before him, showing the greasy inside, and asked her how she was. She said she was fine, abruptly, and shut the door. She could see his eyes spying out the apartment, even as the door closed.

The letter said that her father and mother had talked things over, and had thought that she might like to take a long trip, perhaps to Europe. There would be new things to see, and she could study there if she wanted to. Her mother could go with her, for she herself seemed to be in a nervous condition and the change would do her good, the change and being with Sue again. The letter was signed "Dockie."

She did not answer the letter.

Two weeks later, toward dusk on a rainy spring afternoon, she opened the door of her apartment, to enter, and saw, against the light from the window, the silhouette of the back of a man's head protruding above the overstuffed chair. For a moment she thought it was Slim Sarrett, then the man rose, and turned, and even though the face was black against the light, she knew it was her father. She knew that he was smiling.

She shut the door behind her.

"I had to come to see you, daughter," he said, approaching her. "I hope you won't mind too much." He leaned and kissed her on the cheek.

She stood very straight, not moving, and on the instant when his lips were withdrawn from contact with her cheek, she felt the slightest exhalation of his breath against it.

246

Then he was looking down at her, his face slightly smiling, as from a distance, slightly sad, and strong.

"I had to come," he said. "There are some things you will understand when you are older, my dear. You—"

He hesitated, laid his hand upon her arm, and under that compulsion—though he exerted no pressure—she moved beside him to the window. She sat on the couch, on the edge, not leaning back, and he stood before her.

"I had said to myself—I had written to you—that I would not interfere," he said. "That you had to work out your own destiny. As we all must. But I came—" He smiled again, and moved one hand in a little gesture of deprecation. "When you are as old as I am, Sue, you may understand my weakness."

My God, my God, she thought, and knew that there was nothing in the world for her to say.

"So," he said, "I came."

He sat down, facing her. With her head bowed, she saw his feet set firmly on the floor there, on the frayed carpet, the strong shoes of supple leather, dully glinting, expertly stitched, and the coarse gray fabric of the trousers, scarcely creased, and the brass ferrule of the stick which he held in one hand as he leaned toward her. She knew he was leaning toward her, but she could not lift her head to him.

For some moments, while she felt his eyes upon her, he did not speak.

Then he said—and she seemed to be aware of the slightest edge which had come into his voice—as though his eyes were narrowing, ever so little—he said: "Have you thought about my letter, Sue?"

This was different. This was different now. This was a question. And she thought: *All right.* And lifted her head.

"Yes," she said.

"I want you to do what you want to do," he said. "But I thought —I thought that you might like to go away. Abroad. You have never been abroad. There would be new interests—new places—" A swift movement of his eyes swept the gray walls, the unmade bed, where clothes were piled, the carpet, before they came again to rest on her face.

"I'm all right here," she said.

"It has, no doubt, been a valuable experience. I am sure of that. And—it's strange to say, but it's true—I am glad, in a way, that you never drew on the money I deposited for you—"

"I didn't want it," she said.

247

"But now, you could go away. You have never been abroad. You are young, and new experiences, new people—"

"In other words," she said, "you don't like the people I am friends with now. You never liked them. They're—they're—" She moved her body and looked suddenly about as though to find a word in the air. "Real," she decided, and sank back, feeling empty and cheated.

He shook his head. "You are quite wrong, my dear. I understand there are some admirable and gifted people among them. People of intelligence, and I always respect intelligence. Mr. Blake, whose judgment I admire, has told me—"

"Oh, you've been asking him!" she exclaimed, and stood up, and took two paces on the frayed carpet, and turned, and put her hands together. "Asking him, and he's been spying, and I hate him! That's it, spying for you, and you just want to get rid of me —to get me out of town—"

"My dear," he said, softly.

"—just get me out of town, because I embarrass you. What people say—oh, I know, I know!"

"My dear," he said, and she had to look at him, and he was sitting there, like she hadn't said anything at all, unruffled, like nothing had happened, just sitting there with his hand on his stick.

"You do not know your father," he said then, quietly, "if you think I have ever been a man to be influenced by the whisperings of fools." And for an instant, his face seemed to reflect, fleetingly, an inward smile.

So she stood there, with her hands together, her shoulders moving slightly, and looked wildly about the room, over his head.

"My dear," he said.

Then the knock came at the door.

It was Slim Sarrett.

She was aware of the quick, flicking glance he gave as he stepped into the room; then he moved deliberately toward the chair where her father sat, with his face now turned toward the door and his expression composed by an obvious exercise of will. She watched Slim Sarrett's approach—she had the impulse to count his steps as he approached, watching the grayish, unpolished, patched shoes moving soundlessly, easily, forward—and she felt growing insecurely within her a sense of triumph.

He stopped before her father's chair, his feet close together, and said: "You probably do not remember me. We met some time ago at your home. I am Sarrett."

248

And he regarded Murdock, while Murdock rose, with an effort almost clumsy, from the chair, letting his stick fall, trying to retrieve it, saying, "Yes, of course," and putting out his hand.

She thought she detected—she could not be sure—an instant of hesitation, shaded with theatrical expertness, before Slim Sarrett put out his own hand.

Slim Sarrett released the hand, and, still facing Bogan Murdock, stepped back, with a nice calculation of distance, his body swaying ever so little, into the space between the couch and the table.

Bogan Murdock sank back into his chair, and leaned to secure his stick.

"He—" Sue burst out, hesitating, nodding in the direction of her father, "he is trying to make me go away. He wants me to go away. I told you he wanted me to go away, and he's come to make me go. Abroad. Europe—he wants to send me to Europe—oh, yes—he wants to send me a long way off. He—"

"My dear," Bogan Murdock said.

Slim Sarrett, who seemed to have scarcely listened to her outburst, turned to the table, where a package of cigarettes lay beside a tray heaped with ash and crushed, lip-stick-stained butts. He selected a cigarette, lifted it, and turned to face her, as her words trailed off. "Of course," he said casually, holding the cigarette inexpertly before him with thumb and forefinger, and speaking with the tone of one who mentions a decision long since made, "you won't do it."

"No, no," the girl said.

"Mr. Sarrett!" Bogan Murdock exclaimed.

Slim Sarrett ignored him. "Naturally, you won't," he said to the girl.

"Mr. Sarrett," Bogan Murdock began in a tone of glittering authority, "the decision is my daughter's. I quite fail to see—"

And Sarrett, almost with an air of tolerant discovery, turned to him. "You are quite right, Mr. Murdock. The decision is undoubtedly your daughter's. But—" and he allowed himself the luxury of putting the cigarette to his lips before he continued, "I shall point out that it will be one of the few decisions which she has ever been permitted to make about her life. Without the special type of subtle pressure which you seem to be able to exercise."

He again lifted the cigarette to his lips, turned his head from Bogan Murdock to show his white, carved-looking profile, and looked idly out the window, while the smoke drifted from his nostrils.

"He wants to get me away! Oh, I embarrass him here, that's what he wants, what he—" Sue was saying.

And her father was saying to the face which looked out the window: "I shall not for one moment accept this insolence!"

"Insolence?" Slim Sarrett questioned, idly, not turning. "To a man like you, Mr. Murdock, accustomed to the exercise of large and small tyrannies and gifted with an extraordinary talent for self-deception, any truth comes as an impertinence. Your relation to your daughter has interested me for a long while. For me it has had an interesting symbolic significance. You—"

Bogan Murdock sat very straight in his chair, the white coming around his lips, his hand working on the handle of his stick, saying: "Mr. Sarrett, I shall not—"

"—for instance," the even, detached voice proceeded, "represent to me the special disease of our time, the abstract passion for power, a vanity springing from an awareness of the emptiness and unreality of the self which can only attempt to become real and human by the oppression of people who manage to retain some shreds of reality and humanity. Now, your daughter—"

Bogan Murdock was on his feet, his mouth twitching, his cheeks darkened with fury, his hand grasping the stick at the middle, uncertainly, not quite lifting it. He took one step toward Sarrett, who now turned, and, not laying down the cigarette poised between forefinger and thumb, said: "Mr. Murdock, I think that I could manage nicely to take that stick away from you. And I am an excellent boxer, and I am in excellent condition. And you—" he paused as to assess the potential opponent, "are much older. You are only a middle-aged playboy sportsman. I strongly advise you—"

The girl, not breathing, watched her father as he stood there.

"Besides," Sarrett was saying, "it would make a nice headline: *Prominent Broker Brawls with Student in Daughter's Apartment.* Could you afford that, Mr. Murdock?"

She watched her father as he stood there for a long instant, and his eyes were wide, all black, it seemed, and glittering, above the flaring nostrils, while his mouth worked over the words that did not come.

Then he went out.

He turned once at the door. His eyes were upon her, but she could not make out the expression on his face.

She saw his square, not very wide shoulders as he walked down the hall, quickly, for he had not closed the door after him.

That night she became Slim Sarrett's mistress.

In the months that followed, she did not ask herself whether she was happy or not. Only now and then she remembered times from the past when she had asked herself that question. Those times seemed very far off, now, and—there was a kind of victory in the thought—irrelevant. And she did not think about the future.

But Slim Sarrett, apparently, thought about the future. Occasionally, he talked about going to New York. In the fall, perhaps, instead of going back to the University for his Ph.D. He could make enough free-lancing, he said, for him to live on, and she, she had enough for herself until he could get established. Just for herself, though, he said. He could do enough writing to live on from the first, and he would be established soon. He talked that way, now and then, but the words had no meaning for her, though she said yes, yes.

Words didn't have much meaning for her. You just lived the way you were, anyway. They didn't have much meaning, except when she sat in the studio at night, with the voices going on and the air full of words, and she held the glass in her hand and drank.

Slim Sarrett encouraged her drinking. She became aware of that very gradually. At the studio, when people were there, he would lean sympathetically toward her with a fresh drink in his hand before she had really finished the former one. She liked it, and he knew she liked it, and she said things that made everybody laugh. Or he would come to her apartment in the evening and bring a bottle, and mix drinks for her in the kitchenette, under the bright light in there, while she lay on the couch in the other room, in the dark. He would bring the drink to her, and lean above her and give it to her, and sit there while she drank it. Sometimes he would sit there in the chair, away from her, in the almost dark room, not saying a word, and he would watch her. Then things would begin to blur a little. Your knees and wrists would seem to be away from you, the blood in them throbbing out there in the dark, flowing away from you, yet they were you. Then he would rise from his chair and come to her, not making a sound.

That was the way it was, but she didn't care.

But sometimes he sat there until she was asleep. Then she would wake, and stir, and he would be leaning above her.

Only, once or twice, when she had not had very much, she had seized him, as though vindictively, and had exclaimed: "Oh, Slim, Slim, you know—you know what you are—you know what you want to do. Oh, Slim, you've got to make me know, know about me. You've got to make me, you've got to!"

251

Then he had held her head cradled against his chest, and leaning his head above her, had murmured, "Hush, hush, hush," like a nurse or mother. He held her head cradled in his left arm, and murmured, "Hush, hush, my darling," while the long, steely, cool fingers of his right hand rhythmically smoothed her forehead and disordered hair, or rested upon her eyes.

The night Mr. Billie Constantidopeles knocked on the studio door was a hot night in September, too hot for a night in that season, windless, oppressive, dry, with a full moon, still big and blood-red though well up from the eastern horizon beyond the vibrating lights of the district across the river; and at that moment Professor Hoxley had just been affirming that he was an Aristotelian. He was balancing himself on the little, almost capering feet, waving his cigarette in one hand and his sixth glass in the other, and lifting his face, on which the perspiration glistened dewily, up to Duckfoot Blake, who, with the ivory cigarette holder drooping from the corner of his mouth, regarded him with interest. Professor Hoxley balanced and exclaimed: "Oh, I'm an Aristotelian, I'm an Aristotelian, I'm an Aristotelian!"

"Gawd," said Duckfoot Blake, "you almost make me believe you are, Prof."

"Oh, yes, I am, but Herbert Hoover is a Platonist, he really is, and the trouble with this country is only a Platonist can be elected President—Woodrow Wilson was a Platonist, and Warren G. Harding was a Platonist, and Calvin Coolidge was a Platonist—he really was, just like Saint Augustine and John of Erigena—and Herbert Hoover is a dweat-big, bad Platonist— Oh, what makes you have those dweat-big Platonic teeth, dwand-mother—" he lisped and chanted, "but I, ah *bencite!* oh, little me—I'm an Aristotelian—and I won't ever be President, for I'm an Aristotelian, for I'm—"

At that moment, the knock came on the door, and somebody opened the door before Slim Sarrett could get there, and Mr. Billie Constantidopeles was revealed, of medium height, definitely plump, somewhat sagging, clad in fawn-colored jacket, lemon-yellow silk shirt with low, loose collar, flannel trousers of a skirty fullness, brown-and-white shoes, with a Panama hat big as a planter's in one hand and a Malacca cane in the other, his wispy, dark hair thin and lichenlike on the big skull, and his sun-bronzed face smiling, and he was saying: "Pardon, all, but—"

"Gawd," said Duckfoot Blake, quite audibly, "it's them beans I ate."

"Pardon, all," then the stranger's eyes fell upon Slim Sarrett, and he cried out in a beautiful, operatic baritone: "Ah, Slim!"

Then he rushed across the intervening space, dropping his Panama—which Malloy promptly picked up and promptly inspected—and seized Slim Sarrett by the arms and shook him and patted him on the shoulder and exclaimed: "Ah, Slim, ah, Slim!" While Slim Sarrett said, "Well, well," and smiled an impeccable smile which made no commitments.

Malloy had finished his inspection of the Panama and had set it rakishly upon his own head.

"I just hit town," the stranger was saying to Slim, "on the evening plane, and I grabbed me a taxi and went out to that dump of a University and I tore the place up finding out where you lived. Tell me, says I, the address of the greatest living poet, whose fusion of intellectual power and warm, pulsating passion is unprecedented, whose hand I long to clasp, who renews my youth, for the sight of whom I pant like a wanderer in a weary land—and here I am, here is little Billie—and oh, the difference to me! Yes, sir, and—"

"Let me introduce you," Slim Sarrett said, interrupting, and took him by the arm. "This is Mr. Constantidopeles," he said, and began to move around the circle. "He is a painter, a very fine painter—"

"I have," Mr. Constantidopeles broke in, "been painting nudes in Martinique. Gold bodies glistening in the noon. Great muscled torsos, like black bronze, whose velvet sheen reflects the midnight stars of the tropics like black lagoons—"

"It ain't them beans," Duckfoot Blake pondered, "it was that second slice of mince pie. My mother said not—"

"This is Professor Hoxley," Slim Sarrett began again.

"I'm an Aristotelian, I'm an Aristotelian," Professor Hoxley chanted and managed to seize Mr. Constantidopeles' hand, to which he clung, balancing.

"My people," Mr. Constantidopeles remarked pleasantly, "were Greek. We Greeks must stick together." He winked at Slim Sarrett. "We must maintain the best of the Greek tradition. I meditate upon Socrates in the privacy of my chamber, in the watches of the night." Gracefully, he detached his hand.

"I'm an Aris—" Professor Hoxley resumed, but the problem of balance occupied his attention.

"This is Mrs. Hoxley," Slim Sarrett said.

"I am indeed delighted, madame," Mr. Constantidopeles murmured, bowing, "—and surprised. May I ask, are you Greek, too?"

"No," she said, and Mr. Constantidopeles shook his head, as

253

though the world were too much for him, while Slim Sarrett led him to the next person. "This is—"

They came to Malloy, who shook hands, and said, "Glad to meetcha. You sure got a swell hat." He took the hat off his head and looked at the inside. "I bet it cost fifty bucks."

"You must keep it," Mr. Constantidopeles said.

"Say," Malloy protested, "I ain't taking your hat. Not and it costing fifty bucks. Hell, maybe it cost a hundred bucks. I know them things cost—"

"Really, Mr. Malloy, you must," and Mr. Constantidopeles took the hat and adjusted it, with critical delicacy, upon Malloy's head, and stepped back to survey the effect.

"Say, now—"

"You must," Mr. Constantidopeles breathed, and bowed his head a little, as in boyish embarrassment. "You see, my father peddled bananas. He made practically nothing off any particular banana, but you see, he peddled so many. So many. Wherever hand reached out to grasp that sweet and interesting fruit, my father's genius presided. His white ships sailed distant, palm-fringed seas. My crest should be—and is, I may say—the banana rampant on a field of azure. Do you like bananas, Mr. Malloy?"

"Sure, I eat some."

"Fine," Mr. Constantidopeles exclaimed. "You have no doubt eaten a great many bananas. You have contributed at least something to the hat. Perhaps you have eaten the whole hat's worth. Now I, I never eat bananas. It is, therefore, not really my hat. It is your hat, in simple equity. And I have flown from Martinique—"

"I thought you were in Paris," Slim Sarrett said.

"I—" Mr. Constantidopeles began, but Professor Hoxley stiffened, struck perfect equilibrium for an instant, and plunged across the space toward the stranger, uttering, "Paris!" and reaching for Mr. Constantidopeles, continued, "Paris—Paris—been in Paris—let me touch him—I salute him—I touch the hem of his garment—I—"

Mr. Constantidopeles took Professor Hoxley's uncertain hand tenderly, and patted it, continuing to pat it while he spoke: "I was in Paris three years. Then Martinique—" He sank into a chair, still holding the hand of Professor Hoxley, who was compelled to squat at his knee and who lifted his sweat-and-spectacle-glistening face and chirped softly to himself, like a contented little chimpanzee, over and over again, the syllables, "Paris."

"Ah, Slim, I sat in a café in Paris and read a poem of yours in a magazine, and I leaped from the table and went to a telephone and called the office of that magazine in New York, but they could not tell me where to find you. I telephoned for three days, I telephoned the last address they finally gave me, but I never found you. I thought, I'll write to Slim and tell him how beautiful his poem is. Then I thought, no, it would be sacrilege. For it is sacrilege to write to a dear friend. To put the heart on paper. I only write to my bank. Then in Martinique I thought, I shall write to Slim's magazine and ask them to forward my letter and ask Slim to come to Martinique, but in the tropics—you know how it is in the tropics —and Martinique is so tropical, and you know how tropical little Billie is—and so—"

Professor Hoxley chirped and murmured as though he were the little chimpanzee nursing a nut in one cheek, and Mr. Constantidopeles patted him soothingly, and murmured, too.

"Then in Florida, of all things, in Miami, I ran into your father. I ran into—"

"Did you do much painting in Paris?" Slim demanded, not too loudly, but firmly, interrupting the remark addressed to him.

But Mr. Constantidopeles was not to be interrupted. "—in a bar. He is selling washing machines now, he said. I asked him where you were, and now—"

Slim Sarrett rose noisily, and Sue watched him and thought, *Oh, the liar, the damned, stinking, phony little liar, look at him!* So, still watching Slim's face, which was whiter than ever and in which the dark eyes glittered, she addressed the stranger with excessive sweetness: "Oh, you know Slim's father! How nice! He must be such an interesting man. Slim has told me—"

Slim stood in front of Mr. Constantidopeles, and said, "Let me get you a drink, let me get you a drink," very loud, but the stranger, whose face showed amazement politely suppressed, was leaning toward Sue, and saying, "Sure, I know him."

"Oh, Slim has told me so much about him," Sue said enthusiastically, and watched Slim's face, "so much. I've always wanted to meet him. He told me about the time his father was blown up on the river—you know—"

"Really," Mr. Constantidopeles murmured.

"You must get Slim to tell you all about it," she urged, "you really must—you will, won't you, Slim?"

"Let me get you a drink," Slim repeated hoarsely to Mr. Constantidopeles.

"And Slim's mother—that was such an interesting story—in New Orleans. And how is Slim's darling mother?"

"New Orleans? New Orleans?" Mr. Constantidopeles questioned in some bewilderment, and looked up at Slim: "Say, have your

255

folks left Georgia and moved to New Orleans? Your father didn't say anything about—"

"Yes, New Orleans, yes," Slim answered, speaking rapidly, smiling strainedly, leaning over Mr. Constantidopeles as over a baby's crib, cajolingly, saying, "Let me get you a drink—it's not very good whisky but it is pure—it's pure corn even if it hasn't been properly aged—will you take grapefruit juice in it—it is—"

"It's damned good corn," Malloy affirmed, wearing the hat.

"Everybody wants drinks!" Slim said, very loud.

"Sure," Mr. Constantidopeles agreed, and continued, "no, your old man didn't say anything about moving to New Orleans, but he told me you were here the last he heard from you. So little Billie just caught him a plane, and—"

"Everybody wants drinks!" Slim Sarrett declared, and for one instant, swung his gaze widely, wildly, about, like a man tossed desperately at sea. Then he began seizing glasses, empty or half-full, from the hands around him, and pressing them against his body in the crook of one arm as he reached with the other. "Come on!" he ordered Mr. Constantidopeles, "come on, and help me mix them."

"Sure," he replied, and released the hand of Professor Hoxley, who, without that support, listed back gently on his hams. "Sure," Mr. Constantidopeles said, "I'll go with you. And you will go with me to Chicago. We shall fly. Tomorrow. I have a one-man show in Chicago. All my Martinique stuff." He rose with dignity, and resumed: "You will love it. My portrait of Jose. And Jean—Pierre—Pierre was the color of an orange, and against the blue—blue like the color of my old man's native Aegean. There's something about blue water and islands! Blue and with sunshine. The isles of Greece, the isles of Greece, where burning Sappho loved and sung, whence sprang the arts of war and peace, and little burning Billie sprung!— But Martinique—Emil—Michaud, six-feet-three, muscled like a panther, agile as the pard, black as an assassin's dream—he was my masterpiece—" Walking toward the kitchen with his friend, whose haste he restrained with an arm on the shoulder, he continued, "And little Jacques—ah, little Jacques—"

"I am an Aristotelian," wistfully uttered Professor Hoxley, and made no immediate attempt to rise from the floor.

Sue leaned back in her chair, almost happily, watching the kitchen doorway through which the two figures had disappeared. *The little liar, the little stinking liar,* she said to herself, but the words were automatic in her mind, and if she was angry, the anger was absorbed into a pervasive and delightful excitement, a sense of freedom and power, a tingling exaltation. Oh, she could wait.

She would wait, and just give it to him in small doses. She'd make him squirm. She saw in her mind his face, white, strained, tortured, with the eyes casting wildly about. Oh, she'd make him squirm a long time before she gave him the works. All evening. He'd have something to look forward to, all right.

Slim Sarrett and Mr. Constantidopeles came back from the kitchen bearing trays of glasses. The talk and the noise began again, but she sat in the middle of it, quiet as a mouse, smiling.

It was very hot. The moon, paling, the blood drained from it, had long since climbed beyond the range of vision from the east windows. A second glass jug of corn whisky had been brought from the bedroom and had been opened. Slim Sarrett took glasses to the kitchen to replenish them, and every time, Mr. Constantidopeles went with him. The grapefruit had given out, but there was still some ice, which floated in the pale liquid cut with water. Malloy was very drunk, and wore the hat. Professor Hoxley, in an access of gallantry, tried to persuade his wife to rise from the couch and join in a conversation he was having with Duckfoot, but she said she was all right where she was. Professor Hoxley giggled and said she was always all right where she was. He said she was so lazy she didn't think anything was worth moving for. She said mournfully that she supposed something might be worth moving for but not what she got. Malloy wanted to know if she wouldn't even roll over, and the foreman, who until that moment had been quietly drunk, roared with laughter and beat his thigh, and Professor Hoxley seemed to be on the verge of tears while the foreman pointed at him and roared. But he brightened quickly.

The scar on Sweetwater's face was very white. Little Jenkins tried to recite one of his poems to Mr. Constantidopeles. It was a poem about an island, he said, and he knew how Mr. Constantidopeles said he liked islands. But he couldn't remember the first two lines. Mr. Constantidopeles listened to Jenkins and drank a very great deal and sat in his chair like a raja. He told Sweetwater that he had a very interesting scar, and that he would like to paint him. Sweetwater said, no soap, he was gun-shy.

At three o'clock Malloy took his glass, which had been neglected, and went to the kitchen, where Slim and Mr. Constantidopeles were preparing drinks. He opened the door, which was almost closed, and for a moment hung swaying on the door, the hat on the back of his head; then he whooped like an Indian and pointed into the kitchen. He whooped until people began to run to the kitchen door, Jenkins, the foreman, Betsy, little Frey—and he pointed into the kitchen and laughed and yelled: "I seen 'em, I seen 'em! Slim is a tootsie-wootsie, Slim is a tootsie-wootsie!" And then in childish glee: "Shame, shame, papa shame, everybody knows your name, shame, shame, papa—"

Until Slim Sarrett was suddenly before him, his face white as chalk and perspiration beading minutely at the base of the nostrils, and struck him savagely on the mouth. The people fell back, their eyes on Slim, not on Malloy who clung to the door, whose face was rapt in surprise, and whose mouth oozed blood. The second blow, an uncoiling, whiplike right to the jaw, sent Malloy down, not crashing, but sinking slowly, like a crate lowered into the hold, one hand still on the door. The hat fell off.

"Oh," Alice Smythe screamed.

Malloy felt around behind him puzzledly for the hat, put it on, and got up, all very methodically.

Slim Sarrett knocked him down.

The hat had come off again, and Malloy felt around for it.

It was Sweetwater who got Sue Murdock out. He got her out quickly. At the first blow, he got up from his chair, went to the couch, where she sat, and took her roughly by the arm. "Get up," he said, and while she stared across the room, oblivious of him, it seemed, he jerked her to her feet.

He propelled her toward the door, her gaze never leaving the scene at the kitchen.

As she went out, she saw Malloy, the hat on his head, rise heavily again. She saw Slim Sarrett poised beautifully in that lithe and dexterous crouch, and his face white. She saw Professor Hoxley hanging on the mantel shelf, where he declared detachedly that he was an Aristotelian. And she saw Mr. Constantidopeles seat himself in a big chair, at some distance, move the chair until it gave him a comfortable view, and, with his Malacca cane across his knees, survey the event with paternal interest.

When they were a little way down the first flight of steps, she heard Alice Smythe scream again.

As they walked along the street toward her apartment, Sweetwater gripped her tightly and clumsily by the arm, as though to support her. "Damn it," she said, furiously, suddenly aware of his assistance, "I can walk! I'm not a child."

So he released his hold, and walked along beside her, and a little behind her.

At the door of the apartment house, she held the knob and

turned to him, as he waited there on the steps, but did not seem to be addressing him. "God," she said, "I never—I never—want to see anybody again. Not anybody!"

He studied her there in the shadow of the vestibule for a moment. Then he said: "Cheer up, kid. It was all in the cards."

Twenty

Statement of Ashby Wyndham

IT WAS nigh a year on the river and we come to Hulltown. It was a big town. It was the biggest town I ever seen afore we come to the city here where the Lord has done led us. At Hulltown they was a furnace where they melted the iron out of the rock they taken out of the ground. I got me a job workin at the furnace. And Jasper got him a job. It was the Lords blessin for we needed money bad. Old Sister Lumpkin was down and porely. Marie watched her and tended on her but we needed money to git her somethin to eat as would stay on her stummick and to git her medicine.

In Hulltown we taken Pearl from the house of abominations.

It was summer and I was comin down the street in a part of town where I had not never been. It was Sunday evenin at sun, and I was just walkin for it had come on me so. It was not dark yit but them lights in the street come on just a minute after I seen the house. Them lights in town come on long afore a man had good need. I seen the house and I seen the two of them settin on the porch laughin and talkin. It was a yeller house set by a alley. The other houses nigh it was not houses for folks to dwell in, and they was closed up for a Sunday. It had a fence around it and a gate. I seen the woman and the man settin there, and I stopped at the gate. I give them a good evenin as best I knowed. The woman said good evenin but the man did not say nuthin.

She was a medium size woman and her hair was yeller. The man was a big man. They both had on fine clothes, I seen. They was settin in a swing and the man had his arm around the woman. The woman had on a yeller dress.

I ast could I come in. I had not aimed to but the Lord laid it on my tongue lak he done them days. I seen somebody and the Lord laid it on my tongue may be. If he did not I never said nuthin. But I ast them could I come in a minute.

They ain't nuthin stoppin you, the woman said. The man did not say nuthin. He just looked at me lak I was a mule he might buy but he did not reckin he would.

I said thank you kindly, and I went in that air gate. I come on the porch.

The lady said the other girls would not be back till nigh eight o'clock. She ast did I want to see one of the girls.

I said, no mam.

Well, you better git on and peddle yore apples, the man said to me. You ain't got no business here, he said.

I know I ain't, I said, but the Lord has.

For Christ sake, the man said, and he knocked the ashes off his cigar.

What do you want, the lady ast me.

Hell, the man said, he don't want nuthin he can pay for. Then he said to me, buddy, this is a high class place and you better git.

I was gittin ready to say excuse me please and git on, but the lady ast me what did I want.

Hell, says the man, he wants a dime to git him a cup of coffee. He retched in his pants and he taken a dime. He throwed the dime on the floor in front of me. I let it lay.

I don't want no dime, I told him. I was gittin ready to go, I said, but yore wife ast me what I come for.

Wife, the man said, and he bust out laughin.

The lady did not laugh. He shaken her with his arm lak he was tryin to make her laugh. She said, I don't see nuthin so God damn funny.

He stopped laughin of a sudden and he said to me, you git on.

But the lady said to him, Claude, you act too damn big, you act lak you own the place. She told him to shut up and take his God damn hands offen her.

He got mad. You could see he was gittin mad. You talk that way to me, he said, and you let that God damn trash come in here, and he ain't got a dime.

I am a pore man, I said, but I ain't trash. I am a pore man but I got Jesus in my heart.

This is a hell of a place to bring Jesus, the man said and he laughed agin. I seen his heart was hardened.

She did not pay no mind. She ast me what did I want.

I did not want nuthin, mam, I said, the Lord just laid it on me to come in and ast did you have the peace of Jesus in yore heart.

Well, you done ast it, the lady said, and now you can git out.

You can just take yore bleedin Jesus and git out, the man said to me, afore I knock the bleedin Jesus out of you.

261

Mister, I said to him, I am goin to go. I come not meanin no harm. The Lord laid it on me to come and the Lord lays it on me to go, and not no human man.

Git out, he said.

I am, I said, but I am goin in the Lord and not for you.

I ought never said it. A man can be proud and high in the Lord lak he can in pore human pride and it is a sin. It is a worse sin.

The hell you say, the man said.

I turned round and started down the steps. I never looked back. I did not see him git up from that air swing. I did not know nuthin till I felt him kick me where a man sets down. I was on them steps and it knocked me plum down on the ground and me not expectin it.

The man was standin there laughin. I got up and I seen the lady was laughin too. I was surprised the lady was laughin.

I went to the gate and the lady kept on laughin. Mam, I said, it ain't fitten for you to laugh.

All right, the man said, and I will bust you agin.

He come down off the porch. I walked on slow. I knowed he was comin but I never looked back. I heard him comin on the walk behind me. I got to the end of the fence where the alley was and he hit me on the side of the head. He knocked me down.

I will learn you to talk that way to a lady, he said.

I was layin there. It was night now but he was standin under the light hangin in the street and I seen him good.

I got up and he give it to me agin. I nigh give it back to him, but I never. I knowed it was not the Lords will for me to. I knowed it all come on me because I taken sinful pride in the Lord, and it is a sin. He give it to me three times afore he knocked me down.

The lady come out the gate and was standin there.

I got up and he knocked me down agin. I was layin in the alley.

The lady was laughin. If he won't fight lak a man, she said, kick him lak he was a dog.

I will learn him to fight, the man said.

I come up and he give it to me three times. He knocked me down.

Kick him, the lady said. Kick him lak he was a dog.

She was laughin and goin on but it was not lak folks laughs of a common. It was lak she did not know she was laughin and she could not stop it.

I got up agin when I could. I got up slow because he had shore messed me up. He was a big man. He was nigh as big as they come. He was gittin fat but he had his strength.

I got up and he give it to me. But just then I seen a man come round the corner of the alley. I seen it was a police man. But just then that man give it to me on the jaw just that time the lady stopped laughin and looked at that police man. That police man said somethin but I never understood what it was. I did not understand for it was right then I done it. I did not aim to and I did not rightly know I done it till I seen that man layin there and his head on the brick walk. Somethin must have went pop inside me for I never knowed what I done. That man must have turned round to see who that police man was. He must have got offen his balance. He must have not been careful or somethin to let a man what was fixed lak I was knock him down.

I seen him layin there and I seen the police man. I knowed he was goin to take me.

He said, Miss Pearl what is goin on here.

Miss Pearl was that ladys name.

She stopped laughin and she pointed at him was layin with his head on the brick walk and she said, it is him.

She said somethin else but I never knowed what it was. I did not know nuthin. I just sunk down on the ground.

I come to and I was layin on a bed. It was a good bed and sweet smellin. Then I seen that lady standin there. She ast how did I feel.

I tetched my face with my hand. It was swole up lak a punkin.

You done stopped bleedin, she said, but you ain't no pretty pitcher.

I ast was the police man goin to take me to jail.

Why, that was Mr. Duffy, she said, why, Mr. Duffy has done taken him.

Ain't they goin to take me, I said.

Naw, she said, Mr. Duffy is a friend of mine and he takes what ones I say take. I said for Mr. Duffy to take him and he taken him. They had to take him in a ambylance and I bet he ain't come round yit with his head bust lak it was.

I ought never done it, I said.

It was not yore fault, she said, I just reckin it was Jesus fault. Jesus just taken his eyes offen you a secont lak he had not ought to. He must have winked, may be.

I said I had to git on home.

You ain't fitten to go no wheres, she said.

I said I had to git on home.

263

She ast me where did I stay at.

I told her on the shanty boat. And I got offen that bed.

It is a long way, she said, and you ain't in no shape.

I said I was goin.

She said she was goin to git me there. I am goin to see you git there, she said.

She done it for all of me.

Twenty-one

WHEN Gerald Calhoun, on Monday, back from Saint Louis on the noon train, entered his office, his secretary handed him a pad on which was written a number, and said: "It was calling Friday, but I said you were out of town. And it's been calling all morning. Every half hour. I said you'd be in on the noon train, but they called anyway."

Gerald Calhoun recognized it as his father's number. He picked up the telephone and began to call the number.

The secretary lingered a moment, saying: "And Mr. Blake, he's anxious to see you as soon as possible. He ought to be back from lunch any minute."

The voice came over the wire, from miles away, from the shadowy room where old Mr. Calhoun's big mottled hand clumsily held the receiver, like a bear's paw with an egg, where the old blind woman sat by the fire and breathed asthmatically; and Gerald Calhoun, sitting alone in the office, enclosed by the antiseptically glistening walls, his hand lying carefully on the cold glass top of the big desk, heard the voice: "Son?"

"Yes?" Gerald Calhoun said, "Yes?"

We got to move, the voice said.

Foreclosed, the voice said.

"My God," Gerald Calhoun said, and the sickness was cold in his stomach, and the knot of something, hatred, fury, despair, was there, deep down, as it had been years ago when he stood and watched the big hands fumble the strap, fumble the staple set on the wire, fumble the file, fumble the button—the tiny knot cold and deep like a horrible seed, swathed in the sickness—and he cast his eyes desperately about him as though the walls closed in, into the black, anonymous transmitter, and said: "I thought they'd hold off—they held off before—you paid them something—I thought —I thought—"

It ain't them, the voice said.

265

They sold the mortgage, the voice said, and never said nothing to me.

"I told you, I told you," Gerald Calhoun said, "I can't—everything I've got is tied up—borrowed everything I can—tell them—"

We got to move, the voice said. Five days.

It's a man named Perkins, the voice said.

Son, the voice said.

And Duckfoot Blake came in.

"Jesus," he said, "you look like you swallowed the worm in the peach."

"They foreclosed," Gerald Calhoun said. "On my father. He's got to go. The First State sold the mortgage. They held off before, but they sold it. Hell!—" and his hand struck the glass, furiously, "—I couldn't help it. I couldn't help it! Everything I got tied up in Massey Mountain and Pretty River Quarries— Hell, I've borrowed every penny I can. God damn it, I can't help it—I—"

"Easy," Duckfoot said. "Nobody said you could."

"I couldn't! And the bastards sold the mortgage. God, couldn't they hold off— Right now and the Massey Mountain Bill just passed, and I'd have something. It'd be easy."

"How much is it?" Duckfoot asked.

"Three thousand something. Just a little longer and I—"

"I got a little dough," Duckfoot said, "that I ain't squandered on the devil's pasteboards. I got that much. And it isn't in Massey Mountain, either." He adjusted a cigarette in his holder, flung a cigarette on the glass in front of Gerald Calhoun, and lighted his own. "Now," he said, "you just go to whoever bought the mortgage and— By the way, who is it?"

"His name is Perkins."

Duckfoot removed the holder from his lips, looked at the ceiling, and exhaled the smoke. Then he said: "Pal, it's no sale."

"What?"

"No sale. Don't you know who Jake Perkins is?"

"Hell, no!"

"Pal, Jake Perkins is trigger man for the Happy Valley Hunt Club. He was a four-bit realtor with dirty underdrawers and the conscience of the South American bushmaster at shedding time and now he is trigger man for Happy Valley. Hell, you been asleep? They began getting hold of all those places out by your old man, and restoring them with spinning wheels and flintlocks in the *ee*-poch—"

"I knew, but—"

"—and they gonna ride pink coats across the riotously colored

266

autumn landscape. And you, my somewhat overfed centaur, will be right there giving the view-halloo, unless—" He detached the butt from his holder, and flipped it dizzily, accurately, across to a bronze wastebasket.

"Unless," Duckfoot said, "you are ripe."

"Ripe?"

"Jesus," Duckfoot said, "I got to get off my dogs." And he sank into a chair. He flung an envelope on the desk before Gerald Calhoun, who picked it up and inspected the single sheet enclosed. Then he stared at the other man, his mouth ready to frame the question.

"To quit," Duckfoot said. "Hell, it's written in English. You can just copy it, and sign your name. But you better copy it fast. I'm mailing it this afternoon, to take effect tomorrow. I figure I'll have twenty-four hours' jump on the sheriff."

"You're crazy, you—"

"Listen, here, Jerry," Duckfoot said, "Murdock's bleeding this place white. He's got collateral here would make Continental shinplasters gilt-edged. There's enough phony deposit certificates floating round to provide fuel for Guy Fawkes Day. There's—"

"Those State deposits—it's a lie!" Jerry jumped up from the desk. "I know—I saw those bonds, the ones up for the State deposits. I saw every damned one of them!"

"Sure," Duckfoot said, "you saw 'em. But you saw 'em when they were put up for those last State deposits. And me—I saw 'em, too. When? Last week. Right back in this bank last Friday. Switched. Somebody switched 'em. And, pal, I ain't gonna be here when the roof falls!"

Jerry got his hat from the rack. "I'm going to see Murdock," he said.

"Write him a letter," Duckfoot said.

"I'm going to see him. Right now."

"Heed not the voice of the charmer," Duckfoot said.

Jerry was at the door, his hat on his head. Duckfoot leaned back in his chair to watch him, sadly, biliously. "Well," he said, "remember one little thing. When he puts his hand on your shoulder, and smiles the smile of the Crucified Redeemer, just remember Happy Valley. Bogan Murdock is centaur number one of the Happy Valley. And he is," he turned his gaze to his propped-up feet, "Jake Perkins' boss. Though," and he watched his toes work the soft leather, "he wouldn't admit it. Oh, I don't mean he sicked Jake Perkins on your Old Man in particular. He probably don't even remember your Old Man's place is out there where the Happy

267

Valley boys are going to operate. He's just told Jake to buy up God's green globe cheap so he can put a fence around it and ride a horse over it."

When was the decision made? Later, he was to lie in the dark, and ask himself that. But was not to be able to answer it. Certainly, as he rushed down the street, through the pale autumn sunlight and the traffic, unwittingly shoving other men from the sidewalk, he had said to himself that he would find out, he would find out, he would ask Murdock, point-blank, and if—if— But the *if*, even then, had remained suspended, undefined, and was suspended when he entered the high, quiet office of Bogan Murdock. But perhaps it had been decided long before, and all his own confusion and passion and wrestling of spirit, and his rushing down the street, and the night without sleep, had been nothing but the little bangings and clinkings of the nickel dropped into the slot of the slot machine, while the mechanism whirred and ran, nothing but the senseless effort of the toy tin monkey climbing the string. Or perhaps it had come later.

But with the passion and the *if*—in that delusion, if it was delusion—he had entered the office of Bogan Murdock, and had seen the man sitting there, and in that quietness before he spoke, or stepped forward, and before Bogan Murdock spoke—there was always that infinitesimal delay, the instant of gathering and focus, before Bogan Murdock's simplest greeting— Gerald Calhoun's agitation subsided, as when one walks into the shadowy, empty church and sees only the distant candle-gleam, and the noise of the street outside sinks into an uncompelling whisper.

"Yes," Bogan Murdock was to say, "there have been irregularities in the handling of the Southern Fidelity paper held by the First and Fifth to secure the State deposits. The matter came to my attention last week, and this morning I had a conference with Mr. Jacobs of the First and Fifth." His voice was to be perfectly even, perfectly calm, and his eyes unwavering on Jerry Calhoun's face. "And they are letting the man responsible go—a Mr. Hawkins. The man responsible in the First and Fifth, that is. I shall soon know who was responsible in my own organization. He will, of course" —he was looking away, through the window, over the city—"be dealt with."

"The collateral—" Jerry was to manage to say, "the Meyers and Murdock collateral that—"

And Murdock: "Jerry, you know finance. You know conditions. Values are not, at the moment, stable. A complete review of collateral is being conducted by Mr. Shotwell. I suggest, my boy, that if you are uncomfortable you confer with Mr. Shotwell. All I ask, my boy, is that you make a sober investigation before you come to any decision. You must act according to your best judgment. You must not be swayed by your personal attachments. I do not want"—his eyes were to be steady on Jerry Calhoun's face—"any loyalty to me—any false conception of chivalry—to sway you. Now, as for Mr. Blake—"

"Yes," Jerry was to say, clutching obscurely at that name, "Duck-foot—Mr. Blake—I talked to him—he—"

"As for Mr. Blake," Bogan Murdock repeated evenly, "I cannot say what his views or motives are."

"Duckfoot—he—" Jerry began gropingly.

At that moment the girl had come in—the slight knock, the feet noiseless on the deep, blue carpet—and had laid the newspaper on the desk before Bogan Murdock.

Perhaps, if she had not come at that moment, he was to think. Perhaps, if there had not been that distraction, and the distraction of the news story which was to involve his feelings, things might have been different. Perhaps—but she had brought that little line across the course of his feelings. She had dropped the paper, like an innocent catalytic, into the ferment of his being. "Duckfoot—" he had uttered again, in the moment before he knew what the paper meant. But Bogan Murdock was not listening.

Bogan Murdock was holding the paper in both hands, his knuckles taut and whitening under the brown. The rage was there on his face, like a sudden, and suddenly extinguished, flash in the dark; then his face showed nothing.

He swung to the telephone and dialed. "The scum," he said, "the scum!"

Jerry saw the paper lying on the desk. The black headline ran: *"Murdock" Bill Passed.* Beneath it, down the center of the page, to the bottom, the print ran, in a black box.

"The scum!" Murdock said. And: "There was a time—"

Jerry could not make out the print in the box.

Murdock was talking: "Anse—yes—get the evening paper! Get it—yes—the *Standard.* . . . Don't let my father get it. . . . Do you understand? Under any circumstances. Get it!"

He rose from the desk, very erect. "The scum," he said. "To attack that old man! To attack me through that poor old man. I have stood their attacks. I can stand them. But that old man—" He had come around, and stood before Gerald Calhoun, who rose. "Excuse me, Jerry," he said, softly. "Excuse me, but I've got to go."

269

He took two long paces toward the door, turned, hesitated an instant, and said: "My God, there was a time a man could do it. He could defend his honor. If he had to."

Then he was gone.

The room was, again, very quiet.

Gerald Calhoun leaned over the desk, and read what was there, printed on the paper.

It said: *"Murdock" Bill Passed.*

Below, it said:

The Governor will sign it.

Why?

Because Governor Milam is a creature of the Murdock gang.

Why did Private Porsum support the Murdock Bill?

Because Private Porsum, who was once a hero, has become a creature of the Murdock gang.

Why does the Murdock gang want the Bill passed?

Because the Bill makes it possible for the holding of the Massey Mountain Timber Company, the Atlas Iron Company, and Pretty River Quarries to be dumped upon the tax-payers of this State at an enormous figure.

Who owns this property?

The Murdock gang.

What is the record?

More than two years ago Mr. Bogan Murdock, financier, philanthropist, and sportsman, presented to this State seven hundred acres of mountain land to become a State preserve and park. It was named the Major Lemuel Murdock Park. *It is to become, if Governor Milam signs the Bill, the nucleus of the greater* Major Lemuel Murdock Park.

Who is Major Lemuel Murdock?

He is the man who, on April 4, 1892, in this city, shot and killed, willfully and of malice aforethought, Judge Goodpasture, a political opponent, who in the heat of a campaign uttered certain remarks which offended the vanity of Major Lemuel Murdock. Major Lemuel Murdock was tried and convicted in the courts of Mulcaster County. Upon appeal, the conviction was reversed.

Were the remarks uttered by Judge Goodpasture true?

The remarks were true.

What was the defense offered by Major Lemuel Murdock?

That he shot to protect his honor.

What is honor?

Conceptions differ.

What is Mr. Bogan Murdock's conception of honor?

270

We submit that . . .

There was more, but Gerald Calhoun did not read it.

Instead, he stood in the high, quiet room, and stared unseeingly out the great window, which framed the black roofs of the city, the wisping smoke, the faded landscape beyond; and it all, the distant earth and structures set solidly on the earth to conceal it, heaved like the sea. He let one hand sink to the top of Bogan Murdock's desk, as though to steady himself.

He had not made a decision. He had not said to himself: *I shall do this:* or *I shall do that.*

The old man sat on the step of the tack room, in the stable hall, mountainously decayed, sagging from the big maned head, the gray streaked yellowly as by old rust stains, the whole mass sagging, as by long slip and erosion, from the hunched head and shoulders to the great paunch, which fell between the spread thighs, on one of which was laid the puffed, yellow-and-mauve-streaked old hand; and the hand moved a little, as in and of itself, like some blind subsea creature drawn up, bloated with the release of pressure, mottled yellow and mauve as its color faded, expiring slowly with soundless gasp and twitch.

"Yeah," the old man said, "yeah—" through the ruined teeth, and shook his head twitchingly, and the facial muscles tightened under the loose, stained skin in an effort of painful, groping concentration. The red-rimmed, bloodshot blue eyes adjusted themselves under the disordered dignity of the shaggy brows; peered out from under the brows, sufferingly, resentfully, dumbly-dangerously, like a hurt old beast cornered in the thicket; came to focus upon the little Negro boy who squatted on the stable floor before him.

The other little Negro boy, smaller, five years old perhaps, clad in old overalls too big for him, stood to one side, watching the old man.

"Yeah," the old man said, and exhaled heavily.

The smaller boy swung a little to one side, jumped with excitement a couple of times, with the graceful, stiff-legged, steel-spring quality of a kid, his feet coming clear simultaneously of the floor, and stretched out his right hand, the forefinger pointing like a pistol toward the lighted area of the hall opening, and with enraptured face, the little brown face contorting, the eyes glistening, uttered the word: "Pow!" Then: "Pow, Pow!"

"Shet up!" the other boy hissed at him, snatching the overalls leg, jerking downward. "Shet up, you Peewee!"

Peewee sank slowly down, squatting on his little hams, the rap-

271

ture smoothing from his face, his eyes now fixed on the old man.

The old man swung his head ponderously, twitchingly, suspiciously, from one to the other.

"Yassuh, Maj'r Lem, yassuh," the other little Negro boy said soothingly, whisperingly, almost caressingly.

"He said—he said—" the old man began, stared about him suddenly, and failed. His breathing began again with its hissing, weary, difficult pull and exhalation, while the boys watched, waiting.

A horse stirred in one of the stalls, down the hall.

"He say—" the bigger little boy whispered caressingly, insinuatingly, "he got up thar, and he say, that ole Maj'r Lem—he say—"

The old man's bulk heaved forward a little, and he lifted his head, his wet lips half open to show the old teeth. The children watched him, scarcely breathing, not moving. Their faces were still, caught in a trancelike expectancy; their eyes glistened at him, unblinkingly, the whites showing; they squatted with the patience of worshipers, in the dusky hall, before the hulked, sagging, swollen, idollike mass, waiting for the utterance.

"He say—" Peewee whispered.

The old bulk heaved.

"He say—" Peewee whispered, and the other boy, jerking the overalls leg of Peewee but not taking his gaze from the man's working, slowly twisting and curding face, whispered: "Ssh ssh, he come-en, he a-gonna come."

"At Essex," the old man said.

"At the courthouse," he said, and his face worked.

"He come-en, he come-en," Peewee whispered, and clenched his hands together under his chin and shuddered in prayerful rapture.

"He stood up there—that blackguard stood up there on the steps of the courthouse. In Essex. And he said. That blackguard said—"

"He say—" Peewee whispered.

"He said, Major Lemuel Murdock—Major Lemuel Murdock—but I—I never had a Yankee dollar—"

"Dat whut he say, dat whut he say," the other little boy whispered urgently, leaning forward. "He say, that ole Maj'r Lem, he a ole scalawag son-a-bitch, he a ole sheep-snitchen son-a-bitch, he a—"

"He said—that blackguard said—"

"Ole Maj'r Lem, he a son-a-bitch bastud," the other little boy whispered, "scalawag bastud, a piss-ass ole bastud, a piss—"

"Piss-ass ole bastud, piss-ass ole bastud, ole Maj'r Lem, piss-ass ole—" Peewee shivered in his ecstasy.

272

"He come on the train," the bigger little boy said, "yassuh, and you—"

Peewee, squatting, jerked his knees, saying, "Choo-kee-choo-kee-choo," puffingly, and moved his forearms like the drivers of a locomotive.

"He come," the other little boy urged, "he come, and you—whut you do?"

And the old man heaved and stared at him pitifully, pleadingly, while his wet mouth convulsed without sound.

"Whut you do?" The boy hunched closer, still squatting, sliding his feet forward in little jerks. "Whut you do, huh?" he repeated, and his eyes glittered, and a touch of mastery, of compulsion, came into his voice. He stared upward at the old face, unrelentingly, victoriously. "Whut you do?"

"He came up the steps," the old man managed, croakingly. "I was there, and he came up the steps. The band was playing—" he said. "The band was playing," he said. "I was there," he said, "and the band was playing—" He did not go on.

"Toodle-oo-toodle-oo—too-too," Peewee made the music softly, as though a long way off, and patted his hands in time, softly.

"Whut you do, huh? And he call you, ole Maj'r Lem"—You-Bub hitched himself closer, peering up at the old face—"he say, ole Maj'r Lem, he a son-a-bitch, he a—"

"The band was playing—the band—"

"Toodle-oo—toodle-oo-oo," Peewee made the music. He cocked his head and puffed his cheeks like little brown, slick billiard balls, and his thrust-out, puckered, peeled-back lips were like a little, astonishingly pink-hearted flower.

"Whut you do, huh? And he say—"

The old man heaved up his big head, and the gray, yellow-tarnished mane shook as he cast his eyes wildly, awakeningly, around. "I shot him!" he uttered in a strong, terrible croak. "I shot—"

Peewee had leaped up. His stiff, spread-out legs made twice the kidlike dance, coming clear of the floor together. He thrust his right arm out, the forefinger pointed like the pistol at his brother. "Pow!" he exclaimed, his voice falsetto with joy, "Pow!"

You-Bub half rose, and fell back on the ground, clutching his stomach, his eyes rolling.

"Pow!" the finger pistol pointed at him, and Peewee danced. "Pow, pow, pow, pow!"

"You, Peewee," You-Bub ordered, not ceasing to writhe, "you stop it, he never shot but three times, it was three—"

"Pow, pow, pow!" Peewee screamed, and danced.

You-Bub rolled on his back, twisted in elaborate agony, lifted up his knees and then sprawled them out, rolled his eyes, and moaned, clutching his stomach, making no further protest, surrendering himself completely to the pantomime of death, the delicious fulfillment, the perfection of pain, the bliss. There on the dunged floor, at the feet of the old man, who stared.

"Pow, pow!"

But the old Negro had come in the door, Old Anse running rheumatically, exclaiming furiously and with short breath: "You, Peewee, stop it! You-Bub, I bust you, I—"

Peewee stood frozen, his arm stretched out, his mouth shaped for a *pow* which did not come.

Old Anse snatched up You-Bub by the arm, jerking him to a squatting position, and began to box him on the side of the head, with a creaking, stiff-armed motion, exclaiming: "I done tole you, I done tole you I bust you. I bust you both. You make Ole Maj'r cry agin, and I bust you. I tell Mass' Bog'n—I gonna tell 'im, and he snatch you. I tole you, you make Ole Maj'r cry agin, and I gonna—" while the blows fell, and the breath failed. "—and you, Peewee, I—"

But Peewee, unfrozen, was fleeing down the dusky hall.

Old Anse dropped You-Bub, like something used and forgotten. You-Bub crawled away a couple of yards, then leaped and ran out into the lot, into the sun, and was gone.

Old Anse leaned toward the wet, quivering face, which was lifted toward him. The big, yellow-and-mauve, swollen hand clutched Old Anse by the sleeve of his jumper. Muttering, "Now, Maj'r Lem, now, Maj'r Lem, I done tole 'em, I done tole 'em," Old Anse fumbled with his free hand in the breast pocket of the black broadcloth coat and got the big, snowy linen handkerchief, initialed, and wiped the cheeks, and patted the eyes gently, like a child's, and held the handkerchief to the nose, muttering all the while.

Major Murdock looked up, still clutching the sleeve, and said: "I shot him, I—"

"Ssh, now ssh, Maj'r Lem, it's done long gone, it's—"

"I had to! I had to, I—"

"He said—"

"Shore you had to. You had to. Doan you fret, doan—"

"I'm Major Lemuel Murdock," the old man whispered, and clung to the sleeve, and lifted up his face.

"Shore, you'se the Ole Maj'r. You'se Maj'r Lem, and ever'body know. You'se the Ole Maj'r, and no mis-take."

"He said—" Major Murdock began, but Anse patted him on the

shoulder, and wiped his face, and said: "You jes hush now. You hush, and it's bout time yore paper git here. You go git yore paper and fergit all it. You walk down ter the big road, and meet the man and git it. Maybe it in the box by now."

Major Murdock went out the door, blinked a moment at the light, and started across the lot, beside the stables, toward the house. But he did not go to the house. He cut across to the drive, skirting the dead rose garden, and went around the end of the house. He went down the hill, beyond the cedars, between the bare oaks, blinking now and then, owlishly, at the westering sun, which was not yet going red.

The paper was in the box.

He took it out, and started up the rise, not looking at it at first. Halfway up he stopped for breath, and standing there, opened the paper. He began to read, his heavy head hanging forward over the paper, the eyes not moving, the head swaying from side to side to carry the eyes from one word to the next, from one line to the next, swaying in a difficult, sad, bull-like motion. Then he lifted up his head, and made a sound in his throat. He looked widely around, over the landscape. Then he made the sound again, and the lax skin of the jowls shook.

He started up the hill again, holding the paper in his hand. His breath came heavy, and the sweat began to slide down his cheeks.

He entered the house by the front door, and stood for a moment in the empty hall, while his breath rasped and labored. He seemed to be listening, but there was no other sound. Then he went into the library. He passed through the library, and into the room beyond.

In that shadowy room, the heads of great beasts, with glassy, unrelenting eyes, protruded from the walls, twisted-horned, antlered, spiked, tusked, fanged, hairy, bearded. On shelves, in the shadow, silver cups and mugs gleamed. In the far wall, under the enormous, fungusy moose head, seemingly bearded with moss, rifles were racked under glass, which gleamed. Gun cases hung on the wall. Major Murdock, with ponderous, wheezing stealth, opened another cabinet, and took out a revolver. He found cartridges in the drawer. He loaded the weapon, and left the room. On his way out, he paused cunningly at each door to listen before passing through it. But there was no sound.

He walked down the hill, faster now.

At the stone pillars, he looked up and down the highway. Nothing was visible, except toward the left, a wagon coming in his direction. He turned right, and began to walk beside the concrete slab, on the soft earth, going toward the city, the smoke of which was visible.

The wagon, half on the slab, half off, overtook him. The mules were almost upon him before he noticed, and was forced to step down into the ditch. The wagon drew up even with him, but when he faced it, standing there in the ditch and lifting his hand, the old Negro man who was driving said, "Whoa!" and pulled back on his rope reins, and turned a slow, incurious gaze, beyond surprise, upon him. The hammer-shaped, antediluvian, saurian, earth-colored, as out of the earth, crusted heads of the mules sagged forward, motionless in the late sunlight.

"Are you going to town?" Major Murdock demanded.

"I'se aimen to, Cap'm," the old Negro man said.

Without a word, Major Murdock approached the wagon, laid both his hands on the never-painted, splintery, gray sideboard of the bed, set his foot to the hub, and heavily, puffingly, with veins suddenly violent on his temples, got himself up, and into the bed, and subsided on the loose boards laid across the bed for a seat, in front of the heaped cordwood. The old Negro hitched himself over to make room, took his impartial gaze off Major Murdock and directed it down the long, white road, over the heads of the mules, and uttered, "Gi-ap," without emphasis, as though nothing had happened, as though he were still alone; and the wheels began to turn softly on the right hand where the earth was, metallically, with a grinding patience, on the left, on the slab.

The sound of Major Murdock's breathing abated, somewhat.

"It'll be night fore I git nigh, Cap'n," the Negro said.

Major Murdock did not reply, breathing and looking down the road.

A car snatched past them, whining, whirring, and dwindled toward the city.

"This-here ain't no otty-mobile, Cap'm," the Negro said, and gave a dry snigger.

"Drive on," Major Murdock ordered, not turning.

A quarter of a mile, and the wagon neared a lane bearing off to the right.

"Cap'm," the Negro said, "I takes off this-a way. It's a shawt-cut and ain't no otty-mobiles kin go. It dirt and ain't no bridge on Broadus-Fi-ord. But me—I kin go. It dirt and ain't no bridge on Broadus Fi-ord. But me—I kin go. Ole Sal and Beck, they kin—"

"Drive on," Major Murdock said.

They went down the lane, jolting in the dry ruts, with a crumbling sound.

"It'll be night, Cap'm. And me, I'm gwine stop at my boy's. Jasper, he live on the aidge of town, and I kin take my stove wood on ter town in the mawnen. To Mister Tawm Taylor, lak I done tole him. Cap'm, you know Mister Tawm? Big heavy-set man—" He eyed Major Murdock, who did not answer.

"Cap'm, how you git in frum Jasper's, huh? It a piece, frum Jasper's, and night fore we nigh. How you git in, Cap'm?"

Major Murdock's head swung weightily to face him, and the eyes blinked. "Captain—" Major Murdock said, "captain—" He blinked. "I'm Major Murdock," he said. "I'm Major Lemuel Murdock, and he was at Essex—it was at Essex—"

"Ex-cuse me, Maj'r."

"—and he said—" He began to move his head from side to side. "And he said—"

"Yassuh, Boss, yassuh—"

Major Murdock heaved his bulk, and wheezed, leaning toward the Negro, his mouth working. Then he said: "The band was playing—it was the band—and I—"

"Whut band, Boss?"

"The band was playing—and I—I—" The swollen, sagging face made its effort, "—and I shot him."

"Lawd-God, Boss! Lawd-God, Maj'r," the Negro exclaimed, staring at, drawing back from, the laboring face which leaned toward his own. "Lawd-God, shot who?"

"Judge Goodpasture—the blackguard, the lying blackguard, and I—"

"Lawd-God!"

Major Murdock's hand clutched the Negro's wrist, the flabby mass closing on the withered little stick-thin bone. "I'll tell you," he said, leaning, "I'll tell you. The blackguard—"

"Boss," the Negro pleaded. "Lawd-God, Boss, not me. I ain't a-listenin. Naw-suh, I ain't a-gonna listen. Lawd-God, and I doan wanta know. Not and you shootin nobody. Not nuthen, Lawd-God!"

"The blackguard—and I—"

The Negro's eyes bugged out, as though a hand had been closed on his windpipe, and he made a retarded, squeaking exhalation, like a rubber toy in a baby's fist. His eyes were fixed on the revolver, which Major Murdock now held in his free hand.

"I'll shoot him like a dog!" Major Murdock proclaimed, and lurched, and lifted the revolver.

"Naw, Lawd-God! Lawd-God."

"I'm Major Lemuel Murdock—I'm Major Murdock—and I—"

"Maj'r Lem'el, Maj'r Lem'el, please, Maj'r Lem'el, put it away, please, Maj'r Lem'el Murdock, you gonna put it away, please. You ain't gonna shoot nobody, not no human-man, not nobody, please—"

"He said—he said—"

"I doan like it, I doan like them things, please, Maj'r Lem'el Murdock, what yore name is, please—" He gave up, in his agony, the big old hand on his wrist, clutching, and his gaze riveted on the revolver, which was bright in the last light.

The revolver sank slowly into Major Murdock's lap.

"It was the band," he said.

"Yassuh, yassuh!"

"It was the band," Major Murdock repeated, his voice low in the painful, groping musing. Then he leaned again toward the Negro, shaking his head, begging: "The band—it was the band—I can't remember what the band was playing—"

"Lawd-God," the Negro uttered, like a prayer, and jerked forward on the seat, and with his free hand lashed the ropes over the mules in a frenzy, breathing, "Lawd-God!"

The wagon lunged forward, hammering the ruts, jerking and bouncing down the slight grade.

Major Murdock's right hand, laxly grasping the revolver, bounced and joggled on his lap, like something dropped, lost, and forgotten.

Perhaps the decision was made the next morning, when Gerald Calhoun stood before Bogan Murdock, whose face out of the strain of sleeplessness looked sculptured and hard, as though irrelevancies had been chiseled and polished away, had been so stylized, to exhibit only the simple verity of the fundamental structure, and whose eyes were bright blue-black, brighter than ever and unwavering. The brown of the face was, however, streaked a little, yellowly, so that the slick, hard flesh resembled a carved onyx. On the left cheek was a razor nick, on which a fleck of blood, neglected, had crusted in darker brown, as though the onyx had painfully exuded that one large, rich, dark drop, which had then, in its turn, solidified.

"Yes," Bogan Murdock said, "they struck through him. At me. They struck through him, that—" and he turned away, very erect, the dark, perfect cloth of his coat molding and defining the square, straight, almost too narrow shoulders; and he stared out the window. "That—" he said, and paused. He seemed to gather himself, and concluded: "That poor old man."

Jerry stood there, watching, and could think of nothing to say.

278

He wanted to say something, but he did not know what it was he had to say, as though he were a table, a tree, some natural object with a vitality locked deeply within it, an object about which people moved and spoke, and which observed, eyelessly, and knew, and suffered with the numb, obscure germination within it.

"That poor old man," Bogan Murdock said, softly, and turned and fixed his eyes upon Jerry.

Jerry wet his lips. He felt as though he had been detected in the horrible, dreamlike, submarine circumstances of a crime which he had not committed—no, he had not done it, he had not—and there was one word to clear him, if he could speak it. Or, even, if he could think it.

"That poor old man," Bogan Murdock almost whispered, with his gaze uncompromisingly fixed, "—and they found him—they found him in the railway station. Standing there late last night, with the revolver in his hand. How he got there, God knows." He stopped, and again, for an instant, looked away. "I don't want to know how he got there," he said.

Then he turned his head: "And they found him. A policeman found him. And took the revolver. And do you know what he said?"

Jerry tried, and the word came: "No." But it had no reality for him. He was not sure he had said it.

"He said, 'The band isn't playing. I don't know why the band isn't playing.' Then they took him away. To the police station. They didn't know who he was. And he sat there, in that police station, like a common thief, and all he could say was, 'Get Beau, get Beau.' They stood around and laughed. Beaumont Grey—Beau—he was a friend of my father. He was the lawyer who defended him in the old trouble. A great gentleman. He has—" he said, and hesitated, as though mastering himself and the passage of time, "been dead these twenty years. Did you," he asked Jerry, "ever hear his name?"

"No," Jerry said.

"No," Bogan Murdock said, "no, but he was a great gentleman. One of the last. There are few left." He paused. "My father," he said quietly, "is a great gentleman." And he waited.

"Yes," Jerry said.

"And—" Bogan Murdock blazed, the controlled fury pin-pointed like a jet, "that scum! They struck through him. At me. I have fought them. I can fight them. But they struck through him. And I—" his head seemed to bow infinitesimally, giving only that little under the weight, and he spread his hands in the air before him, "cannot help but feel guilty."

Guilty, guilty, and the word rang in Jerry's consciousness, but it was not like a word, but like a wave, without a name, pulsing out cold from a knot in his stomach, leaving him weak, and clammy at the temples, before the next wave came through him, spreading through him like the concentric, irrevocable ripples from the spot in the very center of his being where the stone had been dropped; and it was like eyes on him, not only those blue-ringed black pupils which were on him, but other eyes, the eyes of people he knew, and strange eyes, fixed on him.

"I should not have been surprised," Bogan Murdock was saying, "for they would stop at nothing. They have struck at me in other ways. Through people in my organization. People who were close to me. They can," he said, "reach people. People," he said, "whom I have trusted."

"Duckfoot—" Jerry said, with an effort, drawing the word up out of himself, like a weight. "Duckfoot—you don't—you don't think he—"

Bogan Murdock sat down in the chair at his desk. He meticulously adjusted a bronze paper weight, under which there were no papers. "There are," he decided, and the fine fingers rested on the paper weight, which he seemed to be inspecting, "things which I do not feel at liberty to discuss."

But Jerry said: "Duckfoot—you don't think he'd do a thing like that?"

"Excuse me, Jerry," Bogan Murdock interrupted, and smiled precisely as he did in the mornings, in the corridors, in the elevator. "Excuse me," he said, "but have you spoken to Mr. Shotwell?"

"No—I—"

"I mentioned the matter to him this morning. I told him you were very much concerned. He—"

"No—" Jerry began.

But Bogan Murdock was going on, evenly: "—expects you to get in touch with him. You remember," he said, "the collateral question—you remember, you were disturbed about that?"

"No," Jerry said, summoning himself, "no—"

But Bogan Murdock, smiling as in a distant, understanding compassion, shook his head gently.

Or had the decision been reached the afternoon before, when, after leaving Bogan Murdock's office, Jerry had gone back to the Southern Fidelity and had found Duckfoot Blake cocked back in his chair, his feet on the desk, the ivory holder hanging from his face, and Ham Murdock standing before him, flushed and surly, with a lock of coarse hair dangling to his brow.

"Well," Duckfoot demanded, as Jerry entered, "did Bogan tell you everything was jake? Did he say that he, Herbie Hoover, and J. H. Christ had just had a little conference and fixed everything up? Did he say—"

"Shut up," Ham Murdock said, heavily, "you think you're so God-damned—"

"Smart," concluded Duckfoot for him, and added: "Not very, Hammie-Wammie, but smart enough to figure out that two and two add up to fifteen years in the pen. And the doctor has prescribed fresh air for yours-truly. You know, weak chest." He coughed theatrically.

"Yeah," Ham said, twisting his face, "yeah, you're smart enough to crawl. You get ready to crawl. You crawl out now and you're a son-of-a-bitch, you—"

"This," Duckfoot said to Jerry, gesturing toward Ham Murdock with the air of an impresario, "is that spirit of tact and persuasion Bogan sends over to fix me up. To take me back into the fold. To soothe the fevered brow, to—"

"It's a God-damned lie," Ham broke in, stepping forward, clenching his fists. "I haven't seen my father. Somebody tipped me. I just came—"

"I," said Duckfoot, "am not Mr. Pinkerton. Nor am I Mr. Holmes. But I can do simple sums. I composed my resignation at nine A.M., in a felicitous prose. My secretary typed it. You, Pal Jerry, saw it at two P.M., Central Standard Time. Three people only— secretary, Pal Jerry, yours-truly—saw it, or knew about it, and at three-ten in bursts our friend with the olive branch in one hand and the brass knucks in the other. How did he know, how—"

"It's a damned lie!" Ham proclaimed.

"Simple," Duckfoot said. "Little Miss Flo Forbes, on whom I built a trust somewhat less than absolute, has betrayed me. She types my piece, heads for the ladies' john, and ducks to a telephone to tip Bogan. And Bogan sicks Hammie on me, thinking that my document is in the morning mail and he will get it at two-thirty. Indeed, Miss Flo put it in my mail basket, but I took it right out again to show Pal Jerry whenever he got here. So Hammie beats the gun. My little piece is right here." And he tapped his inside coat pocket. "And, boy," he added, "do I love it!"

"You son-of-a-bitch," Ham Murdock said.

Private Porsum stepped inside the door.

In his large weathered face, cedar-colored as though hewn out of wood, or clay-colored, earthy, the grayish eyes, which were pale in contrast to the color of the flesh, looked out, moving over the scene with a puzzled, painful candor.

"President Porsum," Duckfoot greeted him. "Well, Private!"

Ham Murdock broke in, stepping toward Porsum, pointing at Duckfoot, saying, "He's quitting—he wrote a letter—he—"

"Right," Duckfoot agreed, meeting the grayish, metal-colored eyes, which were on him.

"Duckfoot," Private Porsum began, "I didn't know, I—"

"My apologies," Duckfoot said. "I wrote my resignation to Bogan. I was just going to tell you as a friend, when you came in this afternoon. A friend, mind you. For, Private, you ain't President of the Southern Fidelity. You are, to be blunt, a sucker. You are a stooge. You are a waterboy."

"God damn you, Blake, you—" Ham shouted, and stopped, as, for an instant, Porsum looked at him before turning his gaze upon Duckfoot, shaking his head, preparing his face to speak, saying in his slow, melancholy voice: "Naw, naw, Duckfoot. You're not leaving now. Not now. Not after all Bogan's done."

"Sure," Duckfoot agreed, "Bogan made you rich. He put you in politics. He makes his friends buy your ponies. But you paid him. Sure, you broke the big strike at Massey Mountain with your silver tongue. You showed your heroic frame on the stump and elected Governor Milam. You don't owe Bogan a thing. You have—"

"You—you—" Ham shouted, pointing at Duckfoot, "my father made you, and you crawl!"

"Pal," Duckfoot replied gently, "nobody made yours-truly, University of Chicago, Ph.D. I was found under a cabbage leaf. I sprang full-armed from the brow of Pallas. The Pixies brought me. And now—" he lowered his feet from the desk, set them lovingly on the floor, and uncoiled his height, "I go back to the burning fountain whence I came. I am, to be exact, hauling ass."

He picked up his hat, the soft black felt hat, like a preacher's.

"Duckfoot," Porsum said, and did not go on.

"I'm leaving, Private," he said. "You can stay, and the ponderous and marble jaws of the bastille yawn. For you, but not for me."

"Look here, look here, what do you mean?"

Duckfoot came around from behind the desk and laid his hand on Porsum's shoulder. "You are a hero, Private," he said sadly, softly, "but the war is over and heroes' wits are kept in ponderous vases. You ought to know what I mean. I mean my little soldier is trying to dump no-good Massey Mountain on the State. I mean the collateral on State deposits has been switched. I mean the paper on Murdock's loans ain't worth a damn and you ought to know it. I mean he's milked this bank, and he's milked this State and he—"

"I'll kill you," Ham Murdock shouted, and slugged at Duckfoot, whose body seemed to sway back like a reed, so that the blow only grazed his shoulder.

But Porsum, not moving from his tracks, had grasped Ham Murdock, and had drawn him, and held him with one big arm across his body, pinning him, while Ham said: "Damn you, Porsum, damn you, let me loose!"

Duckfoot looked at him curiously. "The spit-and-image of your old grandpa, huh?" he asked. "Honor of the family, huh?"

He put his hat on his head, and stepped to the door, moving gingerly as on eggs, favoring his feet, and turned to inspect, above Ham Murdock's head, Porsum's face, ravaged, furrowed like ripped earth, and the pale-seeming eyes, which looked out in dawning horror, pain, confusion, and appeal.

Then to Ham Murdock: "Keep your fingers out of the till."

To Gerald Calhoun: "Coming, pal?"

But Jerry did not reply.

Duckfoot went out the door, down the corridor, and into the street. Jerry could see him poised for an instant on the curb, attenuated, angular, his neck outthrust, his coat tail jerked up above the long legs, standing there gauntly and cautiously above the rickety legs, like an aquatic fowl.

That was the way it had been.

That was the way it had been, and the next morning Jerry stood before Bogan Murdock, who fingered the bronze paper weight and said: "Mr. Shotwell expects you to get in touch with him, Jerry. You know, the collateral question."

"No," Jerry said, summoning himself, wanting to know, afraid to know, knowing that there was nothing to know, while Bogan Murdock, smiling as in distant, understanding compassion, shook his head.

Bogan Murdock said: "Mr. Shotwell will be free to—"

"I don't want to see him," Jerry burst out.

"But the collateral question, Jerry? You were disturbed about the collateral question. You ought to investigate. To satisfy yourself. You owe it to yourself, you know. This is no time for false sentiment. You owe it to yourself, my boy."

"No!" Jerry exclaimed. And: "No."

Just as Jerry was leaving, Bogan Murdock, walking with him

to the door with his hand on his shoulder, said: "I understand there has been a foreclosure on your father's place. Forgive me for mentioning it, but it must have been a blow to you—your feeling for him—the family place—"

"Yes," Jerry said, and that pang, which had been smothered and forgotten in the midst of his more immediate problem, struck him again."

"I don't know," Bogan Murdock hesitated, "but—"

"Time—" Jerry said, not in reply to his friend, the word simply bursting out of his suffering, "I didn't know and all my stuff was tied up. I couldn't get a penny out in time—you know how things are—I didn't guess—if there'd just been time!"

"Yes, yes, of course," Bogan Murdock murmured comfortingly, absolvingly, and continued: "I don't know, I cannot be sure, but perhaps something could be arranged to give a little time. Even now. Yes, a little time. I am not too hopeful, but something, perhaps."

He removed his hand from Jerry's shoulder, and faced him at the door. "We shall see," he said, and shook hands.

Mr. Calhoun was not compelled to move in five days. It was a full six weeks before the execution. At that time, Mr. Calhoun's furniture was loaded on a truck and on his own farm wagon and hauled to a small house, not much better than a shack, on a back road. He had rented the place for thirty dollars a month, with some fifty acres of land. The land was not very good, but he thought, he said, he would try his hand at turkeys. He reckoned, he said, he always had had a hand with turkeys, but he just never gave them much mind before. He reckoned there might be some money in turkeys, with Thanksgiving and Christmas and all.

"Money," Uncle Lew echoed, and spat. "Yeah, money, Mr. Astor!"

Twenty-two

"—AND THAT poor boy lay there on his pallet, racked with pain and giving off an offensive odor from the infection which had set in after the amputation of the leg. He lay there, not an aristocrat, no scion of chivalry, no cavalier he, but a son of the people—· his father a blacksmith, he had told me when he asked me to write his farewell letter—and not a man in whom a settled conviction of the sacredness of a cause had led to martyrdom, nor in whose fibers thrilled the sublime impulse to heroic self-sacrifice, no volunteer dedicated to defend his homeland and its consecrated banner, but a conscript, not a good man but a man who, according to his own confession, had sinned in despite of God and had lived carnally. That same poor, unlettered, willful, purblind boy, who had, when the surgeon approached to do his dire duty, screamed curses upon God and upon his homeland and its consecrated struggle—that same boy, when he knew that the dark clouds were gathering, took me by the hand like a little child, and said, 'Parson, I been a wicked man; you pray fer my salvation.' And I knelt there by his pallet in the mortal stench, and prayed to God for mercy. I prayed until that poor boy whispered that he was at peace. Only one more wish he had, he said. And his face is yet before me, after the many years, and I hear his words: 'Parson, I ain't ne'er seen Gin'l Lee; I'm easy with God, parson, but I'd like wunst to see Gin'l Lee.'

"So I consulted my conscience and wrote a letter to that great man, and gave it to an orderly to transmit to his headquarters, which, at the moment, were not distant from the hospital. And the orderly returned to me with a note from that great man, who, at the time of trial, when he carried the fate of a proud people across his saddlebow, could take time to bend to the feeble voice of one of the lowliest.—That note, I say, yet reposes between the pages of my Bible, like a pressed flower.—That evening, by the flickering illumination of a camp lantern, General Lee stood beside the pallet, and removed his gauntlet, and leaned and took the hand of the poor boy. 'Gin'l,' that poor boy whispered in accents already

285

muffled by the eternal shadow, 'thank you right kindly. And, Gin'l,' he said, 'I'm right sorry I'm sich a stink.'

"Then, ladies and gentlemen, I observed a tear to course down that noble and beautiful and manly face. It glittered in the poor rays of that lantern like a precious diamond, and at that moment I thought how much more precious was that tear than any diamond. Then General Lee spoke, in that vibrant voice now tuned to sadness and to tenderness. He said: 'My son, my son.'

"That was all he said. He laid the now frail hand back on the pallet, and put on his gauntlet, and walked out into the darkness to take up again his own cross. That was all he said. But as the years pass, I have found that enough.

"I only saw General Lee once again, and that in the sad days after the vain carnage had ceased. I stood in my pulpit and saw below me that sainted aspect in which dignity overcame suffering. And I told this story, which I have told so often since, while I looked down upon him. I do not feel that I am mistaken when I say that again the moisture of sublime pity glistened in his eye. And so, ladies and gentlemen, that story which has meant so much to me, I tell again today, for it—" Sweetie Sweetwater said, and his voice dropped the sonorous mimicry, "and by God, he would tell it again, word by every God-damned word of it, till I thought I would puke if I heard it one more time, and you can bet I was always there in the front pew, where I damned well had to be, being the rector's boy. Or he'd tell it at the dinner table. Or at the U.D.C. meetings. Or at reunions. And he had whiskers like General Lee's and he'd turn his profile at you. Oh, God, would he turn that Roman nose! Oh, God, he—"

"It's not a bad story, though," Sue said reflectively, "except, of course, the rhetoric. The rhetoric is—"

"There's not a God-damned thing wrong with the story, except," Sweetie said, "it's a lie. There ain't anything wrong with any story I ever heard except it was a God-damned lie. They're all God-damned lies, which is what makes 'em stories, no matter what kind of rhetoric, and that's a word you picked up off that Sarrett, but it don't mean a thing, and—"

"Your father said it happened to him," Sue persisted, "and he's a preacher and he wouldn't tell a lie."

"My old man is a preacher, all right, and he ain't a liar, but that don't keep the story from being a lie. I don't believe a word of it except that my old man was a chaplain in the Army of Virginia twenty-five years before I was born, and I wouldn't believe that if I hadn't seen the papers on it. And even if every word was true, that only makes it a worse kind of lie, for the worst lies are true every God-damned word by word, but the whole thing is a lie just because it is the kind of story it is. Oh, my old man ain't a liar, but he just can't distinguish cow patties from porridge. Which is just part of being a preacher in the first place, and one reason things are the way they are. Did you ever see one could tell horse droppings from wild honey? Well, my old man can't, and they ought to thrown him out of the Episcopal Church years back instead of making him a bishop, on account of his theology. He's got everything so mixed up, he thinks Jesus Christ was killed in Pickett's charge. He thinks the Virgin Mary was a Confederate spy in Washington and carried documents through the Federal lines done up in her petticoats."

"You talk like you loved and respected him," Sue said, with a prim bitterness, thrusting her arm out straight and flicking the ash off the end of the cigarette she held.

"Sure, I love him," Sweetie said, "and I respect his head, which is hoary with the snows of ninety winters, about like I respect a prize simlin. I love him but he is a menace. He's a menace but he's a simple-minded menace. He ain't a son-of-a-bitch like your old man. Which is what makes it worse, for if he was a son-of-a-bitch like your old man, I wouldn't have to love him; I could just hate his guts the way you hate your old man."

"Yes," Sue said, slowly, "yes," her gaze wandering from Sweetie's face, and out through the window, over the roofs, which were streaked with dirty snow.

"But now I just love him, and go off my nut if I have to get within a mile of him. And I ain't been within a mile of him for going on ten years. I just write him a postcard once a month and tell him I love him and am well and hope you are the same. That is, when I ain't been in jail. And jail'd be a boon beside listening to that silver tongue all day long. When I put on long pants, I said I was through. I'd had my bellyful of the Lost Cause, and believe in winning a fight if I get in one, and I had my bellyful of getting the side elevation of that Roman, aristocratic, chivalric nose—"

"Which," Sue said, "you never inherited."

"I did inherit it," Sweetie said, "but a son-of-a-bitching scab up in Akron broke it in with a length of scantling." He fingered his nose, moving the blunt mass of cartilage tenderly as though the injury were fresh. "Or," he said, "maybe it was a son-of-a-bitching punk of a deputy sheriff did it in Birmingham. But I had it. You can always tell an aristocrat by his nose, and I'm an aristocrat.

Girlie, am I an aristocrat! I am a scion of chivalry. I got inside of me five quarts of the bluest chivalric blood ever distilled in Virginia, and every thimbleful is at the boiling point, and you've got the answer. Come here!"

He lolled back in the overstuffed chair, and motioned to her imperiously with his right hand.

She looked at the hand. It was a blunt, heavy hand, with stubby fingers, which sprang off separately from the palm, like spokes of a wheel, and which did not ever quite straighten out. The dark hair was thick on the back of the hand.

Watching the hand, she said: "Say *please.*"

"It ain't in my vocabulary."

"Say *please,*" she commanded, shaking her head gravely.

"It ain't in my vocabulary."

"*Please,*" she reiterated, gravely wheedling, as to a child.

"Listen, girlie," he said, "I never got a damned thing in my life I said please for. And I want something right now, and I mean it and no maybe's. You heard what I said. Come here!"

"No manners," she announced apologetically to the empty air as though to a friend. She rose in exaggerated resignation from her chair, smoothed her skirt at the hips, with her spread hands, and moved slowly toward him, shifting her shoulders ever so slightly as she walked, her hands still resting lightly at her hips. "No manners, no culture, no *politesse,* no *savoir-faire,*" she apologized tolerantly, swaying her shoulders, "and besides"—she was near his chair now and was narrowly watching the outstretched hand—"he smells slightly. He is—"

She tried to jerk back, but the hand had flicked forward and had seized her by the wrist, and drew her. She jerked back, and pulled, but his weight in the chair did not budge. He drew her to him, then, suddenly, thrust his legs out, one on each side of her ankles to lock them so that she fell toward him, with her free hand thrust out against his chest for support.

"He is," she resumed, flushed from the effort, settling herself in his lap, "slightly stinking. He is a stinking aristocrat. He stinks," she said, "but he is an aristocrat. You can always tell an aristocrat by his—" she set her forefinger to his bulgy, twisted nose, and gently pushed, while he looked cross-eyed, "nose."

"Yeah," he said, "that's the only way to tell 'em."

She leaned to kiss him lightly on the end of the nose, between the little kisses murmuring maternally, "Did the bad scabby-wabby —did him break—my itsy's bewfeefool—aristocratic—nose—up in Akron?"

288

"Or Birmingham," he grunted.

"Um-um," she murmured sympathetically, leaning. Then, all at once, she set her small teeth at the very tip of his nose, and bit.

"God damn it!" he shouted.

"Sh, sh, manners," she rebuked, and laid her finger on his lips.

He leaned his face against her finger.

"Are you sure," she inquired, pensively, "it was just his little nose got broken?"

"Baby!" he exclaimed, "baby, am I sure! Baby, I can produce affidavits from Shanghai in Chinese. I can produce affidavits from Armentiers in French. From Colon in Spanish. Sloe-eyed lasses smelling of whale blubber in the Arctic night will bear witness. In far-off Kamchatka—"

"The bitches," she said.

Near the stained river, not a very large river, which uncoils indolently but with an assured, compulsive dignity between the flat, broom-sage-covered, tired fields of the Tidewater toward the sea, Jason Sweetwater was born some five or six years before the turn of the century. He was born in a red-brick, ivy-draped, story-and-a-half house, with a slate roof, and a chastely designed portico, which had once been white, but from which the paint flaked and fell under the unhurried impact of the seasons, leaving exposed the neutral wood rendered spongy by weather now and so soft that a thumbnail could score it deep or pluck out the relaxed fibers. In the shallow yard the lilac bushes crowded over the picket fence, which needed repair, and the grass encroached upon the uneven bricks of the walk and sprang unremittingly from the crevices. On the left, beyond the picket fence, was the church, brick richly weathered outside; inside, shadow and white panels and varnished pews and the dark, carved pulpit and the cranky, breathless organ; above, the modestly aspiring steeple and the placid bell.

On weekdays, when Jason Sweetwater, a child, tiptoed into the church, and sat in one of the pews, alone, the place was cool and astonishingly quiet. If, somewhere, a man shouted or a rooster crowed, the sound penetrated only as the weak, mystifying irrelevance of a dream recalled in snatches, or as some event of the day remembered just as one drops off to sleep. But there, even in the weekday hush, the astonishing silence seemed to contain the ghostly distillate of the sound sacred to the precincts, the stiff, dry, sibilant rustle of ladies' silk, the decorous cough, the voice of his father, rising and falling, flowing, enveloping, blurring, devouring in its rounded, inevitable rhythm.

Sometimes he felt that if he listened hard enough he might hear them. He was not a religious child. He did not think of God when he went alone into the church, but the practice gave him a kind of perilous pleasure, a satisfaction sweeter because tinged with guilt. Not that anyone, least of all his father, would have forbidden him. His father never spoke to him about the habit, either to encourage or to discourage him, but secretly was pleased, when, from his study window, he watched the chunky, clumsy figure of his small son move warily across the patch of lawn to the side fence, open the gate, and go to enter, almost thievishly, the side door to the vestry. On such occasions he would think: *My son Jason is deeply spiritual; he is a child but he is deeply spiritual.* Then, seated at his desk, torn between pride and a grateful humility, he might bow his head and pray briefly for his son before he resumed his work.

In the church, sitting alone, Jason felt a tingling, tumescent certainty of self, a swelling potentiality of power and excitement so great that sometimes he held his breath until his ears rang like distant bells. His entering and sitting there alone was a kind of avowal of self, a compensation for, a repudiation of, the not-self which he was when he sat there on Sunday amid the rustlings and decorous coughs and under the tidal, silvery swell of the voice.

Once, when Jason sat there alone, the thought came to him that God's wrath was at that moment, and mortally, upon him, because he was what he was, and was there in that spot, filled with what was in him. The first flash of the terrible conviction passed into a cold, reckless defiance, and he closed his eyes, waiting, while the defiance mounted heroically into ecstatic certainty and he whispered over and over again, the evil, filthy words he knew, which blacken man and shame God. His lifted face, a square, blunt little child's face, was smooth and pure, as he sat there under the filtered light of the afternoon, with the eyes squinched tight shut and the lips moving.

But nothing happened. The moment subsided, and the heroic certainty in him. He opened his eyes. He looked about him as one does upon waking for the first time in a strange room. Shadows filled the upper church. Motes of dust danced, below, in a slanting beam of light. A lawn mower began to whir, far off.

He felt like crying, he felt betrayed—the tears burned at his eyes—but he did not cry. He had been too big a boy to cry, for a long time now, years now.

He left the church, carrying his betrayal, his emptiness, carefully as though not to spill his emptiness, as one is careful not to slosh a brimming bucket. He moved toward his house carefully, warily, across the open space, like one who, familiar with danger, shuns the open, and when forced into the open, eyes appraisingly the now inimical converts.

Then he was in the safety of his small hot room upstairs, under the eaves. He lay on his cot, face down, with his relaxed arms stretched out. He knew that after a while the supper bell would ring, and he would have to go down and sit with the others in the house.

There would be his mother, a small woman close to fifty, with a gray face, his father, now in his middle sixties, bearded, maned, erect, with deep eyes and beautiful hands, and his mother's mother, who was a shadow smelling of peppermint and echoing the names of people who had been dead a long time. Or there might be others —there were often others. At any time the boy might enter a room to find, sitting there alone, an old man, with clipped beard and gaiters and silver-headed stick, who would lay a knobby, uncertain hand on his head and wheeze at him. Or an old lady, and the old ladies were the worst. He would have to stand in the middle of a group of them in the sitting room, among the dust-smelling horsehair furniture and under the pictures and flags, and one of them would put her dry hand beneath his chin and peer into his face, so close that her breath, smelling like stale cooked turnips, would delicately fan his face, and she would say: "No, he has the favor of Willoughby Gresham. He has the Gresham eyes." And another would lean and say: "No, not like Willoughby Gresham, like Cassius Calloway, if you will try to recollect Cassius Calloway, he—" And another: "No—"

They would peer and exhale upon him and put the dead names upon him, until he felt that he was nothing, that his own name was nothing and the dead names were everything, although they were dead, too.

The house was full of those people, the wheezing old men and the gray-faced old ladies, who came and went away, and the dead names, which never went away. But, too, it was full of beliefs, and of believing. The gray-faced old ladies and the old gentlemen, his mother and his father, they all believed. They all believed in a great number of things, and they spoke of those things in the same familiar tone they used to name the dead names of people whom he had never seen, whose faces were featureless to him, as they were now featureless under the sod, who had died, long back, of childbed, minnie-ball, weak lungs, burst bowels, or the fall from the horse when the girth slipped. Or, which was worse, they assumed so insidiously that he did believe. And he stood before them, and felt as though he were

291

sinking powerlessly, deeper and deeper, into a great bin of cotton batting where the terrifying softness clung to the eyeballs and blotted all to a twilight, and blocked respiration and the mouth which would utter its cry of protest. He lived in the world of the shadowy poetry which they murmured around him, or enunciated voluptuously as his father enunciated Virgil when he read it aloud to polish his son's pronunciation. "You will do well, Jason, at the University," his father would say, laying aside the book. "You are well prepared, and you will do well if you do not lose your habits of study."

"Yes, sir," Jason would say.

At Charlottesville, he did not study at all. One morning, in April toward the end of his first year, he left his room, leaving behind him his scarcely marked books, his drawers of linen, his suits on their racks, and walked idly across the delicately springing lawns, eying detachedly the young men who hurried toward the gleaming, authoritative buildings, which were so white in the sun, and mailed a card to his father. He thought of the rooms where, after the stroke of the bell, voices like his father's voice would begin to speak beautifully.

He had eleven dollars in his pocket.

A week later, he shipped on a schooner out of Baltimore.

He was eighteen years old, was very strong, and believed in nothing except himself. Fifteen years later, he had learned that his father was right.

He had begun to learn that on the miserable, rat-infested, pest-ridden schooner as it heaved greasily southward toward the Caribbean. He had learned that in the Marine Corps, in which he had enlisted after one year at sea. He had learned it in France, in great bitterness, and it had generated in him a cold ferocity and a capacity for endurance. He had learned it later, in a dozen ships, in fifty ports, San Francisco, Bombay, Aden, Lisbon, Guayaquil, in hotels, barrooms, brothels, flophouses. He had learned it in factories, on docks, in jails, on picket lines, at the point of a gun, under the impact of the sawed-off baseball bat, and from the electric, inchoate delight which tingled clean to the shoulder when his fist found the brittle bone of a jaw or the softness of the belly. He had learned it from great dissipation, from the observation of death, from violence, from loneliness, and from considerable suffering.

He had learned that his father was, at least in part, right. A man could not believe in himself unless he believed in something else. He knew that what he had learned was important. So he did not regret the wasted years which had been the expense of learning it.

He saw that they had not really been wasted. He saw in them, now, an inevitable logic. He could look back on them with a kind of humble gratitude and a sense of peace. He could even look back, for instance, on the night when, in Galveston, he had tricked the mulatto prostitute who had satisfied him. He had pushed off her clawing hands and had slipped the dollar bill, his last one, back into his watch pocket. But she had made such a racket he had had to sock her. He had had to tap her pretty good. He could now look back upon that body lying on the floor of the fusty hole, illuminated fitfully by the soot-streaked kerosene lamp, the blood swelling meagerly from the split flesh at the cheek bone, the muddy eyes staring upward at him, suddenly clean and bright with a focused perfection of hatred, with the purity and certainty of eyes which have been granted the ultimate vision. She had lain there, looking at him, and had not said a word or uttered, after the single scream at the impact, any sound whatsoever.

Now he could think back to that and see it, without the shame and nausea. It was part of what he had learned. It had had to be that way. I reckon, he said to himself, a fellow dumb as I am has to get it the hard way, he has to be a son-of-a-bitch before he can even recognize one.

He had learned that he had to believe in something else before he could really believe in himself, and in the end he came to believe in something other than himself. He believed in it fully, uncompromisingly, with all the directness of his simple, logical nature. And believing in it, he could now believe in himself so fully that he no longer ever gave himself a thought. Life became an objective problem, complicated in its detail, but susceptible to solution in terms of a single principle. It was a tough problem, no denying, but nobody had crooked the deck; it was straight goods.

Now he could enjoy just sitting in a room with people and hearing them talk, as he had sat in the studio of Slim Sarrett, not talking much himself, just sitting there for the most part. He could enjoy almost any kind of people now, and that hadn't been true before, unless his recollection tricked him. He could enjoy people now, like a man who has been sick and penned up a long time can enjoy getting out and sitting in the sun, and not even thinking, just sitting and listening to the voices of people. He had been able to enjoy being with people like Duckfoot Blake, and Ham Murdock, and Alice Smythe, and Professor Hoxley, and Mrs. Hoxley, and Malloy, and Sam Ball and little Jenkins, and Slim Sarrett, even if half of them were goofy, and, God, what goof they could spill! He didn't, somehow, feel any more he had to measure off a man and figure whether he could handle him, or try to figure what every woman he met would be like in bed. The fury, he reckoned, had drained off pretty well, and he could look at somebody else now and know it was just a poor, benighted hunk of bone and gristle and fat meat, wearing pants or skirts as the case might be, just a poor God-damned man or woman moving in the world.

And he could enjoy drinking now, too. He had never used to enjoy drinking before, he knew that, not just the drinking. He had just slugged it in, and waited, while he felt bigger and bigger inside, and everything tightened up, till he felt like taking something in his hands and just tearing it apart while it screamed. He used to feel like just taking the whole son-of-a-bitching world in his hands and tearing it apart and spitting in its face while it screamed. And, by God, he'd sure done all he could in that direction a few times. Well, he could just take a drink now for the pleasure of it. And all he felt was like he had a great big furry Persian cat half asleep in his stomach and purring to beat hell; or maybe like he was a cat.

He had sat there like that, in Slim Sarrett's studio, with that big furry Persian cat in his stomach purring to beat hell, and he had watched Sue Murdock, who was Slim Sarrett's girl, they said, while she made her face grave and candid, and said something—how some God-damned thing or somebody was like something, the sort of thing she said that made all that gang near bust a gut laughing— and then, in the middle of their laughing, she'd look innocently off somewhere at the corner of the room. What she said was sure phony, and no mistake. It wasn't even her own kind of phoniness; it was somebody else's kind of phoniness. Maybe she was phony herself.

Maybe she was. But he knew that he was in love with her. And he knew that wasn't phony.

He was thirty-four years old and had never been in love. Once he had thought he was in love and had married. That was in a coal town in Pennsylvania, and the girl was the daughter of a Polack miner. She was a school teacher, and she looked washed clean and had yellow coils of hair in a town where nothing and nobody looked washed clean. He thought he was in love with her, but, looking back, he had decided the only reason he married her was because every male in town that hadn't slipped and hung himself on a barbed-wire fence in early youth had hot pants over her. He married her just to show he could do it, in a community where old men were ready to throw down their crutches and take out after any laundry wagon that was carrying her drawers to be washed. He did it because he was Sweetie Sweetwater, and he'd prove it. He figured at the time she married him because she loved him.

He decided pretty early she didn't do it because she loved him. She married him because she wanted to use him. She wanted to make him a stooge. Not just a household stooge. He was prepared to admit that any husband not a complete son-of-a-bitch was going to take a little of the garden variety of henpecking. But, no, she wanted to make him a stooge to the whole world. She wanted to make him kiss the world's wide ass. She wanted to make him cuddle up to the Company. To butter some little white-collared office manager. To turn him into an informer, and her the daughter of a back-sprained old mine-monkey. She would do that because she wanted to live in a house like the one that pus-busted biddie that office manager was married to had, and drive a car. She knew he had education and she was just going to manage him so he would rise in the world. Jesus, when he'd been conscientiously and faithfully endeavoring all his life to sink in the world so he could get his feet on the ground and find out what a man was.

So one morning he just put his hat on his head, laid all his pay except five bucks on the bureau, and walked out the door and kept on walking.

He kept right on going, for seven years and several thousand miles, stopping to eat at tables and lie in beds and work in factories and mills and scratch his belly in four or five jail cells and rest up in a couple of hospitals, until he got to the big attic room where Sue Murdock's face assumed that pellucid gravity before she said something which would throw that gang into stitches, and which he knew was phony.

He knew he was in love with her, all right. Well, she was that Slim Sarrett's girl—which sure made him revise his original view of Sarrett—and he wasn't going to butt in. He was through with that sort of thing, butting in for the hell of it. And she was Bogan Murdock's daughter. He sure wasn't unaware of the humor of that. Yep, the situation was practically perfect.

She was Bogan Murdock's daughter, but she had run out on the old man, they said. "What courage!" that Alice Smythe had said. Well, he had his fingers crossed on that. It didn't take much courage just to play at being poor, if you had enough dough to finance the project of playing at being poor. Or to run out, when you knew they'd be paying you to come back when you got good and ready and not tarnish the family name. And meantime she sure didn't have any darns in her clothes and she slept late and led the life of the spirit and read Shakespeare's sonnets and those thin deckle-edged volumes Sarrett reviewed in thin magazines and got high as a kite three times a week—or more, as far as he knew—and provided Sarrett's nookie. Yes, he reckoned she did, and he took a kind of grim satisfaction in being able to think that and not get the jitters. There wasn't any law a man had to get the girl he happened to fall in love with and live happily ever after. And little Sue didn't look like she'd fit in with his scheme of things.

But when she sat up straight from the waist and hitched her shoulders like that—Jesus, where did she learn that trick?—and when her face smoothed to that look of pensive, God-damned inward innocence before she said what she was going to say—then a strut just broke in his insides and he felt soft and sweet like he did when he was a kid and got bilious in the spring and they squirted him full of an enema bag full of warm water to get him ready for the summer and green apples.

Then he would try not to listen to what she would say.

What she said didn't matter, anyway. It was just a lie somebody put in her mouth. Her face was trying to tell the truth, but she didn't have the words for it. Maybe she wouldn't ever find the words for it. It took anybody a long time to find the words for the truth, even if the truth was growing in you and ruining your appetite and not letting you sleep, like a tumor you don't know about. He reckoned he knew how it was. So, in the end, when she said what she said and he couldn't help hearing it and looked around at the faces that would be twisted with laughing, he just felt sorry for her, and sad, like she was one of those little six-year-old girls they put grease paint on and mascara and frizz their hair and dress in a little stand-out skirt up to the little baby crotch and put out on a vaudeville stage in the spotlight to sing some slop in a voice so high it squeaked, in between the comic team number and the pride of the beef trust. *Sister,* he would think then, feeling sorry for her, *sister, you got plenty way to go yet.*

Thinking that—*you got plenty way to go yet*—speaking from the distance of the way he himself had come, that made him feel better. It put some safe space in between them. For the moment at least, it made things feel like they were settled, like she had died, or he had bought a one-way ticket and was on the train. Maybe he ought to buy a one-way ticket, he thought more than once. But he always decided that he had lived long enough to know how to take his medicine, and besides he had a little unfinished business out at the Freeman Foundries, and things were getting hot there. So he would sit in a chair there in Slim Sarrett's studio, and watch her, and sip his likker, which he knew how to enjoy now, and think: *Sister, you sure got plenty way to go.*

Feeling sorry for her, that was what hooked him for good and all, he reckoned. So long as it was just something he wanted to get out of her, he could pass the deal, and just cover up his chin when the punch came. But when it looked like she wanted something out of him, that made the difference. Or maybe that was just the alibi he cooked up for himself. Maybe it was a smoke screen, behind which he was operating. In the end he dismissed the question as not being too important. He wasn't going to get a hernia thinking about it. He said to himself that if something had one side, it was bound to have two sides, and if you turned something over you were bound to find the other side, and maybe that would be the side the grub worm lived under. But he wasn't going to act like a God-damned Liberal. He sure wasn't cut out for a Hamlet. He knew that if you got anything you sure had to pay for it, and you paid for it with a chunk right out of your soul, whatever that was, and all you had to be careful about was that you got something for it, and *caveat emptor,* buddy.

Sister, you got plenty way to go, he would think; but flung down beside her on the lumpy bed, in the late winter afternoons, after he had come in from the Foundries, when the lights were already on in the houses across the river, or in the evenings, after he had come back from a meeting, he would listen to her talk and also think that she had come quite a way. She didn't know what the score was, but she wasn't entirely ignorant of the fact a game was going on. They had put her in there without telling her no holds were barred and the other guy might have anything from brass knucks to a Smith and Wesson. But she was trying to make sense of it, all right.

She would lie there on the bed, talking in the shadowy room, while he sat in a chair, or lay on the bed, too, with a space between them, not touching her. Bit by bit, evening after evening, she would try to put the past together, fumblingly, like a kid working with a jigsaw puzzle. She was talking to him, telling him about it, but he knew it wasn't so much for him as for herself. It was like a jigsaw puzzle, all right, but there was always one piece missing, and she couldn't tell whether it was a picture of a hula dancer or a map of classic Greece. And maybe you couldn't tell either, even if you thought you could.

Like that evening he came by and found she had another letter from Murdock.

"And he signed it *Dockie,*" she said.

"Throw it down the can and pull the chain," he said, "and forget about it."

"He signed it *Dockie*," she said bitterly, holding the crumpled sheet of paper in her hand, tightly as though it were precious, and staring at him as though he were getting ready to rob her.

"Throw it down the can," he said.

"I used to call him *Dockie*," she said, "a long time ago when I was little. He called himself *Dockie* when he talked to me. He'd pick me up, and hold me high up in the air, then bring me down close, and say, 'Give Dockie a kiss.'" Her mouth twisted in repugnance, and pain, as she clutched the piece of paper. "Then he'd kiss me—"

"Listen," he said, "he'd kiss you and give you a thousand bucks right now, if you'd go back. It'd be cheap for him at the price. Don't think you're doing him any good running out this way, right now when the heat is getting turned on him. Oh, he'd kiss you, all right."

"I'd get out of bed at night, sometimes," she said, "and go down where he'd be sitting by himself, and I'd slip in and sit on the floor by his foot and lean my head against his knee, and call him *Dockie*. Dockie," she repeated, twisting her mouth. "I'd get up and—"

"Sure," he said, "all kids do that. Kids don't like to be left in the dark. They think something is going on—"

"He was good to me," she said.

"Sure, he was good to you," he said. "Everybody is good to kids if they've got plenty of dough and spare time. I don't mind thumping a kid in the stomach myself and saying goo-goo, even if it ain't my own. Judas Iscariot was good to his kids, if he had any. It don't prove a thing."

"No," she admitted dubiously, "no, I reckon—"

"Forget it," he advised, and studying her, as she stood there before him, looking at him with eyes which seemed to be drawing farther and farther away from him, as into distance, while her fingers delicately worked the piece of crumpled paper, he added: "Gee, but you sure carry all your baggage with you. Why don't you try forgetting something once in a while?"

She made no answer.

Then he said: "I'm going to a meeting. Why don't you come on with me? I bet you haven't been outa this hole all day."

"No, I haven't," she said.

"Well, come with me."

"No," she said, "I don't believe I'll go."

"Suit yourself," he replied, "but I gotta be shoving."

So he left, and all the way down the dark, slushy street, hearing the wheels of automobiles hiss imperiously through the puddles and the melting snow, and the empty, perfunctory clang of street-car bells a block over, he could see her standing there, her eyes, her face, seeming to withdraw from him while she fingered that damned paper.

He shrugged his shoulders. *Time,* he thought, *give her time.* And with melancholy resolution, he put his mind on the business ahead of him that evening. He ticked off the names of the men who were going to talk. McGinnis would be there; he'd promised to come. If they could hook McGinnis, McGinnis ought to swing a lot of weight with the men. And McGinnis had been with the Freeman Foundries twenty-three years, and still a sucker. But you had to handle those old boys with kid gloves. The old ones were so whipped-down, they'd take a kicking and lick the boot, or they were so bitter and burnt out, they were against everything and everybody, you too, for they figured you had something up your sleeve, too. And he saw McGinnis, gaunt, bitter, the deep-set, dark eyes smoldering with the last, impartial, hoarded malediction for all things he had laid eyes on or would lay eyes on until they shut up his eyes and laid the nickels on them. Until his old woman collected his five-hundred-dollar insurance policy—if he hadn't let it lapse three weeks before he kicked off—and spent half on the funeral, and paid the doctor and the back grocery bill, and the rent one month, and saved out enough to put a stamp on a letter addressed to the last address she had for that boy who had gone out West and hadn't written her for five years, and who was probably dead or in jail or was daffy from having a San Francisco Junior Chamber of Commerce baseball bat wrapped around his skull or was drinking sterno in a flophouse by this time. Well.

But there was Sue before him again, as she had been when he turned to go. And again, as an orderly man folds a paper and puts it away in his desk before he turns to another stack and a new problem, he put aside the thought of Sue Murdock, who carried all her baggage with her.

She sure did.

Why couldn't she forget that Slim? Not that he was jealous. He'd taken his medicine too far back to be jealous now, he told himself. Jesus, he was inoculated. He'd eaten enough of his own bile to use it for a cocktail now and not bat an eye. Jesus, he was Mithridates, all right. He wasn't jealous. He didn't have any reason to be jealous, and he knew it. Sue wasn't exactly stuck on that

Slim, to state it mildly. But he sure couldn't figure her morbid curiosity about the bastard. It was morbid. Every time Al—who wasn't a foreman any more, who was on his uppers, who was living on bread and water or near it now—came over with Betsy to sit with him and Sue, it wouldn't be five minutes before somehow Sue'd get the conversation around to Slim Sarrett. He'd be damned if he knew how she did it, but she did. And natural as could be. It looked like she'd be through with the subject when she found out Slim had pulled out in a plane for Chicago with that Greek banana peddler. "On a honeymoon," Al had said, and bellowed and slapped his knee, and Betsy had snickered at first, then she had bellowed too—she laughed like a man, right out of the belly, when she got really tickled—and had jabbed Al in the ribs, and had screamed: "Now ain't you a card!" And Al had said: "Sue, you better watch them Greeks. You better give Sweetie good grub round here, or he'll be heading for a Greek restaurant." And Betsy had screamed: "Now ain't you a card!"

It looked like that would satisfy her.

But she was morbid.

Slim hadn't got back to town twenty-four hours before Sue knew all about it. How he'd turned up with a new suit, with a wad of dough, and a case of Scotch run in from Canada. And back by plane, Scotch and all, like a God-damned millionaire. And how he'd thrown a party with that Scotch, and Malloy was there, Malloy and the stitches barely out of his face where Sarrett had hacked him down, and Malloy drank a whole bottle of Scotch. That was what they said. It made you want to puke.

It was morbid.

But he reckoned she was doing the best she could.

She had, two nights after the night when he had left her standing there in the room with Murdock's letter in her hand, asked him to take her to his meeting. "If you want to go," he said.

He reckoned she was doing the best she could.

She had gone to the meeting, and had sat in the big, cold room, where the old tobacco smoke stung your eyes, with her fur coat pulled up to her chin, it was so cold, and had listened with unmoving gravity, like a good little girl in church, apparently unaware of the looks the boys gave her when they got a chance, half of them undressing her and half of them wanting to cut her sweet little, pretty little, round little blessed throat, which would pulse and flutter like it did when she put her head back and you laid your hand on her throat—wanting to cut it because she was Murdock's daughter—and a lot of them wanting to do both. She sure took minds off business. Well, he'd keep his mind on his business. She was part of his business—he'd admit that, all right—but by Jesus, he'd keep his mind on his business.

As they walked back together, after the meeting, he had wanted to ask her what she thought of it. But he hadn't, she seemed so wrapped up in herself, the way she got sometimes. Then she had said: "They all want something—really want it."

And he had said: "You're damned tooting, they want something. They want three squares and the rent."

They had walked on ten yards, in the dark, keeping step as best they could on the slick pavement.

Then she had said: "I wish I wanted something."

Which struck him as pretty damned silly, so he had said: "Well, sister, you don't want to be wanting that. You ain't got the taste or the constitution."

She hadn't said a thing to that.

Then, ten yards on, she had said: "I don't want anything."

"I want something," he had said. "Just wait till we get to the apartment, and I'll tell you what I want."

She made no answer. He glanced at her face, in profile, and she looked like she hadn't heard a word he said. She was looking straight ahead up the dark, empty street, and he might just as well not have been there. He might have been a ghost, and a damned transparent one, for all she showed. He might just as well have been a ghost trying to tell something to somebody and making plenty of noise to his own ghost ears but not a whisper to that ear less than twenty-four inches away. And he thought of ghosts keeping step with you, and straining and yammering, but not putting it across. Or maybe they were putting it across to her, for it sure sometimes looked like she had plenty of ghosts, and all of them talking at once and her hearing every word, and not wanting to miss a God-damned syllable, with that listening expression on her face, and her eyes that way, but you could be plenty sure she hadn't been listening to you. Well, maybe the ghosts were real, and he wasn't. He sure wasn't real right now, he had thought, moving beside her in the shadow of the buildings.

What he had said had not been real, and he had known it. And she had known it. He hadn't wanted to go to bed with her at all, then. Trust her—trust any of 'em—to spot you when you pulled that swagger. He had just said it, and it was phony. He had said it because it was just one way of stopping her from saying what she was saying. Sure, and it worked sometimes. It would take her mind off what she was saying, quick as a wink and twice as handsome and a little bit like pulling the pin on a hand grenade. She'd take you up too damned quick, that was the trouble. It was like she grabbed hold of something just because it came to hand and was something to grab hold of. Like somebody in quicksand grabs hold of something. She'd take you up too damned quick to be convincing, you might say. She'd put too God-damned much into it for it to be real. And then, by God, you wouldn't feel exactly real, and by God, if you didn't feel real when you had your hands on that little package something was sure out of gear.

He reckoned something was out of gear, sometimes. But give her time.

Yeah, give her time, talk about giving her time, when every time you pulled a phony like that you sure weren't helping things along. But he couldn't help himself sometimes, not since he'd found out it would work sometimes. It would just pop out, and all the time he'd be back off in a corner of his head with sly, slick, calculating low cunning just gambling she'd take him up. And not necessarily because you wanted to. You might be dog-tired and whipped down like a dishrag, but you just had to change the subject. Oh, you were going to save a soul, you were going to cast out a life line, you were going to cheer someone along life's rocky way, you were going to be the great healer, and you just changed the subject.

Sweetie, he had said to himself as he walked beside her, *Sweetie, you are a son-of-a-bitch.*

Which he couldn't help. He'd just do that, and know he was doing it. He'd do it, or he'd get tough with her.

He'd say: "For Christ sake, I bet you've been up here in this room all day. Why don't you take a walk? Why don't you take up tatting? Why don't you collect tinfoil for an old folks' home? For Christ sake, why don't you do something and quit picking your scabs?"

Which didn't help much, either.

She never got sore, when he talked like that. And she never cried. He'd say that for her, and he sure couldn't stand a crying female. But maybe he wished she would get sore. Maybe he even wished she would cry. He wished she would get it out of her system.

But she just looked at him. Or sometimes she looked like she hadn't even heard him.

But she'd sure pick her scabs.

That Slim.

He reckoned if you'd been around that baby much and had a dose of the hogwash he put out under the label of soothing syrup, it'd take you more than a pissing-spell to come to grips with reality

302

and face the challenge and roll up your sleeves and spit in the palms of your hands. The truth wasn't in him. He just didn't lie when he had to. For some purpose. He was a lie. He had to be the lie. Like that cock-and-bull story he told Sue about his father being a blown-up barge captain and his mother a whore in New Orleans and God knows what all. It was sure funny when that Greek mentioned seeing Slim's father in Florida and him selling washing machines. And he bet the mother wasn't a whore, either. He bet she was a member in good standing of a Baptist sewing circle and sent the bastard a couple of bucks now and then when she could save it out of the house money and wrote him and asked him did he read his Bible. God, it must be a blow to Slim to have a mother like that and her not a whore in New Orleans after all. Gee, it must be tough. It must be tough on you, you dirty little snob. It was sure funny to see Slim's face when that Greek petunia spilled the beans. And Sue sitting right there. At least it would have been plenty funny to see his face, if you hadn't seen Sue's face too. That wasn't very funny. It wasn't very funny.

"Why," she had demanded of him, a long time after that night, "why did he tell me all that? I just don't see why." Accusingly, like he, Sweetie Sweetwater, was responsible. Like he had to answer for that bastard.

"Hell, I don't know," he had said.

"Why did he tell me?" And she had looked at him like he had robbed a bank.

"Forget it," he had said.

"What I want to know is why? Why?"

"Because he's a liar," he had said. "Maybe he told you because he wanted you to feel sorry for him. Or think he was wonderful or something. But the real reason was because he is a liar. He is a liar just like a channel catfish ain't a canary. He swims in a lie, and he is in the lie and the lie is in him and if you could hook him and pull him out he'd hang there with his gills puffing and his eyes popping and not know what to make of it. He just ain't adapted to breathe God's sweet air."

"He told me—" she had begun.

"I bet he told you plenty," he had said. "He told me he had been to sea, which was a mistake because he didn't know I had. And I mean I had me a hitch of it. So I just made him talk out of pure devilment. He talked a lot of stuff he'd got out of books somewhere, which was all right for fooling somebody who'd just been in a rowboat on the city park pond. Well, I never let on."

"Why—"

"Because he lives in a dream world. And God damn it, he makes a living out of it. Writing them God-damned poems. Which are a pack of lies. I can't make a thing out of 'em, but I know they are a pack of lies."

"He told me—"

"Forget it," he had said. "Christ, can't you forget it?"

"I don't want to forget it," she had replied, gravely. "I want to know what—"

He had looked at her. "Are you stuck on that pansy?" he had demanded.

She hadn't said anything for a minute, and he had sat there wishing he had swallowed his fat tongue, like a blue-point on half shell.

"I'd like," she had said, then slowly, "to kill him."

He had believed her. She would like to kill him. Because he had something on her. Because he had a secret. She would like to kill him like you want to kill somebody who blackmails you. He was a part of her now. He was the part of her she wanted to kill. She wouldn't feel clean till he was dead.

She would say: "Oh, Sweetie, I don't know what makes me the way I am. What makes me the way I am?"

He might cock his head to one side, and grin at her, knowing he was grinning, showing his broken tooth, knowing how his face looked just like he was looking in a mirror—*Oh, Sweetie, you are a leering, lousy, insinuating, fundamental, masterful son-of-a-bitch, you are, you are hell on the women, yeah*—and say: "What way are you, huh? I'd like any way you can name, and right now, sister!" And knowing the whole time why he did it.

And maybe it would work.

Or maybe he would get tough. Maybe he would say: "Now look here, quit being so God-damned morbid. Why don't you put your mind on something? Why don't—"

But maybe nothing would work, and she would only pause, and regard him, and then begin with that distant, circumstantial, dispassionate tone to tell him how something had been, every little detail. Like when she told him about Rosemary Murphy. She had liked Rosemary, she said, better than any girl she knew. And he believed her, even if she never saw Rosemary any more, now. "I really like her," she said. "I never knew anybody like her. She hasn't got anything, and she's crippled. She's not very smart, she just barely gets through all right at school no matter how hard she studies, and she has to type all the time to get a little money.

And it'll be like that all her life, and she knows it'll be that way. And she goes right on.

"I used to fight with Jerry about her—that was one of the things —about his not liking her. Oh, he said he liked her, but I could tell he didn't, and I'd accuse him. He acted like he had the itch when she was around; he couldn't sit still. Or like she had the leprosy, or something, and he was afraid to catch it. I knew how he felt, and Rosemary knew it, and I couldn't stand it, and I'd tell him. I couldn't see how he could be that way; I couldn't bear it. But I—" She stopped and laid her hands together in her lap. Her ankles and knees were together, very straight, demure, almost, and she sat up very straight, and looked straight at him. He could see her hands slowly clench in her lap.

"But I—" she said, and stopped.

He knew better than to say anything. He watched her hands.

"But I—what I did to Rosemary. It was horrible, and I knew it was horrible, but I couldn't help it. I just did it. I'd been with Jerry, and when I'd see Rosemary—I'd go up to her room a lot and talk to her—I'd tell her about us. I started out just telling her little things, just the ordinary things a girl tells another girl about a man she's in love with, and not thinking much about it. About what he said to me, and what I said, and sometimes about how we fought—that was before we got to fighting so bad. One time—I don't know how it happened, it was just a slip—I told her about how he kissed me. All I was really saying was that the fighting didn't matter.

"Then I just happened to notice her face. It was changed. It wasn't like it had ever been before. And something just got into me. I couldn't help it. So I said: 'That's nothing. That's nothing beside going all the way.'

"I don't believe she breathed for a minute. She just sat there looking at me. Then she said, and it was just a whisper: 'Do you?'

"I told her, yes.

"She sat there looking at me. Like she was waiting for me to go on. And I don't believe she even breathed the whole time.

"I didn't tell her any more that time. I got up and left. But later on, I'd tell her things. I'd tell her just a little more every time, and she'd get that look on her face. It got so I'd tell her everything. I couldn't help it, even if I did know what I was doing. I'd say things to her you can't say to anybody except somebody you're in love with. And not to somebody you're in love with except sometimes, when everything is a certain way, and it seems all right. I told her what we did. How sometimes we went out in the

305

country, and Jerry always had a blanket in the rumble seat—when I first found out he had a blanket back there, I was furious, I was so jealous, it was an old blanket and you could tell he'd been keeping it in the rumble seat. I told her how we went out in the country, and how it was on the ground, at night, and you could see the stars. And how one time it was on the big couch in the drawing room at home, and my father across the hall in the library, and I could hear him moving around. I'd tell her what Jerry said, and everything. Just exactly. And her face would flush up, and her eyes get bright and glitter, and it didn't look like she would breathe at all. She would look pretty then, she was so different from usual.

"Then one day I told her how Jerry and I had come to her room and she wasn't there. I told it very slow, and I watched her like it seemed I couldn't help doing. I told her how we noticed there wasn't any latch on the door, and what he said and what I said. I told her every bit. And when I got through, and was watching her, she said, just about like a whisper like she didn't have enough breath in her: 'Here—here on my bed?' And she looked at the bed.

" 'Yes,' I said, 'yes. It was right there on the bed.' And I pointed at the bed. 'Right there, Rosemary. It was—'

"Then she suddenly jumped up—as near as she could jump up with her braces and all—and just about screamed at me: 'Shut up! Shut up! Do you hear, shut up!'"

"Then she began to cry. She was sort of hysterical at first, but pretty soon she was just crying quietly. I comforted her the way you do, and she finally put her head down on my shoulder and cried. But I wasn't really sorry for her. I am telling the truth, I wasn't. I enjoyed it, in a way. I got a kind of excitement out of her crying. It was horrible, and I knew it was horrible, but I enjoyed it. That's what I did to Rosemary, and it was horrible. I know it was. It was horrible. Wasn't it? Wasn't it?"

And she leaned toward him a little, demandingly, intently, her face set in a kind of expectancy, as though she begged for a favor, for agreement.

"Yes," he admitted, "it was a horrible thing."

"Oh, God," she said softly, under her breath, not to him.

"Look here," he commanded, "it's not all that bad."

"I don't know what makes me the way I am," she said.

"You're not any different from anybody else," he affirmed.

"That's what I did to Rosemary," she said, not seeming to pay him any attention. "And it was horrible."

"There's something horrible in everybody," he said, "till they work it out. It looks like a man's got to boil the pus out."

"What I did to Rosemary—" she said.

"Listen," he said, "I went to a whore in Galveston one time. It was a mulatto whore, and a mulatto whore in Galveston, let me tell you, is something. She was a one-buck whore. Then I snatched my dollar off her, and when she made a fuss, I tapped her. I gave it to her pretty good, and cracked her cheek open. She lay there on the floor and looked at me. I number it among my greatest achievements."

"Oh, God," she breathed.

She had not heard a word he said.

"Forget it," he said. "Do something and it'll be all right. You'll forget it then. And then it won't matter if you do remember it."

"I'm a mess," she said.

She rose, and came to him, and sat on his lap and let her head sink to his shoulder.

"I'm a mess," she said. "What made you ever take up with a mess like me?"

"You're a right nice mess," he said.

"I don't know what I am," she said, "but whatever I am, I'm a mess."

Whatever you are. There's just one way to find out what you are. Everybody stands for something and till you know what you stand for you ain't anything. You ain't anything in the world, no matter how God-damned fascinating you think your personality is.

Sweetie, he said to himself, his hand lying on her hair, you are a wonderful guy. *You* are not a mess. You are superb. You are Socrates. You are Bruce Barton. You are the Child Jesus expounding the law in the Temple. You are Dorothy Dix. You take away the sins of the world. And your personality is so God-damned fascinating.

In the late winter he became more and more involved in his work. The organization was good enough now. The demands were made on the management. He was on the committee which conferred with the management. He sat in the big, clean room, on the walls of which were big framed photographs of men in rich-looking dark suits, with dark ties knotted small at stiff collar, with tie pins visible in the picture, photographs of men with square jaws and abundance of iron-gray hair which in the real men had contrasted well with the ruddy flesh you knew the faces had had, or photographs of men with sharp eyes and thin jaws and no hair on their high, narrow heads, men whose faces, you knew, had been gray. He sat in a comfortable, leather-upholstered chair, gradually adding to the pile of cigarette butts in the bronze tray on the table before him, and looked up at the photographs or at the men around the table, and he thought that you couldn't tell the difference between the faces in the pictures and the faces there across from him. He attended to the voices, but he knew what they were going to say before they said it. He had known a long time before. It was always the same. Everybody always said the same thing. Things weren't decided by talk. They were decided by things behind the talk. He could predict all the talk. He had known that somebody would say, as the powerful, heavy, washed, ruddy-jowled man with the iron-gray hair was now saying, with his great red fist square on the table with clean, clipped, gray, dead-looking nails, saying: "We'll close down. We'll have to close down, and then where will you be?"

And he had known what he himself would say. He said: "That's our risk, Mr. Burbank."

He had known the thin, high-skulled, gray-faced, hairless man would say: "We can't pay it. We can't pay it. You understand, we can't, and where'll you be?" His voice mounting, and thinning.

And he himself said: "Maybe it's a question of gradually or suddenly."

"What? What?"

And he had said: "Starving."

"We can't. The company can't pay it. I tell you, we can't!"

And he said: "You could if you hadn't let the Foundries be milked dry, all right."

"It's a lie!" That was the ruddy-faced man.

"What? What do you mean?" That was the high-skulled, hairless man, his voice thinning.

And he had looked at them all, and said: "You know what I mean. I mean Murdock."

"It's a lie!"

And he said: "Get out from under Murdock and you can pay."

You almost felt sorry for them. Caught between Murdock and Sweetie Sweetwater. No, not Sweetie Sweetwater—Sweetie Sweetwater wasn't anything, just a name, a voice, an instrument—it was a force behind Sweetie Sweetwater. Maybe Murdock was not anything, either, and there was something behind him. All right, then. That was the way it was. All right.

All right. But crowd 'em. And crowd your own boys, too. They could take some crowding, too. Keep your eye on the ball. Take the risk. Sure, there was a risk, but take it. Just keep your eye on the ball, and crowd 'em all.

During that period he saw Sue very little. About all the time he had was late at night, when he could drop by the apartment for a few minutes. Thank God, it had come this late. She looked like she could take care of herself now. He'd always said, just give her time. Just as soon as she figured out how things were. As soon as she could begin to do something. As soon as she could put her mind on something. Well, she was working with the women now. She was helping organize relief. She was reading something. She was trying to find out how things were. She was smart. She'd find out.

And when that poem, not signed, but dedicated to her, came in the mail, she just laughed at it. She showed it to him, and they laughed at it together. You couldn't make any sense out of it. That Slim was a card, he'd have to hand it to him. And then the copy of the magazine came with the poem printed in it. It was just dedicated to "S.M." now. Jesus, wasn't it sweet?

Then the strike came. Things were hot. And would be hotter. And by God, they'd be hotter for Murdock. Hell was going to pop all over the State. All over ten states. "There's going to be hell popping," he said to Sue. "If you want to collect that thousand bucks and a kiss from your old man for coming back home to be a good girl, you better hurry. Maybe he can still give it to you, since he wrote you again just last week, but you better hurry, or there won't be any thousand bucks. There'll be just a great big old kiss from daddy and that's all."

Then, later: "Well, it's me your old man's offering the dough to now. If I'm a good boy. A guy took me to a beer joint, a guy I never saw, and wanted to buy me a bottle of brew and tell me something. He wanted to tell me something all right. He wanted to tell me he had some dough for me if I'd be a good boy. Even if I didn't do anything but just clear out of town, he had some dough for me. When he got to the point, I had a mouthful of brew, so I just let him have it in the eye. I let him have a mouthful for eyewash. Gee, some folks think money can buy anything."

"Yes," she said, "they think it'll buy anything."

"Well, it won't be dough your old man'll offer me next time. It'll be a length of lead pipe on a dark night. If I'm not careful."

"Just let him," she said, viciously, tightening up, "just let him, and I'll—I'll—"

"Sister," he said, "your old man won't even know about it unless he reads it in the back page of the paper. He won't get his hands

309

dirty. Oh, no! He won't do a thing. He just creates a climate, you might say, in which certain vegetables grow."

It was the next night she said she wanted to go down on to the picket line.

"It won't be like Daisy Day at Vassar," he said.

"All right," she said.

"You might get shoved around," he said.

She didn't say anything to that.

"Your picture will be in the paper," he said. "Some reporter will spot you, and all your friends will see your picture in the paper. In one of the papers," he added, "the one that doesn't like your old man, from motives, I got to admit, somewhat less than noble."

"I'll go," she said.

"Suit yourself," he said.

She went. A reporter spotted her, and her picture was in the paper that night, on the front page.

He brought the paper to the apartment, and showed it to her. "For your memory book," he said. *"Financier's daughter at picket line,"* he read the caption, out loud. *"Miss Sue Murdock, daughter of—"* He dropped the paper into her lap, and laughed.

"It's a very nice picture," she said, regarding it critically.

"It," he affirmed, "will sure roil the waters. It is nicer than you think, sister. It will—"

"It is very, very nice, though," she hesitated, studying it; "it is a little different from the one they used when they announced my engagement the other time."

"Huh?"

"When they announced my engagement the other time," she repeated. "But I like this one better. It is more original. Much. And," she looked up at him, "you can kiss me, now we're engaged."

"Sure," he said, and kissed her, "sure, I like being engaged."

"That's fine," she said. "You can go home and dream about me, and get up early and go right down and buy a license, and get over to your nice little strike only half an hour late. But we can't get married for five days. It's the law. Five days is—"

"Huh?"

"—a long time, and I don't believe in long engagements. They are very trying on the nerves. Especially—" and she smiled primly at him, "when you are pregnant."

"When what?"

"When," she said, "you are pregnant."

Well, he would be damned. He would be teetotally damned. He

310

would be teetotally and fundamentally God-damned, and it was wonderful. It was teetotally and fundamentally God-damned wonderful, and he felt like he had shipped a pint-and-a-half of red-eye.

"Well, I'll be damned," he said, and felt wonderful.

"It's true," she affirmed.

She was wonderful. He looked at her, and she was teetotally and God-damned wonderful.

"Sister!" he said, "sister, let's go out and eat a steak. I feel like eating a two-pound, two-inch-thick Kansas City steak. I got to keep my strength up, if we're going to be pregnant. Let's go to—"

"—to eat a hamburger," she said.

"I said a steak."

"A steak costs nearly as much as a license," she said. "You've got to start saving for the license."

"Look here," he said.

"I know," she anticipated sweetly, "you're married. I seem to recall you told me all about it. She was a beautiful blond social-climbing Polack."

"You're damned right, I'm married. And I've been in the jug for several different reasons, but I'm just too advanced in years to learn to go to jail for bigamy."

"You can get a divorce," she said. "It would take more than five days, and we would just have a long engagement, but you could get one."

"I could get a divorce," he agreed, not looking at her, feeling guilty even though he knew he wasn't guilty, feeling like a son-of-a-bitch, even though he knew there wasn't anything else he could do, "but—" even though he wasn't looking at her, he knew how her face would be, how her eyes would be staring at him, "I can't get married."

"You can't?"

He didn't look at her. Her voice was very quiet.

"I won't," he said. Then, having said that, he could look at her.

He would have to hand it to her. Her face didn't show a thing. She sat there, with the newspaper in her lap, sitting up straight from the hips, and her face was smooth. It was smooth and faraway.

"You mean—" she began quietly, and stopped.

That was what he meant. He meant he couldn't get married. He couldn't and be Sweetie Sweetwater, who had been born in the brick house with the chastely designed, peeling portico on the banks of the stained river in Virginia, and who had come a long way from there, and had married the beautiful blond Polack girl, and had tapped the mulatto prostitute in Galveston, and had been

311

in jail, and had earned everything he believed in, and had learned in a very hard and expensive way to believe in the few things he believed in. He did not believe that people should get married. He believed that marriage was a kind of prostitution which was worse than the other kind. It was worse because in the other kind of prostitution a body was sold for something, and he believed that marriage was a system by which love was sold for something. And he believed in love.

He could honestly tell Sue Murdock that he loved her.

But he honestly believed that if he and Sue Murdock got married he would be making a concession to something to which he could no longer afford to make any concession. And he believed that she would be making a concession to something from which she had scarcely and precariously escaped.

"How long have you been pregnant?" he demanded.

"About six weeks," she stated, detachedly.

Then, as he paused, trying to suppress the unworthy speculation which came into his mind, she added: "Oh, that's not it. You needn't count back to see whether that was the time I began to read your books and stuff, and go to work on the relief committee. That wasn't why I went down to the picket line. That wasn't why I did anything I did."

She had seen right into him, and he felt the blush mounting hot to his cheeks. Love was a terrible thing sometimes. It made somebody see right into somebody else, sometimes. It gave them the drop. He had had the drop on her, he reckoned. Or had thought he had, seeing right into her all these months, thinking he knew what she needed. And now she had the drop on him. "I guess I did have that in mind," he admitted.

"Well, you needn't," she said, bitterly, and he reckoned she had the right to bitterness. "I didn't do anything I did just to make you marry me. I wasn't trying to butter you. I did what I did because I wanted to."

"I'm sorry," he said, but he did not frame in his own mind exactly what he was sorry for. He was sorry he had been mean and low, and had betrayed her in his mind by counting back. He was sorry she was pregnant, and was ashamed he was sorry, because he wanted to be happy because she was going to have a child, the way he had been happy when she told him. He was sorry he could not marry her.

But he could not. Not and be Sweetie Sweetwater, who had earned what little he believed in. Perhaps somebody stronger could behave differently, and be all right. But he couldn't, and he knew it. He knew he had built some kind of a wall, and if he pulled out even one brick, or one stone, it would all come tumbling down. Perhaps his wall wasn't built right. Perhaps you ought to build what you believed in so you could take out a lot of bricks or stones and it would still stand up. But he had built the only way he knew. Perhaps she could make a concession and take out a brick and it wouldn't hurt. He wouldn't say, ever again, what she ought to do. He was through with that. But he knew what he could do. And knew what he could not do.

And he knew that he loved Sue Murdock, and that he believed in love.

They did not go out for the two-pound, two-inch-thick Kansas City steak, which he did not want now.

Instead, he pushed the electric switch, and sat on the floor in the dark which was mitigated only by the little light which filtered up from the city below, and tried to tell her what he knew.

In that way was initiated the period of contest between them. Sometimes, for days, it would be a wordless contest. They would be as they had been before, except for the fact that because of the pressure of his work he had less and less time with her. And, as before, she continued her activities. They were as they had been before, saying the same things and going through the ordinary movements of their life, but with a new, pervasive caution, as of ambush. They were like frontiersmen, who, in a new country, move about in the innocent routine of camp or cabin, apparently intent on those tasks but with a constant though unspoken awareness of the woods or thicket beyond the field.

It was like the moment—though the moment indefinitely and painfully prolonged in equilibrium—when two wrestlers first lay hand to each other, and stand, motionless, while the muscles tense up, while each tries to appraise the strength and speed he has not yet felt or observed, while each tries to sense the heart and cunning and patience of the other.

It was, however, the period of their greatest tenderness for each other. It was as though the fact of her pregnancy could bring them, unperturbed and undistracted by other considerations, closer together than ever before and could give them moments of a charmed poise and happiness, like petals floating on a black water. They could shut the mind to history and future, as to the most trivial irrelevancies, and thereby maintain and define the moment. Each practiced new gentleness with the other, as though to compensate for the cold private reservation made in the commitment to the terms of the struggle. Their behavior had something of the courtesy existing between two opposed champions whose bitter rivalry must work itself out according to a chivalric code and is defined only in the ironical ambivalence of hatred and mutual admiration.

Sweetie Sweetwater knew that he would win. He knew that he would win because he knew that his very being depended upon refusal to compromise. He had decided long ago what points he could never compromise. And, knowing that he would win, he felt a great pity for her, and an admiration for her gallantry in the face of the overwhelming odds against her. She had stuff, all right, and she was going to keep it clean. But feeling that made him feel cheap, and made his own tenderness and pity cheap. He could afford those things. He could afford them, because he knew he would win. He felt like a cheat, even though he hadn't cheated. He had told her how it was. He felt like a man who has the wild deuce in the hole, and the other fellow keeps raising and smiles. You got to play the cards God gave you, but, Jesus, why doesn't the other fellow just call and shut up. You feel sorry for the other fellow, but you got to play the cards. But he had told Sue Murdock what his cards were. He had told her he had that wild deuce.

So sometimes he would lie beside her after she had gone to sleep, and watch her, and sometimes he would be filled with such a sweetness that his eyes swam with tears. He reckoned he could tell anybody what happiness was, if anybody happened to ask him now. He reckoned he knew what it was like, if this was a fair sample. He reckoned there was more where the sample came from, but he knew ne hadn't earned it. *We are sending you this sample absolutely free, and at no cost to yourself.* It certainly hadn't cost him anything. No sir, it had just come in the morning mail. *If you like this sample, just fill out your name and address on the dotted line and we will send you our product.* He would sure-God like some more of that product. *If our product is not according to the sample, or if for any reason whatsoever it does not please you, just return to us and the purchase price will be refunded.* He would sure-God be able to use a hunk of happiness on approval. He sure-God could. But you sure-God couldn't believe what you read in the paper. If that happiness just didn't happen to fit your needs there sure-God wouldn't be any refund of that purchase price. And the purchase price was just a chunk out of your soul. You paid that out and there sure-God wasn't going to be any refund. No matter what they said in the papers and no matter if brilliant young society hostesses served it to their guests and full-page advertisements carried their signed portraits in four-color process. God Almighty himself couldn't refund that purchase price.

He would get up, quietly so as not to wake her, and put on his shoes and go out into the street, where it wasn't so cold now, for it was getting on to spring. He would go to his rooming house, and climb the stairs, and undress and get into his bed and lie on his back, looking up at the ceiling, on which the street lamp below made shadows. He didn't lie there and think very long about happiness. *Happiness* was a word that he just didn't happen to have in his vocabulary. It was an idea that he just didn't happen to have given much attention to. He would go to sleep pretty quick. That was one thing, he always had been able to go to sleep pretty quick. He had always been able to sleep, even in jail, if the God-damned wild life didn't chew on you too much. It was sure an asset to be able to sleep when you were laying up in jail.

One night as he walked home, he saw Slim Sarrett on the other side of the street. It was drizzling and misty, the kind of night you got when winter broke, but he was sure it was Slim Sarrett, all right. He was walking in the same direction, so he just walked faster so he could pass and get a look to be sure, but when he caught up it was a dark block and he couldn't make out the face, but he was sure. Nobody else in the world wore his raincoat hanging over his shoulders loose, like he was a cross between Lord Byron and a Russian duke and a matinee idol playing Hamlet and a bullfighter.

"I saw Sarrett on the street last night," he said to Sue the next evening, when he came by.

"Yes," she replied noncommittally.

"He was out prowling trying to find him a beautiful old panhandler what had passed out from drinking sterno, no doubt," he added, and then was ashamed to look at her face for he knew it was a nasty thing to say to her. It wasn't her fault that bastard was the kind of bastard he was. But that bastard just burned him up and he couldn't help it.

But when she spoke, her voice was absolutely casual. She said: "I saw him the other day."

"You did?" he demanded, and tried to make his own voice normal, but he knew he hadn't been exactly successful.

"Yes," she said. "I met him on the street when I was coming home from the relief office. It was in the next block. He talked to me."

"Look here," he burst out, "you just tell that pansy to leave you alone. That pansy bothers you again, and I'll break his back. You

315

tell that pansy I'll spill his God-damned chlorophyll all over the county. If he bothers you again, I'll—"

"He didn't bother me," she said. "He just talked to me—"

"Just let him talk to you one more time, and I'll—"

"I've got to talk to somebody!" she cried out. Then, watching his face: "Oh, not about us. Don't be afraid! But I've got to talk to somebody. I don't talk to anybody. I don't see anybody. I don't see you ten minutes a day. You never—"

"I'm sorry," he said, and his lips felt stiff like he was having a mud facial, and the barber had gone off and forgot him. "I'm sorry. I—" He didn't know what he had meant to say. He was looking at her body, thinking how long had it been, wondering could you tell it yet.

"Look!" she said. "Look!" And she seemed to thrust her belly unnaturally out toward him, as she stood there. Look! Sure I'm pregnant. Sure I am. You just try being pregnant some time, and see how you like it. See if it doesn't make you nervous. See if it improves your own beautiful Jesus-Christ-like disposition. Just try it!

"I'm sorry—" he began, lost what he had meant to say, gathered himself. "Sue," he said quietly, "I'm doing the best I can. I have something on my hands I can't let go. I've got to see this thing through. We almost got the sympathy strike ready at Holman's, and I can't let go. I'm doing the best I can, Sue."

"Yes," she said, and she crossed the space between them to kiss him.

It was all right then. He reckoned he'd be nervous too, if he was pregnant.

After supper that night, she said she had received by mail the previous day another poem from Sarrett. "It's dedicated to me," she said, and laughed. "Just like the other one."

She got the poem out of the desk, and handed it to Sweetie.

He studied it.

"Jesus," he said, "and that bastard gets money for 'em."

"He doesn't get exactly rich on them."

"This don't mean a God-damned thing," he said, again studying the paper.

"I think I see what it means," she volunteered. "If you take that last image about the bird as the key to the symbol, and see how that's built to with the other implications of flying—of flight—then you—"

"I don't need me any symbol," he said, "to see what it means. It just means, my little sugarplum, that you've just about reformed

316

the talented young fruiter. It means he's realizing that maybe our forefathers knew best." Then he laughed, and tossed it at her.

She caught it, and laughed, too.

"Congratulations!" he said.

He would lie in the dark beside her, after she had gone to sleep, and be happy. He would be happy, at least when he did not think of anything in the world, but just looked at her, as she lay there with her eyes gravely closed.

Once, as he lay there, he reached over to lay his hand, without disturbing her, on the slight mound, which was relaxed now in sleep and which moved, ever so little, with her respiration.

He seemed to see, as it would be there under his hand, the little hunched-up creature, blind, unbreathing, the tiny hands and feet formed like delicate carving—or would they be really formed yet? How long did it take before the nails appeared, he wondered. He wondered when it got a face, a real face which you could call human. He remembered fetuses in jars, the wizened, little, simianwise faces, intent and, for all their wisdom, contorted in profound puzzlement. He remembered the Indian mummies he had once seen at Salt Lake City, how they were hunched, and the eyelids squinting because there was nothing under them any more, and the intent, contorted faces. Those faces were like the faces of the fetuses, the same look, intent, contorted, the same invincible, painful abstraction. Before and after taking.

It would be hunched up there, under his hand. If you could see it, it would look like the drawings he had seen of the way certain primitive tribes buried their dead. Hunched up like that. He reckoned that was where they got the idea, maybe. On the page where the drawings were, there were always drawings or photographs of stuff they buried in there with him, too. A chunk of Sweetie Sweetwater and of Sue Murdock, and of old Marston Sweetwater, LL.D., Chaplain, C.S.A., and old men with congress gaiters and silverheaded sticks and bad breath and old ladies who peered at you and Vyvian Sweetwater who was buried in 1660 in a little brick church which still stood in the dead field beside the salt estuary in Virginia, and a chunk of Bogan Murdock and Mrs. Murdock, who, they said, was a drunkard, and of that old half-wit bastard Murdock, who was a murderer, and of all the Murdocks before, whose names he had never heard of, and chunks of people who had been dead a thousand years. The little devil sure-God had an assortment of junk and plunder stored in there with him while he hunched up and didn't have to do any breathing and try to make sense of it

317

yet. Maybe he would be able to make sense of it. He had him a time trying to make sense of the chunk which was just Sweetie Sweetwater.

But Sweetie Sweetwater—he remembered—he had had a lot of junk and plunder piled around him when he was hunched up like that. Well, he knew what old Sweetie had done with his junk and plunder. Sweetie had just consigned a God's plenty of artifacts to the ash heap. You couldn't catch Sweetie toting arrowheads in this year of grace and of the tommy-gun. An arrowhead would have sure been useful in the Argonne.

He thought that, lying beside her, propped up on his elbow, with his hand on her body. He was happy, even if he did think it. It was the damnedest thing, but he was happy anyway.

When he walked down the narrow hall, where the cracked, earth-colored plaster was lit by the yellow light from the single bulb, and put his hand on the door, it was like any other evening, except that he was late. He was very late, and he was tired. He knocked on the door, heard a muffled voice, which must have been hers uttering its invitation, and entered.

There was no light in the room.

"Hello," he said, not feeling tired any more, "you sure haven't got any light in here."

"No," her voice replied, flatly, "I haven't."

Then he detected the odor of whisky.

"Fire-water," he said, and reached for the light switch by the door, "I reckon I—"

He saw her lying on the couch, near the table. The bottle of whisky was on the table. It was nearly half empty. There was only one glass visible. That glass was on the floor by the couch.

"You needn't look," she said, "because there isn't any other glass."

"I just thought you might have one sitting out for me," he lied, thinking, *My God, she just sees through you.* And, aware of his false heartiness, he added: "I could use me a—"

"There isn't any other glass," she affirmed distantly, judicially, flatly, with her large eyes fixed directly upon him from the pillow, "nobody helped me. I drank it all myself. I have drunk nearly a pint, all by myself. I, Sue Murdock, who am about to become a mother, have drunk a pint. It is one thing little Sue can do. She can drink a great deal of whisky. She can drink a great deal of gin. Her capacity is truly remarkable. Even if she is out of practice. But it is a natural gift."

She lay on the couch, on her back, her long, straight legs neatly together, the toes pointed like a dancer's, one arm trailing to the floor, the hand relaxed, like something forgotten, near the empty glass, her head propped on a pillow. Her eyes, unnaturally wide, were fixed directly upon him, but her face was smooth and composed.

"Well," he said, feeling his skin prick and tingle drily, testing his voice with the word, hesitating, proceeding, "I could use a drink."

He moved across the floor, his muscles tense as though he were trying out ice or were walking a fence.

He leaned to pick up the glass by her hand. The hand did not move.

He poured about three ounces into the glass; then, as he was lifting it to his lips, she said: "Give it to me. It's my glass."

He passed it to her, not saying anything.

She held it in her hand. "If you want a drink," she stated, "you can get a glass in the kitchen."

When he did not turn to go to the kitchen, but stood watching her, she burst out: "It's my glass, and my whisky! I paid for it! If you want a drink you can get you a glass. But it's my whisky, and I'm drinking it. I paid for it, every drop. With my money. And you needn't stand there and look like that! It's mine and I'm drinking it!"

"Sue—" he said, and heard his voice imploring, and was swept by terror and humility like a man suddenly struck by the enormity of a nameless guilt.

"Sue—" he said.

But she broke in: "Oh, Sue, Sue, Sue! That's all you say! Go on and say it. Go on and tell me I'm drunk. Sure, I'm drunk! And because of you; you go off and leave me up here, and I'm the way I am, and you go away, and what do you expect me to do? What do—"

"Do! I expect you to have some sense. I expect you to have some decency. You're going to have a child and you drink a pint of whisky! You don't owe me a thing, but you owe that child something. You owe it enough at least not to get drunk."

"I don't owe it a God-damned thing," she replied, suddenly quiet, and lifted the glass to her lips.

He leaned forward and tried to snatch the glass from her hands. Jerking from him, she spilled the whisky on herself.

He stepped back and took the bottle from the table and broke it against the edge of the table and flung it down, and found him-

319

self trembling and wordless with the sweat on his forehead, and her eyes burning at him.

"God," she said, "you're wonderful! You're so God-damned wonderful. You're Jesus Christ, you're—"

"Shut up!" he said viciously.

"You're—"

She sat up, rose from the couch, wavered, began to laugh, then straightened herself, standing before him.

"—you're just like my father, you don't like him but you ought to like him because you're just like him, you want to run everybody, you want to run everybody for their own good, and you don't give a damn for anybody, not anybody in the world, just yourself, just yourself!" She began to laugh.

"Listen," he said. "It doesn't matter what I am, but you're not going to lie up here dead drunk. Oh, I know what you told me—how you got drunk and passed out or just about with that Sarrett watching you and not drinking—oh, he never touched a drop—just watching you and waiting, because he liked you that way. Because he liked it that way. But listen here, I'm not Slim Sarrett. I don't live in any dream world. I'm going to—"

She was beating him on the shoulders and chest with her clenched fists. She raked him across the cheek with her nails, like a cat. And he stood there looking at her and not feeling a thing.

"I'll have an abortion," she screamed. "I'll get rid of it!"

"Then it'll be the end," he said, but she was not listening to him. She was striking him, and saying, "Oh, oh, oh, oh!" for the terrible force inside her which was beyond words. In between the *oh's* she uttered a throaty sound which was not quite like a sob, while she struck him. Finally, in his massive and sluggish astonishment, not feeling her blows, he deliberately took her by the wrists. She jerked her hands together, as in the position of prayer, and kicked him systematically on the shins, while she said, "Oh, oh, oh!"

Then the tears came in a burst, and she did not kick him any more.

After she had quieted down and quit crying, he stood in the kitchen. He had not turned on the light. Standing there, he could hear her heavy, measured breathing from the other room, where she was asleep now. He stood there and listened to that sound, in the dark kitchen, and stared out the window over the nighttime city, which he did not see.

Twenty-three

Statement of Ashby Wyndham

WE WAS movin on the river. They was me and Marie and Old Man Lumpkin and Mrs. Lumpkin and Murry what was gittin to be nigh a man and Jasper and Pearl. They was sevin of us countin Pearl. She come to the shanty boat that night with me. It was the Lords will she come for I lak not to got there. Just afore we got there she nigh had to tote me. We got right to it and I sunk down and did not know nuthin. I come to and I seen I was on the boat. I seen Marie standin there, and she ast me how did I feel. I said I felt better than I did last night.

Last night, she said, last night, this ain't tomorrer. This is the day after tomorrer and it is gittin nigh to sun.

I had laid there the enduren time and not knowed.

And we is on the river, she said. We is a long way on the river from Hulltown.

How come, I ast her.

She pointed and I seen where she pointed and there was that lady standin. She said for us to git on, Marie said.

She had ast Marie to git on. She said she aimed to pray God and worship and rejoice if he would stretch out his hand and learn her. But she said she did not reckin she would learn good in Hulltown, and her weak and frail.

I seen her standin there and I lak not to knowed her. She was not wearin that yeller dress lak she had been. She was wearin a old dress belonged to Mrs. Lumpkin. Just a old common dress down to her feet and decent.

Marie said how that night she brung me she set there all night or helped her and Mrs. Lumpkin fix for me. When light come she ast them to git on. She taken Marie by the hand and ast her. And when they got started good she ast Mrs. Lumpkin who was nigh of a size did she have air old dress, and she taken off that yeller dress and put on Mrs. Lumpkins dress and she throwed that yeller dress

321

in the river. She said she would not give it to nobody. Said no decent woman would not want to wear a dress of hern.

I seen her standin there in that old dress and barefoot. She had throwed her pointed shoes in the river.

Her hair was still yeller but it was not all curly lak afore. She looked lak she was oldern I knowed. She was oldern me and Marie.

She done her part. When we stopped at them towns she worked when she could git work to do. If she could not git no work she taken care of the boat and cooked the vittles for us. She had laid soft one time and now she laid hard. She had been in a bed was soft and sweet smellin and now it was a pallit on the hard floor. But she did not never complain and she praised God how He taken her from the house of abominations. She prayed the Lord to take her by the hand and learn her to rejoice. She ast us to pray for her and named how she wallered in sin and grunted lak a hog after the worlds slop and taken no thought. She named it and they was tears come in her eyes.

Marie said how of a night when the women was layin on the side of the curtin where they taken their rest and was sleepin she would wake up for Pearl grabbin holt of her hand. Pearl would grab holt of her hand in the dark.

It looked lak Marie was a sister to her.

When Marie come sick it was Pearl set beside her and fanned them flies and give water for the burnin fever and taken no rest or ease.

Marie was sick eight days and she died.

It was sevin days and Marie said to me, Ashby, I am goin to go.

She was nigh too weak to talk.

No, I said, it cannot be.

Yes, she said, it is, for I am flowin and movin away from here lak water down hill.

No, I said, and I did not know. I had yelled it out till the sound come lak I was yellin to somebody acrost the river.

Don't you fret and grieve Ashby, she said. Don't you take on.

No, I yelled.

Yes, she said, and I do not grieve for me. I grieve because I never brought you no good lak it is for women, Ashby.

Oh, Marie, I said, you give me what was to give. I laid in the dark till you come and they was a sparkle in you give light to my eyes. I seen the sparkle and I put out my hand towards it lak a child baby not knowin what it is. I sinned and I made you take on my sin and it was flesh lust. A man don't love no woman true but in Gods eye but if he loves her in his pore man way may be it can

322

learn him to love the Lord. It is lak a school and the young un goes to school and they learns him to spell and if he studies on it he gits so he can read the Lords blessed word. Oh, Marie, I said to her, you learned me to spell, and I see it clear.

She did not say nuthin, but she looked at me and I seen the sparkle in her. It come of a sudden lak long afore, and her layin sick now.

Marie, I said, I see it clear now and not never afore.

She looked at me and she said, I will give little Frank a big kiss and a hug for his Pappy. She said not air other word.

The next evenin her spirit taken its flight and left me to mourn.

It was Pearl washed her and fanned them flies after she was layin dead. We was not near no town or settlemint. We did not see no houses or nuthin but woods and cane thickits all that next day. I did not want to put her in the ground in no woods or cane thickit lak a varmint. It was August and the river was low with drout. The water did not hardly move. I set and looked at a old black stub of a dead tree and it taken nigh all that mornin to git where it was. Then it taken all evenin to git where I could not see it. We taken two days to git to a settlemint. Pearl set there and fanned them flies and tears come down her cheeks.

At the settlemint we bought them boards to make a coffin for Marie. We paid two dollars and twenty cents and Jasper and me made it. We put her in the ground where they was a church and Christian folks was standin there.

I mourned for Marie. When my Pappy died I did not mourn for him. When my Mammy lay cold and dead, it was not in me to mourn. My heart was lak flint rock in me and cuttin, but it was not mournin. When little Frank died it was not mournin I done. I run mad lak a dog on the mountain. But now I mourned for Marie and for all them I seen taste the bitterness and take their flight. When a man ain't in God he cannot mourn. He cannot truly mourn. I seen them not in God as fell down on the ground and tore their hair, but it is a way of puttin a curse on God. It ain't mournin of a truth. After Marie died I set on the boat and looked at the river and smelled the mud stinkin where the water had done gone down low, and I seen how Marie was goin to lay in the stinkin ground, and I nigh put a curse on God. But it was not mournin. It was a wildness and it tears a man in two pieces. But to mourn in God and of His will is a kind of sweetness. It is gittin closter to them as is dead than ever you was and them livin and drawin breath. It is a gift God give, and I give praise.

They put Marie in the ground and I knowed how it is to mourn.

I mourned for her and for my Pappy and my Mammy and for Frank, and knowed Gods will.

We stayed in the settlemint three weeks and we worked and was amongst Christian folks and we give testifyin for the Lord.

Then we come agin on the river.

We come where they was fields and the corn was standin tall and yeller and ready for folks to come with wagins. I never seen no corn lak it in Custiss. And I seen big fields for pasture, and horses and cows standin. I seen them houses. They was big and white with paint on them and I seen folks settin in front or standin. It was lak a country I never heard tell.

Then we come nigh the city. They was smoke on the sky. Murry seen the smoke was fer off, and Pearl said it was the city.

We come in the city under them bridges and seen all the folks walkin and ridin. We come in to the bank and Murry jumped off and taken the rope. They was folks everwhere. More than a man could name. They was thick lak the corn we seen.

They is folks here as walks in sin, I said, and folks as walks in God. It is a field to the harvest. We are here and we are goin to testify to the saved and to the unsaved.

Old Man Lumpkin said amen.

We stood in the street and we testified. Folks was comin and goin. They was them as scoffed and scorned and them as hearkened. We went in the city where the folks was thickest and we stood on the street and sang a song and rejoiced. Pearl sang good and Murry, and me and Mr. Lumpkin we taken the bass burden. We sang about Mary and her only son.

> Mary had a only son
> The Jews and the Romans had him hung
> Keep yore hand on the plow hold on.

> They taken him to Cavalree
> And there they hung him on a tree
> Keep yore hand on the plow hold on.

We sung how they done it and how he died to save. We told how he had done saved our souls and it was peace in our heart.

A police man come and said how we could not sing and testify. I told him how the Lord said His blessed word was for ever man. I showed him the place in the book. He said he could not help what it said, for us to git on.

We went to another place where they was folks movin and

324

standin. We sung and testified. It was another police man come and said to git on.

We taken another stand and it was the same. Everwhere it was the same. I tried to tell them how it was and showed it to them in the book but they said for us to git on. I was sore in my heart.

A saved man has got joy and rejoicin in his heart and he is bustin to tell. He has got Gods word in him and he has got peace and he has got to pour it out to them as has ears. It is a joy to pour it out and the joy is withouten end. But you don't let him tell and pour it out of his heart and his heart is sore. He is lak a woman got a baby and her breast has got milk for that air baby and it is a joy when it takes its suck and is helt to the tit. But you take that woman away from that air baby and her breast is swole and sore for the fullness. My heart was sore.

I told them was with me how it was.

Pearl said for us to git to the boat and git on it and leave.

I said why.

She said she was afeard of them police.

Jasper said he knowed them. He said they could not do nuthin but put you in jail. He said they would not beat no woman.

Pearl said she was not afeard of bein beat.

I am afeard of bein beat, Jasper said. They shore beat me one time when they taken me. I am afeard of bein beat but I will do what Ashby says. I aim to do Gods will.

I ain't afeard of bein beat, Pearl said. But they put you in jail and you lay there and they ain't nuthin for you. You are alone. And they let you out and they ain't nuthin for you or nobody. It does you harm.

They is God for you, I said.

Oh God, she said, I am a pore woman and I am afeard to be alone. I need what help they is. I need them with me as has God in their heart to lift me up. Oh God, she said, I am weak and frail.

I did not say nuthin. We went on down to the boat. I did not know nuthin to say. I was waitin for it to come on me what to say.

We et and I read to them out of the book what is a ever present help. We prayed to God.

What we goin to do, Pearl ast.

I don't rightly know, I said. It will come on me, I said.

We taken our rest for it was dark.

I nigh never slept that enduren night. I laid and called to God.

When light come I rose up and taken the book. I opened it and looked and lo, I seen. It said, and Jesus said unto him no man havin put his hand to the plow and lookin back, is fittin for the Kingdom of God.

I knowed it for a sign and come of God.

What we going to do, Pearl ast me.

I read her what it said.

Oh God, she said.

I laid in jail, Jasper said, when I was a sinful man, and taken it. I reckon I can take it now I aim to walk in God.

Oh God, Pearl said, I am weak and frail.

The Lord will keep holt on you with His hand, I said.

We went in the city lak afore. We sung and we give testifyin. Ever time a police man come and said for us to git on. But it was all. They did not take nobody to jail. And ever time we come to another place and taken our stand.

It was after dinner time. Mrs. Lumpkin come sick. She set on the pavemint and puked. After a spell she said she did not feel so bad. But I said for Old Man Lumpkin and Pearl to git her to the boat. And they done it. Me and Jasper and Murry, we stayed and give testifyin some more. Then we come to the boat.

Mrs. Lumpkin was some better but porely.

She was porely the next mornin. I said for Pearl to stay with her while me and Jasper and Old Man Lumpkin went in the city. We come to a big markit where folks brung vegitibles and chickins and such to sell and folks in the city comes and buys it. We stood where they come in and went out and I read to them out of the book.

A police man come and said, for Christ sake you all git on somewheres else so I won't have to run you in.

I said to him how we done come in Gods name.

Well for Christ sake, he said, you go somewheres else in Gods name and quit worryin folks.

I read to him what the book said.

Save it for Sunday, he said, and git on.

We went round to another door where folks was.

Old Man Lumpkin said how he was worrit how Mrs. Lumpkin was makin out. I said I would go down to the boat and see how she was makin out. He was a old man and it was hard for him to climb back up the hill. I said I would git a doctor if she was not makin out so good and come tell him. I told him and Jasper to wait and not do no readin or testifyin or nuthin. I did not want them to git in no trouble and me not there.

I come to the boat and Mrs. Lumpkin was still porely. I said I was aimin to git a doctor and she said naw, for the money. I said the money was not nuthin and her layin there and not makin out no better. She said naw, and I was argyin with her and of a sudden Pearl yelled somethin. Pearl was out front of the house part. She yelled agin, and I come out.

It is Murry, she yelled.

I seen Murry runnin down the hill. Then I seen a man behind him. It was a police man. The police man was yellin for him to stop but he never paid him no mind. They was another police man back up the hill was comin too. The first police man had a pistol in his hand I seen. I yelled for Murry to stop but he never.

The police man shot off his pistil but I seen he did not mean to shoot Murry.

Murry run up the board we had laid to the boat. He yelled they done taken Jasper and Old Man Lumpkin. He kicked that board in the water and he tried right quick to cut that rope as helt the boat. He taken out his knife to cut it. They says how Murry taken out his knife to cut the police man but he never. He is a good boy and has got true peace in his heart. He did not mean nuthin when he broke loose from the police man up to the markit and tripped him up and run. He was afeard lak a young un, and taken no thought.

The first police man got there and he grabbed that big board out of the water. He was tryin to lay it to the boat. Murry tried to kick it loose but he slipped and fell.

The other police man got there and he was yellin.

Then Pearl yelled right behind me. I looked round and seen her. She had that there old squirril rifle of Jasper in her hand.

It looked lak I could not say nuthin. It all come of a sudden.

Them police men throwed the board on and was yellin. One of them put his foot on the board.

Oh God, Pearl said out loud.

Pearl, I yelled, Pearl. And I aimed to grab holt of that rifle.

She shot off that old squirril rifle.

I seen that police man put his hands on his stummick afore he fell in the water.

Murry had got up and was cuttin on the big rope. He cut it.

I felt the river take holt of the boat. It was not much for the water was low with the drout but we had done slipped out good from the bank. The police man was gittin the other one out of the water.

I seen Pearl standin there. She still had holt of that rifle lak she never knowed she helt it. She was watchin that police man and them folks what come runnin.

Pearl, I said.

She turned right slow, and looked at me.

I said, Pearl, give me that rifle.

Then she looked down at it. Then she said, oh God.

Give it to me, Pearl, I said.

All of a sudden she throwed it in the river.

Pearl, I said then and knowed what she was goin to do. It was lak somebody told me. I made to ketch her by the barest. She nigh lak to got in the river. But I had my holt good.

We laid there where we fell. She was tryin and strivin to git loose but I helt my holt. She was beatin on me with her hands to git loose. Then she started to cry and she said God damn me. She said God damn you Ashby Windham, God damn you to hell you Ashby Wyndham you son of a bitch. She said them things and more what she never meant or knowed. She scratched my face with her fingernails till the blood come out. She bit me on my arm to make me let go my holt, but I never.

I yelled for Murry to help me and he done it. We got holt of her good and helt her hands. Then I said to Murry I could keep holt of her and for him to git the oars and put the boat to the bank. Then he taken the oars lak I said an was tryin when I heard that motor boat comin. It was them police men as taken us.

They come to us and got on and I said I was tryin to put the boat to the bank and wait for them lak it was Gods will.

I bet, one of them said, but it was the truth I spoke.

They taken us to the jail.

I am in the jail now and I lay here. I lay here and I pray to God to show me His face. Oh God make me to rejoice agin and in my salvation. I ast to know and it is my weakness. Pearl laid holt on salvation and come out from the house of abominations. She put off her sin and she was rejoicin. Her heart was full of joy and all she aimed to do was testify to folks and name her joy and salvation. But if salvation had not taken holt on her she would be in Hulltown and smilin yit. She would not be layin and holdin her eyes squinched up and not sayin nuthin nor not takin bite or sup. Oh God she laid off one sin for salvation and salvation taken her to another sin. She kilt a man and it is a bigger sin.

Oh Lord yore salvation it moves lak the wind. It blows the pore mans heart lak a dead leaf. It is lak the wind and no man ain't seen it come or go. Oh Lord yore foot has been set in the dark place and it is not seen. Oh Lord yore will has run lak the fox and sly. The pore mans mind sniffs after it lak a hound dog. But the scent is done lost and the ways of its goin.

Oh Lord have mercy on Pearl where she lays.
Have mercy on me and not turn yore face away.
I have writ down the truth lak it was.
I am rispectfully

Ashby Porsum Wyndham

Private Porsum, sitting in his chair in his own house, lowered the sheets of typescript, and sank back a little into his chair. He had sat very erect during his reading, holding the sheets firmly between his large, freckled, square-nailed hands, moving his head slightly from side to side as though to follow each line he was reading, working his lips ever so little as though to form the words he saw there on the sheet.

Now he looked at the small, dry, acid-faced man, fortyish and almost shabby, who sat in a straight chair opposite him, and asked: "Where did you get it?"

The dry, acid-faced man removed a toothpick from his lips, inspected the toothpick as though to determine whether or not it had achieved its purpose, exposed his bad teeth, and said: "I got it where it says. It comes from the jail, just like it says. It is a true and sworn copy of a statement written by Ashby Porsum Wyndham."

He gave the word *Porsum* a lingering emphasis.

"What are you bringing it here for, Mr.—" Private Porsum asked, and hesitated.

"Tucker," the man said, "Tucker. The name is Tucker, but it doesn't mean anything to you. Unless, of course, you read *The Standard*. Which I don't imagine is your favorite paper."

"What are you bringing it here for, Mr. Tucker?" Private Porsum asked.

"Mr. Porsum, I am a reporter and you are news. You are a hero. I wrote the first story on you when you got back to this State in 1919. *Mountains and the Man,* I called it. It was reprinted all over the country. It was better than anything they wrote up in New York when you came."

"Yes," Private Porsum said, "I remember."

"Well, you are still news. You are a rich man. You are a success story. Boy from Mountains Makes Good. You are a bank president. You are a power behind politics. You throw your weight around. You get on the front page. You got on the front page with the Massey Mountain strikes. *Son of Hills Heals Strife.* Yeah, that was the headline in Murdock's stooge sheet. You are on the front page now for backing the Murdock Park Bill. But not in Murdock's stooge sheet. You have been on the front page of *The Standard* for a month and I know you don't like it. So *The Standard* isn't asking you to do it a favor. It isn't asking any of Murdock's boys to do it a favor."

"I am not one of Murdock's boys, Mr. Tucker, and I'll appreciate—"

"It don't matter to me what you call it, Mr. Porsum. You are a pal of Murdock. You are a pal of Governor Milam. And *The Standard,* as you may have heard, is not. So I'm not asking you to do us a favor."

"Well, what do you want, Mr. Tucker?"

"I just want to do *you* a favor, Mr. Porsum. I am just giving you an opportunity to make any statement you care to before we run the pertinent passages from this poor Christ-bitten bastard's story. I reckon you can figure out some of the passages *The Standard* will consider pertinent."

"You can say—" Private Porsum stopped, and shifted his weight in the easy chair.

"Yeah?" the reporter queried. He got out a pad and pencil.

"You can say I am always sorry to hear of anybody from Custiss County having trouble. You can say I was born in Custiss County and I have always had the welfare and the well-being of my many friends in the mountains close to my mind and to my heart."

"Sure," the reporter said softly, busy writing. "Sure."

"What did you say?" Private Porsum demanded.

"I just said 'sure,' " the reporter said, "but it don't mean a God-damned thing."

"It is the truth, Mr. Tucker," Private Porsum affirmed with a hint of violence.

"I just said 'sure,' " the reporter said. "I ain't God Almighty and I ain't a mind reader and I ain't your conscience. I am just a reporter and I'll put down what you tell me."

"Well, you put down what I said, then. And put down that I will keep right on trying to do what I can to help my people and the people of this State and try to do what is right." He stopped.

The reporter looked up from his pad. "Is that all, Mr. Porsum?" he demanded.

Private Porsum, shifting his weight, slowly closing and unclosing one of his heavy, freckled hands, staring at the reporter, said, "Yes, that's all."

"Well, Mr. Porsum," the reporter said, "it will sure leave our readers wondering whether or not that poor bastard is really your cousin. Like he claims."

"How do I know!" Private Porsum burst out. "My God, how do I know?"

"Do you want me to put that down?" the reporter asked.

Private Porsum stared at him, then said: "No. Don't put it down."

The reporter waited with his pencil poised.

"Put down I have a lot of kin in Custiss County. There are a lot of Porsums, and I am proud to be one of them. I have been away so much since the War I don't know all of them, but I feel for my kin. As for this Mr. Wyndham, it may very well be he is my cousin. If he is—"

The pencil moved, then stopped, waiting.

"If he is—" Private Porsum repeated. His gaze met the brown uncommitting pupils of the muddy, flecked eyes which were now lifted to him.

"Let me see that," Private Porsum commanded, and reached out his hand for the pad.

The reporter passed it to him.

He read it slowly, his mouth silently forming the words, as before. Then, very deliberately, he tore the pages from the pad, dropped the pad, and tore the detached pages of notes into several bits.

"For Christ sake," Mr. Tucker said.

Private Porsum stood up. The bits of the paper scattered to the floor. He stepped across the room to his desk and pressed a button concealed under the ledge. Then he said, "I'm going to the jail."

"I'll ride you in," the reporter said, "and I'll bring you back."

"I'll take my own car," Private Porsum said.

A Negro man came to the door. "Get my car," Private Porsum ordered.

"Can I see you at the jail?" the reporter asked, and picked up his hat.

Private Porsum nodded.

The two men walked out into the hall, and out to the porch. Waiting there for the other car, the reporter looked appraisingly over the lawn and to the left where the white paddocks were. "You've got a nice place here, Mr. Porsum," he said.

"Yes," Private Porsum said.

He lay on his back, on the cot. He wore overalls and a gray shirt. He was so long that the soles of his bare feet projected slightly over the end of the cot. His brogans were placed neatly side by side on the floor near the cot. His arms were folded on his chest, which stirred regularly with his breathing. His eyes were closed. The rather thin lips of his wide mouth were slightly parted in respiration. He did not move, or open his eyes, when the key turned in the lock.

"Sleeping," the man in the uniform said, nodding, "he sleeps a lot. He sleeps ever afternoon. But," he said, with the air of one trying to be fair, "he don't sleep none in the morning. He reads his Bible in the mornings. Ever morning, durned if he don't. And night, durned if he ain't on his knees talking to his Jesus half the night. I bet he's got callouses on his durn knees."

Private Porsum did not answer. He was looking at the man on the cot.

"Well," the man in the uniform said, hitching his shoulders in dismissal, "them as is sleeping don't know nothing."

"No," Private Porsum said, still looking at the man, "I reckon they don't."

"Call me, Mr. Porsum, when you want me," the man said, grinning inward through the bars. "I don't reckon you want to be spending the night in this here hotel."

Private Porsum waited until the steps of the man had died away down the corridor. Then, almost guiltily, with an excess of caution, he approached the cot. He leaned slightly over the man there, but did not touch or speak to him. He peered, almost fearfully, down at the face, the thinning lips now relaxed, the nose jutting upward, almost sharp, the square brow, the matted dark hair. The skin seemed to be drawn tight over the strong bones of the facial structure. Sleep only clouded the intensity of the face as breath clouds a mirror, or steel. He peered dubiously down at the sleeping face, as one peers down at a bright object submerged in water, trying to make out the true character of the object through the distorting medium.

The man on the cot opened his eyes. He looked up at Private Porsum, without surprise, without speaking, or moving.

"Mr. Wyndham," Private Porsum said.

The man on the cot did not answer, but continued to regard, detachedly, the face above him. Then, not moving, he said: "You are the Private, ain't you?"

"Yes," Private Porsum said.

"I am sorry I was layin here sleepin," Ashby Wyndham said, coming to a sitting position," and you come."

"It's all right," Private Porsum said.

"It looks lak I sleep ever evenin afore supper," Ashby Wyndham said. "It looks lak I am tuckered out of a evenin."

"The—" Private Porsum hesitated, fumbling for the word, "the man—he said you prayed at night."

"Pray," Ashby Wyndham repeated. He had picked up one of his brogans and had started to put it on, but now he sat with it in his hands, his bare feet on the floor, turning the shoe over and over in his hands. "Pray," he repeated, but not in echo now, and he cast his eyes suddenly about the cell. "Pray—" he began again, and stopped. He looked down at the brogan, which he turned in his hands.

"The man said you prayed," Private Porsum said.

"Pray!" Ashby Wyndham burst out, gripping the shoe. "I—I can't pray. Lord God, I have tried to pray and call on His holy name. Ever night. Ever night, and on my knees bowed down to God. Oh, God," he said wildly, stopped, looked up at Private Porsum, shook his head. "But He has done turned away His face," he added.

"I read the statement you wrote," Private Porsum said, after a moment, while the man's eyes were upon him.

"There was them as laid in jail," Ashby Wyndham said, "and could pray to God. Paul laid in jail. And Silas laid there and the Lord never turned away His face. He has broke bolts and locks and men has walked out rejoicin in His name. But I don't ask it. I don't ask nuthin. I don't want nuthin and it mortal. I would lay till Judgmint and it His will. Only—" he said, searching Private Porsum's face, "He give me word. Only," and he shook his head, "He unstoppered my heart for what lays swole in it. Only He unbunged it."

"I read what you wrote," Private Porsum said.

"It did not do no good," Ashby Wyndham said, "writin it. I wrote it down and Gospel true, but I can't pray no more."

"You wrote that you are my cousin."

"My mammy was a Porsum," Ashby Wyndham said. "She is dead and in Jesus' arms. But she was a Porsum. She was Mattie May Porsum. Her pappy was Ef Porsum as was brother to Jed Porsum. Jed Porsum walked in God, folks said."

"Jed Porsum was my father," Private Porsum said.

"I never knowed her folks," Ashby Wyndham said, "but her Pappy, and me a young un." He inspected Private Porsum's face, then said: "You got a favor to Ef."

"Listen—" Private Porsum began, but Ashby Wyndham interrupted.

"I am plum sorry," he said, "but I never ast you to set. And you comin here." He rose, his bare toes curling from the concrete floor, and motioned to the hickory chair by the opposite wall.

333

"Listen," Private Porsum said, not noticing the gesture, "I'm going to get you out of here. I know people who will get you out. You didn't do anything, you don't belong in here, you—"

"I belong where it is the Lord's will to put me," Ashby Wyndham said.

"You don't belong here. You haven't done anything—"

"I done things," Ashby Wyndham said, "and it is my shame and ruination."

"Don't be a fool," Private Porsum burst out.

"Let the tree lay where the wind has done blowed it down," Ashby Wyndham said. He sat again on the cot, seeming to withdraw.

"You haven't done a God-damned thing," Private Porsum said angrily, "and you sit here."

"Jacob—" Ashby Wyndham began, "him my brother and what I done."

"You've made it up. God knows you've made it up!"

Ashby Wyndham shook his head, then put his right hand to his forehead, shaking his head, and wiped his hand slowly downward across his face. "No," he uttered, "a man don't make up nuthin. He has done what he has done and it is on me now."

"You've made it up," Private Porsum insisted angrily, "and I'm going to get you out. Do you hear? You being here, it's not right, I—"

The man sitting on the cot slowly shook his head. "Man's rightness ain't nuthin to me. It is trash and a deceivin," he said. "I am here of a God rightness, and here I lay."

"I'm going to get you out. I'm going to take you out to my place. I've got a place and I'll take you out there and fix you up."

"It is toys and garnishments of the world," Ashby Wyndham said, "and it ain't for me."

"You won't come?"

"No," Ashby Wyndham said, distantly, "it ain't for me."

"Because I came to Massey Mountain that time, because I made the men go back to work—is that why?" Private Porsum leaned forward over the cot. "Because you think I was one of them threw you out, is that why? I swear to God I—"

"What happened to me ain't nuthin," Ashby Wyndham said.

"Because you think I was one of them cut the men's pay, because you think I starved them, because you think I robbed them? I tell you that was all the Company could pay. Every cent! They couldn't afford to pay more, I tell you—" His voice mounted, and the brown flesh of his face darkened with the rush of blood, as he

334

leaned. "I'll tell you, I—" He stopped, looking down at the man, and seemed to grope for a word.

Under the eyes that stared inimically down at him from the weathered, contorted, darkening face, Ashby Wyndham let his body sink gradually back until he lay on the cot. Then he drew his legs up and straightened them. He performed the action soberly, carefully, preciously, as a convalescent, alone again, gets back into bed after his first morning up to receive visitors. When he had composed himself, his big hands lying again on his chest, he said: "It ain't in me to judge."

"I tell you I tried to do what was right," Private Porsum said. "I saw the books—the figures—and I tried to do what was right."

"I judge no human man, and it is mercy I crave," Ashby Wyndham said. And added: "I believe you aimed to do what was right."

"All right," Private Porsum announced with decision, victoriously, straightening himself up. "All right, now I'll go get you out. I'll take you out to my place. You are my cousin, but I would do it for any man lying here for no just cause. If you weren't my cousin. But you are my cousin, you—"

But Ashby Wyndham shook his head. "No," he said.

"No!" Private Porsum exclaimed. "But you said—"

"It is the world," Ashby Wyndham said. "I put out my hand and laid holt on the world one time, but it ain't nuthin. Lord put pore man in this world and give it him and said, it is yoren, take it and eat and know yore emptiness. I knowed it. And I know it now."

"You fool," Private Porsum uttered in a low, measured, grating voice, while, slowly, his gaze sharpened to a murderous intensity. Then, suddenly, in fury: "You poor God-damned fool!" And he leaned quickly, and seized the man's shoulder and shook him, saying: "God damn you, God damn you, get up from there. Do you hear, you are going!"

Ashby Wyndham shut his eyes. The cot shook with the violence of the hand which grasped his shoulder. "No," he said, in patience, as to a disorderly child.

Private Porsum released his grip, and straightened up. He was a tall man, and big-boned, now running to flesh. He wore a dark suit, a dark tie, and a white shirt, which looked whiter against the seamed, cedary flesh of his face. He still carried himself erect. His bulk dominated the constricted cell.

"You fool," he said, as though in meditation, and breathed heavily.

He turned toward the door.

Ashby Wyndham was watching him now, but not moving.

"Mr. Porsum," he said.

Private Porsum turned and dully regarded him. The intensity had guttered out of his eyes.

"Mr. Porsum," Ashby Wyndham said, "I didn't aim to go and make you mad."

Private Porsum, in his animal-like, suspicious, smoldering heaviness, regarded him, like a bull aware at last of the meaning of the staff fixed to the nose ring.

"Mr. Porsum," Ashby Wyndham said, "I want you to do me a favor."

"What?"

"Mr. Porsum, when I was not much more than a sprout and the War was fit, and I knowed you done good, and kilt all them Germins but not in no blood-hate—" he sat up on the edge of the cot, "—and was not afeard of none of them, and I knowed you was named Porsum and my cousin and you was a big man and would not let them name you a captain or nuthin—I used to want to shake you by the hand, Mr. Porsum. It is a favor, Mr. Porsum, but I would be a proud man to shake you by the hand."

He drew his feet a little back under the edge of the cot as though to rise, but waited, watching the other man for a sign.

"Damn you to hell," Private Porsum said, not viciously but heavily, and turned, and struck on the steel bars with his fist, and called for the jailer in a loud voice.

The bodies of the platoon which Captain Miles sent down the left side of the little valley lay strung along where from the head of the valley you could see them. There was one man not dead. You could see him trying to roll over even if it was a good way off. I watched him trying to roll over.

They got the first machine gun all right. They got it with grenades. But they never got the second. Captain Miles ought never sent that platoon to try to get across the valley and flank it. Any fool would had better sense.

You could lay there and hear a lot of shooting way off.

The sun was bright in the valley. On the left side there was a patch of woods where the machine gun was laying. It was a separate patch from the big woods where the first gun was. There was no telling how many men there was laying in that little patch of woods. They would stay there till we killed them or took them. We knew they were told to do that and they would do like they were told. Our boys were going forward and those Germans in that

336

patch of woods was told to hold them as long as they could. They would do it.

It was not a big valley. It was just a little cove where the land broke. We were laying at the head where we had some cover. On the right-hand side there was not any cover to speak of. There was part of an old stone wall and there was a few rocks and at the end of the point there was three or four trees. I reckoned they was chestnuts. There was some brush near them.

I could see Captain Miles' face. He was working his jaw a little, rubbing his bottom lip across his teeth, like he did when he got in a tight. I knew what he was going to do. He was working himself up. He was going to send some more men to try and get across from the big patch of woods to the little patch. Any fool would had better sense.

I crawled where Lieutenant Griscom was laying. He was white in the face. He always got white in the face but he did what they told him to do. I reckon he thought Captain Miles would send him with that next platoon. He was white in the face, but he would go.

That machine gun started to shoot and I laid down flat as I could. They could not hit us where we laid, but the bullets come cutting through the brush about high as a man's chest. Then it stopped shooting. Maybe they saw me moving. It was a good piece, but maybe they had spyglasses and saw me moving.

Lieutenant Griscom, I said.

Private Porsum, he said to me. He was white in the face.

Ain't any man can get across there, I said.

Shut up, he said, but he never looked at me. He was looking over to that little patch of woods. He was thinking how maybe the Captain would pick him to take the next bunch over there.

Look over yonder, I said to Lieutenant Griscom. I pointed where there was the chestnuts at the point on the right-hand side.

What, he said.

If a man was there, I said, maybe he could get a shot in.

A man couldn't get there, he said, for it is lower than the gun, and a man couldn't get good and started from here.

There is a little cover, I said.

If a man got there he could not do any good, it is so long across to the gun, he said.

It is not more than seventy yards, I said, and I doubt it is near seventy.

A man couldn't get there, he said. He was still watching the patch of woods.

A man could try, I said. And I said I would try.

For Christ sake, he said, and he took a deep breath and let it out like a man has dived under water a long time and come up.

Then he sort of shook his head. If you was there, he said, I don't reckon it would do any good.

I could try, I said.

He looked at me. Maybe you could, he said.

I could try, I said, if the Lord would hear my prayer.

He did not say a thing, looking at that patch of woods. Then he said, I will speak to Captain Miles. And he said, And you better pray hard. You are a praying man and now is sure the time you better strut your stuff.

I need a feller to go with me, I said, to load for me.

You better take two, he said, in case one feller don't get there.

He crawled off and talked to Captain Miles. They talked a right smart, then he motioned to me with his hand, and I crawled to him. Captain Miles gave me two men to go with me.

It was just as good they gave me two men, for one man never got there. I told them to do like I did and I would pick the cover and go first, but one feller did not get there. It looks like some people have not got a sleight for picking cover and such. They have not got something in them to tell them when it is the right time and such. It was a man named Miller never got there. The man named Percy got there all right, for all those Germans could do.

We laid in the brush behind the chestnut trees, and the bullets come cutting through the brush, over us but too high. Then I saw where the gun was. I kept my eye on it.

I told Percy to get behind the other tree across from me and put something on the ground, a handkerchief or something, to lay his clips on. I wanted him to have them where he could get at them fast and handy and I didn't want him laying them on the ground to get anything on them to foul if he got excited and fast. He did what I said.

I took the first shot. I could see the feller's head. I did not see if I hit him, but it was maybe twenty seconds before they started shooting at us again so I reckoned maybe I hit him and they drug him back so a feller could get at the gun. The aim was way off when they started to shoot again and I saw the feller right quick and I gave it to him. I had to try to get him fast before they could get a good aim where we were laying. We had fair cover but I did not want to take any chance. That was why I wanted a man to load for me and have two rifles if one got jammed and not waste time. Percy was a good man and did like I said.

I missed the next man I tried for and he got good aim and

nearly got me. He came near cutting down that big chestnut. The bullets hit not six inches from my face. It took me three tries to get him. I got the next feller on one try.

Crying out loud, Percy said, four of the bastards.

I got the next one on two tries.

Crying out loud, Percy said, it is five.

Every time I got one, Percy said that, and counted.

But I did not hardly hear him or pay him any mind. It looked like I was not paying mind to anything going on. I knew I was looking across the cove and seeing some feller's head and shooting him and taking the gun Percy would give me and shooting again, but it was all slow-seeming and not real. I felt empty and floating like it was a dream, and my mouth was dry. I was praying. I was not praying with words. I was praying without words like I was praying all over and did not need any words, and I was lifted up.

Crying out loud, Percy said, nineteen of the bastards, they must be a million.

He passed me the gun.

Crying out loud, he said, our boys are shooting at them, our boys are working down in the woods, some of them have got across to the woods. But it was like I heard him but did not know. I heard it and it was like something you remember just before you go to sleep.

I laid there and shot.

Crying out loud, Percy said, it is twenty-two.

I did not see a feller's head at the gun. I could see the place but nobody had his head there and my finger was on my trigger.

They are going out from the woods, Percy said, they are going out to our boys and they have their hands up.

But I kept my eye on where a feller's head would be.

Then I saw some of our boys run up in the patch of woods where the gun was. I saw more Germans come out with their hands up. Our boys was yelling across to us.

I lay on my stomach with my gun aimed across the cove to the patch of woods. I let my gun sink down till it laid on the ground. I let my head just go down and lay on the stock and pressed my forehead against it and smelled the oily smell a good-rubbed gunstock has and the burnt powder smell. But my face was pressed down right at the ground where the dead leaves was laying off that chestnut tree and I smelled the dead leaves and the ground too like when I was a young one and played and laid on the ground, in the woods. I was laying there crying. I was bellering like a snot.

I had laid there and shot and I had prayed but not in words.

*Now I laid there and cried like a snot but I was twenty-seven
years old. I was a grown man and I was crying like a man will
when everything goes out of him and away from him and everything is over and done and he is weak and there is nothing in the
world for him.*

*I had prayed to God, and harder than I ever prayed to him for
the eight years since I found Jesus and tried to put off my sin. I
had prayed to him without words, and he answered my prayer. He
lifted me up and gave me the victory. But I ought to have prayed
to him for one more thing. I ought to have prayed to him to let
that last bullet coming out of the gun hid over in that patch of
woods hit me clean between the eyes.*

Milt Porsum, who was known as Private Porsum, sat in an easy
chair in the big clean living room of his house on Mercer Pike.
His powerful freckled hands lay on his knees. A setter slept on the
floor at his feet. Now and then the dog twitched and stirred.

He rose from his chair and stood there in the middle of the
room, with his arms hanging limp at his sides.

He switched off the reading lamp on the table by the chair
where he had been sitting. Now the moonlight made a rectangle
of whiteness on the floor under the big window at the south end
of the room. He walked to the window.

There, washed by the moonlight, beyond the lawn, were the
white stables and the white paddocks.

He stared out of the window and struck his two heavy hands
together, once, fist to palm.

"Oh, God damn him," Private Porsum said. "What did he have
to come here for? God damn him to hell!"

Twenty-four

WHEN, shortly after three o'clock on a Saturday afternoon, Private Porsum stood under the high, white, spacious porch of Bogan Murdock's house, and, having lifted and let fall the great bronze knocker, which was shaped like a lion's distended paw, hairy and regal, he thought: *A door is where a man goes in and he comes out. I am going in this door in a minute and I am going to come out. When a man goes in a door he is a different man and he is a different man when he comes out.* He waited, sensing the reverberations which would be dying away in the rich dimness of the big hall inside, and felt the comfort of the sun on the back of his head and neck.

Then the door opened and he saw the smooth, coppery, inquiring face and oiled, cast-metal-looking hair of the young Negro who stood there. "Howdy-do, Mr. Porsum," the Negro said.

Private Porsum looked at the smooth face sharply, as though he were meeting it for the first time and must have its secret. But it was a familiar face, and it told him nothing, just as it had never told him anything. Then he said: "Howdy-do, Anse." And asked: "Is Mr. Murdock in?"

"Yes, sir," the Negro said, and held the door wide, and said: "Won't you come in, Mr. Porsum?"

He entered, the door was closed behind him, and he stood in the hall and inspected it with the promptings of a new curiosity— the firm sweep of the stairway, the chandelier which hung like formal and luxurious ice, the tremendous mirror, set in curling gold, which repeated the scene in its icy depthlessness—while he waited for the Negro to announce him in the library. He had known that Bogan Murdock would be in that room.

Bogan Murdock was standing there, as he had known he would be, smiling to show the white, firm-set teeth, his hand extended, saying: "Well, Private, I'm glad you've dropped by."

"Thank you," said Private Porsum, and took the hand.

"Have a seat, Private," Bogan Murdock invited, gesturing with

341

that easy, controlled hypnotic resistless motion which focused, finally, at the tip of the poised brown forefinger. "Have a seat," he invited, "and I'll call in a little Scotch and we'll anticipate the hour."

"No, thank you," Private Porsum said, not moving, not looking at the chair to which he was being invited, feeling obscurely that he must not look at it.

"Oh, sit down," Bogan Murdock said, smiling, but with the slightest imperious glint in his tone.

"I have just come by for a minute, Bogan."

"Sit down, I've been trying to get you this morning. I wanted to talk to you about the Massey Mountain affair. The State is not called on to make payment for more than two more weeks, you know, and Meyers and Murdock holds a good deal of Massey Mountain stock. I just wanted to see you about raising some money on a chunk of our stock at your bank. But sit down and we can talk. I called you at the bank this morning, but they said you were out."

Private Porsum did not sit down. "I was not at the bank this morning," he said meditatively; "I was with Mr. Blake all morning."

"Well, and how is old Duckfoot getting along?" Bogan Murdock demanded. "They tell me he hasn't located yet. Maybe he is beginning to realize that he was a little hasty in leaving us. Jobs aren't too plentiful these days. Even for bright boys like Duckfoot."

"I went to see him on some business," Private Porsum said.

"Well, you might do worse than take him back," Bogan Murdock said, and laughed. "Provided, of course, he has seen the light."

"We didn't talk about him coming back, Bogan. I don't think he would come back. I wanted to talk to him about some bank matters. And," he reached into his inner coat pocket and drew out a folded sheet of paper, and held it in his hand, "about this."

He held the paper in his hand, not proffering it, and Bogan Murdock took one step toward him and grasped the paper, as if he were picking it up from a shelf.

"Read it," Private Porsum said, and looked out the window.

He kept his eyes fixed on the far-off, smoky-blue line of the horizon beyond the lawn and the fields and the trees while Bogan Murdock read.

"In God's name!" Bogan Murdock exclaimed.

Private Porsum did not take his eyes from the distant scene.

"In God's name!" Bogan Murdock exclaimed, and the paper rattled in his grasp, and Private Porsum slowly, heavily, turned his head and saw the suddenly chiseled face, which was now streaked sallow with its tan, and the blazing, pin-pointed eyes directed upon him.

"You don't realize, Porsum—you don't realize," Bogan Murdock was saying, and read aloud: "I, Milt Porsum, have used my influence to bring about the purchase by this State of the Massey Mountain Lumber Company and Atlas Iron Company properties for the establishment of a park and preserve. I wish to say to the people of this State that I acted in full awareness of the true value of the said properties and that I take full responsibility for my action. I cannot undo the evil which I have done, but I—" He stopped. "My God, Porsum!" he demanded, "what are you up to, what have you done with this?"

"It will be in the evening *Standard,*" Private Porsum said tiredly. "I gave it to a Mr. Tucker. Mr. Tucker is a reporter for *The Standard.* I told him to—"

"You call him, you call him now," Bogan Murdock burst out, and seized the telephone on his desk, and set it back in its cradle and picked up the directory and flung it open. "You get that Tucker. Tell him you want it back. Tell him you've got to make some corrections, and take the God-damned thing. Get it some way. You—" He flung the directory down. "Four-seven-eight-two, four-seven-eight-two," he muttered and dialed with the straight, strong, flickering forefinger. "You tell him to hold it, tell him you'll repudiate it, tell him—"

"I gave him a signed copy," Private Porsum said, and his eyes again sought the horizon.

"Tell him you'll sue him—tell him you've seen your lawyer and you can prove duress—get that God-damned thing!"

"No," Private Porsum said.

"You don't realize, man! You don't realize what this will do to the financial structure. You can't do this. It doesn't matter what that property is worth now. You owe it to the people of this State to keep your God-damned mouth shut. You owe—"

"I reckon I owe it to myself, Bogan, not to," he said. "I reckon a man owes himself something, Bogan," he said, not looking, thinking: *It will be over soon, it will be over.*

"You owe it to yourself not to be a fool. You've got responsibilities. You're president of a bank, you—"

"No, Bogan," he said, "I was. But I'm not now."

"What?"

"I'm not any more."

"You're quitting? You're quitting!" Bogan Murdock had stepped

343

to him and had seized him by the lapel, and strained, shaking the weight of the man's body, but the man did not even look at him. He shook him, saying: "Listen, you've got responsibilities, responsibilities, do you hear?"

"I had 'em," Private Porsum said, "but I reckon I didn't do so good by 'em. Things went on that had no business. I tried not to know about them, but I reckon I did all right."

"Not a thing went on that wasn't legal," Bogan Murdock said firmly. Then, searching the man's face, which was above his own, he said quietly, patiently, as though explaining to a sick man or a child: "It was all perfectly legal, I swear to you, Private. That," he said, almost whispering, peering at the big, sad, immobile face, "is perfectly true."

"I am going down this afternoon to make a statement," Private Porsum said.

"All right, Private," Bogan Murdock said. He released his hold on the lapel, almost with a motion of distaste, and stepped smartly back. "All right," he said, and his voice took on a sudden flash of triumph, like the voice of a man who suddenly sees the truth, "you are perfectly right! It was not legal. It was decidedly illegal. Go, and make your statement. And do you know what will happen? Listen—" Bogan Murdock lifted his hand, his fingers together as though in benediction, "and I will tell you. You will go to jail." Bogan Murdock smiled in invincible pity.

"I reckoned I would," Private Porsum said.

"Not," Bogan Murdock said, and leaned toward him, "if you aren't a fool. Not if you stick with the bank, if you don't make that statement, if you will call that reporter. Now!" And he swung to the telephone.

Private Porsum shook his head. "No," he uttered. "I'm going now, Bogan, and go down and make that statement. I reckon you might call it a confession."

"But while you're confessing, Mr. Porsum—" it was Dorothy Murdock's voice; she stood just inside the half-opened door, leaning against the jamb; she wore a pale blue negligee and her bare feet were in mules, her face was fixed in a distant, unapproachable, abstract, pale, saintly smile—"don't you think, Mr. Porsum, you might start confessing right here?"

Then, while the two men stared, speechless, at her, she continued: "Why don't you start right here, Mr. Porsum? Why don't you tell Bogan about you and me?"

"Dorothy!" Bogan Murdock spoke demandingly, but she lifted her pale forefinger, delicately, chidingly, at him, and shook her

344

head, while she said: "Hush, Bogan. Give Mr. Porsum time. He will confess. Mr. Porsum is a man of honor. Mr. Porsum is a hero. Aren't you, Mr. Porsum?" And she turned to him. "Aren't you, Mr. Porsum? He was your friend, Mr. Porsum, and you should tell him the truth. Friendship deserves that much."

Private Porsum's face worked and he seemed to be trying to speak, staring like a paralytic whose desperate plea cannot be articulated.

"Dorothy!" Bogan Murdock demanded.

"Oh, I'll tell you, Bogan, if Mr. Porsum lacks the manhood. Yes, we had an affair. Didn't we, Mr. Porsum? Oh, and I loved you passionately, Mr. Porsum, and I thought you loved me. Won't you admit that you loved me, Private? That day when I first came out to your place, to look at the horse—you know, Bogan, White Star, the horse I bought—it was the day Sue left, and everything seemed to be confused and I felt lost and there was Mr. Porsum, so quiet and simple and strong, so—" and she burst out laughing, with a brittle, glassy intonation, with her head thrown back and her mouth unnaturally wide to show the secret pink of her inner mouth and the whiteness of the inner teeth, where a little gold gleamed.

"You came out," Private Porsum managed to say, "you came out there, Mrs. Murdock, but—"

"But nothing, Mr. Porsum," she snapped at him, and the blue veins leaped on her temples. Then, suddenly, she smiled in sweet melancholy, and shook her head, saying: "You were so strong and gentle, Private—Mr. Porsum—something I missed here at home, here—Bogan, you were so busy—but I should have known, Mr. Porsum, it could not last forever. I should have known it would come to this. Oh, a hero like you can have many women, Mr. Porsum. But I—I am getting old—I am getting old—old—" and her voice faltered and her white hand wove in the air, deliciously and impeccably as though toying with a gossamer, before her bosom, which was partially exposed by the looseness of the blue robe. "Old—old—old," she whispered, and her eyes filled with tears.

"Dorothy," Bogan Murdock demanded, savagely, "are you telling the truth?"

"See, Bogan," she said, "I am crying. Would I cry if it were not true? The truth—oh, it's true. We always intended to tell you the truth. Didn't we, Mr. Porsum? It was the only honorable thing to do, we wanted you to know, and—and—" she whispered, "everybody else knew, you see."

"Everybody—else—knew?" Bogan Murdock said, spacing the

345

words out preciously, half in question, half in echo. And, with his inquiring, bright glance fixed upon her, he retreated to his desk.

"Oh, everybody," she said, "everybody in town, for we were indiscreet—but when you love as we—when—" and her voice trailed off into a bemused, voluptuous sigh as she stared at her husband, who, standing beside an open drawer of his desk, held a pistol in his hand, pointed at Private Porsum.

Private Porsum looked, dully, at the pistol, and then at Bogan Murdock's face above it. He shifted his weight and half turned, for he had been facing Dorothy Murdock. "Bogan," he said tiredly, "I don't care if you shoot me. It don't matter to me, shooting. But I never did it."

"He is lying, Bogan," Dorothy Murdock insisted softly, insinuatingly.

"I'm not lying," Private Porsum said. "Mrs. Murdock came out to my place like she says. I saw her out there more than one time, Bogan. And I might have done it. Only I didn't, Bogan. I didn't even try. Because I thought you was my friend, Bogan, and I haven't ever done it to a friend."

"He's lying, Bogan!" Dorothy Murdock screamed.

Bogan Murdock held the pistol steadily on the man, but did not fire.

"Do it, Bogan," she screamed, "do it!"

The pistol sank a fraction of an inch, but steadily, as though meticulously probing for an exact spot of aim.

"Don't be afraid, Bogan!"

But he did not fire, and Dorothy Murdock, curling back her lips as though for expectoration, said: "You're afraid, Bogan."

Watching him, she repeated: "You're afraid, Bogan."

Private Porsum stood in the middle of the room, waiting in a sad, heavy indifference like a tired servant waiting to be instructed for a final errand.

"Get out!" Bogan Murdock suddenly commanded. And lowered the weapon.

Private Porsum turned slowly toward the door, and stopped just in front of Dorothy Murdock. He studied her a moment. "I reckon," he said to her, "I just don't know how you came to do it, Mrs. Murdock."

She returned his gaze. Then, as her bosom heaved, she struck him across the face.

"Get out!" she said.

She leaned back against the door jamb for support and shut her eyes, breathing irregularly. She stood there while his steps retreated across the hall, and the hall door was shut with its solid, dull, authoritative sound. Then, an instant later, there was the sound of a motor starting.

When the sound of the motor had died away, she opened her eyes and turned her head toward her husband, who waited by the desk. The revolver lay upon the polished wood. She moved unsteadily into the room, watching him. She stopped, swaying slightly, almost at the spot where Private Porsum had stood, and said: "You were afraid, Bogan. You are a coward, Bogan."

"You're drunk," Bogan Murdock said.

"Yes," she agreed, swaying, "yes, I am drunk. Sure, I'm drunk. But you shouldn't care. Oh, you didn't care about me. But, Bogan—listen, Bogan—" she moved a step nearer him, "you ought to have cared about yourself. He's going down to tell people about the bank, Bogan, and you could have shot him. Oh, that's why you started to shoot him, Bogan. Oh, I know you, Bogan. Just for that. When I said everybody knew, that's when you started to do it. And use me as an excuse. But not because of me. Not because of me. Oh, no, Bogan, not because of me. For yourself, for yourself—"

"Shut up!" he ordered.

"—for yourself, and not for me—"

"So he wouldn't have you?" he asked, mastering himself, articulating his words carefully. "And I scarcely blame him. Scarcely. For not taking on a drunken, sodden, self-abusing, middle-aged bitch. Oh, no," he said, and began to laugh, "oh, no, for that is not exactly what a man wants."

"—and not because of me, not—because—of—me," she repeated, and seemed not to have heard him, and cast her glance wildly about the room, with her dark hair slipping down girlishly over the pure blue sheen of the silk robe as she sank to the floor.

Twenty-five

THEY sat in Sue Murdock's apartment, the man who had been a foreman at the Freeman Foundries before he was fired, his girl Betsy, who, they said, had once been a prostitute, Sweetie Sweetwater, and Sue Murdock. It was about half past ten, on Sunday morning, the day and the hour when little children—the little girls in careful, pastel-colored ribbons and cute dresses, clutching miniature purses, the little boys in belted wool jackets and white collars, with plastered hair curling unrulily at the ends and faces scrubbed until they have the appearance of being varnished—sit on hard chairs in the basements and annexes of churches, and scrooge and twist secretly and dangle their legs, and in thin, uncertain voices raggedly repeat in unison the Golden Text. When black limousines whisk, and a few sedate electrics amble, up the sunlit, tree-lined avenues—the trees are bare now and a few final colored leaves, just fallen, lie in the dry gutters and stir to the passage of the cars—and the automobiles presently will stop before the great piles of brick or still new-looking Gothic limestone, and old ladies, with the help of colored chauffeurs, will creakily descend and, with the concealment of a lace handkerchief, place a peppermint drop upon the tongue, which is dry and gray, and will go in to worship. When Negro cooks take a look at the roast in the oven and, knowing there is no danger of the mistress bursting into the kitchen, spit into the sink and boldly insert a gob of snuff on the lower gum. When laborers stretch their feet, shoeless, toward the coal stove and belch with the comfort of the late breakfast. When children scream in the slum street. When newsboys congregate on the corner by the drugstore and scuffle and exchange obscenities and hail passing cars. When red-faced, tweedy men step out of cars at the country club and inhale deeply, two or three times, the brisk air, then light cigars and, followed by a caddie carrying the bags of clubs, stalk toward the locker entrance, grinding the gravel under their cleated feet. When young lovers, free for a whole day together, begin to prick themselves deliciously, half consciously, in

348

the deeps of the mind with the thought of dark hallways or the car parked in the country lane. When the bedridden invalid knows that before dark people will call, bearing too perfect, ceremonial greenhouse blossoms, which will be disposed about the room in an ironic prematureness.

But the foreman sat in an overstuffed chair in Sue Murdock's apartment with the front section of the newspaper spread on his knees, the other sections and the funny papers scattered about his feet, and said: "Jeeze, if he didn't spill it, Jeeze, if he didn't!"

"Yeah," Sweetwater agreed.

"Whatever made him do it," the foreman said, "that's what I can't figure, and him a buddy with Murdock and them."

"*What*," Sweetie said, "don't matter, but he did do it."

"Gimme another one, Sweetie," the foreman ordered and held out his glass, "and I'll shore drink to whatever it was. Gimme another one, it's Sunday."

Sweetie got out of his chair and received the glass.

"Yeah," Betsy said, "and every day's Sunday since you got fired."

"It'll be all right now," the foreman affirmed. "You boys'll win that strike now, by God, and they'll throw Meyers and Murdock out of the foundry—God, they'll have to after all what the Private spilled—"

Sweetie passed the glass of corn to the foreman, and turned to Betsy and held out his hand for her glass. "It's Sunday," he said, grinning.

She handed him the glass.

"—yeah, they'll have to reorganize. And throw out Murdock, and—"

"Yeah, and they'll make you president," Betsy Dodd said, and gulped from her glass.

"—get out from under Murdock and they can pay decent—"

"Maybe," Sweetie said.

"Hell," the foreman said, "but I'd shore like to see Murdock's face this morning when he opened his paper and seen—"

"My father," Sue Murdock remarked distantly, from the bed, where she was propped up, on top of the covers, "never reads the papers on Sunday morning. He does not," she added, "intrude business upon the refinements of life."

"Well, I bet he shore played hell with the refinements of life this morning, and I wish to God I had seen him."

"I wish I had, too," Sue Murdock said.

"God, it's all cracking up," the foreman said, "all them bastards is cracking up. That God-damned hunting club cracking up—

Happy Valley, Happy Valley," he slapped his leg and laughed, and drank, and repeated: "Happy Valley!"

"Happy Valley," Betsy Dodd echoed and laughed. She was showing the liquor.

"And they gonna let them they throwed off them farms come on back if they want to and wait and see what them trustees and receivers and lawyers and such are gonna do. And live in them houses they done fixed up so fine. Jesus, Happy Valley," the foreman iterated, and slapped his leg. "Jesus," he said, "it is all cracking up!"

"Yes," said Sweetie, "it is."

"Boy, and does it suit me. It is sure all right by me."

"Sure," said Sweetwater, "it is gonna be all right."

"Yeah," the foreman agreed.

"Yeah," Sweetwater said, "it is gonna be wonderful. It is gonna be too God-damned wonderful. We are gonna sit on our tails and light two-bit cigars with five-dollar bills while soft music is rendered by a string quartet."

"Well, you'll win that strike," the foreman affirmed, "and it suits me."

"Win it and what have you got?" Sweetwater demanded indifferently.

"Well, and it was you so hot on the strike. It was you whooped it up."

"And I'd do it again," Sweetwater said grimly.

"Well, what are you griping about?"

"Jack," Sweetwater declared dourly, "you make me want to puke. You win a strike and you think you have done something. You think if you see Murdock in jail that you have done something. You don't know a God-damned thing. You make me sick, Jack."

The foreman set his glass on the floor and regarded Sweetie. "What the hell's the matter with you?" he demanded.

Sweetie did not answer.

"Oh, it's just his beautiful nature," Sue remarked airily.

The foreman stood up. He turned to Betsy, who was sitting on the bed. "Look for me when you see me," he said, and to the others said, "So long," and went out.

"Yeah," Betsy said, "and when I'll see him, it'll be about two in the morning and he'll crack his cookies in the sink and I'll have to put him to bed. Jesus, Sweetie, you don't get drunk with him and he's out to find somebody will. He'll be all over town telling them how he done it single-handed. God damn him, he will come in and do it in the sink, but—" she exhaled a deep, bed-shaking sigh and lifted her now bleared eyes heavenward, "I love him. Jesus, I love him, he's a no-good bastard, but, Jesus, I love that man and I tell you and I don't care who knows." She rocked herself gently back and forth on the edge of the bed and her luxurious breasts swayed and jounced a little and the springs creaked with her not inconsiderable weight. "I love that bastard," she crooned, "and I—"

Sweetie rose abruptly from his chair. "Aw, shut up," he said. He walked to the window and stared morosely down over the roofs and the river.

"Oh, you must excuse him," Sue Murdock said, "for he's not responsible today. It's because he's so happy he's going to marry me."

"Honey!" Betsy exclaimed in ecstasy. "Honey, ain't it wonderful?" She leaned over and laid her very white, slightly inflated-looking hand, with its crimson nails, on Sue Murdock's knee, saying: "Oh, Honey, it is sure wonderful, I always say there ain't nuthin like gitting married, that's what I tell Jack, but that bastard—"

"The hell I am," Sweetie said, not turning from the window. He took a knife from his pocket and began to pare his nails, glumly.

"Yes, you will, Sweetie," Betsy said, nodding sagely at the stocky, unresponsive back, which was black against the window, "you gonna marry Sue, for Sue is a sweet kid, she is a darling kid, I ain't never seen a kid sweeter'n Sue and you're a lucky bastard, and I always say to Jack, I say—"

There was a knock at the door.

Sue Murdock said, "Come in," and shifted her body so that she could see the door.

Sweetie did not turn from the window.

The door opened with an almost theatrical retardation. Slim Sarrett stood there, framed in the doorway, tall, his old raincoat draped like a cape from his shoulders, his face lifted.

Betsy Dodd giggled. "Look," she said, "if it ain't the fruiter!"

Slim Sarrett's eyes shifted slightly in their sockets, moving like slick, twin chocolate-colored agates geared to perfect synchronization, and momentarily rested, with a dispassionate contempt, upon the blowsy, too fat, blondined, giggling woman.

Sweetie had turned from the window to face the room. He observed, but seemed to hold himself detached from, the scene. The blade of his knife still moved punctiliously over the edge of one of his fingernails, scraping it smooth.

Slim Sarrett's eyes left Betsy and focused upon Sue Murdock. "I want to talk to you," he announced, flatly and expressionlessly.

351

"Well," she said, "I don't want to talk to you."

"That's telling him!" Betsy applauded, and giggled. "That's telling the fruiter!"

Slim Sarrett stepped formally into the room, and pushed the door shut behind him.

"I told you I didn't want to talk to you," Sue Murdock said venomously, and sat up. "I told you I didn't want to see you again. I told you that and you hang around, you follow me on the street —oh, I've seen you, hanging round a block behind me when I go out and spying on me and thinking I didn't see you—and writing those poems and sending them to me. They make me sick. I told you, and haven't you got any pride? And you come sneaking up here on Sunday morning because you think I'll be by myself then. Oh, you make me sick," she concluded, and let herself sink back to her elbow as though in weakness. With her head in its slanted position, the yellow hair hung sleekly from the part to brush the tip of her lower shoulder.

"I came at this time," Slim Sarrett announced, "because I thought you would be alone. You were right. I want to speak to you alone."

"Oh, the fruiter wants to be alone with Sue, oh, the fruiter wants to be alone with Sue," Betsy chanted, and gently swayed in a motion of which her breasts partook.

"I want to speak to you alone," he said in his distant, unchanged voice.

"Oh, the fruiter wants to be alone with Sue," Betsy chanted and swayed.

"Get out," Sue Murdock said, not loudly but staring at him with a weary malevolence.

"I must speak to you, for," he affirmed composedly, "it is very important."

"Get out," Sue Murdock said.

"No," he said.

"Get out!" she commanded with violence, and pushed herself up to a sitting position, and shook back the hair from her face with a taut, vicious motion of her head.

"No," he replied, even more quietly.

Sweetie stopped scraping the nail of his left forefinger. With the knife held diagonally across the palm of his right hand, the point of the blade at the tip of his forefinger, and the thumb resting on the haft, he snapped the blade up, then let it snap shut in the palm of his hand. It made a small click. "You heard what the lady said," he remarked.

Slim Sarrett did not move, nor even glance toward Sweetie. His

352

eyes, depthless, accurate, uncompromising, were fixed upon Sue Murdock's face.

"All right," Sweetie announced.

Betsy giggled.

"All right," Sweetie repeated indifferently, and put the knife in his pocket, "I reckon I'll have to throw you out." He took two steps into the room, from the window.

Slim Sarrett watched him, then said in little better than a whisper: "I'll kill you."

Sweetie took another step, then measured the distance between them like a man getting ready to do a carpentering or a plumbing job.

Slim Sarrett let the raincoat slip from his shoulders and fall to the floor behind him. For an instant he stood very erect, his head lifted. Then his left foot slipped forward and the knees flexed a little. His hands still hung at his sides, idly like instruments in a rack.

"Stop!" Sue cried, "stop, Sweetie!"

"Shut up," Betsy said.

"He'll hurt you, Sweetie, he'll hurt you, he's a boxer," Sue cried, but Sweetie had, at the instant, lunged forward.

He had guarded his face, and had lunged in, his head low, almost at his opponent's waist.

Slim Sarrett placed one blow glancingly on the side of Sweetie's head, before Sweetie was upon him, gripping him, lifting him from the floor, plunging forward to fall upon him so that one shoulder drove into his upper abdomen.

"Jesus," Betsy giggled, and drew her feet back to make room for the men, who rolled and thrashed on the floor before her. "Jesus," she said, and leaned solicitously, maternally, forward over them.

Sweetie managed to pin Slim Sarrett's left arm with his crooked leg, and seize the right wrist with his own left hand. Then, while Sarrett heaved and writhed and jerked his legs up to try vainly to hook Sweetie's head or shoulders into a scissors, Sweetie, grunting, methodical, chunked him in the face with the heel of the palm of his right hand and slapped him.

"Slap him, slap him," Betsy crooned deliciously, "slap the fruiter."

He would chunk him solidly with the broad, heavy heel of his palm, so nastily that Sarrett's head would roll and snap; then he would grunt; then he would slap, his palm making a flat sound on the flesh.

"Slap him," Betsy crooned.

Slim Sarrett's attenuated legs, with the trousers slipping to show the polished flesh of the calf, threshed and jerked in the air spasmodically, like a grasshopper's when one holds it by the pinched-back wings, upsidedown. Sweetwater chunked, grunted, slapped.

"Slap the pee out of him," Betsy sang.

Sarrett's legs suddenly collapsed, the heels striking the floor, the knees crooked upward. Then the knees slipped flat. He was weeping softly.

Sweetie chunked and slapped him two or three times more.

Sweetie got clumsily up, breathing raspingly. He stood astride Sarrett, above Sarrett's knees, and looked down at the bleared, swollen, teary face. Then, just as he seemed about to step back, Sarrett kicked sharply upward. Sweetie swung so that the impact missed his privates and struck him on the thigh.

"Huh," he grunted.

"I'd kill him," Betsy cried, "I'd kill the fruiter!"

Sarrett had rolled over on his side now with the force of his kick, but his neck was craned so that he could see Sweetie. Deliberately, Sweetie kicked him in the tail. "Get up," he ordered.

Sarrett did not move.

"Get up, or I'll kick your tail off," Sweetie said.

Sarrett rose uncertainly. The instant he was erect, Sweetie plunged at him, driving him back against the wall by the door, pinning him there while Sarrett clawed and kicked, and with his free hand reaching out to jerk the door open. Then he half shoved, half threw Sarrett into the hall. Sarrett came down upon one knee, not weeping now, screaming: "I'll kill you, Sweetwater, I'll kill you!"

Sweetie turned and picked up the raincoat from the floor. He flung that, too, into the hall, and shut the door upon the sound of Slim Sarrett's voice.

He turned back into the room, fingering the place above his ear where Sarrett had hit him.

"Jesus," Betsy breathed devoutly, "you done it. You sure done it. You sure threw him out."

"Oh, he done it," Sue echoed in smiling, acid mimicry, her eyes glittering. "Oh, never you fear, what Sweetwater says, he does, oh, never you fear. Sweetwater is wonderful, Sweetwater is sublime, Sweetwater throws people out. Every Sunday morning Sweetwater throws people out."

Sweetie directed a slow, stolid gaze upon her, still fingering his head.

354

"Look at him," Sue commanded, "behold him, so strong, so silent, so true. He throws people out."

He withdrew his gaze from her, and went into the bathroom, leaving the door open. He turned on the tap at the basin, and leaned forward and applied cold water to the spot on his head, while Sue, beyond the open door, said: "Oh, he throws people out every Sunday morning. Like my father, he reserves every Sunday morning for the refinements of life. Oh, he is wonderful, oh, he is good, he is marvelous, he—"

Outside, Betsy Dodd was saying: "I'm shoving along. I'll see you."

"Oh, he is grand, Sweetwater is grand, behold the great Sweetwater, behold—"

There was the sound of the outer door.

"—the great Sweetwater, he will defend me, he will guard me, he will throw anybody out who says boo to me, he will love me, he will cherish me, oh, his belly is a sheaf of wheat set round with lilies, he—"

Sweetie cut off the tap, dropped the wet towel into the basin, and came out into the room.

"Behold the marvel, the patrician, the paragon, the dilly, the daisy—"

"Shut up," he said.

She stopped, and sank back against the piled pillows, half sitting. She watched him with glittering eyes, her face smooth and passionless, her glinting hair falling symmetrical and pure on each side of her face. With the thumb and forefinger of her right hand, she plucked at one of the little knots on the counterpane. "Are you going to marry me?" she asked with childlike gravity.

"No," he said.

"In which case," she said, unchanging, "I shall have an abortion."

He studied her expressionlessly. "You know what I said," he said.

He waited but she answered nothing, looking at him with sweet gravity. So he picked up his hat from the table, and went out the door.

After he had gone and the sound of his footsteps had been absorbed into the massive silence of the room, she remained on the bed, in the same posture, carefully plucking one of the little knots on the counterpane, with her eyes directed at the spot in the middle of the room where he had last stood.

Finally, she rose, and went to the kitchen. There she laid a place on the table, poured a glass of milk, and put out bread and butter. She put butter into a skillet, lighted the gas beneath it, and when the butter had dissolved and begun to rustle, broke two eggs into it. She scrambled the eggs lightly, and then dumped them into a plate. She ran a little water into the skillet and set it in the sink. Then, with an air of formality, she seated herself, picked up her fork, and tasted the first mouthful. She masticated it very slowly, looking out the window, swallowed it, took a bite of bread, a drink of milk, another mouthful of egg. When she had eaten it, she lifted a third bite to her lips, and actually took a morsel into her mouth. She laid the fork down with most of the egg still on it. With her tongue, she forced the uneaten morsel back to her lips, and wiped it away with a paper napkin. She inspected the smeared mess on the napkin, then with a sudden positive gesture, crumpled up the napkin and threw it to the floor. She managed, however, to drink the rest of the milk.

She scraped her plate into the garbage pail, washed the dishes, and put them away. From the cupboard she took down a bottle of corn whisky and poured herself a drink. Having swallowed that, she went to the bathroom, washed her face, combed her hair, and applied lipstick, studying her face in the mirror. Then she began to straighten the room. She picked up the papers, stacked them neatly on the table, smoothed the bed and adjusted the pillows, took the ash trays to the kitchen and emptied them. In the kitchen she took another drink. Back in the room, she got a fresh nightgown from the closet and her slippers and robe. She laid the robe and gown upon the bed, neatly, and set the slippers on the floor. Then she turned back the covers, as though it were evening.

She looked at her watch. It was two-thirty.

She sat in the easy chair near the window. She felt very calm and empty and secure with finality. She felt like a mother, a widow, who enters the quiet rooms, still scented by flowers, after the marriage of her last child. She felt like a statesman who closets himself alone upon receiving news of the victorious armistice. She felt like a plunger who has sold at the peak, at the precise turn of the market, and sits alone, drifting in the dead waters to the leeward of the violent moment of intuition, and numbly, reverently, timorously, fondles his acumen. She felt like one who, after vomit, relaxes in the relief from pressure and retch, and is ready to sleep.

Once she looked out the window at the big, bright sky of autumn, and thought how it would be to sit her mare, after the gallop, alone in the middle of a great, windless, sun-drenched meadow, where the grass was still green.

At a little after three, she again looked at her watch, and rose. She got her purse from the closet, and from one corner of the bureau there, took out, from under handkerchiefs and stockings, a roll of bills held by a rubber band. She counted out one hundred dollars in twenties, put that into her purse, and detached another bill, a five-dollar bill, from the roll. Then she counted what she had left. It amounted to nine hundred and forty-three dollars. She started to replace the money in the drawer. Upon second thought, however, she put it, too, into her purse.

She went into the kitchen once more, then left the apartment, locking the door behind her.

She reckoned it would hurt, all right. People said it hurt like hell. But that was what people would say. She reckoned she could stand it if anybody else could.

. . . and when I was little they put me to bed as soon as I finished my supper, as soon as it began to get dark, as soon as the whippoorwill was calling, it was Lizzie who put me to bed and said, honey, said honey chile, and Dorothy came to the bed and Dockie came and Dockie came and he blew in my ear, Dockie came and blew in my ear light as a feather and tickly-nice, and blew in my ear, and said, go to sleep, whispered go to sleep, baby, go to sleep, sleep, but I can't go to sleep, sleep, God damn it I can't go to sleep for it hurt so God-damned much, oh!

So she reached out in the dark—it was very dark, for the curtains were drawn to cut off any reflection of the lights from the street below—and her hand touched the bottle, which was on a straight chair by the bed.

. . . but I didn't go to sleep, I lay in the dark and I didn't go to sleep because I was by myself in the dark and I am afraid of the dark and the teddy bear is no good and a teddy bear is full of sawdust and stuff and does not love you and isn't any good, and people are downstairs and Lizzie is in the kitchen eating and sucking the gravy and watching the cook and Dorothy is with people and pretty and laughing and Dockie is there, Dockie is there, and they laugh and talk where the lights are and they love me, they love me they say, but they put me to bed in the dark and they are laughing but they put me to bed in the dark and by myself and a teddy bear does not love you, but it was not Callie or Dorothy or Dockie, not Dockie, not Dockie, oh, put me to bed in the dark by myself, but he had a sharp beard and his eyes behind the glasses were wet and sad and his hands were the color of lard and he says, my dear, my dear young lady, my dear, it won't hurt, it won't hurt very much, hold tight, and he is a liar a God-damned liar, oh!

She put out her hand in the dark to the chair.

. . . but I didn't go to sleep for I was afraid and I cried for I had lost something, for I had lost my little gold ring or my locket which was shaped like a heart or the silver spoon I took from the pantry to play in the dirt with, and I don't know where down by the big oak or back in the barn where the cows chew or under the bushes where I hid and heard Lizzie calling and heard Dorothy calling and heard Dockie calling and he called baby, baby, where are you baby, it's Dockie, don't be afraid, but oh!

She put out her hand.

. . . but there were people downstairs laughing and talking, I knew, and I had lost something and I was afraid to tell and I cried in the dark where they put me while they were laughing and talking and I had lost something and I had put something away in the dark, my little gold ring or my locket or the silver spoon, I had lost something, or the silver spoon, oh! oh, it looked like a spoon, oh!

Even as she put out her hand, she heard the rap at the door. She lay still, but it came again. It came again, more peremptorily. Then, after a moment, she was aware of a slight scraping sound. Raising herself on an elbow, she peered toward the door and saw the white object sliding in beneath it. She waited in that position until she heard steps retreating down the uncarpeted hall. Then she rose laboriously, switched on a lamp, put on her robe and slippers and went to the door to pick up the letter. Cautiously, holding the letter in her hand, she unlatched the door, and looked down the hall. She could hear feet moving down the stair a floor below.

She saw that the letter was from her father. Gazing at the envelope, she pushed the door shut behind her, and moved toward the lamp. She tore open the envelope, withdrew the rich, crackling sheet, and with her head bowed over the sheet, as though she were nearsighted, began to read the letter:

> Dearest Sue:
>
> This is one more appeal to you to think of your future, if you cannot be moved by the thought of your parents, who truly love you and want you with them. I do not write this last in bitterness, for I understand that you feel that you must work out your own problem. But I want to call your attention—for I am, after all, a business man, you know—to the fact that the investments on which you have been depending are likely to be much less profitable in the future.

The judgment of the young lawyer who has been handling your affairs is not of the best. And I happen to have discovered—quite by accident, I assure you—that you have been drawing heavily against your little capital. Daughter, I wish that you had been willing to draw against the funds which I have been depositing in the bank to your account. I beg you to do so now. I beg you to go away, to New York, let us say, and try to adjust yourself to a new life, where you can make new friends, where perhaps you can light upon a line of endeavor which will interest you. I want to assure you that I will stand behind you financially, and with my thoughts and prayers. I will—

She crumpled the sheet and flung it to the floor.

"Oh, I'm going away," she said out loud, "don't you worry. But not on you, don't you worry, don't you worry. And don't you worry about my little capital, oh, don't you worry, I've got it safe in my purse, every penny of it, nine hundred and forty-three dollars, nine hundred and forty-three dollars, my little capital, and it will last forever, nine hundred and forty-three dollars, it is all the money in the world—" And she began to laugh, and kicked the wad of paper on the floor. It bounced away. She pursued it, laughing, and kicked it again, like a soccer player. Suddenly, she stopped, her body drawn over tautly, and said, "Oh!"

She turned off the light. Not quite straightening up, she moved cautiously to the bed, took off her robe, and lay down again. She drank heavily from the bottle, in the dark, and set it back on the chair.

. . . and I lay in the dark and cried but I had hunted for it, I had hunted for it, I had hunted and hunted, for I had lost it but I didn't know where, down at the barn or under the bushes where I lay hid and they called, Dockie called, he called, baby, baby, but I have hunted and hunted everywhere, everywhere, I have hunted everywhere—

Her mind slid slowly, then swoopingly, off into blackness, and she did not feel or think anything. Then she felt that she was rising slowly to a surface, like a diver who has gone down deep.

. . . and they put me to bed at dark every night and it was the man with the eyes always wet and sad behind the glasses and he said, my dear, it won't hurt, it won't hurt a bit, it—

She slipped off again, feeling like a trapeze performer who, at the end of a long, wonderful arc, releases her hold on the bar and

sails effortlessly, superbly, royally over all the lights and faces up-
turned so far below, the darling of the circus sailing away from
them into the dark, for there is no tent at all and it is dark and
there are no stars in the sky but you go sailing and smile in the
dark and hold out your hands to touch the strong hands held out
to you in the pitch dark and you know they will catch and hold
your hands.

. . . *won't hurt a bit, it won't—*

No, she had not let go; she was swinging again.

. . . *it won't.*

She had let go.

When she first came, painfully, back to consciousness, she was
aware of nothing but the darkness before her eyes. She did not
know, at the instant, whether her eyes were open or shut. Then
she knew that they were open. Then she was aware of her heart
beating.

Then, not moving, hearing her heart beating faithfully in the
warm darkness which was herself, she became aware, or thought
she was aware, of a presence in the room. She tried to remember
whether or not she had locked the door again. But it did not seem
important. And she slipped back into unconsciousness.

Then, waking, she was again aware of the presence. She was
sure it was there, but she was not afraid. She did not feel anything, for everything was so far away. She tried to stir, and spoke.
At least, she had tried to speak. She had intended to speak. She
had intended to ask who it was.

But there was no answer.

For a moment she thought that she had been deceived, and that
there was no one there at all. She spoke again; then decided that
there was nobody there.

But there was.

She felt the hand, which was very cool and firm, laid lightly on
her forehead, and her breath froze in the constriction of her throat
and her heart gave one astounding knock, which shook her.

Then she heard, as from a considerable distance, the voice saying: "Sue, Sue, my darling, my darling."

It was Slim Sarrett's voice.

"Go away," she said. She was sure she had said it.

"My darling, my darling, my little beautiful darling," the voice
whispered, and the cool hand moved caressingly, comfortingly, on
her hot forehead, brushing back the hair.

360

"Go away," she tried to say, or said, but the hand moved so lightly, so soothingly.

"My darling, my darling, forgive me but I had to come, I had to see you, I had to see you, my darling, my darling—" but she was not hearing the words.

The other hand in the dark began to smooth her bare shoulder, gently pushing aside the strap of the gown, moving lovingly over the shoulder, caressing the throat.

"Go away," she said.

"My darling, my darling," the whisper said.

"You can't," she said thickly, "you can't," and tried to rise up, but the hand lay firm on her forehead and her body seemed to be nothing, to be flowing away strengthlessly.

"Lie still, lie still, my darling," the whisper kept saying.

"You can't," she said, "you can't, you can't because—oh, I'm drunk, I'm drunk like I used to be, but you can't this time, because—" and it struck her as the funniest thing in the world, as the funniest joke there ever was in the world, "and you can't," and she laughed, "oh, it's a joke on Slim Sarrett, you came in the dark but you can't, you can't, he comes in the dark and I'm drunk but he can't this time, he can't—" and she laughed two or three times, wildly.

"Oh," the voice said, "oh."

The hand had moved from her forehead now and had twisted itself in her hair.

"Oh, he can't this time," she said, laughing.

"Shut up," he breathed the words gently, like an endearment, prayerfully, "oh, please shut up, oh, please, please."

But she did not. She laughed delightedly, like a child, seeming to be floating in the dark with the hand tangled in her hair binding it to the pillow and the hand lying upon her throat.

The laughter faltered, stopped, began again, died away in a contented little sigh. Her eyes were closed. Her breathing, which had become slightly raucous, steadied itself.

He waited for some minutes, listening to her breathing.

Sitting by the bed, on the chair, Slim Sarrett gradually increased the pressure upon her throat, until he strangled her. She did not struggle, really. She did not bring her arms out from beneath the covers under which they were, as it were, pinioned. Her body stirred laboriously, twice, twisting, and her knees drew up somewhat, tenting the covers. Then they sank down, slowly, and the legs straightened, as though she were composing and adjusting herself. After that she did not move at all.

361

He sat beside the bed for some time, with one hand on her throat, the other tangled in her hair. He leaned forward toward her, like a physician who, at the bedside of a patient, awaits the result of the crisis. Still with his hands stretched out, he shut his eyes. If he shut his eyes, it might not be this time, it might be any other time and not this time. It might be one of those other times when he had sat beside her in the dark with his hand tangled in her hair, or touching her throat, listening to her breath. But, leaning forward with his eyes shut, he could not hear a thing, no matter how hard he listened. But it was her fault. It wasn't his fault. It was her fault. All her fault. *She shouldn't have done it,* he thought, *she shouldn't have laughed at me. I asked her, I said, Please, please, please. But she kept on laughing. I said, Darling, darling, please, please. But she kept on laughing. And Malloy laughed, and they all stood there and laughed at me, but Sue didn't laugh, and he threw me down and kicked me and Betsy Dodds laughed, but Sue didn't laugh, she didn't laugh, but then she laughed, she laughed too, and they shouldn't laugh at me, they can't laugh at me, I'm Slim Sarrett, I'm Slim Sarrett. But she laughed, and it isn't my fault. It isn't.* His mind was full of the faces and the faces were laughing. They wouldn't stop laughing, and she was laughing, she laughed, too. His hand tightened again, without thought, upon her throat.

Then he knew that he didn't have to do that. She wouldn't laugh at him. Poor little thing, poor little Sue, she wouldn't laugh at him. She never would have laughed, if she had known. She hadn't known that they shouldn't laugh at him, that she shouldn't laugh at him. She never would have laughed, if she had known. His closed eyes were wet with tears, and he was filled with a great, beautiful, elegiac pity, for her, for himself, for everybody he knew—for they didn't know, nobody told them—for everybody in the whole world who struggles and errs and suffers and dies.

After a while, but long before light began to creep into the room, he got up from the chair. He was cold, and stiff from having sat so long in the strained posture. He flexed his arms, and worked his hands together. Then he carefully examined the apartment, pulling out drawers here and there and disordering or rumpling the contents. To perform these operations, he covered his right hand with a handkerchief. In the top drawer of the bureau, he found the purse. He took out the roll of bills, still fastened with the rubber band. He held them in his hand a moment, then put them into his pocket. In a box in the drawer he found two rings and a bracelet. These articles, too, he took. Then he left the apartment.

Before he reached the building where he lived, he picked up a sheet of newspaper which was lying in the street. He wrapped and wadded the rings and bracelet into the paper. Continuing to walk, he looked sharply over his shoulder, then ahead. There was nobody in the street, anywhere. He stopped, leaned quickly, and thrust the mass of paper down through the grating of a gutter sewer.

As he proceeded at his brisk normal pace, he congratulated himself upon the idea. Nobody would ever find those things there. Those things had belonged to Sue Murdock, and now nobody would ever find them. Yes, it was an excellent idea.

Twenty-six

MR. CALHOUN leaned over the big chair where, swaddled in a comforter and a shawl, which had once been blue but was now streaked and ambiguously faded, Aunt Ursula was propped. Her hands, with the beauty and cunning of their bony structure scarcely concealed by the dry yellow skin which sheathed it, protruded from beneath the shawl, curling, palms downward on the lap. Her head was lifted slightly, the sightless sunken eyes fixed inquiringly as on a distant object, squinting as against too bright a sun, the lower jaw drooping in anticipation of the spoon which Mr. Calhoun was lifting, so carefully, to her mouth.

"Take it, Aunt Ursula," he was saying, "take it, it's got plenty of sugar in it."

But he did not need to urge her, for the lower lip of the open mouth twitched with a feeble pleasure as the spoonful of hot milk and soaked bread approached.

She closed her lips and he carefully withdrew the spoon from between them; then straightened up a little, still watching her face for the sign that she was ready for another spoonful. He knew that face perfectly. He knew what the lightest twitch or movement meant. There was no need for her to speak to him, and she rarely spoke, and then with a creaking, fretful little voice which made a sound like an old hinge disturbed by a night breeze and which said nothing to him but simply defined irrelevant fragments drifting up to the surface from a life which she had lived long before he had ever laid eyes on her, or on the grave-eyed girl who had married him and who had borne him a son and who had died. And there was no need for him to speak to her. But he did speak to her, murmuring to her when he gave her food, when he adjusted her match-stick, musty body in bed or chair, when he entered the room after an absence. He felt, sometimes, that she was what he had, the priceless vestige which he had saved out of everything, and felt, with a faithful certainty, that she would stay with him as long as he had need of her.

364

For she did not change. She had ceased to change long back, her constancy was such. Other things changed. The chair in which she sat changed: an arm had been broken off in the moving and he had mended it with nails and copper wire. The table, the carpet, the bed, the chairs changed, and were changing daily under his touch. He had an index now, as it were, for the change, for now, since the return to his house, which was no longer his but which he inhabited on the sufferance of people whose names he did not know, the objects which he had so long been accustomed to were, though set in the old locations, in contrast to the new, discreetly gleaming walls, the even floors, the tight glass. He himself had changed, and was changing. He knew that when he lay awake at night and felt the cold crawl into bed with him like a dog, a great dog haired with frost and with an icy muzzle and an icy tongue which licked him lovingly, confidingly, licking through his ample flesh to the bone. He knew it when he stooped by the woodpile to get sticks for the stove. Lew had changed. To look at, at least, more angular, more spare, with, even, moments when the accusing, vindictive eyes filmed, as though he were willing, at last, to compromise, or at least, to call a temporary truce. Or perhaps, it was not a truce, but a piece of perfidious strategy, a device for lulling the enemy, for luring him out into the open.

And there, now, was Lew, sitting hunched beside the oil lamp, his game leg thrust out before him, his hands clutching the evening paper, saying: "They got him, by God, they got it pinned on him, by God, they ought to hang the black bastard, by God, I'd hang him, I'd hang him, I knowed it, by God!" And the newspaper quivered in his grasp.

"Take it, Aunt Ursula," Mr. Calhoun murmured, leaning, lifting the spoon.

"I knowed it," Lew uttered victoriously, "by God, I knowed it from the first. It was the nigger, it was the nigger—they knowed he come up there that night, and I knowed it was him. Nigger doings, it was, and I knowed it, and not that white feller, and they done let that white feller go what had the key. He's done proved where he was that night, he's done proved it—"

"Take it, Aunt Ursula," Mr. Calhoun murmured.

"I coulda told 'em, yeah, I knowed it, by God, listen, listen here—" and he began to read: *"Jason Sweetwater, who is known to have been intimate with the dead girl and who was held yesterday on suspicion, has satisfactorily accounted for his movements on the night of the crime and has been released. T. A. Sarrett, a graduate student at the University, with whom Jason Sweetwater*

365

*had had a violent altercation in the slain girl's apartment the morning preceding the crime, was questioned but not held—*I coulda told 'em, but they never asked me, oh, no, they never asked me, and I knowed it was the nigger, it was—"

"There wasn't any way to know," Mr. Calhoun said, not turning, holding the spoon, "not for certain. It is hard to know a thing for certain."

"For certain, for certain!" Lew jerked forward and spat and rattled his heavy, chunky shoe of the outthrust clubfoot, "Oh, there you go, Mr. Astor, oh, you know so much, Mr. Astor, but I coulda told 'em, and they'll hang him, by God, they'll hang that nigger, they oughta take him out and hang him, I'd hang him, I'd swing on the rope and stomp on his neck till the neck bone scrunched, by God! Listen here: . . . *a servant of the Murdock family, in whose education the family had assisted. It had been planned to send him to Columbia University in New York last year, but the execution of the plan was postponed, and Lieutenant Hotchkiss, of the homicide squad, has suggested the theory that disappointment caused by postponement of the plan may have been a factor in the motive for the crime.*" Lew enunciated each word with a quivering intensity, rattling the paper, thrusting his face toward it. *"The revenge motive, Lieutenant Hotchkiss says in a statement given out this afternoon, may have led to the murder and robbery—*by God, by God, them Murdocks, oh, they can't have no common nigger, oh, they are high-stepping, they got to have educated niggers—" he paused in the height of their excitement, breathing, "and it serves 'em right, by God!"

Mr. Calhoun turned heavily toward Lew. "No," he said, "no, Lew. It don't serve anybody right. It don't serve that poor girl right." And he put the spoon back in the bowl, giving his attention to the bowl, seeking the hunk of bread which floated there.

"Oh, it serves her right," Lew cackled, and leaned forward and dropped the paper on his knees, his excitement mounting rapidly, "oh, it serves her right, her laying round with men, her high-stepping, her drinking likker and laying round with men and not caring who, her—"

"You don't know," Mr. Calhoun said, "not for certain."

"It says—the paper says—listen here—" he snatched up the paper, "listen here, Mr. Astor—" Then he stopped. He leaned toward the paper, thrusting his sharp face devouringly toward it, and emitted, once, a slight, whining breath like a hound straining on a leash, then burst out: "By God, I told you, I told you, Mr. Astor, I told you I'd rather lay in a ditch and lap like a dog than work for old

Lem Murdock's boy. Listen here—but oh, no, you wouldn't listen, Jerry wouldn't listen—but listen here! They got Jerry in jail."

The spoon, which Mr. Calhoun dropped, clattered on the hearth.

"No," Mr. Calhoun said, staring at Lew, shaking his head massively, saying, "no, not Jerry. Jerry wouldn't be mixed up in nothing like that—not Jerry—" under Lew's whetted, exultant gaze.

"Oh, no, Mr. Astor—but look here—" he jerked himself up, clattering the boxlike shoe, thrusting the paper at Mr. Calhoun, whose head did not cease to move, slowly, from side to side in its ponderous, faithful negation, "they took him today, for fooling round at that bank, for fooling with folks' money—look here!"

Mr. Calhoun took the paper in one hand. With the other he still held the bowl of milk. He looked about helplessly, holding the bowl, seeking a place to put it.

He set it on the mantel shelf.

Then, while Lew, standing, hunching toward him, rocking on his twisted leg, avidly eyed his face, Mr. Calhoun opened the paper and bowed to read.

It was there. It was there on one side. On the right side. *Bank official in custody*, it said. It was there.

"I'd rather laid in a ditch," Lew rejoiced, "and lapped like a dog—"

Mr. Calhoun lifted his head, fumbling numbly to draw the thong which led to the watch in the watch pocket of his trousers. He managed to draw the watch out. "It's late," he said, mumbling as to himself, "it's nigh seven-thirty. If I get hitched up quick, I—"

"I'd laid in a ditch," Lew said.

"—I can make it by ten. If I get hitched quick. I reckon they'll let me in to see Jerry. I reckon they will and me his daddy and come a ways. If I get hitched quick—"

But he stood there, clutching the newspaper in one hand and the watch in the other, working his lips to make the words, but seemingly incapable of motion.

"Well," Duckfoot Blake said, as the cell door clicked shut behind him and he fastidiously adjusted a fresh cigarette into his ivory holder, and surveyed the man who sat on the cot before him, "if they'd just put us some decent mahogany in here and lay out a box of Corona Coronas, you and me and the Private could have a bank meeting."

Jerry Calhoun regarded him dully, unresentfully, leaning forward with his wrists hanging off the inside of his spread knees.

"It would be just like old times," Duckfoot said, and lighted his cigarette, and took the first drag, and blew two rings of smoke, blue and perfect in the still air.

"What did you come here for?" Jerry said, not moving.

"To gloat," Duckfoot affirmed. He waved the long holder, tracing a meticulous arabesque in the air with the glowing tip of the cigarette. "After supper, as soon as I saw it in the evening paper, I said, Now I shall go to the bastille and gloat." He studied the big, sagging-over, apathetic form, and demanded: "To gloat—what do you think of that?"

Jerry Calhoun did not answer.

"Yeah, to gloat, so I just telephoned my pal Bugger Kahn to come over to the jail and help me gloat. Unfortunately, Bugger cannot come until nine P.M., Central Standard Time, so I just came on to gloat privately until his advent. I shall not be able to gloat like Bugger, who plays stud poker for a profession and gloats about two o'clock every morning when they start counting the chips. But Bugger is a pretty good gloater when he gets round to the jail, too, for Bugger, in his spare time, is a hook-nosed, fawn-eyed bail-broker with the manners of a Sister of Mercy in a maternity ward."

He looked down at his biscuit-thick gold watch, dangling the Phi Beta Kappa key on the chain, and said: "It is eight-forty."

He put the watch back in his pocket, and looked distastefully at Jerry Calhoun. "For Christ sake," he snapped, "why don't you say something?"

Jerry Calhoun stirred a little, and worked his fingers, but avoided the eyes of his friend.

"You make me sick," Duckfoot declared. "They throw you in the can and you sit here and mope for six hours and don't get bail. Didn't you ever hear of *habeas corpus?* For Christ sake, why didn't you get bail?"

Jerry Calhoun did not answer, lifting his thick-fleshed face.

"Oh, you just prefer to sit here and suffer," Duckfoot said. "Who do you think you are? Jesus Christ declining to wipe from his brow the sputum of the holiday-spirited *hoi polloi?* My God, why don't you snap out of this sweet despair? My God, snap out of it. My God," he reiterated, stepping back into the middle of the cell and looking down at the man, "why didn't you call me up?"

"Shut up," Jerry said tiredly.

"So the cat hasn't got your tongue," Duckfoot said. "So you can talk? Now just get yourself spiritually prepared to get out of here. You don't have to stay here. Sweetwater got out. The Private could get bail but he don't want to, for he's a hero. That pore mountain Jesus don't want to get out, for he is Christ-bit. And the nigger can't get out, for they won't let him.— My God," Duckfoot interrupted himself, and lifted his gaze heavenward, "the social circles I move in!" Then again to the man on the cot: "But you—you can get out."

"Duckfoot—Duckfoot—" Jerry said, and slowly heaved his weight on the cot and exhaled like a man surrendering something.

"Yeah?" Duckfoot questioned.

"Was it the nigger killed her?" he asked.

"She's dead," Duckfoot said brutally, appraising the lifted face on which the dullness was beginning now to crack and shift and sag like old ice, "and it don't matter who killed her. But," he paused judicially, and inhaled from the cigarette, "I don't think it was the nigger. But," he said, "it will be the nigger hangs. And—"

"Sue—" Jerry Calhoun uttered wrenchingly, "who killed Sue?"

"And," Duckfoot continued unperturbedly, but narrowly watching his friend, "it may very well be tonight they hang him. For—"

"Who killed her?"

"—for things," Duckfoot continued, "unless I miss my guess, are stirring in the alleys and pool halls and faubourgs of this community. And—" he jerked out his watch and looked at it, "why doesn't that Bugger come on?"

"Who killed her?" Jerry demanded.

"Damn it, I didn't kill her," Duckfoot said. "And you didn't kill her. So why don't you shut up about it?"

He strode across to the window, plopping his feet on the cement floor, and peered out.

"I don't like it," he said. "There're people hanging round over yonder," he said, turning from the window. "There's too damned many people. Over there across the square." Then, fretfully: "Why doesn't that Bugger come on so we can get out of here?"

"She's dead," Jerry said.

"Sure, she's dead," Duckfoot said, still fretfully. "Somebody squeezed her windpipe and she's dead. And you'd better be dead than the way you are, sitting there like that. For God's sake, buck up. My God, if I couldn't buck up, I'd shoot myself."

Jerry Calhoun did not speak, but leaning forward on the cot, his elbows on his knees, he stared heavily at the other man.

"And stop looking at me like that," Duckfoot snapped. "Stop feeling so damned sorry for yourself and pretending you're feeling sorry for her."

Jerry Calhoun heaved his weight on the cot. "Say that and I'll—" he said, and clenched his hands.

"Fine," Duckfoot encouraged, "get mad at me. Show some sign

of life. Sure, she's dead and you ain't, and we got to get out of here. Damn that Bugger, why can't he come on?"

He looked at his watch and went to the window, looked out, turned, and said, "There's a hell of a lot of cars stopping round the corner. And in the square."

A man came to the door of the cell and said: "Mr. Blake."

"Yeah?" Duckfoot inquired. Then: "Has he come?"

"He telephoned," the man said, "and says tell you he'd be late. He said he couldn't come right now, he—"

"Afraid to come," Duckfoot said. "Damn his bail-broking soul." Then savagely to the man: "What the hell is going on out there?" He gestured to the window.

"Folks," the man replied sagely, with his finger smoothing the blue cloth over his paunch, "is just a leetle bit excited."

"Well, what's going to happen?"

"Nuthin," the man said, "not nuthin."

"Hell," Duckfoot said irritably, "I'm not asking what they're going to do. I know what they're going to do. They're going to try to hang the nigger. Sooner or later. I'm asking you what you brave boys are going to do. Are you going to let them hang the nigger?"

"We ain't going to let nobody do nuthin," the man said surlily.

"Nuts," Duckfoot said, and turned away from the bars of the door as though he were the free man outside, and the man in blue, who clutched a bar with one hand, were the one locked in.

The noise came from across the square, for the first time, not loud, a sound like the sound of surf which you pick up when the wind changes right.

"Yeah," Duckfoot said, turning to him again.

The man watched him truculently.

"Where is the nigger?" Duckfoot demanded.

"He's downstairs with the niggers," the man said.

"Well," Duckfoot advised, "you better put a white mark on his forehead so they'll be sure and get the right one."

The noise came again.

"No doubt," Duckfoot said, "your friends are expecting you. Don't let me detain you."

"Buddy," the man retorted, not grinning, "you ain't de-taining nobody."

He went away.

"Damn that Bugger Kahn," Duckfoot said aggrievedly.

Somewhere in the building, there was a crash, and the tinkle of falling glass.

"The classic instrument of the sovereign people," Duckfoot announced, "the half brick, the alley apple, the seed of democracy, the fruit of the popular will." Then: "Damn that Bugger." Then he swung toward Jerry, saying, "And damn you, you sure picked a night to go to jail."

There was another crash, and the falling of glass. One of the prisoners down the corridor began yelling. Duckfoot cocked his head, listening. "I can't make out what he's yelling," he complained.

There was another crash of a window, then a scattering of shots.

"Conscience shots," Duckfoot said. "Shooting over their heads." He went to the window and peered out. "Why don't they shoot a couple of 'em in the guts?" he demanded.

More of the prisoners down the corridor were yelling now. They were yelling, "Get the nigger, get the nigger, get the nigger!" They yelled like the cheering section at a football game.

Two men, half running, passed down the corridor before the cell.

"Hey, Sheriff," a prisoner called, "why don't you give 'em the nigger, so I can git some sleep?"

Duckfoot went to the door and tried to see down the corridor. The prisoners were yelling, "It ain't the Private, it ain't the Private, it ain't the Private they want, it's the nigger!"

"It looks like they're talking to the Private," Duckfoot said.

The prisoners kept on yelling.

The two men, with Private Porsum, running, repassed in the corridor.

"It beats me," Duckfoot admitted, and turned back into the cell.

There was a roaring in the square.

"God," Duckfoot said, "why don't they come on in and get it over with? Those cops won't do anything. Why don't they get it over?" His face looked white and streaked.

He looked down at his feet. "My dogs," he mourned. "I got to get off my dogs." He sat down on the chair, and lifted his feet alternately from the floor, with the careful motion of a man trying the temperature of a footbath.

Then he seemed to be listening, trying to sift the sounds from the square; then he returned his attention to his feet. "It'll be a long winter night," he said. "I do wish I'd brought my knitting," he said, and settled his uneasy frame back into the chair.

But all at once, he jerked himself up, saying: "Damn it, why don't they do it, if they're going to?" He glared balefully at Jerry Calhoun, while the prisoners shouted, and demanded: "Why don't they go on and do it?"

He went to the window and peered out, and turned to Jerry. "I can't tell what's going on," he complained. "They're just milling around." Then he looked at his watch. He thrust the watch back into his pocket, and said: "Damn that Bugger, leaving us here."

Unmoved, Jerry Calhoun said, in bitter satisfaction: "Well, it don't matter."

"The hell it don't!" Duckfoot retorted ferociously, his voice rising and cracking like a boy's, his paper-thin, white nostrils twitching; "everything matters, and don't you say it don't! Everything—"

There was a crash, the falling of glass again, and the shouting.

"—matters, every God-damned thing. And you say it don't and I'll slap you, you fool. I'll slap the pee out of you. It matters that Porsum's in here, and that half-wit mountain Jesus, and—"

There was a scattering of shots outside.

"—it matters you're a complete damned fool, a complete, thumb-sucking, self-pitying fool, and it matters you're here and that bastard Murdock is enjoying his bereavement in comfort—"

The prisoners were beating on the bars with their chairs.

"—and it matters Sue is dead, that poor little, pretty little, flat-buttocked blonde, and it matters they choked her to death, and it matters the nigger is here—"

"Sit down," Jerry Calhoun said, looking up at the white, twitching face.

"—and it matters they're going to hang him, it matters they're going to take him out and—"

"Sit down," Jerry ordered.

"—hang him and cut his pecker off, those bastards, those bastards, those poor, murdering, miserable, God-damned bloody bastards, and those cops—"

And he stood in the middle of the cell, and the nostrils of his pointed nose worked in the middle of his high white slick face and he stretched his arm out toward the noise outside, which was terrifying now, and the coat sleeve slipped back off his long white blue-veined bony wrist and he shook his fist at whatever was out there beyond the walls, filling the square, coiling and curdling and swelling blackly under the buildings and the sky and the lamp posts, on which the bulbs had been knocked out.

He knew that it mattered. Duckfoot Blake knew that everything mattered. He knew that everything he had ever done or said or thought mattered. He knew that all those years which had been full of his goings and comings and his loneliness and his pride and his pitiful pleasures mattered. He had never known it before, but he knew it now. He knew it, at last, and all the years he had lived were there all at once in him and around him, and that was horrible, more horrible than the thing which was about to happen.

He knew that it mattered, but he did not know how it mattered, or why, but he only knew that it did, not how, not why, as he stood there with the long, unpowerful arm uplifted, and felt sick and exalted with his knowledge.

"Sit down," Jerry said tiredly.

"My dogs," Duckfoot said, and sat in the chair.

They sat there for a moment without speaking, Jerry Calhoun sunk in upon himself, Duckfoot Blake taut and straining to catch the meaning of the sounds, the shouting inside and the shouting outside and the sound of chairs beating metal.

Then he said meditatively: "It's all worth a million dollars."

Jerry did not respond.

"A million bucks to Murdock," Duckfoot said glumly, "a million. Getting Sue killed. Public sympathy. Getting the nigger killed. It takes folks' minds off Murdock. But getting Sue killed—oh, he'll know his cue, all right. They'll never get a conviction. They won't even get an indictment."

"God," Jerry uttered, "God!" and rose abruptly from the cot, "if they get him, if I could just see Bogan Murdock here!"

"It's healthy you feel that way," Duckfoot said, shaking his head, "but it wouldn't mean much."

"God," Jerry said, and his big hands closed into fists at the level of his waist.

Duckfoot shook his head. "No," he repeated, "it wouldn't mean much. Because Bogan Murdock ain't real. Bogan is a solar myth, he is a pixy, he is a poltergeist. Son," he said, "you can't put ectoplasm in jail. But Bogan ain't even ectoplasm. He is just something you and I thought up one night. When Bogan Murdock looks in the mirror, he don't see a thing."

"God," Jerry Calhoun breathed, not listening, shaking himself like a big dog emerging from the water.

"Bogan Murdock is just a dream Bogan Murdock had, a great big wonderful dream. And you can't put a dream in jail, son. Bogan Murdock is just a wonderful idea Bogan Murdock had. And that," Duckfoot said sadly, "is why Bogan Murdock is a great man."

"There isn't any noise out there," Jerry Calhoun said.

"He is a great man, son, and no mistake," Duckfoot continued, "but they aren't ever real. You were almost a great man yourself, Jerry. But—"

"There isn't any noise," Jerry said, and moved toward the window.

Duckfoot jumped from his chair. "Something's happened," he said excitedly, "something's happened!"

They pressed to the window, side by side. The crowd was falling back from the building. Some policemen, not many, were across the square at the head of a street, working against the crowd, breaking it up. To one side there were a few mounted men. There were not many policemen, but the crowd was breaking up, scattering into the side streets.

"I'm damned," Duckfoot said, "I don't savvy."

The space in front of the building was empty now.

"They're not going to do it," Duckfoot said. "They're not even going to try to do it. Look at 'em. They're not even going to try."

They stood there and watched the crowd recoil and dissolve.

"The poor bastards, the poor miserable bastards," Duckfoot said, "they didn't even want to hang the nigger. They just thought they wanted to."

The shouting in the corridor had stopped, too. There was only the distant sound of the policemen across the square, and now and then the sound of a whistle.

"They just thought they wanted to," Duckfoot said. "But they didn't even have that in 'em. Not even that. You might have some kind of respect for 'em if they'd really wanted to. But they didn't even want that, the bastards."

The clanging of an ambulance bell drew nearer. Then the machine itself rushed into the square, and with screaming brakes stopped in front of the building beyond their range of vision.

"The cops must have made a mistake and winged somebody," Duckfoot said.

But he was wrong.

The ambulance had come for Private Porsum. In fifteen minutes everybody in the cells along the corridor knew that. Private Porsum had agreed to speak to the crowd. He had stepped out on a balcony for that purpose. Before he had spoken more than a few words, before any word could have been understood in that hubbub, a brick had come hurtling from the darkness and had struck him on the head. He had fallen forward, had hung for an instant against the railing, then had slipped over.

That fact, and not any word he had spoken, had accomplished his purpose. The men at whose feet he lay, with blood over his forehead, looked down at him, and did not know why they were there. "Somebody ought to git a doctor," somebody said, and with those words the purpose of the mob dissolved. It was no longer a mob. There was only the mass of individuals, men and boys, aimless and futile and confused, waiting for the handful of policemen from a district station to arrive and herd them off like sheep.

Now deputies walked up and down the corridor, quieting the prisoners.

"How bad is the Private hurt?" Duckfoot asked one of them.

"No telling," the man said, and passed on down the corridor.

Duckfoot and Jerry stood for a moment longer, looking out into the corridor. Then Duckfoot said: "I reckon I better go and get that Bugger Kahn out of bed. Maybe there's still such a thing as *habeas corpus* in this town."

Twenty-seven

"WILL YOU please put the large bag here," Slim Sarrett ordered the bellboy, indicating, with outstretched arm and accurate forefinger, the rack at the foot of the bed.

The bellboy complied, laying the very large suitcase, of glossy, rich, unscarred tawny cowhide, on its side on the rack, then turned to the patron.

Slim Sarrett held out to him a leather pad of keys, saying: "It is the larger of the two brass keys."

With impassive face, the boy took the pad, selected the proper key, and opened the suitcase.

Slim Sarrett held out his hand to receive the pad of keys. "The small bag will do on the foot of the bed," he said.

The small bag, a handy replica of the large one, was placed on the foot of the bed.

The boy moved to the window, lowered the top sash a few inches, and raised the bottom one an equal distance, while Slim Sarrett regarded him appraisingly. "Will you please raise it a trifle more," he requested, "another six inches, I should say?"

The boy executed the command, toying with the sash to bring it to the precise point, cocking his head critically, touching the sash again to push it down a hair's breadth, and touching it once more, delicately, like an artist who, stepping back from the easel on the last day, picks up another brush and in a spirit of grateful reverence applies to the canvas the last, minute, fulfilling point of color, too precious for discernment by the vulgar eye. Then he turned blandly to Slim Sarrett, who stood erectly in the middle of the room, under the mellow light, beyond the glinting cowhide bags, clad in a dark blue suit of coarse, expensive cloth, draped with a cunning, almost too loose elegance from the shoulders, in a gray shirt cut low at the collar, with a black tie knotted carelessly below the firm, lifted chin.

"Will that be all, sir?" inquired the boy in a perfect voice.

"Yes, thank you," Slim Sarrett said, and stretched out his hand, holding between thumb and forefinger a coin.

The boy received the coin, murmured his gratitude, and under Slim Sarrett's impartial gaze, retreated to the door. At the door, just at the instant of his withdrawal, his posture seemed to slip—as a coat is slipped off to reveal the braces and rumpled shirt—and he bore a fleeting kinship to those indolent, gawky, insolent boys who lounge in pool halls and on drugstore corners, in the evening, and spit on the pavement and whistle to passing girls and shove each other and say, "Yeah, Jack, yeah, Snipe, yeah, Bull, yeah."

Slim Sarrett saw the door close upon the withdrawing, transmuted face, then swept his glance over the room, like a commander upon mounting the bridge. Deliberately, he went to the larger bag and began to unpack. He laid out two suits on the bed, one dark chocolate tweed, one gray with a decisive chalky stripe, both new, both expensive, both confident. He transferred his linen to the drawers of a bureau. Then he hung up the suits in the closet, each time stopping, as he passed under the light, to inspect the object which he carried. From the smaller bag he took out a silver-mounted set of brushes, which he placed on the bureau, a toilet kit in black leather with silver clasps, and a maroon silk robe and slippers.

He undressed to his shorts, hung up the suit which he had been wearing, and for thirty minutes put himself through a vigorous routine of calisthenics. The sweat came soon, and made his body glisten under the light, tinting the flesh from white to the merest suggestion of gold. Through all the violence of his movements, his face remained expressionless, except for a light parting of the lips, as though that chiseled face were, somehow, detached from, and superior to, the strains and contortions and rhythmic agonies of the glistening body.

When he had finished the exercises, he picked up his slippers and toilet kit, and entered the bathroom. He took a shower, dried himself meticulously, and applied a lotion to his flesh. He put on pajamas and the maroon silk robe. Standing before the mirror, he combed his hair until it plastered to the high even contours of his skull like black lacquer.

That done, he observed himself thoughtfully in the mirror, then went to the desk, where he took paper and dipped a pen. For a long time he did not write, his lips moving as in prayer and his eyes fixed unseeingly upon the blank, neutral-colored wall before him.

Then he began to write, forming each letter carefully, cleanly, and decisively upon the white paper. He wrote:

377

It is your enemy but has breath sweeter than myrrh.
It has the old Biblical cunning but sits in a sunny place.
It came from your mother's womb, and she screamed at the moment
  of egress.
The family doctor slapped breath in, relighted his bitten cigar
While the old nurse washed it and washed it, without complete suc-
  cess.

Feet passed in the hall beyond the latched door, and he only looked up once. Then he began to write again:

By shores where all kindly monsters wallow and welter and mourn
And lift their gaze unto your crocus-tread . . .

He studied the lines, touching the tip of the penstaff to his teeth. Carefully, he ran bold, heavy strokes through the lines.

He got up from his chair and went to the window. He looked down, far down, into the canyon-street below him, where the lights of vehicles moved, jerked, flowed, and minute figures shifted and swarmed before the glowing base of the buildings which lifted invincibly up—he looked up—against the black sky.

He returned to his seat, and his labor. He wrote:

By cliffs where whales—oh, I saw them numb-eyed and motherly—
  mourn
And lift gaze unto your crocus-tread; in the crowded square
When the mayor coughs and unveils the high frock-coated bronze
  of your father;
In the library where the great folios, chained like a beast, blink and
  mourn;
There he will come, and smile like the future, and hand you the
  letter.

Feet passed in the hall, and he listened until there was no sound. He wrote:

In hired rooms he sits by your side and in dark dreams of fields of
  lilies

"In dark dreams of fields of lilies," he said aloud, lifting his gaze up to the neutral wall.

Feet moved in the hall, scarcely making a sound on the depth of carpet out there, approaching, passing; and listening, he murmured, "and in dark dreams of fields of lilies," and picked up the pen and wrote:

While feet conspire in the calumnious corridor.

"While feet conspire," he murmured. He stared at the wall. "While feet," he murmured; and suddenly rose from his chair.

He began to pace about the room. He stopped, stood stock still in the middle of the room, held his right hand in his left before his chest and gently rubbed the knuckles, and listened. Somebody was in the corridor, somebody was coming. But the feet passed on. He remained for a moment longer in the posture of listening, but there was only the distant surge and roar of the city ascending into the room. He began to pace again, holding his hands in that position, and working his mouth to make words which were not audible.

At last he flung himself down across the bed, face down. He lay there, trying to think of nothing, nothing, nothing at all, while life stirred and swarmed and uncoiled in its dim, undulant, rhythmic, fulfilling roar far below, where the lights were, and while the great towers of New York heaved massively into the black sky and hedged him about.

On the evening when Gerald Calhoun was released on bail, his father reached the jail some forty-five minutes after Duckfoot Blake had left to get Kahn. Jerry, sitting on the cot as he had sat before, hunching forward, his elbows on his knees, his wrists drooping forward, did not even look up when he first heard the sound of approaching feet. Even when the sound ceased, and he knew that someone stood before the cell, he did not look up until he heard the chink of metal as the key was applied to the lock.

There, beside the man with the key, was his father, wearing jean pants and an old brown wool coat, and a white shirt, crudely starched but very clean, a button missing at the collar but the collar held almost together by the awkward knot of the black tie, which hung below the slight gap of the collar. Mr. Calhoun, holding his black hat in his hand, stood there, waiting for the manipulation of the lock, looking in through the bars, not saying a word. His breath came with a spasmodic heaviness.

Jerry, looking at him, felt, for the moment, nothing, nothing at all. He stared at him, noting with dispassionate clarity every detail of appearance; but the big old man, with the knotted hands clutching the black hat before him, might have been a stranger getting ready to say, "Mister—mister, I was just wondering if you'd —if you might be wanting to buy—" Or getting ready to say, "Mister, I musta got off the road—I was wondering if—"

The door swung open and Mr. Calhoun stepped into the cell, and stood there, as before, regarding his son but not able, yet, to find the words.

Then, after the door had clicked to behind him, he took one step forward, stopped, and with his face gathering itself for the effort, said: "Son." And then, again, said it: "Son."

Until that moment, the moment when the big old man said, "Son," and again, "Son," Jerry Calhoun had not seen his own situation as related to anything in the world except himself. His confusion, his apathy, his grief, his bitterness, and finally, his single flash of triumphant and releasing ferocity at the thought of Bogan Murdock—Bogan Murdock jailed, Bogan Murdock seized and flung into a cell, Bogan Murdock ruined—had been, simply, his own being, almost absolute in themselves, lacking relationship even to the events and persons of the tangible world which had caused his own situation. For those events and persons, from the time when he had opened a newspaper and seen the photograph of Sue Murdock above the savagely laconic statement, *Slain Girl,* had been as shadowy as frosted breath on the air. There had only been the flow of feeling which was himself.

But now, with his father's voice, his father was real, and demanding, demanding to break in upon that privacy of pain, which was himself, in which, now, he was almost jealously, preciously, at home. He looked at his father's face above the white shirt, the buttonless collar with the wisp of thread, the twisted tie. Looking at that wisp of thread, he saw with a horrible precision his father leaning over the open drawer, fumbling for the white shirt, dropping it in his haste, fumbling with the buttons, tearing off the button, his big knotted swollen hands shaking and his breath coming hard. And that scene was there before his eyes clearer than reality, and it was the last indignity, the last assault upon him, the last betrayal. No— it was more—it—

"I came as soon as I could, son," he was saying. "I saw the paper, and soon as I could, soon as I could get hitched up."

—it was more, it was the cause, the very cause of everything, of everything that had happened to him, of Sue Murdock dead, of himself in jail, of everything. And with that blaze of conviction and accusation in him, he stared at the man there before him, who was saying: "Why, son, why didn't you let me know—you ought to let me know, son, you ought—"

With a vindictive delight, he cut in, his voice rising in triumph: "You couldn't have done a thing—not a thing. And you can't do anything now!"

"Maybe not, maybe not, son—maybe I couldn't done a thing, but I could come. And they'd let me in—they let me in now and it late

380

and against the rules, but I told them how I'd come a long piece, and—"

"Oh, God damn it, God damn it!" Jerry burst out, and watched the surprise come on the big, sagging, clay-colored face, as though it had been slapped, and then saw the surprise not there, the face as it had been, looking down at him, saying: "Son."

Mr. Calhoun took a step forward toward the cot.

Oh, God, if he puts his hands on me, if he touches me, Jerry thought, and his muscles went tense as though to brace himself, for that was the one thing, the last thing, which he could not bear.

But Mr. Calhoun did not touch him. He took that single step toward the cot, then stopped, and merely looked at his son, not saying a word.

Then Duckfoot Blake was in the corridor, waiting for the man to unlock, and saying: "Well, Jerry, let's get going. It's all O.K." Then, inside, to Mr. Calhoun: "I'm mighty glad to know you. Jerry's been a buddy of mine for a long time. Yeah, I'm glad you turned up to help me take a hand with that loafer over there. Gawd, look at him, ain't he a sight?" And he wagged a long brittle forefinger toward the cot, where Jerry sat.

Duckfoot drove them out to the Calhoun place, in his car. He had proposed that they spend the night at his house, but Mr. Calhoun had said, "I'm much obliged, Mr. Blake, and I know Jerry's obliged, but I reckon we ought to be getting on home. You know how 'tis on a farm, you got to be getting home."

Home, Jerry had echoed in his mind, *home,* and had seen Lew's face and Aunt Ursula's face and his father's, and had felt the wild impulse to run across the square—for they were standing in front of the jail then—and run down the street under the murky lights, and keep on running, out where it was dark, where there wouldn't be anybody, where they would leave him alone, where everybody, everybody, would leave him alone.

So, over Mr. Calhoun's protest, they went in Duckfoot's car. Mr. Calhoun had said that he couldn't leave his horse and buggy standing out in the street all night. He said it used to be a man could put his horse in a livery stable, but he didn't know as there was one for a man now. But Duckfoot went to the telephone in the all-night restaurant on the square, and got hold of a Negro he knew to get the horse and bring him on out in the morning. They didn't even have to wait for the Negro to come to the square, for the man at the restaurant said he'd attend to it. Duckfoot knew the man at the restaurant, too. Duckfoot knew everybody.

Jerry sat in the back seat of Duckfoot's old car, and his father in

381

front. They rattled across the square, over the tangle of streetcar tracks, out through the wholesale district, out through the suburbs where the few street lights showed the huddled, paintless houses. There were no lights in the houses. Then they were in the country. On both sides, the fields, stripped, empty, dark, heaved toward the sky. The sky was starless, streaked with dark clouds. The woods beyond the fields were darker than the sky.

Duckfoot was talking to Mr. Calhoun. He was telling him some preposterous, endless tale of the time when he had been an auctioneer at a jewelry joint. He would release the wheel and gesture, and the car would swerve; then he would seize the wheel in the nick of time, and his high, nasal voice would go on and on. But Jerry did not follow the words. His body swayed and lurched with the motion of the car.

They turned off the highway at last, up the lane to the Calhoun place. He observed with some surprise that the house was white now, solid and serene among the leafless trees, under the dark sky. There was a new fence, a white fence. As the car drew up to the gate, he saw that the dead gum by the gate had been cut out. Even the stump had been dug out and the hole sodded over, he could make out even in that light. With a sardonic self-irony, he realized that everything was as he had planned to make it—oh, he had been going to paint the house white some day, oh, he had been going to put up a fence, oh, he had been going to take out that gum, he had been going to do all that when he got a little extra change. Oh, he had been going to fix up the Old Calhoun Place, and drive out Saturday afternoons and look at his herd of pure-bred Herefords— sure, he was going to have them, sure—and see how his setters were doing and maybe go down across the pasture beyond the wood lot, with a gun across his arm and a dog skirting the sage and some friend from town beside him, and knock down a couple of quail, and go back up to the house and sit in front of the fire with a glass in his hand and talk to that anonymous man from town whom he had brought out to the Old Calhoun Place. And where would Lew and Aunt Ursula have been? Gone—dead, perhaps—not in the picture. He had never said to himself, *After they are dead.* They simply were not in the picture. There was no place in the picture for them. Had there been a place in the picture for his father? The question flashed through his mind with its obscene candor. But he refused the question—he hadn't asked the question, nobody had asked the question, it was no question and nobody had a right to ask it. And the spasm of rejection in his mind transmitted itself to his limbs, so that he twitched as at the start of a rigor.

There was his father standing in the road now. So he got out and followed his father and Duckfoot through the white gate and up the brick walk to the glimmeringly white mass of the house beyond the dark trees.

Old Mr. Calhoun fumbled with his keys, found the right one, finally opened the door. "Just a minute," he said, "just a minute and I'll get some light."

The room was almost black dark. Jerry could see a few red chinks on the hearth, where Lew had banked the fire, red coals showing where the ashes had dropped off the chunks of wood. Mr. Calhoun struck a match, peered about with the tiny flame held up, and located the lamp. "We just never got the electricity turned back on since we got back," he said, in a voice of careful explanation, not apology. "And coal oil not costing nothing to speak of."

As the wick caught, the rays of the lamp flickered on the pale walls and on the high white ceiling; then steadied. Jerry stood by the door, staring at the clean room, which was so big and bare, dwarfing and devouring the old pieces of furniture, stripping them of their old meanings and functions, leaving them clearly and pitifully what they were, junk. His gaze traveled slowly around the room, which was familiar and yet so treacherously unfamiliar now, as in a dream.

"Shut the door, Jerry," his father was saying, "and I'll stir up the fire. And you, Mr. Blake, you just have a chair, and I'll get some coffee on. It's a ways for you to be going back in, and the air's got some nip."

"I'm afraid it's no sale, Mr. Calhoun," Duckfoot said. "I'd sure like to have a cup and jaw a little, but it's late. How about fixing me a quart when I come out tomorrow or next day? That is—" he continued, and turned to Jerry, "if you want me to stop by your apartment and bring you anything out here?"

"You might get me some clothes," Jerry said.

"Sure," Duckfoot said, "I'll get your duds. I'll bring you your crate, too, if you'll give me the keys. Then you can drive me as far as the car line when I go back to town."

Jerry took the key pad from his pocket and detached his car keys and held them in his hand.

"You figure on staying out to supper, Mr. Blake," his father was saying, "when you come out with Jerry's stuff. We'd be proud to have you."

"Sure thing," Duckfoot said, and reached over and lifted the keys from Jerry's hand as though he were taking them off a shelf, "sure thing, Mr. Calhoun, and I'll plan on having an appetite. But now I got to shove."

Mr. Calhoun crossed the space toward Duckfoot, stood ponderously in front of him, seemed about to speak, then spoke. "Mr. Blake," he said, "Mr. Blake—you don't know how me and Jerry feel—what you did—" And he thrust out his hand.

"Aw, for Christ's sake," Duckfoot said, almost fretfully. Then he seized the hand and shook it, dropped it suddenly, and said: "I got to shove."

"I'll see you, pal," he called back to Jerry, as he stepped out of the door.

Mr. Calhoun had got to the door too late to open it for the guest. Now he held it ajar and looked out. After a moment Jerry heard the sound of the motor, then the grinding of gears. Mr. Calhoun closed the door. He crossed to the hearth, and spread his hands over the embers, which gave forth a little flame now. He seemed to be studying the flame.

Jerry still stood near the door. He stood there like a stranger who, neglected, waits to be asked his errand, and looked at the humped-over figure above the embers and the small flame. That figure would straighten up in a minute, it would straighten up and turn its face toward him. He knew that. He became aware of the ticking of a clock. He listened to the clock, and knew that in a minute that big, sagging, creased old face would turn toward him, not in accusation, not in rancor, not even in despair, but simply in recognition and acceptance, which would be most horrible of all. For against that there could be no defense.

Mr Calhoun turned from the fire.

"I reckon it's about time we went to bed, son," he said.

Jerry did not answer.

"You can sleep in your room, son," the man said. "The bed's not made up, but there's sheets and stuff up there."

"I'll make it up," Jerry said, and started to move across the room.

"Naw," his father objected, "naw, I'll help you," and followed him into the hall, and up the stairs, carrying the lamp, which threw Jerry's shadow enormously up the stairs ahead of him.

Jerry laid his hand on the iron latch, and in the light the room leaped from the chaos of darkness to its proper proportions, the pale, flowered walls, strange to him, the white ceiling here as below, the wide bare floor. The panes of the windows gleamed blackly, with the faintest iridescence, like a film of oil on black water, like a film laid over the coiling immeasurable depth of darkness outside.

384

The single flame of the lamp was reflected winkingly in the black glass.

Mr. Calhoun set the lamp down on the mantel shelf, over the cold, black square of the fireplace. Then he went to the walnut wardrobe, which seemed to lean perilously out from the flowered wall. The door of the wardrobe stuck; then under Mr. Calhoun's uncertain fingers, gave raspingly. He took out two folded sheets, and a blanket and a patchwork quilt, on which the colors had faded and run.

He stood on one side of the bed and Jerry on the other, and they spread the first sheet over the uneven mattress. Then the other sheet, then the blanket and quilt.

Mr. Calhoun went back to the wardrobe, and for some moments, leaning over, fumbled in the interior gloom. Then he straightened up, shaking his head. "A pillow slip," he said. "It looks like I don't find any pillow slip." He stood there seemingly lost in indecision, marveling and sad, holding in his hand a piece of cloth which was not a pillow slip. "It looks like there'd be a pillow slip," he said. He took a step toward the door. "Maybe," he said, "maybe I could—"

"Let it go," Jerry ordered, and seized a pillow from the chair where the two were piled, and thrust it under the lower sheet. Then he straightened up, and stood by the bed, which was ready.

Mr. Calhoun looked at the bed, then at Jerry, and moved a couple of steps toward the door. "I reckon I better let you get on to bed," he said, but, for the moment, he did not move, looking at his son, who stood by the bed, on the side toward the door, and did not answer. Mr. Calhoun seemed about to approach him; then, as though answering the unphrased impulse in himself, said: "Naw, naw—you better get on to bed, son."

He turned to the door, reached it, and laid his hand on the latch. He opened the door, and about to go out, hesitated on the threshold, again looking at his son's face. "Don't you take on and fret, son. Mr. Blake—" he paused, then continued, "Mr. Blake said he figured it would be all right. It's gonna be all right, son."

"All right, all right," Jerry uttered. "What the hell does he know about it?"

"You go to bed, son," Mr. Calhoun said. "It's gonna be all right." Then he closed the door, and Jerry could hear him feeling his way down the stairs.

"All right," Jerry repeated out loud, bitterly, to the closed door. What the hell did Duckfoot know about it? What the hell did his father know?

He began to undress, flinging his clothes down across the foot of the bed, shivering a little as the air struck his bare flesh. When he had stripped to his underwear, he walked across, barefoot, to the fireplace, and blew out the lamp. Then, in the darkness which was absolute in the moment before his eyes had adjusted themselves, he felt his way to the bed, and laid himself down. The springs creaked painfully with his weight.

The springs had always made that sound when he got into this bed and shifted his body to find the position for comfort, always, ever since he could remember. Then, thinking that, he seemed to be sinking, not into the old mattress, which accepted his body now as it had years ago, but into those years themselves, into the self he had been. What had he been? And what did he share with that Jerry Calhoun who, long ago, had lain here?

He could make out objects now in the gloom—the chair and the table where once he had leaned over his books on Sunday afternoons when his father had come up to sit and watch with the absorbing, pitiless patience, the wardrobe, which was a pile of blackness against the pale paper of the wall. The objects were there in the same old places, waiting, and he had come. Under the paper there was the old wall, secret, aware, with eyes to see the old Jerry Calhoun under the new. And here he was, and they had received him, as the old self had received him, as the mattress had received him, as the past had received him, as he was drawn back into Aunt Ursula, and Lew, and his father, and the mother he had never known, and all the nameless people who were dead. Here he was, and the mattress was like a quicksand into which he would sink, imperceptibly but steadily, forever, drawn down by the numberless, nameless fingers that plucked feebly but inexorably, ceaselessly.

He lay rigid, as though any motion, any struggle, might plunge him deeper. Oh, he had come back. He had come back, all right. *All right, all right,* he thought, and thought how his father had said it would be all right.

All right, all right—what right had his father to say "all right"?

He had stood by the door and had said, "All right," and he couldn't even know what *all right* was, for nothing had ever been all right for him, for he had always failed, the cord broke in his hands, the strap twisted in his fingers, the nail bent under his hammer, the dish slipped from his grasp. And he saw his father as he had seen him so many times, leaning over some small thing, some task too precise, breathing heavily with the sweat on his face; and the old sense of outrage and fury started in him. *All right, all right!* Nothing had ever been all right, and it wouldn't be now, and the old man would be alone in the house, alone with the old woman and Lew, and his son gone to prison and disgraced. Oh, that was part of the picture, that was the perfect ending. Thinking that, Jerry suddenly felt a kind of grim glee, a vindication, a vengeance.

He had come back. He had come back to have the old man stand there and say: "It's gonna be all right." He had come back to find out what he knew now. He had come back to lie in the old bed, in that dark which you couldn't tell from the old darknesses. He had left it for other beds, for other nights. He had gone a long way to come back to it. Something in the old self which had lain here had driven him out, but if you are going to come back, why do you leave?

What had driven him out? What had he wanted? Oh, the crowd had cheered in the autumn sunlight and the band had played and people had slapped him on the back and Bogan Murdock had smiled and money had been in his pocket and Sue Murdock—Sue Murdock had stood in the middle of her apartment that last night and had looked at him and had uttered that small, throaty cry, and he had known that she loved him. He had had those things and he had wanted those things. He had wanted so many things and had had all of them, and had had none of them, for what you had came wrong or too soon or too late, or it wore another face, and your three wishes always came true but the last undid all the rest, and you were where you had begun.

You get your wishes, all right, every one. You wanted to fix up the place that your great-great uncle had built. It was the Old Calhoun Place. To paint it white and put on new shutters. To paper the walls and get the grime off the floors—oh, what beautiful floors, oh, yes, the original floors, oh, you don't see ten-inch flooring like that any more. To put up the white fence. To take out the dead gum by the gate. And you had your wish, all right. You came home, and found it all the way you had wanted, but it wasn't yours any more, and you had come in the middle of the night. You came home from jail in the middle of the night.

You didn't come home in the middle of the afternoon and go out to look at your pure-bred Herefords and take your gun and your prize setter and go across the back pasture and knock down a couple of birds and sit by the fire with the glass in your hand and the smiling friend and nobody there but the friend and the nigger with the tray and no Aunt Ursula and no Lew and no—

Had you ever wanted your father dead?

No, you had never said that. You never said that. It's just that he isn't in the room. He is out somewhere. But where is he? Damn

387

it, he just isn't here. Damn it, he's just out somewhere. There's nobody here but me and my friend and the nigger, in this beautiful room in the firelight. He just isn't in right now, that's all. And it's not my fault he's not here.

Why, there he is! Coming in the door. See, there is my father, and your suspicions were completely unjustified, but I'll accept your apology. See, there he is, wearing that beautiful new one-hundred-and-twenty-five-dollar gray suit Larkinson made him in New York and looking unusually well and handsome and carrying his stick and smiling hospitably and looking at me with his fine eyes, which have large black pupils ringed with smoky-blue. I want you to meet my father. Father, this is Mr. ——

But your friend stares at your father and bursts into extraordinary laughter. He laughs and laughs, and the terror grows in you. Then he controls his laughter a little, and points at your father, and says: That isn't your father, that's Bogan Murdock!

And you see that it is not your father. It is not your father at all. Where is your father? You better run, you better run quick and find him. Before they say you killed him. Before the police come and dig in the leaves in the woods and drag the river and look in the old well where you hit the drowning puppy with the brick and pry under the hay in the loft.

Jerry Calhoun heaved himself up in bed, and the springs creaked.

Did I want my father dead? he thought.

And said out loud: "No—no—"

He lay back down on the pillow, thinking, *No, no.*

Did I want my father dead?

No, no, he thought, lying there stiff on the mattress, with his eyes closed, and saw his father's face.

Father, father—I—I—

Yes, son.

Father, I wanted Aunt Ursula dead.

Yes, son.

I didn't really want to give her the blue shawl, father.

Yes, son.

I wanted Lew dead.

Yes, son.

Father, I wanted to sit by the fire, and they wouldn't be there—they wouldn't be there—and—and you wouldn't be there—

Yes, son.

I wanted you dead—I wanted you dead, father—I wanted to sit by the fire—

Yes, son.

388

You knew? Did you know?

Yes, son.

Oh, father—

Yes, son.

There was frost on the ground when Mr. Calhoun came out of the kitchen door, and moved across the backyard to the woodpile. His feet cut through the white frost and left tracks where the dun color of the frozen mud showed through. He leaned above the woodpile, the breath puffing whitely from his mouth, and began to pick up stove-lengths. After he had placed three in the crook of his arm, he had some difficulty in picking more up, for his balance was bad and his hand was cold and unclever. But he finally managed.

While the fire caught and the water for Aunt Ursula's two eggs came slowly to a boil and her pan of milk began to simmer, he laid places for two on the kitchen table. Then he prepared the tray, broke the two eggs into a cup, poured the hot milk into a bowl, and went to feed the old woman, whom he had already propped up in bed on pillows, swathed to the chin in blankets, whose fire he had risen twice in the night to build, and whose face he had, that morning, already wiped with a cloth dipped in water heated in a kettle at her fireplace.

When he came back, Lew was hunched in a chair drawn up almost into contact with the stove.

"Good morning," Mr. Calhoun said.

"Yeah," Lew said, "ain't it, Mr. Astor?"

Mr. Calhoun put a skillet on the stove and in it two thick slices of shoulder meat. While the meat began to uncongeal and the grease to ooze from it on to the black iron, he broke four eggs into a bowl and stirred them. The odor of coffee was already beginning to drift in the air. The breath of the men now did not show white.

"Do you mind setting the bread on?" Mr. Calhoun asked.

"Naw," Lew said, and lurched up, clumping his foot on the hollow boards. He got a plate of cold biscuits and a pat of butter from the safe. As he leaned to place the objects on the table, he observed the plates there. "Ain't Jerry eating?" he demanded, eying Mr. Calhoun's heavy, curved back.

"He'll eat when he wakes up," Mr. Calhoun said, not turning from the stove.

"Yeah, yeah, he'll eat when he wakes up," Lew mimicked. "Yeah, and what'll he eat? Oh, he'll take a morsel of angel-food cake if you please, and a little peach ice cream."

"Being it's the first night," Mr. Calhoun said apologetically, "I figured I'd just not call him."

"Well, I'll call him," Lew announced, "him laying up there sleeping and it broad day. He ain't in no city now, he—"

"Naw, Lew, naw," Mr. Calhoun repeated steadily, occupied with the bowl, the eggs, the frying meat, "don't be bothering him this morning. Just let him sleep now. Tomorrow morning, that'll be different."

"Him laying up there, and work to do!"

"Tomorrow," Mr. Calhoun said. "Jerry, now—he never was no hand to slack, and the need there."

"Laying up there, laying up there!" Lew exulted bitterly, and swung from the table toward the door, and his boot rattled and clumped in victorious tattoo as he lurched and lunged toward the inner door.

"By God!" Mr. Calhoun uttered in a terrible voice.

In the moment of ensuing silence, Lew, his hand already on the knob, turned to confront the powerful, hulking figure, the working face and unsheathed, baleful eyes, the heavy hand lifted to heaven clutching the iron spoon, from which dripped a gout of egg.

He took his hand, almost surreptitiously, from the knob.

The place is the library of Bogan Murdock. The time is about eleven-thirty on a bright wintry morning.

A fire leaps and crackles cleanly in the big fireplace. On a table are set a siphon of soda, a bottle of Scotch whisky, a tray of glasses, and a box of cigars. At that end of the room four men are seated, nondescript men, with pads and pencils in their hands and cigars in their mouths. On the floor beside each of them is a partly filled glass. A fifth man stands behind the tripod of a camera, holding aloft the reflector and flash bulb. The camera is trained across the room.

There, directly in front of the camera, sits Bogan Murdock, erect, smiling, firm-jawed, with his eyes gimleted unflaggingly upon the black spot where, at the appropriate instant, will be exposed the flash of lens. On his right sits his father, who breathes heavily and observes nothing. On his left sits his wife, who, dressed in black, is beautiful and pale as wax. Behind him stands his son, dark-browed and sullen. One unruly lock on the son's head falls forward almost to his eyes. Now and then he twitches his head as though to free himself from that irritation.

The bulb gives its explosive, blinding, veracious flash.

"Thank you," the camera man says.

"Not at all," Bogan Murdock replies.

Bogan Murdock rises from his chair, and moves to the fireplace, moving with a controlled, tautened grace, which is as innocent as though he were alone. The eyes of the seated men follow him. He spreads his fine, brown hands to the blaze, then turns to face them.

"You have," he says, "asked me for a statement."

"Yes, sir," one of the men says, "if you don't mind."

There is a rustling sound as the men adjust themselves in their chairs and shift their pads of paper.

"You want me to make a statement about the failure of the firm of Meyers and Murdock, of which I have the honor to be president."

He looks at them with perfect candor.

There is no answer. So he smiles at them, slowly, in the security of strength and the melancholy of wisdom.

"I have only this to say," he says. "I say that I am completely responsible. I am responsible because I followed too faithfully my larger vision and trusted too much in friends, in subordinates in whom I thought I had found loyalty. But now—under these circumstances, which we need not discuss—I have found a loyalty which I never suspected to exist. In my friends, who have rallied round me. In my family, a great staunchness and loyalty in the midst of their bereavement." He pauses and regards the three people—the old man, the beautiful woman, the strong sullen boy. "So," he says, "in the confidence born of that loyalty, I look to the future. Courage—I hope that I may have a little of it. Courage—" he says, and nods to indicate the mountainous, wrecked old man, who wheezes slowly, "my father had courage. Courage, it is the heritage of all of us—of all citizens of this State. Courage," he says, and turns and indicates with a glance the portrait, as large as life, above the fireplace.

It is the portrait of a man who, more than a century ago, endured cold and hunger, who killed men with his own hand, who survived steaming malarial swamps and long marches, who was ruthless, vindictive, cunning, and headstrong, who was president of his country, who died in the admiration, or hatred, of millions of men. There is the painted face: the sunken flesh over the grim jawbone, the deep, smoldering eyes, the jutting beak of a nose, and the coarse crest of grayish hair, like an old cockatoo.

New Directions Paperbooks – A Partial Listing

For complete listing request free catalog from
New Directions, 80 Eighth Avenue, New York 10011   † Bilingual

For complete listing request free catalog from
New Directions, 80 Eighth Avenue, New York 10011   † Bilingual